REUNION AT CARDWELL RANCH

BY
B.J. DANIELS

MILLS
BOON

First Published in Great Britain 2016
By Mills & Boon, an imprint of HarperCollins*Publishers*
1 London Bridge Street, London, SE1 9GF

© 2016 Barbara Heinlein

ISBN: 978-0-263-91891-5

46-0116

Our policy is to use papers that are natural, renewable and recyclable products and made from wood grown in sustainable forests. The logging and manufacturing processes conform to the legal environmental regulations of the country of origin.

Printed and bound in Spain
by CPI, Barcelona

B.J. Daniels is a *New York Times* and *USA TODAY* bestselling author. She wrote her first book after a career as an award-winning newspaper journalist and the publication of thirty-seven short stories. She lives in Montana with her husband, Parker and three springer spaniels. When not writing, she quilts, boats and plays tennis. Contact her at www.bjdaniels.com, on Facebook or on Twitter, @bjdanielsauthor.

There are books that seem to write themselves. And there are books that try to kill me. This one drove me crazy. But thanks to an escape to the Bahamas with people I love, I was able to finish the book. This one is for Danielle, Travis, Stelly, Leslie and, always, Parker. Your faith in me keeps me going.

Chapter One

The moment she'd stepped into the dark house, she could feel the emptiness surround her like a void. The owners wouldn't be coming to Montana for Christmas this year. The couple was getting a divorce. The man's third marriage, the woman's first.

She'd gotten her information from a good source, but she'd learned, though, that you can never be certain of anything, especially the rumors that ran more wildly than the river ran through the Gallatin Canyon past Big Sky.

Standing stone still in the dark, listening, she waited for a few moments before she snapped on her tiny penlight. There were no other homes close to this one. The owners of these expensive spacious second homes wanted to feel as if they had the mountainside to themselves. Because of that there was little to no chance that anyone would notice if she turned on lights. But she didn't like playing against the odds when it came to the chance of being discovered.

As she moved through the house, she saw sculptures that she knew had cost a small fortune and paintings like some she'd sat for hours studying in museums back East. She hurried on past them, reminded that time was never on her side. In and out as quickly as possible was her personal motto. Otherwise she knew all too well things could go very badly.

She found the painting in the master bedroom on the third floor. A twenty-by-sixteen-inch signed Taylor West original depicting a rancher on horseback surveying his herd. It was one of her favorites. She stepped to it quickly, admiring the brushstrokes and the skillful use of shading as she let the penlight move over it until she found what she was looking for.

Lifting it off the wall, she checked the time. She was running a little over five minutes on this job because of the three stories she'd had to search for this piece.

Quickly she replaced the painting with the one she'd brought, noticing that the bag she'd carried it in had torn. Wadding up the bag, she stuffed it into her coat pocket and tucked the painting from the wall under her arm.

She made her way back through the house, pleased. If only they were all as easy as this one. She'd barely completed the thought when a set of headlights washed over the room.

LARAMIE CARDWELL MENTALLY kicked himself for driving up this snow-packed narrow mountain road in the dark. But according to his sister-in-law, and the real-estate agent for the property, if he wanted a house in the Big Sky area, he had to jump on it the moment it became available.

"Why would you want to buy a house up here when you can stay in one of our guesthouses on the ranch whenever you come?" his cousin Dana Cardwell Savage had argued.

While he appreciated her hospitality at Cardwell Ranch, as much time as he found himself spending in Montana, he wanted a place of his own. It had been family that had brought his brothers back to Montana. But it was love—and barbecue—that had them staying.

He often marveled that it had all started with barbecue—the one thing all five brothers knew. They'd opened a small barbecue joint outside of Houston. Surprisingly, it had taken off and they'd opened others, turning a backyard barbecue into a multimillion-dollar business. It had been his brother Tanner "Tag" Cardwell who'd first come up with the idea of opening their first Texas Boys Barbecue restaurant in Montana in Big Sky.

While some of them had balked at the idea, it had proved to be a good one. Now his brothers were talking about opening others in the state. His four brothers had all returned to their Montana roots, but Laramie was a Texas boy who told himself that he had no desire to live in this wild country—at least not full-time.

With his entire family here now, he wanted his own place, and he could darn sure afford a second home. Though he suspected the one he was on his way to check out would be too large for what he needed.

But there was one way to find out. He figured he'd get a look at the house from the outside. If it wasn't what he wanted, then he wouldn't waste his sister-in-law McKenzie's time looking at the interior.

As he topped a small rise in the road, a moonlit Lone Mountain, the peak that dominated Big Sky, appeared from behind a cloud, making him catch his breath. He'd seen the view numerous times on his other visits to the area, but it still captivated him.

He had to admit this part of Montana was spectacular, although he wasn't so sure about staying up here
for the winter. While the snow was awe inspiring in its
beauty, he still wasn't used to the bracing cold up here.

"You wouldn't mind it if you had someone to cuddle with at night," his brother Tag had joked. All four
of his brothers had fallen in love in Montana—and
with Montana—and now had wives to snuggle up to
on these cold winter nights.

"I only want a house up here," Laramie had said.
"I can kick up the heat when I spend time here during the holidays."

As he topped the rise in the road, his headlights
caught on a three-story house set against the mountainside. Laramie let up on the gas, captivated by the
design of the house and the way it seemed to belong
on the side of the mountain in the pines.

That's when he spotted the dark figure running
along the roofline of the attached garage.

Chapter Two

Laramie remembered hearing that an alleged cat burglar had been seen in Big Sky, but so far the thief hadn't gotten away with anything.

Until now.

Slamming on the brakes, he threw open the door of his rented SUV, leaped out and took off running. It crossed his mind that the robber might be armed and dangerous. But all he could think about was catching the thief.

The freezing snowy night air made his lungs ache. Even though he'd been the business end of Texas Boys Barbecue, he'd stayed in shape. But he felt the high altitude quicken his breathing and reminded himself he wasn't in Houston anymore.

The dark figure had reached the end of the roofline and now leaped down as agile as any cat he'd ever seen. The thief was dressed in all black including a mask that hid his face. He was carrying what appeared to be a painting.

Laramie tackled the burglar, instantly recognizing his physical advantage. The burglar let out a breath as they hit the ground. The painting skidded across the snow.

Rolling over on top of the thief, Laramie held him down with his weight as he fumbled for his cell phone. The slightly built burglar wriggled under him in the deep snow.

"Hold still," he ordered as he finally got his cell phone out and with freezing fingers began to call his cousin's husband, Marshal Hud Savage.

"You're crushing me."

At the burglar's distinctly female voice, Laramie froze. His gaze cut from the phone to the burglar's eyes—the only exposed part of her face other than her mouth. The eyes were a pale blue in the snowy starlight. "You're a…*woman*?"

In a breathless whisper, she said, "You just now noticed that? Could you let me breathe?"

Shocked, he shifted his weight to allow her to take breath into her lungs. This was the cat burglar?

She freed one arm and wiped away the powdery snow from her eyes as she whispered something else.

He cut his eyes to her, suddenly worried that he had injured her when he'd taken her down. She motioned for him to lean closer. He bent down.

Her free hand cupped the back of his neck, pulling him down into a kiss before he could stop her. Suddenly her lips were on his, her mouth parting as if they were lovers.

The next thing he knew he was lying on his back in the snow looking up at the stars as the cat burglar took off. Her escape had been as much of a surprise as the kiss. He quickly sat up. He'd lost his cell phone and his Stetson. Both had fallen into the snow. He plucked them up as he lumbered to his feet. But by then she was already dropping over the side of the ridge.

He took off after her, but he had gone only a few yards when he heard the roar of a snowmobile engine.

Scrambling after her, he turned the corner of the house in time to see the snowmobile roar off through the snow-heavy pines and disappear. He listened to her get away, feeling like a fool. He'd let her trick him.

She'd taken advantage of his surprise and the extra space he'd given her to breathe. She was a lot stronger and more agile than she had appeared and she had a weapon—those lips. He groaned when he thought about the kiss—and its effects on him.

As he turned back, he saw a corner of the painting sticking up out of the snow. Laramie trudged to where it had landed. The only good news was that she hadn't gotten away with the painting.

Surprisingly the frame was still intact. He carefully brushed away the snow, thinking about the woman who'd gotten away. He'd known his share of women in his life. A few had tempted him, a couple had played havoc with his heart and several had taken him for a ride.

However, none of them had tricked him like this. He could well imagine what his brothers would say.

But would he be able to recognize her if he ever saw her again? She'd never spoken above a whisper and he hadn't gotten a chance to remove her ski mask before she'd dumped him in the snow.

Those eyes. Those lips. He told himself if he ever saw either again, damn straight he'd recognize her.

She thought she was smarter than he. She thought she'd gotten away. But he had the painting. And he would find her—if she didn't find him first, he thought, glancing at the painting in the moonlight.

To the fading sound of the snowmobile, he walked back to his rental SUV. Placing the painting in the backseat, he called his cousin's husband, the marshal.

THAT HAD BEEN too close. As Obsidian "Sid" Forester pulled the snowmobile around to the back of the cabin, she glanced over her shoulder. No headlights. No lights at all. She hadn't been followed.

She'd taken a longer route through the trees. At first she'd thought the man who'd tackled her was the owner of the house. But she'd done her research on him and knew he was much older than the man she'd just encountered.

So who was that cowboy with the Southern drawl? Moonlight on snow did strange things to one's vision. But she had gotten a good look at him—a better look than he'd gotten of her, she assured herself. Thick dark hair. Ice-cold blue eyes. Handsome, if you liked that clean-cut, all-business kind of man. She did not.

The only thing that had thrown her was his accent. Definitely from down South. Definitely not the New Yorker who owned the house.

That wasn't all that had thrown her, she had to admit. The kiss. It had worked just as she'd planned and yet… She touched her tongue to her upper lip, remembering the electrical shock she'd felt when they kissed. Worse was the tingling she'd felt in her belly. True, she hadn't kissed a man in… She couldn't even remember when, but she'd never had that kind of reaction. She certainly hadn't expected to feel…anything.

Her pulse was back to normal by the time she entered the cabin. The air smelled of oil paint, turpentine and linseed oil. She shrugged out of her boots and coat at the back door, hung up her coat and kicked her boots aside as she moved to the painting she'd been working on earlier that day.

She gave it a critical perusal before moving into the small kitchen. Unfortunately she hadn't been to the grocery store in several days. She was always starved after one of what she called her "night jobs." With a bottle of beer—her last—a chunk of cheese and some stale bread, she stepped into the living area where a half dozen paintings were drying.

The cabin was small with only a living room, kitchen, bedroom, small bath and a storage room off to one side at the back. The moment the owner had shown it to her—and told her about all its peculiarities—she'd had to have it and had quickly signed the papers.

Sitting down now, she considered each of her paintings as she ate her snack and sipped her beer. It was hard to concentrate after what had happened earlier, though. She'd come close to getting caught before, but nothing like tonight. What would the man do?

Go to the marshal.

She considered that and decided she wasn't worried about the law catching up with her.

What did worry her was that he had the painting.

Taking another bite of cheese and bread, she chewed for a moment before washing it down with the last of the beer. She really did have to go to the store tomorrow.

Just the thought of going out in public made her wonder if she would run into him. That was the other thing about her cabin. It was nestled in the woods, far from urban Big Sky.

What if she did see him again? She had no doubt

that she would recognize him. She'd gotten a good look at him. He had high cheekbones, a patrician nose and generous mouth. She felt that ridiculous stirring again over that one stupid kiss.

She assured herself that there wasn't any way he could recognize her since she'd had the black ski mask on the whole time. Nor could he recognize her voice since she hadn't spoken above a whisper.

Shaking her head, she tried to put him out of her mind. There was more than a good chance that she would never see him again. Obviously he was a tourist, probably only here for the holidays. Once the holidays were over, he'd be on a jet back to wherever he'd picked up that Southern drawl.

Still, she wondered who he was and why he'd driven up to the house tonight. Probably lost. Just her luck. What other reason could he have had to be there?

But while she'd gotten away, it hadn't been clean, which upset her more than she wanted to admit. She prided herself on her larceny skills. Worse, she'd failed. She didn't have the painting.

Losing her appetite, she tossed the crust of stale bread in the trash and put the cheese back into the fridge before she returned to her work in progress. She always did her best thinking while she painted.

"SO, YOU DIDN'T see her face?" Marshal Hud Savage asked as he looked up from his report at the marshal's office later that night.

"She was wearing a ski mask with only the eyes and mouth part open. Her eyes were this amazing… bluish-silvery color." Laramie frowned. "Maybe it was the starlight but they seemed to change color." He realized the marshal was staring at him. "Just put down blue. If I ever see those eyes again, I'll recognize her." Or those lips, he thought, but he wasn't about to tell Hud about the kiss.

It had taken him by surprise—just as she'd planned. But for a moment, his mouth had been on hers. He'd looked into her eyes, felt something quicken inside him, then her warm breath on his cheek and...

He shook his head, reminding himself that it had only been a ploy and he'd fallen for it, hook, line and sinker. He'd kissed a *thief*! What annoyed him was that he had felt anything but disgust for what she'd done.

"How about height and weight?" Hud asked after writing down *blue*.

Laramie shrugged. "Small. Maybe five-five or -six. I have no idea on weight. Slim. I'm sorry I don't have a better description. It all happened too fast. But I have the painting. Maybe you can get her fingerprints—"

"Was she wearing gloves?"

He groaned.

"And you say she got away on a snowmobile?"

All he could do was nod.

"Did you get a make or model?"

Another shake of his head.

"And she overpowered you? Was she armed?"

Laramie groaned inwardly. "Not armed exactly. She was much stronger than I expected and she moved so fast... She caught me off guard."

Hud nodded, but he appeared to be trying hard not to laugh.

"You wait until you find her. She's...wily."

Hud did chuckle then. "I'm sure she is. Here. Sign this."

"So what are the chances you'll catch her?" Laramie asked as he signed the report.

"With a description like the one you just gave me…" Hud shook his head. His phone rang and he reached for it. "Marshal Savage." He listened, his gaze going to Laramie. "Okay. Yep, that'll do it." Hanging up, he picked up the signed report and ripped it in half before tossing it into the trash.

"What?" Laramie demanded.

"I just spoke with the owner of the house. He hadn't planned to come up this holiday, but apparently McKenzie called him yesterday and told him you would be looking at the house. Seems he's anxious to sell, so he flew in tonight." Hud met his gaze. "When I called the maintenance service and asked them to check the house, they found him there. He looked around to see what was missing and found nothing out of order."

"There wasn't anything missing? Was he sure?"

"It seems he has a painting, just like that one…" He pointed to the one leaning against the wall on the floor near Laramie, the painting the cat burglar had dropped. "It isn't missing."

"That's not possible."

Hud shrugged. "The owner says he has the original—the only one of its kind. Also, he said his house hasn't been broken into."

"That can't be right. I saw her coming out of the house."

"Or did you just see her on the ridge of the garage roofline?" the marshal asked.

Laramie thought back. "Maybe I didn't see her come out of the house."

"Since the first report we received about a cat burglar, we've had several sightings. But in all three cases, nothing was taken, the house showed no sign of forced entry…"

Laramie could see where this was going. "So it was a…hoax?"

Hud studied him openly for a moment. "You didn't happen to mention to your brothers that you were going up to that house tonight, did you? They also didn't happen to tell you beforehand about a cat burglar in the area, did they?"

He would kill his brothers. "You think it was a setup?"

Hud shrugged. "You know your brothers better than I do, but I'd say you've been had."

Had in more ways than the marshal could even imagine. He got to his feet. "I'm sorry to bother you with this, then. I just hope they haven't planted counterfeit money on me, as well." His brothers had told him that Hud was investigating a counterfeit operation that had been passing fraudulent money in the canyon.

"Let's hope not," Hud said with a groan. "I get a call a day about a bad twenty. Someone's churning them out," he said getting to his feet. "In the old days it took a lot of expensive equipment and space along with some talent. Now, all you need is a good copy machine. A video online will walk you through the entire process. The good news is that these operations are often small. We aren't talking millions of dollars. Just someone needing some instant spending money."

"Well, good luck finding your counterfeiter and, again, I'm sorry about this. You have enough going on." But as he turned to the door, he said, "What about the painting?"

"The owner swears he has the authenticated original with paperwork on the back." Hud shrugged. "I would imagine this is nothing more than a cheap prop."

"Then you don't mind if I keep it?" Laramie asked.

The marshal chuckled. "It's all yours."

Laramie considered the painting on the floor. It was what he would have called Old West art, a rancher on horseback surveying his herd. It was titled "On The Ranch" and signed by an artist named Taylor West. The painting looked expensive to him, but what did he know?

"If someone comes looking for it, I'll let you know. But I have my doubts." Hud grinned. "If you ever see that woman again, though… I'd be curious just what color her eyes are since they seem to have made a real impression on you."

"REALLY?" LARAMIE DEMANDED when he saw his brother Tanner "Tag" Cardwell at his house the next morning. "That wasn't funny what you and the others pulled last night." He couldn't help but wonder if the kiss had been planned, as well. It was a nice touch, something that would have had his brothers rolling on the floor laughing. "Hud got a real kick out of it since he has nothing to do but take bogus crime reports. I hope he arrests the whole bunch of you."

"I don't know what you're talking about," Tag said as he poured coffee for them.

Laramie looked to his sister-in-law and real-estate agent McKenzie. He'd been staying with them this holiday and, while he enjoyed being with them, he was anxious to get his own place. McKenzie had been helping him find a house.

"Tell me you weren't in on it, too," he said to her.

"I abhor practical jokes." McKenzie shot a disapproving glance at her husband. "What did you and your brothers do?"

"*Nothing. Honest.* I have no idea what he's talking about," Tag said holding up his hands. He looked genuinely innocent.

But Laramie wasn't buying it. He knew his brothers too well. They'd all treated him as if he was the bookworm who ran their family business, Texas Boys Barbecue. They would all have said he was the brother who never had enough adventure in his life.

So it would be just like them to set this up to add some spice to his life, as they would call it.

"Who was the woman?" Laramie demanded.

"There was a *woman*?" Tag asked and grinned.

McKenzie shook her head. "You'll have to tell me about it on the way to the house, Laramie. I promised the owner we'd be there by nine. You can deal with your brothers later."

On the way up the mountain, he told McKenzie about what had happened last night.

"That doesn't sound like something Tag would do," she said. "Are you sure your brothers were behind it?"

"It's the only thing that makes any sense. I saw her leaving with a painting. So, of course, I thought she'd stolen it. I guess that's what I was supposed to think."

"Are you sure the painting you have is a fake?"

"It doesn't look like it to me, but I'm no expert by any means. The owner says he still has the original. So maybe I stopped the woman before she could make the switch, but I could have sworn she was coming *from* the house."

McKenzie seemed to give it some thought. "Maybe she saw your headlights coming up the road and took off before she could make the switch."

"I suppose. If she really was a cat burglar. Or it could be just what the marshal thinks it is—my brothers' idea of a joke.

"I know an art expert if you're interested in finding out about the painting. Or, if it is by a local Western artist, you could take it right to the source," she said.

"Have you ever heard of Taylor West?"

McKenzie looked over at him in surprise. "He's a well-known artist in these parts. He lives farther up the canyon near Taylor Fork. I'm sure if you took the painting to him, he'd be able to tell you if it was his or not."

"I just might do that." He looked up the mountain road ahead and thought about what he'd seen last night as he'd come over the last rise. He couldn't help thinking about the woman. She'd certainly played her part well. If his brothers had been in on it.

He thought about what he'd seen in her eyes just before he started to call the marshal. She'd looked scared. But that could have been an act, too.

"First thing I want to do is see the original," he said to McKenzie.

"You think the owner lied about having it? Why would he do that?" she asked as the house came into view.

"I don't know. To collect on the insurance, maybe. He could be in on some scam involving the artwork if this artist is that well-known."

McKenzie raised a brow as she parked next to a

white SUV next to the house. "Cowboy art doesn't go for that much. A Taylor West might sell for near a hundred grand to the right market. But we aren't talking the Mona Lisa."

He didn't know what the original was worth, but he was anxious to see it. "I looked up the artist's website last night. Most of Taylor West's original work sells for twenty-five to seventy-five thousand depending on the size. Some of his older works are worth more."

"Did you see this particular painting on the artist's website?"

"No."

The owner, Theo Nelson, turned out to be an older distinguished man who'd apparently made his money in real estate back East. "If you have any questions, just let me know. I'll be in my study." Nelson disappeared up the stairs, leaving them alone.

"So what do you think, so far?" McKenzie asked as they stepped to the bank of windows that looked out on Lone Mountain. The snow-covered peak glowed in the morning sun against a robin's-egg-blue sky.

"The view is incredible," Laramie said. Then he dragged his gaze away to look at the paintings on the walls.

"This open concept is nice," McKenzie said as she went into the kitchen. "Great for entertaining. Granite countertops, new top-of-the-line appliances, lots of cupboard space, a walk-in pantry and even more storage for multiple sets of china and glassware—if you ever get married to a woman who collects both... You aren't listening to me," she said when Laramie didn't take the bait.

"Sorry. Let's see the second story," he said, already starting up the stairs.

The next floor had a large second living area, two bedrooms and a study. The study door was partially open, the owner at his desk, head down.

Laramie scanned the walls quickly. The painting wasn't there.

"Another great view," McKenzie was saying.

He agreed, taking a moment to notice the house. He liked it. "Let's see the top floor." He saw her shake her head, but she followed him up to the third level.

This, he realized, was a huge master bedroom. It cantilevered out so when he stood at the bank of windows, he felt as if he was flying.

"Impressive," McKenzie said. "But I'm not sure I could sleep in here. I have this thing about heights. The master bathroom is really nice, though. Check out this shower." She turned, no doubt realizing she'd lost him again.

Laramie stood in front of a painting, shaking his head. "This is the one."

"Does it look like the painting you took from the woman last night?" McKenzie asked in a whisper as she stepped closer.

"It looks *exactly* like it. How can he be so sure it's the original?"

"Because I had it authenticated." Neither of them had heard the owner come up the stairs to join them. Now the man stepped past them to take the painting off the wall and show them the back.

Laramie could see that it had a small card taped to the back. He realized how easy it would have been for the cat burglar to make the switch—including the authentication.

"You must be the man who thought you saw a burglar here last night," Nelson said as he put the painting back on the wall. "I'm glad it was a false alarm."

"Me, too," Laramie said, still not sure he believed it.

"So what do you think of the house?" the man asked.

"I like it."

"We'll be looking at some others," McKenzie said quickly. "How long are you going to be in town?"

"Only as long as it takes. So if you're interested…"

"You'll hear from us," she said, motioning to Laramie that it was time to go. "I have several other houses for us to look at this morning," she said once they were in the SUV heading off the mountain.

"Don't bother. I want that one."

She shot him a look. "But you haven't even—"

"That's the house. Find out what furniture stays. Also I want that painting."

As they dropped over the rise, the house disappearing behind them, McKenzie hit her brakes and skidded to a stop in the middle of the narrow snow-packed road. "You want the painting?"

"I'm pretty sure he'll part with it. If he's selling the house, then he's leaving Montana. His next wife won't want any cowboy art in her house."

McKenzie laughed. "You are definitely decisive once you make up your mind, but did you even look at the house or do you really just want the painting?"

He smiled over at her. "I want both. See what kind of deal you can get me, but don't take no for an answer."

She laughed and shook her head as she got the SUV

going again. "You're more like your brothers than I thought you were."

She had no idea. "I think you're right," Laramie said. "It wasn't my brothers who put that woman up to that stunt last night."

"I'm relieved to hear you say that," she said.

"I think she really *is* a cat burglar."

McKenzie shot him a look. "But she didn't steal anything."

He rubbed his jaw, surprised that he'd forgotten to shave. He'd been so anxious to confront Tag this morning. "I'm not sure about that."

"Why am I getting a bad feeling that you're thinking of trying to catch this woman?"

He smiled over at her. He knew he could go to his brothers for help. Hayes was a private investigator and Austin, who'd been a deputy sheriff, now worked for Hayes at his investigative business.

But his cat burglar had made this personal. He wanted to catch her himself.

Chapter Three

"I know Taylor West's work well," the art dealer said when Laramie called. "Who did you say gave you my name?"

"Local Realtor McKenzie Sheldon Cardwell. She said she's worked with you before."

"Oh, yes, McKenzie," Herbert Darlington said. "You have a painting you'd like me to authenticate?"

"If you can."

Darlington made an unpleasant sound. "If it is a true Taylor West work, I will be able to tell at once. When would you like me to take a look at it?"

"I'm parked outside your gallery right now."

The gallery was in a narrow building along the main street of Bozeman. Laramie had driven the forty-five miles first thing that morning. He was anxious to know about the painting. Even more anxious to know about the woman who'd gotten away.

Golden light shone on the paintings on the old brick walls of the gallery as he entered. He looked for any by Taylor West and saw several of Native Americans as well as one of cowboys. This one, though, was a cattle drive filled with longhorns and cowboys driving the herd through a canyon. It looked so real he could almost smell the dust the cattle were kicking up.

"Bring it back here," Darlington said motioning to a door at the back. The man was short and thick with thinning hair above a round red face. He wore a dark suit like an undertaker and sported a narrow black mustache above narrow thin lips.

Without another word, Darlington took the framed painting from him and moved over to a table. He snapped on a light, pulled on a pair of glasses and bent over the artwork.

"Where did you get this?" he asked after a moment.

"I picked it up from an unknown source."

Darlington shot him a look over one shoulder before returning to the painting. "It's quite good."

"But it's not a Taylor West."

"I didn't say that."

Laramie waited impatiently as the man pulled out a magnifying glass and went over the entire painting again. So much for being able to tell at a glance.

After a few minutes, Darlington let out a sigh, took off his glasses, snapped off the light and turned. "It's an original Taylor West."

Laramie let out a laugh as he raked a hand through his hair. How was that possible? How did any of this make sense? It didn't. "You're sure?"

The art expert gave him a pained, insulted look. "I'm guessing you picked it up for a song."

"Something like that." He reached for the painting.

"So you're interested in selling it," Darlington said. "I suppose I could make you an offer."

"It's not for sale." He reached again for the painting and this time the gallery owner handed it over, though reluctantly.

"I would be happy to authenticate it for you in writing," the gallery owner said.

Laramie wondered if he'd authenticated the one now hanging in the house he hoped McKenzie was getting for him. "I'll think about it." The art dealer walked him toward the front door.

Just then a tall, thin older man with a shoulder-length mane of white-blond hair and a handlebar mustache came in on a gust of wind. He looked like something out of an Old West movie.

"Cody can verify what I've told you," Darlington said.

Laramie eyed the man, wondering if he was also considered an art expert.

"Cody Kent is another of our Western artists," the gallery owner said. Then he turned to Cody. "Mr. Cardwell brought in a Taylor West painting. He was questioning its authenticity."

"Really?" Cody tilted his head to look at the painting in Laramie's hand as Darlington explained to him that while this was a one-of-a-kind piece, apparently there was another one owned by another collector.

That definitely got the man's attention. "So you're saying one of them is a forgery?"

"I'd stake my reputation that this is the original," Darlington said, puffing himself up. "Do you agree?"

Laramie handed the man the artwork and watched him as he inspected it. He noticed that the man's hands seemed to tremble as he stared at it.

The artist handed it back. "Sure looks like the real

thing to me." Cody Kent's gaze met his. "Where did you get it?"

"Just picked it up recently," Laramie said. He took it back from the older man. "Glad to hear you both agree it is an authentic Taylor West."

As he headed for the door, Darlington followed. "Well, if you decide to get rid of it..."

Laramie shook his head but then stopped just short of the door to ask, "How much would you say it's worth?" He noticed that Cody Kent had moved to one of the paintings on display only yards from them, clearly listening to the conversation.

Darlington seemed to give a price more thought than was necessary since he'd just offered to buy it. "I could give you...thirty," he said, keeping his voice down.

"Thirty?"

"Thirty *thousand*," Darlington said. "It would be more but it's an older piece. His work has improved over the years."

Was that right? Laramie smiled to himself. From what he'd seen online last night, artists' older work appeared to have more value—especially if the artist was now dead. Taylor West was still kicking, apparently, but Laramie suspected the painting must be worth a lot more that what he was being offered.

"Thanks, but I think I'll keep it," he said as he tucked it under his arm. "It has...sentimental value."

SID PUT ON clean jeans and a sweater to go to the grocery store. Often she went in her paint-streaked pants and shirts. Anyone who paid any attention was aware that she painted since she spent most Saturdays at the local craft show selling her wares.

Not her paintings, but haphazardly done Montana scenes on everything from old metal saw blades and antique milk cans to ancient tractor parts and windmill blades. Amazingly, her crafts sold well, which proved to her that most people didn't know the difference between good art and bad.

But today she wanted to fly under the radar. No reason to call attention to herself as an artist. It might be too risky if the man from last night was still in town. She knew she was being silly. He'd probably completely forgotten about her.

She assumed he would have gone to the marshal last night with a story about her robbing that house. Since the painting wouldn't be missing, she wasn't worried.

Her only regret was losing the painting. She needed it. Which meant she had to get it back. Or taking all these chances would have been for nothing.

Where was the painting now? She'd learned at a young age to make friends where needed. Now she picked up the phone and called her friend who worked at the marshal's office as she drove to the grocery store.

After the usual pleasantries, she said, "So what's new down there?" Dispatcher Tara Kirkwood loved her job because she got to know everything that was going on—and she loved to share it.

"Counterfeit bills keep turning up," Tara said, keeping her voice down although the office was small and she was probably the only person down there right then. The marshal and detectives were probably out.

She and Tara had established long ago that anything Tara told her wouldn't go any further—and it never had. "The marshal is chasing one right now that was passed at the Corral Bar."

"No more cat burglar sightings?" she asked after listening to what Tara knew about the counterfeit bills.

"Actually, before Hud left, he said his wife's cousin who is in town caught the cat burglar last night." She laughed. "According to him, the burglar turned out to be a *her*."

"No kidding? So is she locked up down there?"

"Naw, she got away." Tara laughed again. "Hud got a chuckle out of it since apparently there was no crime and his cousin-in-law was quite taken with the woman."

Sid laughed even though this was not what she wanted to hear. The marshal's cousin-in-law? Just her luck. Not to mention "quite taken with her"? *Really?* She thought of the kiss. It might have been a mistake since she'd had a hard time forgetting about it, as well.

"What's the guy's name?" she asked.

"Laramie Cardwell."

Cardwell? Anyone who lived in the Gallatin Canyon knew that name. The Cardwell Ranch was one of the first established in the canyon. But she'd never heard of a Laramie Cardwell before.

"You said he was in town. So he's not from here?" she asked even though she knew his accent was way too Southern.

"His father is Angus Cardwell. Apparently his mother got a divorce years ago and took her five sons to live in Texas. Laramie's up here from Houston. He and his brothers own that new place, Texas Boys Barbecue."

"Huh."

"Have you tried it yet?" Tara asked.

"No. I've been meaning to, though," she said, realizing it was true.

"It's really good."

"So did the so-called cat burglar get away with anything?" she had to ask. "You said no crime was committed?"

"Laramie found a painting, but it wasn't stolen from the house. I overheard Hud say Laramie is hanging on to it. Kind of like a souvenir."

Sid mouthed a silent oath. She'd reached Meadow Village and the grocery store. "So now it's hanging at Cardwell Ranch," she joked.

"More than likely at his new house," Tara said.

"His new house?"

The dispatcher dropped her voice even further. "The house that he caught her allegedly robbing? He's *buying* it."

Sid pulled into a parking spot in front of the store. Tara was always a wealth of information. "Now that is a coincidence," she said. "So apparently he's staying."

"At least for the holidays I would think. You really should try their barbecue. It is *so* good."

"I just might do that. Got to go. Sure hope they catch those counterfeiters."

"Me, too. Hud is fit to be tied. It will be nice when things die back down around here."

Disconnecting, Sid parked in front of the grocery, thinking about everything Tara had said. How was she going to get the painting back? She'd never been one to push her luck and hitting the same house twice was more than risky, especially since now Laramie

Cardwell might be expecting her. But did she really have a choice?

Her stomach growled. Still hungry and realizing it was almost lunchtime, she looked up the hill at the sign for Texas Boys Barbecue.

THE FAMILY HAD gathered at the Cardwell Ranch for lunch. Everyone but Laramie.

"What's going on with him?" Austin asked. For years he had been the no-show brother, the one who caught grief because he didn't play family well. Since meeting Gillian and returning to his birthplace, he'd changed. He loved these family get-togethers.

"He's looking for the cat burglar," McKenzie said. "And the four of you can blame yourself for that if you're behind this."

"What?" Austin asked, looking around the table. Tag told him what he knew, Hud added his part and McKenzie finished it up. *"Seriously?* Laramie is trying to find this woman?" He turned to Tag. "You told him we had nothing to do with this, right?"

"I swore we didn't."

Austin groaned. "So he might actually be chasing a real cat burglar."

"Only if the cat burglar is a young woman with silvery-blue eyes," Hud said, shaking his head. "This whole cat burglar thing started when a few residents saw a dark-clad figure sneaking around a couple of houses. But the bottom line is that no one has reported being burglarized. No valuables or paintings are missing."

"So you think it's a hoax," Austin said.

"I do," the marshal agreed. "Probably the local security company put the woman up to it to drum up more business. A lot of the people in Big Sky are from urban areas so security is a concern for them. The rest of us locals don't even bother to lock our doors."

"He told me he was going to visit the artist whose painting the woman dropped," McKenzie said between bites. "Taylor West. He lives up the canyon near Taylor Fork."

"Why didn't he come to us?" Austin asked his brother Hayes. "We are actually trained for this sort of thing." He'd gone to work for Hayes's detective agency after quitting the sheriff's department in Texas—he hadn't been satisfied being simply retired. Gillian had been right. He'd been miserable. He was too young to retire and he enjoyed investigative work.

"Seriously?" Dana asked. "You don't understand why your brother might want to solve this thing on his own? It involves an apparently attractive woman who tricked him and escaped. Laramie is related to all of you. Enough said. He probably thinks she's in trouble and is off to save her."

They all laughed, but Austin couldn't shake the bad feeling he had.

"I know that look in your eye," Gillian said to Austin. "Don't do it."

"She's right," Jackson said speaking up. "We need to stay out of this. I think Laramie's been getting bored running the business. Why not let him have a little… fun, since there is nothing to the cat burglar stories?"

They all agreed. Except Austin. *"Fun?* What if this woman is dangerous?"

"Laramie can take care of himself," Hayes said. "He hasn't just been sitting behind a desk for the past ten years. He's worked with some of us on cases. I think Jackson's right. He needs this and he needs us to stay out of it."

Austin couldn't help being protective of his youngest brother. While he and Hayes had both worked in law enforcement, Laramie had no experience dealing with criminals.

"I hope you're right," Austin said as he watched his family finish their lunches. Still, he couldn't shake the feeling that Laramie had no idea what he was getting into.

For the time being, he'd stay out of it since, if Hud was right, it had been nothing but a prank. But if a woman was involved…

Chapter Four

Artist Taylor West was a tall drink of water. At least that's how Laramie had seen him described on his website. The man who opened the door at the West home *was* tall. He'd aged, though, since he'd put his photo on his website. Laramie guessed he must be in his sixties and had once been very handsome. The gray hair at his temples gave him a distinguished look, but his complexion told the story of a man who drank too much.

"I don't usually meet clients at my home," West said, looking put out.

Laramie was glad he hadn't called ahead. "This was a matter that couldn't wait." A photograph on the wall behind the man caught Laramie's attention. It was of Taylor with a pretty young green-eyed blonde. He was staring at the photo more intently than he realized—especially at the eyes. Could this be the woman he'd tackled last night? She looked the right size but the eye color was wrong.

"My wife, Jade," West said.

Laramie blinked in surprise. Given the age difference between the artist and the woman in the photo, he would have thought it was West's daughter.

West's gaze went to the painting Laramie was holding in one hand. "Is that one of mine?" He sounded like a man worried that Laramie had come here to complain.

"That's what I'd like to know. I promise not to take any more of your time than necessary."

"What makes you think it's mine?" West asked.

"Because it has your name on it." He didn't mention that the so-called expert at the gallery had authenticated it.

"Well, fine, come on in out of the cold. This shouldn't take long." He didn't look less perturbed, but he did step back to let Laramie in.

But that was as far as the invitation was extended. Standing in the entryway of the house, Laramie uncovered the painting and handed it to the artist. Past West, he could see that the house was a huge mess. So where was the young wife?

West looked at it and said, "I don't see what the problem is," and started to hand it back.

"So it's yours?" Laramie asked.

"Obviously," the artist said with impatience.

"Then there *is* a problem." He told him about the one that Theo Nelson owned, the one that had been authenticated. "How do you explain that?"

"One of them must be a forgery since I only painted one."

"And you're sure this one is the original?"

West snatched the painting from him and with a curse headed down a hallway. Laramie followed, stepping over boots and shoes, jackets, dirty socks and assorted dog toys.

"The cleaning crew comes tomorrow," West said

over his shoulder before turning into what was obviously his studio. It, too, was in disarray.

Laramie suspected the man didn't have anyone to clean the house. Or the young wife to do so, either, for that matter.

West snapped on a lamp and put the painting under it. "Where did you get this?"

"I picked it up recently."

"Nelson is right. If he has the original, then this one isn't mine," West said.

"Are you sure?" Clearly he wasn't. "I should tell you that before I came here, I took the painting to a local expert," Laramie said. "He confirmed it was yours and offered me thirty thousand for it."

The artist's eyes widened in surprise. "The original is worth over fifty."

Just as Laramie had suspected. "But the question is, which is the original?"

West swore. "If this is a forgery, it's a really good one." The man was frowning at the artwork, clearly angry and also seeming confused.

"I've looked at both. They appear identical. So if you didn't paint the copy, then who did?"

The artist shook his head. "How would I know?" He was upset now.

"It would take some talent, wouldn't it?"

West sighed impatiently. "Sure, but—"

"Otherwise, you're saying any art student could copy your paintings?"

"I see what you're getting at," the older man said angrily. "Yes, it takes talent. A *lot* of talent. They would have had to have studied their craft and have some natural ability, as well. Also they would have had to

study my work. Not just anyone could make a repro-
duction this good."

"So has this person been hiding under a rock, or is
it someone you know?"

West seemed shocked by the question. "It couldn't
possibly be anyone I know."

"Why not? I would think the cowboy art market is
very small. It must also be competitive. There can't be
that many of you painting at this level, right?"

The artist nodded. "There are only twenty of us in
the OWAC." Seeing Laramie's quizzical expression, he
elaborated. "The Old West Artists Coalition."

Laramie considered that. "Only twenty? That
sounds like a pretty elite—and competitive—group."

"We're all *friends*. We encourage and support each
other. The only competition is with ourselves to get
better."

"But some of you must make more money than others," he prodded. "Who is the best paid of this group
of cowboy artists?"

West met his gaze with an arrogant one. "I am, but
there are several others who do quite well."

"And you're telling me there is no jealousy?" Laramie scoffed at that. He knew too well, being one of five
brothers, that competition was in male DNA. "So who
are the others who are doing 'quite well'?"

"Cody Kent and Hank Ramsey, in that order. Rock
Jackson quite a ways behind those two."

Laramie couldn't help but laugh. Just the fact that
West knew that proved *he* at least had a competitive
spirit. "So what exactly does this group do?"

"I told you. We support each other. We came together because of a desire to keep this art form alive

in memory of the greats like the late Frederic Remington and Charles M. Russell. But also to ensure the work is an authentic representation of Western life. Without standards of quality and a respect for each other and the work..." He sounded as if he was quoting the group's bylaws.

"And you belong to this group?"

"I'm one of its founders along with Rock, Hank and Cody Kent," he said proudly.

Laramie had heard something in the man's tone. "What does it take to be a member?"

"You have to apply. The members decide if your work and your character meet our standards."

"Your *standards*?"

"Originally, you had to have cowboy experience as well as talent. That's changed some. Why are you asking me all this?" West demanded.

Laramie wasn't sure. "So it's an exclusive...club."

"None of my fellow artists would have any reason to rip me off by duplicating my work, if that's what you're getting at," West said. "Not to mention, most of them don't have the talent to copy my work."

Laramie tried not to smile. No competition here.

"Look," West said as if he knew he'd said too much. "There aren't that many of us. We're a dying breed of artists who care about our work. The satisfaction comes from painting and selling our own work—not copying someone else's and passing it off for money."

"Even if they needed money badly?" Laramie asked.

He saw something change in West's expression as if the question had made him think of someone. Laramie knew money could be the most obvious reason for making forgeries of Taylor West's work. Or maybe to rub West's arrogant face in it.

West picked up the painting, frowning harder as he studied it again. "This is definitely the original," he said, but he seemed to lack conviction.

"If no one in your group is talented enough to make you question if this painting is yours or not..."

"I'm telling you," West snapped, "there's no one alive who could have copied my work well enough to fool an expert, let alone me."

Laramie thought that was a ridiculous statement given that someone obviously had, and he said as much.

West suddenly looked even more upset. "There is one man," the artist said after a moment. He'd paled. "H. F. Powell."

"Where would I find him?"

West didn't seem to hear him for a moment. He shook his head as if clearing away cobwebs from his brain. "Find him?" His laugh was more of a grunt. "Six feet under, last I checked."

TEXAS? SO THAT was Laramie Cardwell's accent, Sid thought. The barbecue restaurant had opened in Big Sky Meadows just last year. She'd heard it was owned by five brothers from Houston. Since she didn't get out much—at least during the day—that had been all Sid knew about the place.

Good sense told her to go into the store, buy some food and take it back to the cabin. The sooner she got home, the sooner she could get ready for tonight. Last night's close call was a good reminder that she needed to finish this and move on.

But barbecue sounded good. More than anything, she was curious. She quickly shopped for what groceries she needed, telling herself she would get a barbecue sandwich to go. She knew she was taking a risk, but then again, she'd been taking risks for some time now. Putting the groceries into the back of her SUV, she walked quickly up the hill to Texas Boys Barbecue on the recently plowed sidewalk. The sun glistening off the snow was almost blinding. It was one of those clear, cold winter days in Big Sky when she could see her breath as she walked. She looked up at Lone Mountain, momentarily stunned by how beautiful it was this morning.

Sometimes she got so busy she forgot to notice what an amazing place this was. Once she was done with all of this, maybe she would take a few weeks off and snowboard up on the mountain. She deserved it after this.

A bell jangled over the door as she entered the restaurant. It was early so the place was busy but not packed, and there were enough people that she didn't think she would stand out. Not that she believed Laramie Cardwell could recognize her.

The aroma of smoked meat filled the air, making her stomach growl again. Slipping into a booth, she pulled out a menu from behind an array of barbecue sauces with names like Hot in Houston and Sweet and Spicy San Antonio.

She'd just opened it when she heard a male voice with a distinct Southern accent coming from the kitchen. Looking up she saw a head of dark hair. The man was talking to another man with the same accent. As the first man turned, she realized he wasn't the one from last night, but the resemblance gave her a start even before she laid eyes on the second man.

It was him!

Suddenly, as if sensing her staring at him, he glanced in her direction. Sid quickly ducked behind her menu as a young waitress approached her booth.

"What can I get you?" asked a teenaged girl with a ponytail and an order pad.

"I'll try the pulled pork sandwich with beans and coleslaw," Sid said from behind her menu. "Can I get that to go?"

"Great choice. What would you like to drink?" the girl asked.

Sid peeked out from behind the menu. Through the window into the kitchen she could no longer see the two men—nor could she hear them. Maybe they'd left.

"And a beer."

The girl nodded, then shyly asked if she could see her ID. "I'm sorry, but I have to ask."

Sid might have found that amusing since she was thirty. But she was aware that she didn't look a day over twenty. Behind the waitress, she heard the men's voices coming from the kitchen again. They sounded as though they were arguing.

She heard one say he didn't like what the other one was doing. "Austin, if I need your help I'll ask for it. I can handle this." Laramie Cardwell's voice. Handle what?

Sid looked up at the waitress. Today of all days, she didn't want to show her ID. She knew it was silly since Laramie Cardwell hadn't seen her face last night. But he might have a few moments ago. She remembered him above her in the moonlight and the way he'd looked into her eyes…and felt a shiver.

"You know, just make it a cola. I have work to do this afternoon."

The poor girl nodded without looking at her and wrote on her order pad.

"The owners of this place, are they really from Texas?" Sid asked.

The girl brightened. "They sure are. Five brothers. They just opened this place, but I heard there's another one going to open at Red Lodge."

"Really? Five brothers, huh?"

"Yep, all raised in Texas. They were born here, but left when they were kids. Four of them have moved back."

"The fifth one?" Sid asked, remembering how strong the man's Texas accent had been.

"Laramie still lives in Houston. That's where the main office is located. He's the one in charge of all the restaurants. They're cousins to Dana Cardwell of Cardwell Ranch, if you're familiar with the area."

Anyone who lived in the Canyon as the Gallatin Canyon was known had heard of the Cardwells of Cardwell Ranch.

"Their story is on the back of the menu, if you're interested. I'll get your order right out," the girl said. "You want that cola while you wait?"

Sid would much rather have had a beer and felt foolish for not showing the girl her ID. What were the chances that the waitress would remember her name or have any reason to mention it to her bosses?

Glancing toward the kitchen, she didn't see the men. Or hear them, but that didn't mean they weren't still back there. And if the man from last night had seen her a few minutes ago...

"Sure, I'll take the cola now, but make it to go," she said as she picked up the menu and turned it over.

The Cardwell brothers' story was on the back along with their photos. What surprised her was that Texas Boys Barbecue was a franchise the brothers had started. She'd just assumed they only owned this one restaurant.

Less surprising was that all five brothers were drop-dead gorgeous. In the photo on the back of the menu, the photographer had lined them up along a jack-legged fence, a ranch house in the background. Each brother wore jeans, boots, Western shirts and Stetsons. Each was equally handsome.

Her gaze went to Laramie. He was definitely the one who'd tackled her last night. She felt a shiver as she looked at his photo. His blue eyes stared back at her almost challenging. She told herself she had nothing to fear. He didn't know who she was or the marshal would have been to her door already. Even if he had bought that house, he'd be like most of the residents—staying only a few weeks of the year.

She wished she could wait for him to return to Texas. Unfortunately, she couldn't. Time was running out. She had to get the painting back—even knowing there was a chance of crossing paths with Laramie Cardwell again. She would just have to make sure that didn't happen.

Chapter Five

Laramie left the restaurant, his mind on the painting and the woman, of course. The winter day sparkled under a blinding sun that ricocheted off the new-fallen snow. At loose ends waiting to hear if McKenzie got him the house, he went for a drive up the canyon.

Next to the highway, the Gallatin River snaked through the canyon under a thick layer of aquamarine ice. He tried to enjoy the beauty of this alien winter place. The snowcapped pines bent under the weight of their frozen burden, reminding him that it was less than a week until Christmas. His cousin Dana loved the holidays and went all-out surrounded by her family. He smiled at the thought.

Glancing in his review mirror, he realized he'd seen the large dark brown older-model sedan behind him before—right after he'd left Taylor West's house. It was behind him again.

He tried to laugh off the thought of someone following him. First cat burglars now this? Well, there was one way to find out, he thought as he neared the Corral Bar. He slowed and pulled in. The car went on past.

The windows on the vehicle had been tinted, so he hadn't gotten a good look at the driver. If he had to guess, he'd say male. As it disappeared up the road, he told himself the driver hadn't been following him anyway.

He thought about going inside the bar and having a burger and a beer. This was his father and uncle's favorite bar. Their band often played here.

But he was too antsy. He wanted to get back and find out if McKenzie had gotten him the house…and the painting. He pulled back on the road headed toward Big Sky again, his thoughts going to his cat burglar. The forgery at the house had to have been painted by someone with a whole lot of talent as Taylor West had said.

So if it was a forgery, who had painted it? Not some dead man named H. F. Powell unless he'd painted it before his demise. But the big question was why would his thief take it instead of the authenticated original?

She wouldn't. So if he was right and she'd been coming out of the house when he'd arrived, then she'd been in the process of stealing the original when he'd stopped her.

Which meant McKenzie was about to make a deal for a forgery.

Shaking his head at his own foolishness, he glanced in his rearview mirror. The brown car was back.

He felt a start at the sight of it behind him again. As he glanced in his rearview mirror again he saw that the vehicle was coming up fast. The canyon road had been plowed, but the dark pavement was still icy. Add to that the twists and turns the highway took as it wound through the Gallatin Canyon and the driver of the car was going way too fast.

Laramie had only a moment for his brain to take it

all in before he realized that the driver had no intention of slowing down. A curve was coming up, one with a steep rock face on one side of the road and a precarious drop to the frozen river on the other.

He felt the vehicle's bumper connect with the back of his rental. Just a tap. But on the icy road that was all it took. The rental SUV began to fishtail on the ice as the dark car bumped into him again. He could feel the tires lose traction and the next thing he knew he was sliding toward the river. He felt the tires go off the pavement. A wall of snow rushed over the hood.

Expecting the SUV would be pitched into the river and break through the ice, Laramie braced him. Moments later, heart in his throat, he was shocked when the deep snow off the side of the highway stopped his descent just yards from the frozen river. He sat, so shaken he didn't notice the dark car backing up on the highway above him until he heard the roar of the engine.

Looking up, all he saw was the dark tinted windows on the passenger side as the car sped away.

THE PULLED PORK sandwich was to die for, just as Tara had said. Sid couldn't believe she hadn't been to Texas Boys Barbecue before this. The beans and coleslaw were quite good, too. She had downed the cola on the drive back to the cabin but had saved the rest until she'd reached home. Once there, she'd pulled a cold bottle of beer from the grocery bag and sat down at her kitchen table to devour the barbecue. She couldn't help licking her fingers.

Her father would have loved the food, she thought, and then pushed the thought away. While he was always with her, driving her more than ambition, remembering him often brought aching pain. One day that pain would go away, once she accomplished the job she'd set for herself, she told herself as she cleaned up the mess and changed her clothes.

Back at her easel, she considered the painting she was working on. It was one of her father. He was standing by a horse next to the corral. His battered straw cowboy hat was pushed back, sunlight on his weathered face. Behind him were the rocky cliffs and scrub pine of her youth. She was painting it from memory since all the photos had been lost.

She thought of the stash of original artwork she had hidden all these years. It had been years since anyone had seen those paintings—herself included.

Until recently.

LARAMIE CALLED 911 the moment he was out of the SUV and standing at the edge of the highway. He couldn't believe how lucky he'd been. Just a few more yards and the rental would have been in the river.

Marshal Hud Savage came on the line. "What's this about you being forced off the road?"

He told him and Hud promised to have a wrecker sent down to get his rental out of the snowbank.

Laramie had given him what little description he could of the vehicle that had forced him off the road. As with the alleged cat burglar, he had little information other than the car was large and brown with tinted windows.

"It happened too fast," he said. "But there was no doubt of the driver's intent." He could almost see Hud nodding.

"Had you passed the driver? Or had any interaction before this?"

"No. I saw the car earlier up by Taylor Fork, then again later when I went for a drive up the canyon." He could tell that Hud had little hope of finding the vehicle. "Can you do me a favor? Find out what Taylor West drives."

"Taylor West, the local artist?" Hud asked with obvious surprise.

Hud told him that West owned a large SUV and an older-model pickup. Neither matched the description Laramie had given him.

"What makes you think Taylor West had anything to do with running you off the road?" Hud had wanted to know.

"Nothing really," Laramie said. "That's just the first place I noticed the car following me, after I visited the artist. I'm probably wrong about there being a connection." And yet he had a feeling that if Taylor hadn't been behind it, then someone he knew definitely was. But he had no idea why. "Maybe I ticked off the driver somehow."

"Maybe," Hud said. "You sure you weren't going too slow?"

"Maybe."

TAYLOR WEST PACED the floor after the Texan left. He'd been so shaken that he would have poured himself a drink if there'd been any booze in the house. But his wife had dumped every drop she could find down the drain before she'd left. He'd dug out enough from his hiding places that he'd been fine. Until now.

"When are you coming back?" he'd demanded as

he'd watched her throw her clothes into two suitcases and head for the door.

"When you get some help with your drinking."

He didn't need any help. He drank fine without it.

The old joke fell flat. He knew it was more than his drinking. She'd been trying to let him down easy, he thought as he looked around the house. He hadn't realized what a mess it was until he'd seen it through his visitor's eyes. What had Laramie Cardwell been thinking, showing up unannounced at his door like that?

"It's that damned painting," he said as he opened one kitchen cupboard after another, not even sure what he was looking for—then he remembered where he'd hidden a bottle of bourbon months ago and felt better.

In the laundry room, he moved the washer out a little. Reaching behind it, he groped around, feeling nothing but air and cobwebs. Panic filled him. The drive to the nearest liquor store was a good ten miles. He couldn't go to the nearest bar since he'd been kicked out of it.

His hand brushed over the cold throat of the bourbon bottle. His relief rushed out in a laugh that sounded too loud in the small room. Clutching the bottle, he'withdrew it, wiped off the dust with one of his dirty shirts lying on the laundry room floor and headed for the kitchen.

Unable to find a clean glass, he took his first drink straight from the bottle. The liquor bathed his tongue in bliss, warmed his throat and quenched his thirst. He took another drink as the first one reached his belly and sent a golden glow through him.

That's when he knew he was in trouble. There was only one man who could have painted the forgery. He'd be kidding himself if he thought it was anyone but H. F. Powell. He thought of Powell's last words to him. "I could paint one of your pieces and you wouldn't know the difference, that's how good I am."

Taylor shook his head. He hadn't let himself think of H.F. in years. Some things were best forgotten. Everyone knew that the painter had become a recluse in the last years of his life. No one had seen him for almost two years before the tragedy. There hadn't been a funeral—at H.F.'s request. No memorial service. No family.

H.F. must be rolling in his grave since his paintings were now worth a small fortune. Taylor admitted grudgingly, the man had been one hell of a painter. But look where it had gotten him. The arrogant old fool had died alone and miserable.

Just like you're going to die. Taylor snorted at the thought and the one that came after it. *What goes around, comes around.* He shuddered and took another drink, regretting the calls he'd made the moment Laramie Cardwell left. But he'd been so upset and he wasn't in this alone.

Rock Jackson had sounded as if he'd been asleep before the call.

"I'm telling you this painting was so good… I'm not even sure it isn't the original," he'd told Rock. "Tell me there isn't any chance—"

"Take it easy. You're jumping to conclusions. Who brought you the painting?"

Taylor told him.

"The guy's gone, right?"

"He just left."

"Then there is nothing to worry about," Rock had

said. "Look, I have to go. Have a drink. Everything is fine."

Artist Hank Ramsey had told him pretty much the same thing, only Taylor had heard more worry in Hank's voice.

"If you had seen this painting..." Taylor had said feeling sick to his stomach.

Hank had asked the name of the man who'd stopped by and what painting it had been. Hank had tried to calm him back down. "Taylor, we're all painting cowboys, horses and Indians. We've all had someone copy our paintings. Since you're at the top of the heap, your paintings are going to be forged the most. Let me see what I can find out. In the meantime, don't do anything crazy."

He'd hung up, thinking about the other members of OWAC, picturing each of their faces and telling himself that none of them were good enough to paint such a perfect forgery.

He'd tried to call Rock back, but the number had gone to voice mail. "This is Taylor West. Call me. We really need to talk. If that painting is what I think it is... Call me." He'd disconnected, wondering where Rock was. Or if he just wasn't taking his calls after the first one. Which would make Rock look pretty suspicious, wouldn't it?

Now he took a long drink, admitting that he never should have trusted Rock. Rock wasn't that much different from H. F. Powell when it came to women. Now Rock was in trouble because of another woman. In the middle of an ugly divorce, he was probably desperate for money. But how far would he go?

Taylor knew his suspicion of Rock could also be because Rock had always been jealous of him—especially when Taylor had married Jade.

Jade. Where was his beautiful young wife? She'd probably gone to her mother's back in Indiana. He shoved the thought of her away as he took another drink. He had a lot more to worry about than Jade.

"THE HOUSE IS YOURS," McKenzie announced when Laramie stopped by her office after getting his rental SUV pulled out of the snowbank. He was still shaken, but even more determined to get to the bottom of whatever was going on.

"And the painting?" he asked expectantly. He told himself he couldn't be sure which was original and without it, he might never know.

She chuckled. "Yours, as well. He wanted extra for it, but I convinced him that you wanted pretty much everything in the house except, of course, any items that he couldn't possibly part with. If you don't want the furniture, I know a consignment place—"

"No, furnished is perfect. So what is he leaving?"

"Everything, including the kitchen sink, except for the other paintings and sculptures. He has an art dealer coming to take the lot of them this afternoon."

Laramie couldn't hide his relief. He wasn't sure why the painting was so important. But what had happened after he'd left Taylor West's house had him convinced the painting was at the heart of it. He thought about the house—where he'd seen his alleged cat burglar. "How soon can I take occupancy?"

"Right away, I suppose, if you're in that much of a hurry."

He'd been staying with Tag and McKenzie and

didn't want to hurt her feelings. "No hurry, just anxious to get settled."

"I can understand that. Since the house will come completely furnished, there won't be much that you will need. He's leaving bedding, all of which he said is brand-new. Apparently they haven't gotten to use this house much. I take it that his soon-to-be-ex wife didn't like it up here. Too isolated. Since you're paying cash, I can arrange a rental agreement until the sale is final. You should be able to move in this evening. The owner is in a hurry to get out of town."

"Great."

"But this…urgency to get settled, it wouldn't have anything to do with your…cat burglar, would it?"

Laramie smiled to himself. "You sound like Austin. I ran into him earlier at the restaurant. Like I told him, I know what I'm doing." He wished that was true.

But he didn't think the earlier incident was an attempt to kill him. Then what had it been? If the driver had wanted to scare him off, then he'd failed. Laramie was more determined than ever. He was counting on his cat burglar coming back for the painting. It was just a gut feeling, but a strong one, that for some reason she really needed that painting. And he really needed answers.

He stood to leave.

"Don't forget this," McKenzie said reaching behind her. She handed him what Theo Nelson believed to be the original painting.

He stared at it, anxious to compare it to the one in his rented SUV. "Question, if I wanted everyone to know I'd bought the house, how would I go about getting the word out?"

McKenzie laughed. "In a small community like Big Sky? Are you kidding? Everyone knows everyone else's business. It's probably already out there since the owner informed me to go ahead and change the security information to yours. You'll need to change over the utilities and everything else as soon as you get into the house. But if you were to stop by the furniture store or the grocery and happen to mention you'd bought a house…"

"Let me know when you have my key, and thank you so much. Oh, and one more thing. Have you ever heard of an artist by the name of H. F. Powell?"

"Of course. In fact, one of his paintings is coming up for auction at the Christmas ball this year. It's expected to go high. This interest in cowboy art…"

"Just curiosity."

She laughed. "Uh-huh."

Laramie realized how little he knew about art in general as he left for Meadow Village. His plan was to do exactly what McKenzie had suggested. He had a feeling that his cat burglar kept her ear to the ground. How else had she known that the house was supposed to be empty last night?

Chapter Six

Sid rubbed her back. It ached from hours spent painting. She hadn't realized how long she'd been working. When she painted, time flew by. She hadn't even noticed that her back was aching until a few moments ago when she finally laid down her brush.

She also realized she was hungry. Going to the fridge, she peered in. She'd bought the basics at the store, but nothing appealed to her. The pulled pork barbecue sandwich came to mind. Why not go back there? Several good reasons came to her. Except once she thought of barbecue, nothing else would do.

This late in the evening, Texas Boys Barbecue was quiet. Only a few booths were taken. She slipped into one and was thankful when a different waitress came out with a menu.

"We have a special, if you're interested," the young woman said. She rattled off a variety of items, but all Sid keyed in on was the words *ribs*. Her stomach growled.

"I'll take the baby-back rib special." She started to say "to go" but stopped herself. "And a beer." As she started to whip out her ID, she realized the waitress wasn't even going to ask for it. With relief, she put it away, sat back and took in the place in a way she hadn't done earlier. It was nicely done. Comfortable and homey but without kitschy knickknacks. The atmosphere was warm and welcoming and the smells coming out of the kitchen were making her mouth water.

It felt good to be out of her cabin. She sat back, relaxing—until she heard voices in the kitchen as the waitress brought out her beer. Taking a sip, she watched the back, hoping to get another look at Laramie Cardwell. From where she sat, she could hear the conversation. This time there were three men, all of them speaking with a Texas drawl. But no Laramie.

"So he got the house?"

"He's moving in tonight."

"What was the rush?"

"Apparently he's anxious to get settled."

"I hope that's all it is."

"Bet Dana is already planning a housewarming."

Laughter before the three left.

Laramie was moving into the house *tonight*?

So Tara's information had been right, not that she'd doubted it. Sid thought about Laramie showing up so late the night before at the Nelson house on the side of the mountain. He'd only been interested in the house, but he'd stumbled onto her. Just her luck.

"I'm sorry," Sid said getting the waitress's attention. "But could I have that order to go?"

Laramie was at the grocery store when McKenzie called to say she had the key to the house. "Do you want to meet at the house?"

"Sounds great. I'm picking up a few things. I can meet you there in thirty minutes."

He quickly got what he needed and headed for the checkout. In a matter of minutes he would have the key to his house. He owned a high-rise condo in Houston, but he had never been this excited about the purchase even though the condo had an amazing view of the city.

The house was perfect for him since he didn't plan to spend that much time in Montana. But he needed his own place when he did. If anything, he thought he might spend more time here—during the summer months.

Would he love the house as much if his cat burglar didn't come back for the painting? He pushed that thought away, telling himself he was in the market for a house long before he'd laid eyes on the dark-clad figure running along the rooftop. Long before the kiss.

At the checkout, he was impatient to get into the house. He had to wait in line behind a half dozen people and wished now that he hadn't bothered. Glancing around, he studied the other people in the line. The tourists were easy to spot in the latest ski gear or after-ski wear.

Out of the corner of his eye, he noticed a bulletin board. Dana had mentioned that there were always people looking for housecleaning jobs around Big Sky, if he needed help.

A poster with cowboy art on it caught his eye. A name jumped out at him. H. F. Powell. Leaving his basket to save his place in line, Laramie quickly stepped to the board. Western Art Exhibit at the Museum of the Rockies in Bozeman. H. F. Powell was one of the artists featured in what the poster said was a rare exhibit of the Western masters.

Hurriedly, he searched the poster for the date, fearing he had missed the exhibit. With relief, he saw that it opened tomorrow. Until today, he'd never heard of H. F. Powell. Now he was curious about the man and his work given that Taylor West swore he was the only man who could have duplicated his work so perfectly.

His cat burglar had certainly piqued his interest in Old West art, he thought. After he checked out, he put his groceries in his SUV and walked up the hill to the restaurant for his dinner. The special tonight at Texas Boys Barbecue was ribs so the cook had saved him a slab along with sides.

As he entered the back door, he breathed in the smell of the food, still amazed that his and his brothers' love for barbecue had led to their Texas Boys Barbecue success. None of them ever had to work another day in their lives, but of course they all did have some job because that was the way they were raised. As promised, the cook had his dinner wrapped and ready to take home to his new house.

It was on his way out that he saw a woman as she came out of the front of the restaurant and climbed into a blue SUV.

The woman caught his eye because of the way she moved. No wasted motion, her steps so fluid—and familiar—as she hurried toward her vehicle. He stood there watching her get into the SUV, feeling like a man who'd just seen a ghost.

A thick, long curly mane of strawberry blond hair hung around her shoulders, catching the last of the day's light and making it shine like copper. He held his breath as he watched her slide behind the wheel. The engine revved. She seemed to be in a hurry to get somewhere. Just like that night.

It was her.

All common sense told him that he couldn't possibly have recognized her simply by the way that she moved. There must be dozens of slim young women like her in the area. And yet…

He looked down the hillside to where he'd left his vehicle as she backed up and sped off up the road toward the mountain. There was no way he could reach his vehicle in time. All he could do was watch her get away.

Which was good, he realized. His first impulse had been to go after her. And then what? If only he had been close enough to see her eyes. And those lips. He told himself that if he saw those again, he'd know for certain.

He was thankful he hadn't gone after her and made a fool of himself. He could just imagine what his four brothers would say if he shared this "sighting" with them.

"You need a woman," Tag would say. "Stalking is illegal," Hayes would warn him. "Get a grip," Austin would say. "I agree with Tag. You need a woman bad," Jackson would add.

As the blue SUV disappeared over a rise, he thought they would have been right. What was going on with him? This wasn't like him. He always thought things out before he reacted. And yet last night, he'd gone after what he believed to be a thief without any thought to the risk.

And now he'd almost chased that woman down, and

yet what were the chances she was the same woman?
Big Sky wasn't a large community. If McKenzie was
right, then the woman might already know who he was.
If that had been her... Would she dare go to Texas Boys
Barbecue if she knew who he was, though?

He thought of the woman, of those silver-blue eyes,
of those bee-stung lips, thought of how she'd tricked
him and gotten away. Yes, she would go to the restaurant he and his brothers owned. The woman was
a risk taker.

That thought sent a current of excitement through
him.

What if she had gone there looking for *him* because
she needed to get her hands on the painting—just as
he'd suspected?

Laramie went back inside Texas Boys Barbecue. It
only took a minute to find the young waitress who'd
served the woman. "She didn't happen to use a check
or credit card to pay for her dinner, did she?" he asked,
crossing his fingers.

"Cash."

He couldn't hide his disappointment.

"Is there a problem?" the waitress asked.

"No, I was just hoping to get her name."

The teen laughed. "All you had to do was ask. I
know her. That is I've seen her at the craft shows.
Her name is Obsidian Forester, but she goes by Sid
for short."

"Obsidian." He nodded, silently cheered. He had
her name. "Wait, you said craft shows?"

"Yeah, she's one of the exhibitors like me. I make
candles and sell them. It's just something I like to do
in my spare time since I like crafting."

"What does...Sid sell?"

"She paints scenes on stuff like handsaws, milk jugs, anything that is kind of old and rusted."

He couldn't help the thrill that moved through him. Maybe that really had been her. "So she's an artist," he said more to himself.

"I think she's wasting her talent painting on old junk." The teen shrugged. "But what do I know? People seem to like what she does. She sells more of those paintings than I do candles."

"You don't happen to know where she lives, do you?"

As SID DROVE HOME, she told herself not to let the Texas cowboy rush her. But she could feel the clock ticking. Any good thief knew not to play against the odds. She'd been lucky, but lately she'd been seen. Then last night, almost caught.

Once at the cabin, she ate her ribs. It was already dark. This time of year in the canyon it was pitch-black by five. The ribs were as good or even better than the pulled pork. She licked her fingers after finishing the last one, then cleaned up the kitchen and herself before dressing in all black. Picking up the black ski mask, she headed for her snowmobile.

The next house on her list wasn't far from her cabin, but she took the long way. The owners were spending the holidays in Hawaii. At least that was the intel she'd gotten on them. It would be easy to find out if it was true. The couple drove a huge ivory SUV and left it in the drive when they were there.

For months, she'd done endless research on the houses she planned to hit and the people who owned them. This one was owned by an older couple. He'd been a pilot, she a homemaker. The house was modest by Big Sky standards.

Sid had met both of them at the local art shows. She often struck up conversations, especially with people who had a piece of art she was interested in. Art lovers were quick to talk about the artists they liked. It hadn't been easy to find the owners of the pieces she still needed, but she'd finally tracked them all down.

As she came over a rise, she saw the house. It loomed up out of the darkness. No lights on inside. No large SUV in the drive. The couple kept it in the garage for the next time they flew in.

She killed the engine on the snowmobile some distance from the house. There were no other homes around, one of the benefits of this affluent community. No one wanted neighbors. At least not ones they could see from their houses.

The snow was deep on this side of the mountain. She'd brought snowshoes for the last part of the hike up to the house. Strapping them on, she grabbed her canvas bag and started up the mountain. The moon had come up and now poured silver over the snowy landscape.

Sid could see her breath. The house sat on the side of a mountain at about six thousand feet above sea level. She stopped to catch her breath and look back down the mountain to where she'd left her snowmobile. Nothing moved in the darkness of the pines.

Ahead, moonlight shone a path to the house. Sid listened. Hearing nothing but her own breath, she headed for the house.

In and out. She set her watch. Five minutes. Then

she slipped in through the back door that had been unlocked for her by Maisie at the precise time. She knew exactly where the painting she needed would be hanging and, turning on her penlight, headed right for it.

The exchange didn't take more than a few seconds. She put the painting into the large canvas bag, remembering the night before when the other bag she'd used had a hole in it. Another mistake. She was getting sloppy. Not because of overconfidence, she told herself. No, it was that she'd done this so many times it was becoming routine.

She thought of Laramie Cardwell as she locked the door behind her, texted Maisie "Lunch tomorrow?"— their code—and headed for her snowmobile. As she drove the snowmobile toward her cabin, she realized that once she had the painting she'd lost last night, she'd be done with these kinds of night jobs.

It filled her with a strange nostalgia. She'd been at this for several years now. When she'd started, she had questioned her sanity. Why do this when it could go so badly if she were caught?

Last night that had almost happened. Unfortunately, it wasn't in her nature to leave anything undone—even if she *hadn't* needed the painting to finish what she'd started. She would get that painting back and end this once and for all.

"So what do you think?" McKenzie asked as Laramie used his key to enter his new house.

"I love it," he said as he stepped in and took a deep breath. Through the wall of windows at the front of the house Lone Mountain glistened in the twilight.

"From what I can tell, he left everything but the art-work—other than the one you bought," she said. He looked around, realizing he would have to get more art for the walls, especially with these high ceilings. Walking through the house, he didn't see much that he would change. Theo Nelson's decorator had done a grand job of furnishing the house.

"He even left dishes, flatware and stemware," McKenzie said shaking her head. "He must not have been very attached to the house." She sighed. "There is a used furniture shop down the valley that we call the Second-Wife's Club. Most of it comes from Big Sky. New wife, all new furnishings. You can get some great deals, if you're interested."

Laramie shook his head. "I can't imagine anything more that I would want or need. It is clear that Theo and his wife didn't spend much time here. Everything looks brand-new. I expect to see the price tags still on everything. Let me get some things from the car and then let's take a look upstairs."

The second floor looked the same except for the study. Theo's computer was gone, but that seemed to be the only change. "He didn't even take any of the books on the shelves," McKenzie commented.

In the bedrooms, the beds were still made up with new linens, down comforters and expensive duvets, she noted. "He left all the linens in the bathrooms and the closets for the entire house."

Laramie glanced around and then headed for the stairs to the master bedroom with the two paintings he had acquired. The room looked much the same, save the spot on the wall where the Taylor West had hung.

He took the painting he'd purchased from Theo Nelson and hung it back where it had been. On the wall next to it, he hung the one his cat burglar had dropped.

He turned on the small spotlights that shone on the paintings and stood studying the two, still unable to find anything to distinguish either of them.

"I'm glad you like the painting," McKenzie said joining him. "I could have gotten the price of the house down another twenty grand without it."

He chuckled. "According to the artist, the original is worth fifty. Your art expert offered me thirty thousand for the one I acquired from my mysterious alleged thief."

She let out a low whistle. "Wow, so you got a deal on both of them. That makes me feel better. But I get the impression you would have paid even more for it and the house."

Laramie smiled. "You did great, McKenzie. I can't thank you enough."

"But which painting is the real McCoy?"

"That is the question, isn't it?" he said. "Meanwhile, I love the house." He walked over to the wall of windows. In the darkness of the winter night, the snow-covered Lone Mountain looked ghostlike.

He stood, admiring his view and wondering when his cat burglar would be back. *If* she would be back. He thought of Obsidian "Sid" Forester and wondered how he could make sure they crossed paths if she didn't come back.

Logic, something he'd always prided himself on, reminded him that he couldn't be sure Sid was his cat burglar.

"Not yet," he said to himself as he looked out at the Montana winter night. But all his instincts told him he'd already found her. Now it was just a matter of catching her in the act.

Look you too and it is not against you, but against you. You will know what all the business left in is closed, thought here. Now it was gone even little to hit him live in this way.

Chapter Seven

The next morning, after a rough night, Taylor West woke up hungover and upset. He hadn't gotten a moment's sound sleep last night, worrying that he'd been betrayed. Worse if the truth came out...

He picked up his cell phone and saw that it had been turned off. He had four calls from Cody Kent. He listened to the voice messages, then returned the man's call.

Clearly either Rock or Hank had called him—or they both had. And they'd both pretended to him that there was nothing to be worried about. He swore as he tapped in Cody's number.

"What's this about some forgery?" Cody demanded, sounding both angry and worried. Cody related that he'd been by the gallery yesterday and had run into a man with one of Taylor's paintings.

"Laramie Cardwell. I know. He came by my house."

"Was...it...*the*...original?" Cody asked.

"I don't know."

"What do you mean you don't know?"

"I would swear it was."

"So the other one is a forgery. Have you seen it?"

"I know what you're getting at," Taylor said. "The

other one has to be a forgery, right? And anyone could have painted it."

Cody agreed. "So stop getting everyone all riled up over nothing."

"You're right." Still Taylor had a bad feeling about this.

"You'll let me know if there is a reason to worry, right?"

"Of course." He hung up and tried Rock's number. It went straight to voice mail. Where the hell was Rock? He'd gotten off the line so quickly yesterday...

Taylor felt sweat break out under his arms even though his house was cold this morning because he hadn't bothered to turn up the heat.

He'd had a long night to think about it. If anyone had betrayed them, it would be Rock.

LARAMIE HADN'T SLEPT well the first night in his new home. There was nothing wrong with the bed, the Egyptian cotton sheets or the house's ambiance. Still, he'd had trouble getting to sleep. Even after he'd dozed off, he'd awakened often thinking he'd heard something. All night he'd lain in the king-size bed, listening and waiting for the woman to return and thinking about the vehicle that had tried to put him in the river yesterday.

The incident had to have something to do with the painting, right? Which meant it had something to do with the cat burglar. What, though?

Before going to bed, he'd had a thought. Taking out his pocket knife, he'd carefully scratched a very small mark on the back of the canvas on the painting he'd purchased with the house.

He was sure she'd come back for one—or both— of the paintings. He figured if he ever saw them again after that, he'd know which was which. And if she only took one, he'd know which one she'd left behind. He was pretty sure she knew which one was the real one.

With that, he'd turned out the lights and gone to bed. When he'd opened his eyes this morning, he'd half expected to see the paintings gone. He wouldn't have been surprised if she'd sneaked in and taken them both.

But upon waking, he was almost disappointed to see both paintings right where they'd been when he'd gone to bed. She hadn't come for either one. What if he was wrong and she wouldn't be back?

His phone rang. Seeing it was from the marshal, he quickly took the call. "Do you have some news for me?" he said without preamble.

"Yesterday you asked me to check on vehicles owned by Taylor West," Hud said.

"Right. And you told me he didn't own a large brown car."

"No, he doesn't. But his wife, Jade, does. I got to thinking and checked to see if there were other vehicles that might be registered to someone other than Taylor."

"His wife?" Laramie remembered the photograph he'd seen of the pretty young blonde.

"I've put a BOLO out on it," Hud said. "We could get lucky. But why would Jade West—or someone using her vehicle—want to run you off the road?"

Laramie hung up convinced that it had something to do with the painting, but what, he had no idea. As he headed for the shower, he wondered if Obsidian Forester was indeed his cat burglar. The only way he'd know for sure was if she came back for the painting. He realized how much he was counting on it.

Showered and dressed, he went downstairs. He'd just poured himself a bowl of cereal that he'd bought at the store yesterday when the security company he'd called rang his doorbell.

Theo Nelson had a security system but it hadn't gone off the night Laramie had seen the woman on the roofline. Which meant that the woman had disarmed the alarm before entering the house or she had outsmarted the system.

So he wasn't going to bother adding more security. All he wanted were cameras, and nowadays they made such small ones, she wouldn't know she was being captured on video.

He glanced at his watch. He needed to know more about cowboy art. McKenzie had handled everything including changing over the utilities and contacting the alarm company for him. Leaving the security people to do their work, he drove to Bozeman to the Museum of the Rockies. It was another beautiful winter day, not a cloud in the sky, the blazing sun bright on the snow.

He found himself watching his rearview mirror, looking for the large dark car that had run his off the highway the day before. But by the time he reached Bozeman, he hadn't seen it.

Parking near Montana State University, he entered the museum. While known for its dinosaur collection, the museum also held a variety of other exhibits throughout the year, according to the clerk who took his money, stamped his hand in case he wanted to come back later and handed him a map.

Since the museum had just opened for the day, there

were only a handful of people in the new exhibit featuring Old West master artists. There were paintings by both Charles M. Russell and Frederic Remington, two well-known Old West artists from the 1800s.

They had apparently painted what they saw around them, capturing a lifestyle that they romanticized with their art. While four-wheelers had replaced horses at a lot of ranches, his cousin had told him, the cowboy life survived even to this day out here in the West.

Laramie had just stepped into an adjoining exhibition room when he saw a young woman standing in front of a large painting of a Native American chief in full headdress.

It was the same woman he'd seen coming out of Texas Boys Barbecue yesterday. Obsidian "Sid" Forester.

At seeing the woman again, his pulse jumped as excitement raced through his veins. He reminded himself that she was an artist in her own right, so of course she would be here. That didn't make her guilty of being the cat burglar.

She wore jeans and a canvas jacket over a rust-colored sweater. Her coppery hair was tucked up under a Cubs baseball cap, which pitched her face into shadow, making it impossible to see the color of her eyes at this distance. Nor could he get a good look at her mouth. But even in silhouette he could tell that her lips were full.

He remembered the taste of her mouth and felt an ache that had nothing to do with cowboy art. His reasons for wanting to find this woman had gotten all tangled up with a desire to kiss her again. He knew it was crazy and could just imagine what his brothers would say. But he couldn't wait to get his hands on her as if to assure himself that she was actually real. That what she evoked in him that night was real, as well.

Warning himself to take it slow, he moved closer. As if sensing him staring at her, she looked in his direction, then quickly turned away. He felt a start. Was it possible? He wouldn't know until he got a better look, but all his instincts told him he had her.

IT DIDN'T TAKE Taylor West long to drive to Gallatin Gateway, a small, almost forgotten town at the mouth of the canyon. Once billed as the Gateway to Yellowstone, the town back then had a train that brought tourists to the beautiful large hotel, before ferrying them into the park.

Rock Jackson owned a small ranch against the foothills overlooking the Gallatin River. The place was run-down, the house small and old with some outbuildings behind it, including Rock's studio.

As Taylor pulled up and got out, he thought he saw movement at one of the front windows. But when he knocked hard at the front door, there was no answer from within.

"He probably saw me and doesn't want to deal with me," Taylor told himself. The drive had sobered him up since he'd been drinking before he'd left home. He hated that the drive might have been for nothing, until he reminded himself that he needed to go to a liquor store anyway.

He pounded again. Still no answer. Moving to peer into a front window, he saw that the place was neat and orderly inside. That made him all the more angry since his own house was a mess. Somehow that convinced him even more that Rock Jackson was guilty of something.

Walking around the side of the house, Taylor noticed Rock's art studio. Was he back there working? Raging inside, now positive that Rock had betrayed him, he stormed toward it. This time, he didn't bother to knock. He grabbed the door handle and turned it. Locked.

Cursing, Taylor cupped his hands against one of the windows. The studio was exactly like something he'd always talked about building on his property. He could see only one painting from where he stood. It appeared to be one of Rock's in progress.

As he started to turn away, he saw that there was another room behind the studio. When he got around back, the door into that part of the building had a padlock on it. That alone seemed suspicious.

He picked up a rock and tried to break the padlock but, failing, tossed the rock away and swore. The mellow he'd had earlier was starting to wear off along with the booze, leaving him with a headache and a worse mood. Furious, he stood outside the studio feeling as alone as he'd ever felt. The temperature had dropped with the appearance of clouds obscuring the sun. He shivered and looked around, not sure what to do then.

He could smell snow on the freezing air and wondered why he hadn't gone south this winter. Jade had wanted to go, but he hadn't wanted to make the long drive to Arizona. Now he wished he had. Laramie Cardwell wouldn't have been able to find him and he wouldn't have known about the painting.

Taylor knew that kind of thinking was crazy. Even if he'd been in Arizona, the painting would have surfaced. He'd seen it with his own eyes. He knew what that meant.

Behind him, he spotted an old barn on the property and walked toward it, thinking he'd look around and wait for Rock to return, since he now realized there was no vehicle here. He didn't want to have to drive all this way again if he could help it.

He pushed open the barn door and stepped into the dim darkness. It took a moment for his eyes to adjust, but he didn't mind. It was warmer in here and with the booze wearing off...

Taylor blinked as a large dark object in the barn took shape before him. At first he couldn't believe what he was seeing. He thought for sure it must have been the beginning of a hangover making him only imagine it.

But there was no doubt. The question was what was his wife's car doing in Rock Jackson's barn?

Sɪᴅ ᴛʀɪᴇᴅ ᴛᴏ calm her racing heart. Her mind raced, as well. What was Laramie Cardwell doing here? Her first impulse was to flee, but that would be the worst thing she could do. Seeing him here had been so unexpected. She hadn't been prepared. That's why her pulse thrummed and skin prickled at the memory of his touch.

Why *was* he here? Maybe he was simply interested in cowboy art. She groaned silently as she moved from painting to painting, aware of him tracing her steps like a wolf on the scent of its prey.

Wasn't it possible that his interest in cowboy art had been sparked by the painting she'd dropped and nothing more? Which meant he hadn't forgotten about the painting any more than she had.

Was he here trying to find out more about the painting? Or was he looking for her? Her heart took off like a wild horse running in the wind. Was it possible he'd followed her? That thought turned her blood to ice.

Sid prided herself on her quick thinking when cornered—thus the kiss that had gotten her freedom two nights ago. But she was too aware of him—and vice versa. Good sense told her to leave, but she would have to walk right past him. Also, it might call more attention to her.

Even if she was right and this had something to do with the painting she'd dropped… Even if he was looking for her… He didn't know the importance of the painting in his possession any more than he could prove she was the woman he'd tackled that night.

Telling herself to play it cool, she forced herself to relax. She was safe and she had to admit, she was curious about the Texas cowboy. Wouldn't it be to her benefit to learn as much about him as she could? After all, she needed that painting.

As she moved through the exhibit, taking her time looking at each painting, she studied Laramie every chance she got out of the corner of her eye. He was taller than her few stolen glimpses of him had led her to believe. And since he was the business end of the Texas Boys Barbecue empire, she would have expected him to be some computer geek. But the man who'd tackled her had been anything but.

His dark hair was longer than she first thought. Was that designer stubble on his jaw? She smiled to herself, thinking that she might be wrong about him. He might not be as straitlaced and uptight as she'd thought at their first encounter. Either that or he'd loosened up since then.

Laramie moved slowly, studying each painting, stopping longest, she noticed, at an H. F. Powell painting of a cattle drive. The painting was beautiful, a masterpiece. Even someone without an artist's eye would see that.

He seemed so intent that she hadn't realized she'd been caught staring until he turned suddenly in her direction. She quickly swung back to the painting she had been pretending to examine. The intensity of his look had rattled her again. Could she be wrong about him not knowing who she was?

Just as she started to move away, he stepped up beside her.

"I know nothing about this kind of art," he said in his Southern drawl. "Do you really have to be a cowboy to paint it?"

She didn't look at him. "Sorry, but I wouldn't know. I'm not a fan of cowboy art."

"Really?" He sounded surprised. "And yet here you are." She could feel all of his attention on her. "So you just wandered in here like me?"

"It would seem so," she said, and quickly looked at her watch.

"Take this, for example," he said clearly ignoring her subtle attempt to escape. "Is the idea to portray the life of the cowboy? Or romanticize it because these guys look too happy when you know they have to be freezing?"

Sid looked at the painting of cowboys standing around a campfire drinking coffee from tin cups as cattle milled in the background and snow began to fall. He was right. She couldn't help but smile.

Just as she couldn't help looking over at him.

He seemed startled for a moment as he met her gaze. Then his eyes shifted slowly to her mouth. She fought the urge to lick her lips as she recalled his mouth on hers. His gaze returned to hers. She tried not to shiver.

"I know this sounds corny," he drawled, "but I feel as if we've met somewhere before."

She did her best not to react to his words. "If that's your best pickup line—"

He snapped his fingers as if it had only just come to him. "Texas Boys Barbecue. I saw you coming out of there yesterday." While his intent gaze was still probing, his smile was all sincerity. "I'm betting you had the rib special. Tell me I'm right."

She tried to relax. "So you're a betting man?"

He laughed. "Not usually, but then again I'm a long way from home and out of my element. Right now I'm betting that if you agreed to have a cup of coffee with me, it would make this Texas boy feel more at home this far north."

She laughed, as well. "You seem very much at home to me."

"Laramie Cardwell," he said and extended his hand.

Sid felt she had no choice but to shake it. Her hand disappeared into his large, warm, suntanned one. She tried not to react to the jolt she felt. "Obsidian Forester."

"Obsidian? What a beautiful and unusual name."

"That's why I go by Sid."

"Well, Sid, I hope you take me up on the cup of coffee. I haven't met many people since I've been here."

She was tempted, which surprised her. Playing with fire was one thing. Stepping into a blazing furnace was another. Still, he had no way of knowing—let alone proving—that she'd been the woman whose path he'd crossed that night. And if he did suspect, what better way to prove him wrong than by taking him up on his invitation?

Not to mention, he had the painting she needed. Maybe there was another way to get it, other than stealing it outright. Anyway, what would it hurt to have one cup of coffee with him?

Chapter Eight

Violet. It was the color of her eyes. But Laramie realized as they walked the block to the coffee shop that her eyes changed colors in different light. No wonder he hadn't been sure that first night.

But there was no mistaking the lips. They were bow-shaped, wide and full, and a delicate shade of pink today. He'd remembered the feel of them against his the moment he saw them. Crazily, what he'd wanted more than anything right there in the museum was a repeat kiss. He couldn't be sure, with everything that had been happening that night, exactly what he'd felt when she'd kissed him. It had happened too fast. But the next time she kissed him…

Where had these thoughts come from? He reminded himself that she was a *thief*. His plan was to catch her. The chance of there being another kiss was beyond remote.

He was still surprised that she'd agreed to have coffee with him. He'd worried that he'd come on too strong. He'd never been like his brothers, who seemed to all have a way with women. He was more reserved. More cautious, usually. While he'd done his fair share of dating, he'd never met a woman he'd been serious about.

He figured he knew less about women than he did cowboy art, which was saying a lot. So he felt he was out of his league if Obsidian "Sid" Forester was who he believed she was.

"So fess up," he said once they were seated in a small coffee shop a block from the museum. "You did have the ribs, didn't you?"

She had a nice laugh. An amazing smile. The woman was striking from her coppery hair to her heart-shaped face and the row of freckles that graced her cheeks. But it was her eyes that fascinated him. They'd been violet, but now in the winter light coming in from the coffee shop window, they were almost silver. Like a wolf's, he thought. Silver like they'd been in the moonlight the night they'd met.

"You caught me," she said. "I had the ribs. They were wonderful, but I guess I don't have to tell *you* that. I'm betting you're one of the Texas boys."

"Yep. My four bothers and me," he said, figuring she probably already knew that if she'd looked at their story on the back of the restaurant menu. Wouldn't only an innocent woman go to the barbecue restaurant after his encounter with the cat burglar?

No, he thought. This woman was gutsy. She'd go there almost as a dare.

"Barbecue was the only thing we knew, so we started cooking out behind a small house we turned into a restaurant in Houston." He shrugged. "The business just kind of took off."

"What brought you to Montana?" she asked and took a sip of her coffee. He could feel her watching him over the rim of her cup and wondered what game they were playing. She was definitely his cat burglar. He'd stake his life on it. The thought made him think of the car that had run him off the highway. If he didn't stop this, what would happen next?

Laramie knew he should be worried about that. But there was no way he was backing off. "My brothers and I were all born here in Montana. When my parents divorced, Mom took us to Texas where she had relatives. My dad still lives near Big Sky, so one after another my brothers have returned, and each has fallen in love with Montana and a woman… Opening a restaurant up here seemed like a good idea."

"It appears to be doing well. I heard you were opening another one in Red Lodge."

He smiled, nodding. "I handle the business end of it, so it's one reason I'm here, along with wanting to spend time with my family over the holidays."

"So you aren't staying?" she asked and took another sip of her coffee.

"As a matter of fact, I bought a house yesterday partway up the mountain."

"Really?" She didn't sound that surprised. "So you're planning to move up here?"

He shook his head. "I'll only spend part of the year here like most of the residents, it seems. I still own a condo in Houston and operate things from there."

She nodded.

"So tell me about *you*," he said.

Sid shrugged. "Not much to tell."

"Come on, I just told you my entire life story." He took a sip of coffee and asked, "You live in Big Sky." She nodded. "What do you do there?"

Her silver-blue eyes met his. "I paint." Her full mouth quirked into an amused grin.

"Paint?" He pretended to be surprised. "You're an *artist*? Or do you paint houses?"

She smiled as she shook her head. "I'm more of a hobby-craft person. I paint Montana scenes on old rusty things I find like saw blades and old milk cans. I definitely wouldn't consider myself an artist."

"That explains what you were doing at the exhibit," he said studying her. "You really like cowboy art."

"I admire the artists, but cowboy art isn't my cup of tea, trust me."

"What is?" he asked.

The question seemed to surprise her as if no one had ever asked her that before. Maybe that was why it took her a moment. Or, he thought, maybe it took her a moment to come up with a lie. "Abstract. I like lots of color. I prefer impressionism over realism when I paint."

"My sister-in-law McKenzie would love one of your pieces, then." He studied her. She seemed to be relaxed, but he felt a tension just under the surface. He could feel it buzzing like a live wire between them. "I'd like to see your work sometime."

She said nothing as she finished her coffee and looked again at her watch. "I really need to go."

Laramie mentally kicked himself, but he'd never been patient when he wanted something badly. He pushed his coffee aside and stood as she rose. "It's been a pleasure meeting you. I do hope our paths cross again."

"Maybe they will," she said. He could smell the

citrus scent of her morning shower. "Enjoy your new house."

"Speaking of my new house… I am in desperate need of artwork. The ceilings are ten to twelve foot throughout. I have only one painting I'm partial to, but nothing else. With all these walls to fill, I need help. I sure would appreciate it if you could advise me." She started to decline. "Come on, who better than an artist who loves color to help me?"

Don't do it. Sid met the handsome Texas cowboy's gaze. He'd just told her he had only one painting. She didn't have to guess which one that was.

"I doubt we like the same things," she said.

"You might be surprised," he drawled. "I'd love to show you my house whenever you can come by."

"There are plenty of designers around who could advise you on artwork. I'm not the person you want."

"Oh, I suspect you are exactly the person I'm looking for."

She looked at him, wondering how true that was.

"I have a confession," he said leaning toward her. "I have no artistic talent. I'm betting you have a better eye for art than you think. I'd love to see what you come up with."

Was he trying to tell her that he knew who she was? Or that he at least suspected? Or was he hitting on her? That thought almost made her laugh. Wouldn't that be her luck? A good-looking Texas cowboy interested in her and she had to avoid him for obvious reasons.

"You might not like what I come up with," she challenged.

He seemed to study her. "I think I might surprise you."

She feared that was definitely what might happen.

He walked her back to the museum where they'd left their vehicles. A brief thaw had left the streets of Bozeman bare, but there was still plenty of snow in the mountains. Laramie commented on how beautiful it was.

"So do you ski?" he asked as they neared the museum parking lot.

"No." Sid wondered why she'd lied. But then again she was lying just being with this man.

"Snowboard?"

She shook her head.

"You must do something to enjoy winter since you live in Big Sky. Snowmobile?"

He had stopped beside a white SUV. She assumed it was the same one she'd seen the night he caught her leaving Theo Nelson's house with the painting.

"I hate how loud snowmobiles are," she said truthfully and mugged a face. "They ruin the winter quiet, don't you think?"

Laramie smiled at that. "But they seem to be a necessity if you're going to get around in the mountains in the winter and want to avoid the roads."

She looked away. She could feel her heart thundering in her chest. Oh, yes, he suspected her all right. "Don't you ski?"

He laughed at that. "I'm a Texas boy. I doubt I'll be staying here long enough in the winter to learn. But my cousin has invited me to do some horseback riding on her ranch. Do you ride?"

She thought of the horses she'd loved when she was

younger and the many hours she'd spent in the saddle. Surprisingly, she hadn't realized how much she missed it until that moment.

"I love to ride." The words were out before she could bite her tongue.

Laramie's eyes brightened. "Then we have to go for a ride. When are you free?"

"With the holidays and all…"

"I'm staying until after the holiday masquerade ball that I'm told by my cousin Dana I can't possibly miss." He eyed her openly. "You don't happen to be going?"

She shook her head. "I wouldn't be caught dead there." And this time bit her tongue.

He laughed again. "I feel the same way, but my cousin is very persuasive. Listen, I'm serious about that horseback ride and about your help with artwork for the house."

"Speaking of being very *persuasive*." Their eyes locked for a moment and she felt a warning chill sprint up her back. *Be careful.* This was not a cowboy to fool with. Admittedly, he definitely had his appeal. She recalled the jolt she'd felt when she'd shaken his hand, not to mention the strange reaction to the kiss. "I'll think about both."

"Do that. This is mine," he said motioning to the SUV. "It was nice meeting you, Sid. Oh, I should tell you where I live in case you take me up on my offer. It's the three-story one off Lone Mountain Trail. You probably know it, right?" His gaze met hers and held it. She felt a shiver wind its way up her spine. One minute she was convinced he was hitting on her and the next she was positive again that he knew exactly who she was and was setting her up. "Why don't I give you my phone number in case you can't find it."

"I'll find it," she said as she turned and walked away, mentally kicking herself for this cat-and-mouse game she was playing since she was the mouse and the cat was a much craftier adversary than she'd first thought.

As she climbed into her vehicle, she warned herself to let it go. But that meant letting the painting go. She couldn't do that, she thought with a curse. And Laramie Cardwell was practically daring her to come steal it.

"WHAT IS GOING ON with you?" his brother Austin demanded when he showed up at Laramie's door later that afternoon.

He gave him a confused look. "I bought a house?" Motioning his brother in, he headed for the kitchen.

"*This* house?" Austin said from behind him as he closed the door and followed him. "The house where you saw what you believe was a cat burglar? I know what you're doing and I don't like it."

Laramie laughed. "You're the one who encouraged me to buy a house up here." He opened the refrigerator and offered his brother a beer.

Austin declined with a shake of his head. "I'm not talking about the house and you know it. Hud told me that someone ran you off the highway."

"Just some crazy driver," Laramie said, wondering how much Hud had told his brothers. Apparently nothing more than that since Austin didn't ask him about Taylor or Jade West.

"Is this just about the woman?" Austin asked instead.

"I didn't buy the house for that reason." *Well, not completely*, he thought as he closed the refrigerator. "Come take a look. You'll have to admit the house is perfect for me."

Austin stepped into the living room, still looking skeptical.

"Check out the view," he suggested as he walked to the front window in the living room area. "Open concept. Granite counters. State-of-the-art appliances. What's not to like?"

His brother looked out at Lone Mountain glowing in the afternoon light and seemed to relax a little. "It's nice."

"There are two more floors. The second floor is great for company, two bedrooms, another living area, another bath. The master is on the third floor."

"Where is the painting?" Austin asked.

Realizing there would be no getting rid of him without showing him the painting, Laramie led the way up to the third floor. "Check out the view from here."

"Impressive." But clearly he'd come to see the painting.

The painting was where it'd been when he moved in. And now the alleged original was hanging next to it.

"That's what all the fuss is about?" his brother asked, clearly not that impressed by the artwork.

"It's cowboy art."

Austin shot him a look. "I'm aware of that. What is the original worth?"

"Fifty K."

His brother's eyebrow shot up. "And you bought it with the house?"

"I got a deal on it."

"Not if it's the forgery," Austin pointed out. "Now you have *two* of them?"

"Unless Hud catches the cat burglar and needs them back for evidence."

Austin gave him a "knock off the bull" look. "You think she'll be back for it." Laramie said nothing. What would be the point since it was obvious Austin knew him too well? "Have you considered just how dangerous this might be?"

"I've already found the thief."

His brother's eyebrow shot up. *"What?"*

"I met her today at a cowboy art exhibit in Bozeman. We had coffee."

Austin shook his head as if trying to clear it. "You need to go to Hud and—"

"Without proof? Not a chance. Also I don't want to scare her away." Laramie headed down the stairs.

"So how do you plan to catch her? That is what you're doing, right?" his brother asked, catching up with him.

"I asked her to help me decorate the house."

"Why would you do that?" Austin let out a curse. "If you're right and this woman really is a criminal, then you are in over your head already. I'm serious. What has gotten into you?"

"Isn't it possible that I know what I'm doing? Just because I've always been the brains behind the business doesn't mean I can't do what you and Hayes have been doing for years."

Austin ignored the part about "the brains behind the business."

"Damn it, Laramie, you aren't trained for undercover work."

He leaned against his kitchen counter. "What about the times I've helped the two of you on cases? Give me a little credit."

"At least tell me what you're planning to do."

"I need to know what her game is. She's been seen leaving other houses, but nothing according to the owners was taken. Don't tell me that doesn't intrigue you."

Austin frowned. "I smell a scam, either with the artist, the owner of the painting and/or your cat burglar."

"I have no idea, but," Laramie said, smiling, "I hope to find out."

His brother seemed to run out of arguments. "What is this woman's name? I'll run a background check on her and see if she's had any arrests or convictions."

"Thanks, but I'd rather—"

"Your instincts aside, you need to know who you're dealing with. Unless you don't want to know the truth because... You haven't fallen for this woman, have you?"

"Of course not," he said and looked away, remembering the kiss.

"Laramie—"

"I just don't want you getting involved."

Austin sighed. "How did this woman get under your skin so quickly?"

Laramie shook his head. There was no denying it. Sid had gotten to him.

"If this is about proving something to yourself or to the rest of us—"

"Maybe it started out that way," Laramie admitted. "But if anyone can understand getting hooked on a case, it should be you."

His brother rubbed his neck for a moment before he smiled. "Apparently you are a lot more like me than I ever realized. Okay. All I'll do is run a background check on her. Just let me do that. Unless you're afraid of what I'm going to find out."

"Her name is Obsidian Forester. But I don't want you going to Hud with this yet."

"We'll keep it between us, for now. Obsidian Forester. With a name like that, I shouldn't have any trouble. In the meantime, be careful. You're sure she isn't the one who ran you off the road?"

"I can't imagine how she could be." That was at least true enough.

Chapter Nine

Sid looked around her cabin at all the work she had to do. Since coming back from the museum and her encounter with Laramie Cardwell, she'd gotten little done. Nor had she slept well last night. All her instincts told her to forget about the painting Laramie Cardwell now had in his possession.

If only she could. The painting was a loose end, one she had to take care of, which meant she would have to deal with Laramie Cardwell.

She kept rerunning their conversation in her head. She wavered between, *he knows it was you* and *he can't possibly know* and *even if he does suspect you, he can't prove it.*

Still, getting closer to him—and the painting—felt like a trap. She had no doubt that she could steal the painting back. He would be spending some of the holidays with his family. It would be the perfect time to take it.

But then he would know that, as well. Her head hurt as she considered what he might be up to. If he suspected who she was, then he would try to get proof. She couldn't shake the feeling that he was just waiting for her to show up in the middle of the night to try to retrieve the painting she'd dropped so he could catch her red-handed.

Was Marshal Hud Savage in on it? She didn't think so. Since none of the paintings were missing, he wasn't apt to think that a crime had been committed.

So what was Laramie up to besides tempting her? The fact that he seemed to be tempting her for more than the painting unnerved her. During coffee a couple times she'd caught him looking at her as if…as if he was interested in her? Of course he was, but not because he was attracted to her. And yet, she had felt an electric spark between them. A stirring she hadn't felt in a very long time—if ever.

The thought made her laugh. If it wasn't complicated enough, she could never fall for a *businessman*. She bet that most of the time he wore a three-piece suit and spent his time behind a desk. Definitely not her type. And yet that image didn't quite seem to fit Laramie Cardwell.

No one who spent all his time behind a desk was in that great shape. No, when she closed her eyes, she saw him in boots, jeans and a Western shirt. He'd mentioned going horseback riding. Maybe she would take him up on it and see just how "Western" he really was.

The idea had too much appeal. If she were smart, she would keep her distance. But then how could she find out what he was up to, let alone get the painting back?

She picked up her keys before good sense could stop her and headed for her SUV. It was time to pay Laramie Cardwell a visit.

AUSTIN RAN THE name Obsidian Forester the moment he reached his computer at the small office he kept at his wife's gallery.

"You look awfully serious," Gillian said from the doorway.

"Laramie's met a woman."

She chuckled. "And that's bad?"

"It depends on whether or not she's a convicted felon or worse."

"There's something worse than a convicted felon?"

Austin watched as the information came up on the computer screen. He knew what he'd been expecting. A record that showed the woman was a thief, a forger… at the very least a con artist.

"Well?" Gillian asked as she came into the room.

"No record. Nothing."

"Why don't you sound relieved?"

Austin raked a hand through his hair. "He's my little brother."

"Maybe the woman is fine."

"Maybe she is just starting her criminal career and my little brother is her first victim."

"It sounds to me like you're just looking for trouble," Gillian said as she turned to leave.

LARAMIE HEARD THE sound of the vehicle coming up the road. Another of his brothers? They'd always been protective of him because he was the youngest. He hadn't minded, liking that they had watched his back. But this was different. This was something he wanted to handle himself.

He sighed as he looked out and was pleasantly and

unexpectedly surprised to see Obsidian Forester's older-model blue SUV coming up the road. He hadn't expected her to take him up on his offer—let alone so soon.

Hurrying upstairs, he stashed the painting she'd dropped that night in the closet and then rushed back down. He would show it to her, but not right away.

As the blue SUV pulled in, his heart jumped in his chest with expectation. Even though he knew she was probably only here because of the painting, he still smiled to himself as he watched her get out of her vehicle from a window.

Laramie ran a hand through his thick dark hair and braced himself to see her again. Chimes filled the house as she rang the doorbell. He hoped that the reason Austin hadn't gotten back to him yet was because he hadn't found out anything worrisome about Sid. Bracing himself, he opened the door.

Sid looked out of a fur-trimmed hooded coat. Her face glowed from the cold and the afternoon light. Her breath came out in white puffs, her eyes clear blue like the ice on the river. Snowflakes danced in the air around her. She was a winter wonderland vision standing there.

"Did I catch you at a bad time?" she asked as a few moments passed without either of them speaking.

He mentally shook himself out of his reverie. "Sorry, you looked so…"

"Cold?" she suggested with a smile.

"Exactly, come on in." He stepped aside to let her enter.

"I probably should have called."

"Except you didn't take my number. But your timing couldn't have been more perfect. Let me take your coat. I have a fire going in the fireplace if you need to warm up, and I can make some coffee."

"Thank you," she said, shrugging out of the coat. Her ginger hair was loose and now fell around her shoulders in a sunset wave of color. Her freckles seemed to stand out even more on her pale face. "It's Montana in late December." She shrugged as if being a little cold was expected.

"So you're used to winter," Laramie said as he hung up her coat in the closet by the front door. "I never asked you if you're from here or a newbie like me."

"New to this town. But I was raised in Montana not too far from here." She followed him into the kitchen.

"So where exactly are you from?" he asked as he poured her a mug.

"I grew up outside of Maudlow," she said with a laugh. "You've never heard of it, right? It's to the north. Not much of a town there anymore." She glanced around. "Nice house."

"Thanks. I didn't want anything too big, but by my condo standards, this place seems huge. It does make me want to stay here more, though."

"You aren't planning to stay long this time?" she asked as she wandered into the living room, then turned. "Do you mind?" she asked nodding toward the stairs.

"No, please. Take a look around. As you can see, the walls are all bare down here." He followed her up the stairs, again noting how fluidly she moved. Also how quietly.

On the second floor, she made a lap through the main room, then headed up the second set of stairs to

the master bedroom. To the casual observer she didn't
seem to know the house. But it was clear to him that
she knew exactly what she was looking for.

On the third floor, she entered his bedroom slowly.
Fortunately, he'd made the bed this morning and he
hadn't left any clothing lying around. Because he'd
been expecting her. He was pleased that he'd been
right. In fact, she'd shown up even sooner than he had
hoped.

She stepped in, seeming to take in the view before
she turned first to the right, then slowly to the left as
if leaving the painting till the last.

Laramie had to smile to himself. This is what she'd
come to see, he thought, as she took in the painting.
Everything else had been pretense—he was sure of it.

"This is the painting you told me you bought from
the owner?" she asked without looking at him.

"That's it. There was just something about it, if you
know what I mean."

"No. Like I said, I'm not a fan of cowboy art, but
as long as *you* like it…" She glanced around. Looking
for the other painting?

"I'm not sure what I like, to tell you the truth."

"Isn't there art in your home in Houston?" she asked
as if actually interested.

"I bought the condo new. It came decorated."

She shook her head as if she couldn't imagine doing
something like that.

Her eyes were darker in his bedroom, a deeper
blue. He wondered what color they would be when she
opened her eyes in his bed in the morning. The thought
shook him to his boots. Of course he was attracted

her. What red-blooded Texas boy wouldn't be? But to think that there was a chance they might be lovers...

"What's funny about this painting," he said, drawing her back to it, "is that I have two of them."

That definitely got her attention. "Why would you buy two of them?"

"Good question, since, when I visited the artist, he told me he painted only one of them," Laramie said as he stepped past her to open the closet and pull out the second one. He hung it next to the first. "So which one is the original?"

SHE LOOKED AT THEM for a moment. "I have no idea."

Sid strangled back the cry that rose in her throat. Only moments before she had been looking at all the wonderful wall space he had in his house, thinking how fun it would be to fill it with art. She'd been excited about the ridiculous thought of helping him. How she would have loved it. She had tons of ideas. Not that it would ever happen, but it was fun to fantasize about a lot of things when it came to Laramie Cardwell.

Then he'd said he'd talked to Taylor West about the two paintings, and all the air had rushed out of her. The room suddenly felt too hot, too small, too bright.

She'd barely been able to get the words out. "You showed the work to the artist?" He nodded, hopefully unaware of how upset she'd become. "I would think he would know his own artwork," she said carefully.

"I thought the same thing. Apparently one of these is the original. The other, a forgery. A very good forgery."

"That's remarkable. Did he have any idea who might have been able to forge it?"

Laramie shook his head. "West said the only man good enough to have done the work was one H. F. Powell. Have you heard of him?"

She could only nod.

"But apparently he's dead. So it remains a mystery. Just between you and me? What makes it all the more crazy is how I came to have both paintings."

Sid listened as he told her what she already knew. "That is quite the story," she said when he finished.

"It's a mystery."

"I'm sure you'll solve it," she said, hoping she was wrong.

"Maybe," he said meeting her gaze. "I'm sure hoping I do."

Sid reminded herself that the only reason she'd come over here was to get the painting back, which meant getting closer to Laramie Cardwell. But being here with him, standing this close to him, looking into those blue eyes...

She felt a small tremor move through her. *He knew.* It was time to quit kidding herself. He was just waiting for her to make a mistake. But that wasn't all she saw in his eyes or felt being this close to him. Some kind of chemistry was arcing between them and he felt it, too.

Sid tried to convince herself this was about nothing more than foreplay, flirtation. But the attraction was so strong between them that there was no denying it.

Worse, she *liked* him. Look at the interest he'd taken in Western art since the first night they'd met, she thought with a hidden smile. He'd become intrigued, just as she had become intrigued by him. She couldn't say that about most of the men she'd dated. Her last

serious relationship had been in high school. Fortunately she'd been smart enough not to marry him.

But whatever feelings she might have when it came
to Laramie Cardwell, the question now was how far
she would go to get the painting back.

LARAMIE SAW THE WAY Sid was clutching the coffee mug
in both hands. "Your coffee must be getting cold. Let's
go back down. I want your opinion on that big wall in
the living room."

He'd noticed the change in her. What he'd told her
had upset her. But by the time they reached the kitchen,
she seemed her cool, calm self again.

This woman would be the death of him. The thought
surprised him as if it was a warning. But there was no
denying whatever was going on between them under
the surface. It wasn't his imagination. This woman did
things to him. That alone made her dangerous—not
to mention the fact that she was a criminal. A thief.
Or worse.

He told himself he wouldn't be stupid enough to let
her steal his heart.

"If I'm going to help find the right art for you, then
I'll need to figure out what you like," Sid said after
he'd warmed up her coffee and showed her the large,
high-ceilinged wall in the living room.

"How do you suggest doing that since I don't know
what I like?" he asked, inexplicably still intrigued and
attracted by this woman. He really had to be careful.
Austin was right. He had no idea what he was getting into.

She smiled as she looked up at him, her eyes locking with his. "I guess we'll have to spend more time together so I get to know you better."

He felt a dart of desire puncture his already weak reserve. *She was flirting with him.*

"I completely agree," he heard himself say, all the while reminding himself who he was dealing with. Austin was afraid this woman was dangerous. His brother had no idea given the mix of emotions Sid evoked in him.

She smiled. "Any suggestions?"

She *definitely* was flirting with him. Laying some sort of trap for him?

He decided to play along. "We could start by going horseback riding, but it's supposed to snow this afternoon."

Sid laughed. "I love riding in the snow, but if you—"

"No, I'm in. Just let me call my cousin Dana."

TAYLOR WEST TRIED his wife's cell phone number again. It went straight to voice mail—again. Only this time, the message said that her voice mail was full.

He slammed down the phone. Since seeing Jade's car in Rock Jackson's barn, he hadn't been able to sleep—except for the hours he'd drunk so much that he'd passed out.

"Don't do anything crazy," fellow artist Hank Ramsey had told him. Taylor hadn't wanted to tell anyone, but he was going out of his mind, so he'd called Hank for advice.

"Don't do anything *crazy*?" he'd demanded after hearing Hank's advice. "Rock has stolen my *wife*! And who knows what else he's done." He'd stopped short of telling Hank what else he suspected Rock Jackson of doing. Did he trust either Rock or Hank? Not anymore. Not since he'd seen the painting Laramie Cardwell had in his possession.

"You don't know for a fact that Jade is with Rock."

"Her car is parked in his barn," he'd said between clenched teeth. "And he has a room behind his studio with boarded-up windows and a padlock on the door.

"There could be another explanation than the one you've jumped to."

"What would that be if it was *your* wife?"

"Jade could be storing her car there. Didn't you say she was planning to go to Ohio to visit her sister for a while?"

"Indiana to visit her mother." He'd cursed under his breath, sorry he'd called Hank. "I thought that was where she would go. She never said—it doesn't matter where she went. *Her car is in Rock's barn.* Even if she flew to Mars, why would she leave her car with him?"

"Probably because she didn't want to pay the overnight fee at the airport. Gateway isn't that far from the airport. Rock probably gave her a ride."

He hadn't thought that Jade knew Rock that well. True, she'd been to enough cowboy artist conferences that maybe she'd come to know the artists better than he did. He spent most of his time at those things getting to know the bartender rather than listening to the bull the other artists were spouting.

"Also, I'd be careful about making any accusations since you have no proof about anything. You might want to watch the booze, too. The one thing we have to do is stick together."

Taylor had heard something in the man's voice. Was he warning him? "*I'm* not the problem."

"We don't even know there *is* a problem."

Hank wasn't talking about Jade any longer. "You didn't see the painting," Taylor'd said, trying to keep the anger and the fear out of his voice.

"I'll talk to Rock. I'm sure there is nothing to worry about."

Right, Taylor thought as he went to unlock his gun cabinet.

Chapter Ten

On the way to Cardwell Ranch to meet Sid and go horseback riding, Laramie's cell phone rang. It was his brother Austin.

He braced himself as he took the call. "So what did you find out about Sid?" he asked, just wanting to get it over with.

"*Sid?* You're using her nickname already?" Laramie could practically see his brother shaking his head.

"So did you find something or not?"

Austin sighed. "She appears to be squeaky clean. No arrests, no speeding tickets, nothing. She lives alone, owns a small, older cabin back in the woods outside of Big Sky and drives an older-model SUV." Not a large dark car. "No debt. Makes a modest living with her artwork."

Laramie wanted to laugh with relief. "So why don't you sound happy?"

"Because she's *too* squeaky clean."

"There is no satisfying you, Austin," he joked.

"You still think she's the woman you saw that night with the painting though, right?"

"I'm not sure." He knew he was hedging because he was starting to like Sid—and he *could* be wrong about her being the woman. It had been dark and she'd been wearing a ski mask. All he'd seen were her eyes, and there were a lot of women with blue eyes, right? But those lips... Not every woman had those.

"Just be careful. If you need my help..."

Laramie thanked his brother and drove on to Cardwell Ranch, where he and Sid had agreed to meet. Sid hadn't arrived yet, but his cousin Dana was waiting for him.

"So you've already met someone?" As they stood in her warm, ranch kitchen, Dana sounded too happy to hear that it would be a woman going riding with him.

"You're responsible for marrying off all my brothers, aren't you?" Laramie joked. "Well, this time you've met your match. Marriage is the last thing that is going to happen with this woman."

"I hope you don't have to eat your words," Dana said smiling.

"You'd *better* hope so."

She suddenly quit smiling. "This isn't the woman you caught with the painting?"

"That stopped your matchmaking cold," he said with a laugh.

"You're going horseback riding with *her*? Does Hud know?"

"We don't know for sure that it is even her. Also your husband is convinced this whole cat burglar thing is nothing more than a hoax."

"Well, *I'm* not convinced. What if the woman is dangerous?"

Laramie laughed. "You sound like Austin. Look, if I don't make it back from the horseback ride, you'll have your answer."

"I don't think that's funny."

"Dana, it's just a horseback ride. If you want to worry…she's helping me purchase art for my new house."

His cousin looked aghast. "You be careful, Laramie Cardwell. I've been through enough with your brothers. I don't need you getting into trouble."

Outside, the ranch wrangler had saddled two horses. Laramie told his cousin he was more than capable of saddling his own horses, but Dana had insisted he come inside and visit with her while he waited for his "date" to arrive. Sid had said she needed to run some errands and would prefer to meet him at the ranch.

As a blue SUV pulled into the yard, he went out to greet her. Not surprisingly, Dana followed on his heels.

"Sid, this is my cousin Dana Cardwell Savage. Dana, Obsidian 'Sid' Forester."

Sid held out her hand. "It's a pleasure to meet you," she said. "Thank you for offering the use of your horses. I'm looking forward to it."

"You ride?" Dana asked.

"I grew up on a ranch and rode every day for years."

Laramie noticed that Dana seemed to soften toward the woman, ranch woman to ranch woman. "Then I am especially glad you're going to get to ride today," his cousin said. She turned to Laramie. "How far were you planning to ride?"

"Not far," he said. "We'll be back in a couple hours."

The wrangler handed each of them their reins. Laramie watched Sid swing up into the saddle. Clearly she was comfortable on a horse. He followed suit and they headed along a trail that followed the river. Fresh snow rose in the air around them as they rode.

The day was crisp and cold. Ice crystals hung in the

air and the promise of snow rode on the breeze. But it felt good to be back in the saddle. Laramie had ridden often on his brother Jackson's place. He'd missed it since Jackson had sold his ranch in Texas and moved to Montana.

"Your cousin seems nice," Sid said as they rode.

"Dana? She's amazing. She's also responsible for getting us all to Montana."

Sid cut her eyes at him. "She seemed a little worried about you."

"She's overprotective when it comes to family. But I could tell she liked you. Wait until you get to know her. She's great."

Wait until you get to know her. He made it sound as if they would be spending a lot of time together. Sid said nothing as they rode through snow-laden pines. Water rushed under the thick aquamarine-colored ice on the Gallatin River beside them. The air smelled of snow. She could see that it was already snowing on the top of Lone Mountain across the narrow river valley.

Was she wrong about Laramie's suspicions? Maybe he really was attracted to her and wanted nothing more than a date.

"I was surprised to hear you'd grown up on a ranch," he said.

"Why is that?"

"You don't like cowboy art."

She chuckled. "You think they go hand in hand?"

"I guess not."

"What about you? Where did you learn to ride?"

"We had relatives with horses when we were young. Then my brother Jackson bought a small ranch. I used to ride there almost every day. I've missed it. I've missed my brothers since they've all moved to Montana. Even my mother is here now."

"You're so lucky to have such a large, close family."

He looked over at her. "You don't?"

She shook her head. "My mother died when I was three. My father passed away some years ago. He taught me—" she hated the tremor she heard in her voice "—to ride."

"I'm so sorry for your loss. It sounds like you were close."

Sid just nodded, afraid to speak for fear she would cry. It surprised her, all this emotion. Let alone the fact that she had opened up to Laramie—the last person she should be letting her guard down with.

"You don't have any siblings?" he asked.

"An older sister who travels a lot."

"You must get lonely," he said glancing over at her. Catching a whiff of Laramie's fresh-from-the-shower scent, she felt a longing wash over her. But it was more than a desire to be in this man's arms. It was a need to trust someone other than herself. For just an instant, she wanted to tell him everything. What a weight that would be off her shoulders to confide in someone. To confide in this strong cowboy.

As if sensing the way she was feeling, Laramie reined in next to her. It happened so fast that she didn't have time to react. He reached over and she felt his thumb on her cheek. Until that moment, she hadn't realized she'd been crying as he smoothed away a tear.

His gaze locked with hers as he leaned into her, his mouth finding hers. She tasted the saltiness of her tears and the cold scent of the winter day on his lips. Her own lips parted as she leaned into the kiss. He cupped her face, the kiss sweet and soft, then more demanding. She felt heat run like hot water through her veins, warming her to the toes of her boots.

As if realizing what he was doing, he pulled back suddenly. "Sorry. I couldn't help myself."

She swallowed, desperately wanting to grab the collar of his winter coat and pull him into another kiss. His mouth, warm against hers, had kindled a flame in her like nothing she'd ever felt. She ached to lose herself in this man, which was so not like her that it terrified her. She was always careful. But at this moment, she wanted to throw caution to the wind and let her heart have what it wanted.

"I'm not sorry," she heard herself say, although she knew she should be. Did she have to remind herself how dangerous it was to get too close to Laramie Cardwell, of all men?

It was the second time they'd kissed, she realized with a start. Was that why he'd kissed her? If so, then did he now know she was his cat burglar?

Now what? she wondered as they rode back toward the ranch house. Was he setting her up for a fall? After that kiss, she feared she had a lot more to worry about than the painting.

ROCK JACKSON OPENED one eye to see the time on the clock beside the bed. He'd forgotten for a moment where he was. Then he remembered. He was hiding out in a friend's condo in Bozeman and he wasn't alone. He groaned pleasantly, surprised that he'd slept this late. Even more surprised that he could be this happy.

Rolling over, he looked into Jade West's young,

beautiful face. He couldn't believe she was in his bed. The hours they'd spent making love since she'd shown up at his door were a blur.

The moment he'd laid eyes on her the first time at an Old West Artists Conference, he'd been smitten. The worst part that first time was realizing that she was that old fart Taylor West's trophy wife. He'd said then that the marriage wouldn't last.

And he'd been right. But he never thought he had a chance with her. He was more than surprised when she'd shown up at his door and had fallen into his arms. The satisfaction that gave him was shameful, but he still enjoyed every moment of it. Jade was *his*.

Her lashes fluttered and a moment later her green eyes opened. She smiled, making him laugh with delight.

"What?" she asked as she rolled over onto her back. She had the best rack he'd ever seen and this morning she was displaying it for the world.

"I'm just happy." Happier than he had ever been. With two bad marriages and an imminent divorce, he'd had his share of heartbreak. Jade was his compensation for those hard times. It didn't hurt, either, that he'd stolen that smug SOB Taylor West's wife.

"I need to call Taylor."

Her words burst that moment of pure joy. Like a soap bubble, it popped right before his eyes. "Is that necessary?"

She turned onto her side to look at him again. "I need to *tell* him."

"You could let me do that."

Jade shook her head, her delightful lower lip protruding as she said, "I have to do it myself. It's the right thing to do. I don't want him thinking I'm coming back."

She was young, Rock thought. Barely legal to buy alcohol in Montana. What did she know about these things? "He isn't going to be happy. I'm sure he'll beg you to come back. Or threaten to kill us both."

"He wouldn't do that."

Rock wasn't so sure about that. Taylor could be a loose cannon when he was drinking—which was most of the time. Worse, there was bad blood between them and had been for years.

"You don't have to do it *right* now, do you?" he asked as he pulled her to him.

She purred in his arms and he felt his happiness level rise again. He had what he wanted. Well, almost. He was tired of feeling second rate because of Taylor West. Now that he had Jade, he told himself that nothing could stop him from getting what he deserved. He had Taylor's wife. Soon, she would have Taylor's money.

Life was perfect. Almost. After a quick shower, he checked his emails and found the message from Taylor about the painting.

DANA HAD A pot of chili and a pan of warm-from-the-oven corn bread ready for lunch when Laramie and Sid returned from their ride.

"You can't say no, Sid," Dana insisted as they handed over their reins to the wrangler. She stood on the porch wearing an apron, her hands on her hips. "Hud doesn't think he can make it home for lunch, the kids are with their aunt Stacy. I desperately need adult conversation."

Laramie glanced at Sid. She looked torn. He'd felt

so close to her on their ride, but then he'd felt her pull away again as they'd neared the ranch house. Now she looked as if she wanted to run—and yet was tempted to stay. He might have wondered what she had to fear if he hadn't already known.

"Chili and corn bread," he said. "Did I mention that my cousin is a great cook?"

"I would love to," she said to him, "but I can't. Thank you so much. It sounds wonderful," she called to Dana on the porch. "But I have to go. Thank you again for the horseback ride. It was lovely."

Laramie watched her head for her SUV. The kiss had confirmed what he already knew. Obsidian "Sid" Forester was his cat burglar. There was no doubt now. "Maybe I'll see you later?" he called after her, wondering what would happen next. He knew what he wanted to happen.

She smiled and nodded. "Maybe."

"Well?" Dana demanded once the two of them were seated, chili and corn bread in front of them.

"I don't know what to tell you," he said honestly.

"You don't have to tell me anything. The look on your face says it all," Dana said with a grin. "The woman has gotten to you."

He wanted to deny it but didn't bother. "She told me she lost her father some years ago. I can tell that she is still hurting over that. Apparently, he was all the family she had other than an older sister who travels all the time."

"Oh, that's awful," Dana said, sounding close to tears. She knew what it was like to lose someone she loved. She'd lost her mother, Mary, a few years ago and then, because of a dispute over the ranch, nearly lost her sister and brothers. "I wish she'd stayed for lunch. You should invite her to the masquerade ball."

"I already mentioned it to her."

"And?" Dana asked hopefully.

"She wasn't interested."

"I'm sorry to hear that." He could tell that Sid's refusal had surprised her as much as it had him. "Well, *you* have to come. Don't even try to get out of it," Dana said. "We're all going, including all of your brothers. Everyone wears a costume and doesn't remove their masks until the stroke of midnight. It's the biggest event in the canyon."

He cringed inwardly just as he had the first time Dana had mentioned it. "Like I told you before, I'm not much on—"

Dana shook her head. "I'm not taking no for an answer. Believe me, you don't want to get on my bad side."

Hud laughed as he walked into the kitchen. "Trust me, she is so right about that," the marshal said as he bent to give his wife a kiss. "Whatever she wants you to do, just do it."

Dana slapped playfully at her husband as she said, "I thought you couldn't make lunch."

"I got to thinking about your chili and corn bread," he said with a shrug as he helped himself and joined them.

"I was just talking to Laramie about the masquerade ball. Now that he is going to own a house here…"

"You bought that house?" Hud asked he sat down at the table.

Laramie nodded.

"Did your brothers ever admit to playing that trick on you?" the marshal asked.

"Tag swears they know nothing about a cat burglar. Any news on the vehicle?"

"What vehicle?" Dana said. "Did something happen?"

"Some fool ran Laramie off the highway yesterday," Hud said, keeping his head down as he ate.

"What? And this is the first I'm hearing about it?" Dana demanded.

"I didn't mention it because I thought you would overreact," Hud said. "Seems I was right."

"Are you all right?" Dana demanded of her cousin.

"You can see that he is all right," Hud said.

Dana shot him an impatient look. "Why would someone run you off the road?"

"The person must have been drinking," Laramie said. He felt Dana look from him to her husband as if sensing there was more to the story.

"As to the vehicle," Hud said to him. "Haven't found it yet." He took a bite of chili and chewed. "Ever see the woman again?" he asked after a moment.

Dana shot Laramie a conspiratorial look and gave him a slight shake of her head.

"You haven't had any more sightings?" Laramie asked, avoiding the question.

Hud shook his head. "Fortunately not. I have enough problems with whoever is behind the counterfeit twenties floating around. I got a call earlier from the gas station. Someone passed off another bogus twenty. Once they start circulating…"

They ate in silence for a few moments. "I can't wait to throw a housewarming party for you," Dana said.

"Give him a break, sweetheart," her husband said

with a laugh. "You're going to scare him away with all this talk of parties."

"Well, be thinking about your costume for the ball—and a possible...date." She gave him a sly wink. "I promise you, you don't want to miss the masquerade party," she said, undeterred. "I'll write down the name of a local costume shop. You'll want to get yours soon."

Hud ate quickly and went back to work. Laramie stayed to help Dana with the dishes even though she protested.

"Why didn't you mention the horseback ride with my possible cat burglar to Hud?" he asked Dana.

She laughed. "Hud would have just turned into his marshal persona and started asking a lot of questions you clearly can't answer."

"Austin is already doing that."

"Exactly," she said, eyeing him thoughtfully. "Anyway, as far as we know she hasn't committed any crimes, right?"

He nodded.

"Also, I can tell that you're smitten with her. I liked her. Your brothers told me that you've dated a lot but haven't found *the one*. I guess time will tell with Sid, won't it? I hope she changes her mind about the ball."

"I don't see her doing that. She said she wouldn't be caught dead there."

Dana shuddered. "Those were the words she used?"

"It's just an expression," he said, seeing that Dana was now upset.

"Maybe it's for the best. Every year at the ball there's a silent art auction of several paintings to help continue funding the event," she said slowly. "Last year they were local watercolors. This year they are three works by cowboy artists."

"Who are the artists?" Laramie asked as his interest was piqued.

"Rock Jackson, Taylor West and H. F. Powell."

UPSET WITH HERSELF, Sid drove through Big Sky and turned on the road back to her cabin. She had let down her guard with Laramie. What was wrong with her? She knew what her best friend, Maisie, would say about it even before her friend answered her call.

"I kissed him again."

"You *what*?"

"Well, he kissed *me*, but I kissed him back."

"Sid. How did this happen?"

She told her about the horseback ride. "He caught me at a vulnerable moment. I was talking about…about my father dying and—"

"You went horseback riding with him and told him about your father? Have you lost your mind?"

"I only told him that my father had died." Sid sighed. "He could see that I'm clearly not over it."

"You need to be more careful. If you're right about him suspecting you…"

"I know, but there is something about him that makes me think I can trust him when I'm with him. And when he kissed me…"

"It didn't feel like a kiss from a man who was looking for an art thief?"

"No," Sid said with a groan. "It felt like kiss from a man whose reasons were strictly carnal. And I liked it," she cried.

Maisie laughed. "You know what you need, don't you?"

"If you are going to say a man—" As she pulled up beside her cabin she saw tracks in the snow where someone had walked along the back of the property. The tracks disappeared behind the house. "I have to go. If I don't call you back in five minutes..."

"I know what to do," her friend said solemnly.

Stuffing her cell phone into her pocket, she opened her glove box and pulled out the gun. Dropping it in her other coat pocket, she opened her car door and stepped out.

The snow crunched under her feet, a sign that the temperature was dropping as snow drifted down from a blinding white sky. She'd heard that another winter storm was coming in and was surprised it hadn't hit sooner.

Instead of going in the front, she walked along the side of the cabin to the back and looked toward the woods where the fresh boot prints in the snow had apparently come from. She saw a snowmobile parked some distance from the cabin. She could still smell the exhaust. Whoever was inside hadn't been here long.

Her hand in her coat pocket, her finger on the trigger, she opened the door and stepped in.

Chapter Eleven

Laramie had always been the sensible one. He was the brother the others came to when they had financial questions. He was the one who tried to keep them out of trouble. He was the one—though the youngest—they all expected to be the rational, clear thinking one.

Given what had happened in the past few days, he shouldn't have been that surprised to see that all four of his brothers were waiting for him when he returned to his house. He suspected they hadn't come to see his new residence as he got out and walked toward the waiting vehicle—and his waiting brothers.

"I hope you brought me supper from the restaurant," Laramie said as his brothers all piled out of Austin's SUV. "And more beer." None of them even smiled. He braced himself for the lectures that he knew were coming as he opened the front door of the house.

"Why don't we all have a cold one?" he suggested as he walked into the kitchen. Behind him, they all trudged in, stopping to take their boots off at the door. He turned around to stare and then laugh.

"What's so damned funny?" Jackson demanded.

"All of you. You're all so well…trained now. Is that what marriage does to you? If so, I'll pass."

"Don't try to change the subject. You're in enough trouble," Hayes warned.

"I'll take that beer you offered," Tag said. The other three brothers shot him an annoyed look. "Hey, we can lay into him and still have a beer while we do it."

"If this is about Sid…" He opened the refrigerator and brought out five bottles of beer.

"We just heard about someone running you off the highway in the canyon," Hayes said. "You didn't even bother to tell us?"

"I'm fine," Laramie said. "But I appreciate your concern," he said as he handed them each a bottle.

"Where have you been?" Austin asked, sounding as though he was interrogating one of his suspects back when he was a deputy sheriff in Texas.

"At Cardwell Ranch having lunch with Dana and Hud," Laramie said, twisting off the cap from his beer. He took a drink, then added, "Before that I went on a horseback ride."

"Alone?" Austin asked, then sighed when Laramie said nothing. He wrenched the top off his bottle of beer. "I told you to be careful. A horseback ride?"

"You probably want to see the house," Laramie said. He was still too happy about his afternoon ride with Sid to want to argue with his brothers. Not that he didn't understand their concern. He was too smart not to realize he was playing with fire.

"I want to see these damned paintings," Tag said. He looked toward the stairs. "Are they up there?"

"They were when I left," Laramie said.

SID EASED HER FINGER off the trigger of the gun in her coat pocket. Her older sister stood over the painting on her easel—after having picked the lock on Sid's back door. Sid tried to tamp down her annoyance. Seeing her was like seeing a ghostly image of herself. People used to think the two of them were twins. They looked that much alike, especially when Zander had gone strawberry blonde.

The fact that they were half sisters wouldn't have surprised anyone to see them together—same father, different mothers. But few people knew they were even related because Zander was always gone and they were never seen together.

"Zander, what are you doing here?" Sid hated the edge to her voice. But from past experience, she feared a visit from her half sister didn't bode well.

Zander turned and smiled. "Merry Christmas!"

She slipped out of her coat and hung it on the hook by the back door. "You're here for *Christmas*?"

"Don't sound so surprised," her sister said, stepping to her to give her a hug. "We've missed too many holidays. I decided not to let another one go by without spending it with my little sis."

She caught a whiff of her sister's favorite perfume, a scent that transported her back to their teen years. It also reminded her that it was Zander who'd taught her about breaking and entering. And that was the least of Zander's crimes.

"So you just happened into the area, grabbed a snowmobile and decided to visit?" she asked as she stepped back from the hug.

Zander sighed. "You've always been so suspicious. I came by snowmobile because it had been too many years since I'd gotten to ride on one and I wanted to surprise you. Clearly, I did. Come on, we're all the family we have left."

"And you thought after several years of me not hearing from you that you'd just stop by and surprise me," she repeated.

Her sister laughed and shook her head. "Sid, in case no one has told you, it's *Christmas*. I've heard families get together, exchange presents, sit around the Christmas tree and drink eggnog. At least that's what they do in movies," she said, glancing around Sid's cabin. "But it certainly doesn't look like Christmas here. Where's the tree and the eggnog, the stockings hung with care?"

"If I'd known you were coming for a visit—"

"Not to worry. I'll take care of everything, including filling up your refrigerator. Sid, what do you eat...? Or do you?" She continued, not expecting an answer apparently. "You look thin. I hope it's because you're painting and not because of that crazy quest you've been on."

Sid didn't want to talk about either with her sister. "Where have you been this time?" Zander had taken after her mother, a model who'd disappeared a few years before Sid was born. Her sister had apparently picked up that wandering gene.

"I tend to follow the sun. You know me," Zander said noncommittally as she moved around the cabin. "Unless, of course, I get a hankering to spend Christmas in Big Sky with my sister."

Zander couldn't seem to let grass grow under her feet. According to their father, the photographs she'd seen of Zander's mother hadn't captured her wild spirit. Her father, who'd loved women to distraction, had moved on at fifty after Zander's mother had left, and had another child sans marriage. Even though Sid's mother was younger than he was, he'd managed to out-live her by twenty years.

"I don't have an extra bedroom," Sid said, unable to turn her sister away, "but you can take mine and I'll—"

"I already have a place to stay. I didn't come to move in. Or to keep you from your…work. But don't make any plans for Christmas Eve. I'll bring every-thing."

Sid looked at her sister and felt that old blood bond between them as well as the memories that would al-ways link them. Her timing was questionable, but it *was* almost Christmas, wasn't it? It had been too long since she'd even seen her sister—Zander was right about that. Also, they were the last of their family and the last link to their father.

Sid hugged her again, harder this time while silently praying her sister was telling the truth about her reason for being here now. "I've missed you, Z."

"THE PAINTINGS ARE identical right down to the picture frame," Hayes said as he studied them. "I would swear they were painted by the same artist."

"I took the supposed forgery to an art expert. He offered me thirty thousand for it and offered to docu-ment it as the original," Laramie said. "Even the art-ist who painted it believed this was the original. At least at first."

"Are you sure the one you bought with the house isn't the forgery?" Jackson asked. "McKenzie says most forgeries are easy to spot. All you have to do is look at the colors, the brushstrokes, the canvas…but this one…" He shook his head.

"It is perplexing," he admitted. "But there is a certificate on the back claiming it is an original and one of a kind. That was good enough for its original owner."

"Something isn't right," Hayes said, looking worried. "Either the artist painted more than one of these and lied, or this is a masterful forger. What about the other houses where this…cat burglar was seen?"

"Hud said the owners checked their artwork," Austin said. "It hadn't been taken."

"That's why the marshal thinks the whole thing is a hoax," Laramie pointed out.

"Except you caught the woman and have a second painting that is identical or damned close," Austin said. "If she's switching the originals for forgeries, she has one profitable scam going, and so far she's gotten away with it. Which means she can't let you keep this painting." He glanced over at Laramie and swore. "That's what you're counting on, isn't it?"

"Or maybe the artist is in on it," Hayes said. "You said you talked to him?"

"Taylor West seemed as perplexed by it all as I was," he said. "But according to him, he's the top moneymaker with his art. So if you were going to forge anyone's, it would seem smart to copy his."

"You were run off the road after you visited this Taylor West?" Austin asked, clearly knowing that was the case.

"Coincidence," Laramie said, shrugging. Austin mugged a face at him.

"Whoever is doing this is good, really good," Hayes said studying the artwork.

Laramie nodded. "I asked West who he would

suspect of forging his work. The only artist he could think of who was that good was H. F. Powell."

"I've seen his work," Jackson said. "He was one of the originals like Charles M. Russell and Frederic Remington. But didn't I hear that he's dead? Unless he forged this painting before he died…"

Laramie had thought of that. "What do you know about him?"

His brothers all shrugged.

"I just know that one of his paintings is going to be auctioned off at the ball," Tag said. "McKenzie expects it to go for a lot of money because there aren't many of them around. Most of his work was lost in a house fire the night of his death. Apparently he was a character. I guess in his old age, he locked himself in his studio and no one saw him again. He died destitute with what would now be hundreds of thousands of dollars worth of his paintings going up in flames with him."

"The paintings all burned?" Laramie asked.

"McKenzie said the fire turned out to be arson. The old man apparently started the blaze himself."

"What about the one being auctioned off at the ball?" he asked.

"Apparently it was one that he'd sold before his death," Jackson said.

"I WAS HOPING you'd be glad to see me," Zander said, pretending to pout. "After all, I taught you everything you know."

"Not *everything*." Zander had taught her how to pick locks at a young age, how to break into houses through windows and not leave any evidence. She'd taught her how to steal—and how to get away with it.

For that she owed her since that talent had certainly come in handy.

But fortunately, Sid had learned other things that had helped her in life that her sister could have benefited from. Everyone in Big Sky thought she had no siblings. She'd kept Zander a secret for reasons she didn't want to admit. Now she regretted that—and the times she'd wished it was true.

"So what have you been up to?" her sister said, studying her. "Is there a man in your life?"

Sid shook her head and turned away. "Why would you ask that?"

Zander laughed. "Because you're young, somewhat attractive," her sister joked since she was clearly aware how much they resembled each other, "and this place is crawling with rich men."

Sid groaned. "We're not all looking for a sugar daddy." She wondered now where her sister was staying. It would be just like Zander to have met some man who was letting her stay in his guesthouse—if not his master bedroom.

"Well, don't wait too long to find one," her sister said. "It gets harder as you get older."

Sid started to point out there was only seven years between them. But in the bright light reflecting off the snow outside, Zander looked as if the years they'd been apart had taken a toll on her. Her sister lived hard and fast as if that, too, was in her genes.

Zander walked around the cabin, picking up things and putting them back with no apparent real interest. "So are you almost finished with your diabolical plan?"

She sighed and gave her sister an impatient look. "Diabolical?"

Zander shrugged. "You are almost done, though, aren't you?" She turned to look at her. "You have all the paintings?"

"Not quite."

Her sister nodded. "Then what?"

"I really don't want to talk about this with you. Like you said, it's nearly Christmas. Let's not dig up the past."

Her sister looked angry for a moment, but then nodded. "You're right. We never agreed on much anyway, but we are still blood. Daddy would have wanted us to be friends."

The mention of their father brought tears to Sid's eyes. He was the one person in their lives they could agree on. They had both loved him in their own ways.

"I'm not here to keep you from your...work. But if I can help, you'll let me know. I might be a little rusty at the undercover stuff, but I doubt it would take much to bring it back." Zander grinned. "In fact, I'd welcome the diversion. Life has been too tame for too long."

Sid doubted that. "You didn't seem to have any trouble breaking into my cabin."

Her sister waved that off with a laugh. "Hardly a challenge. You really should consider getting better locks. You don't even have a security system," she said, looking around the small cabin and frowning. "Which means you don't keep anything you value here."

Sid had wondered how long it would take her sister to get to the heart of the matter. But she ignored it, determined not to discuss this with her. "If you're coming back Christmas Eve, I should tell you I don't like eggnog. But if you still remember how to make nachos like you did when we were kids..."

Zander's smile never reached her eyes. "Got the message."

Sid doubted she did. Before the holidays were over, her sister would return to her real reason for being in Big Sky. In the meantime, she wondered what her sister might be up to and asked as much.

"I thought I'd do some skiing and maybe lay around in the hot tub at the place I'm staying."

Sid said nothing, but that didn't sound like the sister she'd known and loved. Since she was fourteen Sid had pretty much been on her own. Growing up with a father who worked all the time and a sister who was a thief, she had learned to take care of herself—any way she'd had to.

Unfortunately, Zander, the firstborn to the mother with the movie-star looks, had been pampered as a child—until her mother disappeared. After that, Zander had merely taken whatever she wanted—including any money she could steal from their father and, finally, the ranch itself.

"I have to run, but I'll be back Christmas Eve with bells on." Zander laughed as she left, her perfume lingering along with the good—and bad—memories she brought with her.

Sid listened to the sound of the snowmobile's motor as it died away in the distance. She couldn't let Zander jeopardize everything she'd worked so hard for. Sinking into a chair, she put her head in her hands and fought tears of anger and frustration. As much as she loved her sister, she couldn't trust her. That alone broke her heart.

She thought of Laramie Cardwell. This house of cards she'd built felt as if it was about to collapse around her. But she had no choice. She had to get that painting back from him. And, knowing her sister, she had to stop Zander from whatever she'd come back to Montana to do.

Chapter Twelve

Later that day, Sid stopped by the grocery store to pick up a few things. She couldn't be sure that she would ever see her sister again—that was until she got a call from someone that Zander was in trouble.

But she would buy a few groceries anyway, just in case. She couldn't depend on Zander not to show up Christmas Eve with only bells on.

Pulling a twenty from her purse, she handed it to the clerk. When the clerk hesitated and began to inspect the bill, Sid felt a chill race up her spine. In that instant, she realized that she couldn't be sure she'd had a twenty in her purse this morning.

With a groan, she also realized that she'd gotten out of the habit of checking her wallet when her sister was around. But it wasn't like Zander to take money and leave change.

"I'm sorry, but I can't take this bill," the clerk said as she motioned for her supervisor to come over.

Sid could feel her face heat with embarrassment as other customers began to stare at her. Her stomach roiled. "What is wrong with the bill?"

The clerk didn't answer. It wasn't until the marshal showed up that Sid learned she'd somehow picked up a counterfeit bill.

PARKED IN THE trees so he could see Rock Jackson's driveway, Taylor West checked to make sure the gun was loaded as he waited. He thought about his wife and took another pull on the bourbon bottle. Jade had called earlier.

"Where are you?" he'd asked as nice as he could the moment he answered.

"Bozeman," she'd said in a small, guilty voice.

He'd hoped Hank might be right about Jade leaving her car in Rock Jackson's barn so she wouldn't have to pay to leave it at the airport. Instead, she was still in the state? Only miles from home?

"What are you doing there?"

"Taylor, I have some news that might upset you," she'd said in that innocent voice she used when she needed money—or now wanted something much worse.

"You think?" he'd asked sarcastically. "I found your car in Rock Jackson's barn."

"*What?*"

"Don't tell me you didn't know it was there."

"Taylor—"

"Jade—"

"She's leaving you, Taylor," Rock had said after taking the phone. "I wouldn't try to fight her, if I were you. From what she's told me, she has more than enough grounds for a divorce. To avoid all the bad publicity, you would be smart to give her what she wants." With that, the bastard had ended the call.

What had Jade told Rock? The mere thought sent Taylor back to the quart of bourbon he'd picked up at the liquor store. The quick swig hit his stomach like a hot brick. He tried to remember the last time he'd eaten. He'd been a mess ever since Jade had left and now she was leaving him for good? Leaving him for Rock Jackson? Had she lost her mind?

On top of that, he'd heard that Rock Jackson had been spending money as if he had it. Taylor was familiar enough with Rock's art career to know that the money hadn't come from the sale of his paintings.

Taylor had a pretty good idea where the money had come from, the lying, cheating bastard. Rock hadn't just stolen his wife, he was jeopardizing everything.

He told himself to be patient as he waited for Rock and Jade to return. He turned on the car radio to keep him company. A holiday song began to play on the radio. With a groan, he realized Christmas was only days away. "Merry Christmas," he said bitterly as he turned off the radio.

Rock would have to come home at some point. He laid the gun in his lap, took another swig of bourbon and listened for the sound of an approaching vehicle.

When Taylor woke up, Rock still hadn't returned. Now almost sober, he started the engine and drove home, determined he would be back, though, tomorrow.

SID WAS ONLY a little surprised to find her sister waiting for her at the house. Zander had let herself in, of course, and was unloading into the refrigerator groceries that she'd apparently picked up in Bozeman.

"I was questioned by the marshal today," Sid said as she brought in what she'd purchased after the marshal had let her go.

Zander lifted a brow in alarm. "Does he know—?"

"No, not about that. Seems I picked up a counterfeit twenty-dollar bill somewhere. You wouldn't know anything about that, would you?"

"Me?" Zander slammed the refrigerator. "Why is it that no matter what happens, you are always suspicious of me?"

Sid laughed. "Yes, why is that? You haven't been in my purse?"

Zander turned to roll her eyes. "You know me so well, do you? Can you imagine me getting into your purse and *leaving* money? This...plot of yours has clearly destroyed your common sense."

"Stop trying to change the subject."

"Why? Don't you think it's time that we had a talk?" her sister said, coming back into the room and plopping down on the couch. "Come on, sit down and tell me what's going on. Remember when we used to talk for hours."

"About the boys you had crushes on," Sid said going into the kitchen and putting away the perishables she'd purchased. As she finished she looked into the living room at her sister.

Zander smiled at her as she patted a spot beside her on the couch. "You can talk to me. Clearly something is bothering you." Her sister cocked her head at her. "You sure there isn't a man? I've never seen you so... off balance."

That her sister knew her so well bothered Sid more than she wanted to admit. She didn't think she was that easy to read. Clearly, she was wrong. Laramie threw her off balance. He made her heart beat too fast. He destroyed her common sense, because she'd actually been thinking of telling him the truth about the painting— and why she so desperately needed it back.

Sid sat down on the couch, curling her legs under her, remembering, not the times she'd had to save Zander, but the times her big sister had saved her. When had the tables turned? When they'd lost their father during those months before his death?

"What would you like for Christmas?" Sid asked, not wanting to confide in Zander about Laramie or anything to do with her so-called quest.

Zander shook her head, looking disappointed. "I didn't come back for presents."

"Why did you?"

Her sister rose to pace the cabin floor. "Isn't it possible I wanted to see you?" She turned to stare at her. "Isn't it possible I was worried about you?" Sid hoped that was the case. "You think you know me, Sid? Well, I know you."

That was what scared her.

"I wish I could trust you, Z," she said, speaking her innermost wish at that moment and then wishing she hadn't.

Zander smiled as she sat back down and took one of Sid's hands, squeezing it. "I guess I'm going to have to prove it to you."

"I'm sorry I thought you'd put the counterfeit twenty in my purse." She actually had thought Zander had switched it for a good twenty. "I probably picked it up somewhere without knowing it."

"See?" Her sister was all smiles. "So while you're in this trusting mood—"

She pulled her hand free. "Z, if this is about money—"

Her sister laughed. "I love it when you call me Z. It's been too long. But I wasn't going to ask for money. I was going to offer my help on your...project."

Sid eyed her. "I thought you were against it."

"Not really. I thought it was dangerous, a waste of your talented time. I didn't see the point. And, while I'm being honest, I felt guilty for making things even harder for you before Dad died. But you've brought me over to your side. You're almost done, right?"

She nodded, studying her sister, wondering if she could trust this. But she felt herself weaken. She had adored Z growing up. She'd missed their connection in the years since.

As much as she didn't like to admit it, Laramie Cardwell *had* become a problem. Her own fault. She shouldn't have gotten this close to him. That had been foolhardy—and dangerous.

But she wasn't quite ready to ask for her sister's help in dealing with him.

WHEN ROCK AND JADE finally came up for air the next day, they left the condo where they'd been staying. Rock hadn't thought far enough ahead as to what they would do now. He'd been in a state of happy delirium, but now that he'd come out of it, he began to worry.

Since her talk with Taylor, Jade had seemed upset, making Rock all the more nervous. For a while he'd been able to forget about his soon-to-be-ex wife, Carla. She'd been looking for ammunition in the divorce. It was one reason he'd borrowed his friend's condo. He'd been so careful not to give her anything she could use against him—until Jade had turned up at his door.

All he could hope was that Carla didn't get wind of this until the divorce papers were signed. She knew he didn't have any money, but she wanted everything else, including his family ranch. He'd told her he would see her dead first.

But now that Jade would be able to take half of

Taylor's money according to Montana law, he was willing to give Carla everything just to get his freedom. That would take care of that problem.

Unfortunately there were other things to be dealt with. He hadn't liked hearing that Taylor had been on his ranch and had found Jade's car in the barn. What else had he discovered? Had he been looking for Jade? Or something else?

He tried not to worry as he looked over at Jade and counted his blessings. She was every man's dream. Jade had modeled for lingerie catalogs, so maybe she wasn't a supermodel, but she was a beauty. He'd been jealous of Taylor from the first time he'd seen them together. Everyone knew the only reason she was with that old man was his money and fame, two things that had ruled Rock out from the get-go.

But then there she'd been, standing on his doorstep and then crying in his arms. It hadn't taken a lot to get her into his bed, once he'd assured her he would help her take Taylor to the cleaners in the divorce.

What he hadn't thought about was his own life. What was he going to do with Jade now? If only his divorce was already final. What if Carla was at the house waiting for him? She'd rented a house up Bear Canyon but she often stopped by the ranch without warning. How was he going to deal with her with Jade on his arm? It could get ugly fast.

Also, he realized belatedly, he needed some time to clear out a few things at his house. Now that he had Jade and, soon, Taylor's money, he would be making some changes—more than just getting rid of Carla. But it would be better if Jade never found out how he'd been able to live the past six months.

He looked over at her, realizing he would have to drop her off somewhere. He couldn't take her home.

"I have an idea, a treat for you to make you feel better while I take care of some things," he said.

She looked at him expectantly. She'd been moody since talking to Taylor. She wouldn't be thinking about going back to the old fool, would she?

"I know of this great day spa."

That picked up her mood considerably. Jade liked the finer things in life. Nothing wrong with that, he thought.

"I don't have any money," she said in that little-girl voice he thought charming.

"My treat." He smiled over at her as he drove toward the day spa. "I'll pick you up later and we'll go see this lawyer I know."

"Don't you think I should talk to Taylor before I talk to a lawyer?" she asked. "Maybe he won't fight me on the divorce."

"Baby, trust me. He isn't going to let you go without a fight. That's why we need to beat him to the punch." He just hoped Taylor wasn't hitting the bottle. No telling what the man would do then. "Trust me, Jade. I'll take care of you." *And you'll take care of me*, he thought.

She leaned over to kiss him on the cheek. "I don't know what I would have done without you."

"You'll never have to find out."

Jade still had the body of a model. But sometimes, he wondered about what went on in that pretty head of hers. The fact that she'd married Taylor to begin with had always bothered him. Was it just for the money or had she really cared about him?

"Just out of curiosity," he asked as he parked in front of the day spa, "why did you *marry* Taylor?"

She frowned. "I was in Mexico, drinking tequila at this cantina. He came in with a painting he'd just finished. I couldn't afford to buy it, but I really liked it."

"You married him for a painting?"

"That, and he told me he owned a ranch in Montana." She shrugged. "You know what's funny. Once I sobered up, I didn't even like the painting."

Rock laughed as he reached across to open her door. "Maybe half of everything Taylor has will make you feel better about it."

AFTER HER SISTER LEFT, Sid knew she had to end this before Christmas Eve if at all possible. Zander being in town added a new complication to her plan.

It didn't take Sid long to find out what new alarm systems Laramie had installed in his new house. She'd used different approaches to get past security systems in the past. But she'd found the best way was the most direct.

She'd gotten her old friend Maisie French to get a part-time job at the local security company. Almost all of the Big Sky residents used the same firm. She called her now to ask if Laramie Cardwell had contacted her office yet.

"He's sticking with the security system already in place but adding cameras around the house," Maisie said.

Sid laughed. He thought he could catch her on video?

"I can send you the location of the cameras," her friend offered. "Or, if I'm working that night, I can shut them down long enough to let you get in and out." Big Sky in winter was prone to power outages so if the system went out for no more than ten minutes, it wasn't anything anyone would question. Unless of course there was a burglary.

"I thought you had a rule about going back a second time?" her friend said after Sid told her that she now had no choice but to get the painting back from Laramie Cardwell.

"I know, but it can't be helped. I can't have that painting floating around out there."

"Can't you just offer to buy it?"

Sid laughed. "He's already suspicious—if not downright convinced I'm a thief."

"But right now he has no proof. If he catches you trying to get the painting back…"

"It's a chance I have to take. He mentioned that he has a family thing tomorrow night."

"And you don't think that sounds like a trap?" Maisie cried.

Sid had to laugh again. "It absolutely does. That's why I have to hit his house tonight." She sighed. "But there's another problem—Zander."

Her friend groaned. "Let me guess—she's broke, she needs help, she wants money." Maisie had known her and Zander since they were kids growing up.

"She says she's only in town to celebrate the holidays with me. She's coming over Christmas Eve. That is why I have to take care of this before then."

Maisie groaned. "You don't trust her, right?"

"She's my sister."

"Exactly."

"I have a plan."

"Of course you do." Her friend laughed, but quickly sobered. "Be careful. I don't like this. But since I am the new kid on the block, I'm working tonight. Just let me know what time. And watch Zander."

"I always do. This is almost over."

"And it's no coincidence that Zander shows up now. It's almost as if she…knows."

Sid had thought the same thing. She disconnected and looked across the room at the costume she'd rented along with the mask for the upcoming ball. She'd told Laramie she wouldn't be caught dead at the ball. She hoped she was right.

Chapter Thirteen

Taylor was getting sick of waiting again outside Rock Jackson's home. More than that, he'd run out of bourbon and found himself sobering up for the third day in a row. All of which wasn't good news. Today, he'd been determined to wait for Rock and Jade until the cows came home, if that's what it took.

But he decided a quick run into the packaged goods store to get another bottle wouldn't take that long. It took a little longer than he'd expected because he'd run into a couple of men he knew and they'd bought him drinks, trying to get a free painting out of him.

Sometimes it felt as if everyone wanted a piece of him. He thought of Jade and the first time he'd laid eyes on her. He'd had to have her, no matter the cost. He was no fool. He'd known why she'd agreed to marry him in Mexico. He'd talked up his ranch, his paintings, his fame and fortune. He hadn't had to look at her to see her disappointment when they'd gotten back to Montana. He'd felt it come rolling off her in waves.

Jade had expected a place like out of one of those fancy home magazines. His ranch house was newer but it wasn't as posh as she would have liked. Nor was his fame and fortune up to her standards. Not to mention how quickly she'd gotten bored living in the canyon. She'd spent most of her days burning the rubber off his tires running back and forth to Bozeman.

Marrying Jade had been a mistake. He admitted that as he drove back toward Rock's place. Every bit of his common sense told him to let her go. Good riddance. He could afford to hire a housekeeper to cook and clean for him since Jade hadn't been good at doing either. He would be better off without her.

Except he didn't want Rock to have her.

LARAMIE HAD DONE his best to get Sid off his mind. He couldn't even explain it to himself, but there was something about her.

"What is your attraction to this woman other than the obvious?" Austin had said when he'd stopped by earlier.

"You mean that she's beautiful, intelligent, talented?"

"No, surely it hasn't skipped your attention that we Cardwell men have a weakness for women in trouble."

"She doesn't seem to be in trouble," Laramie had said.

Austin had chuckled. "You don't believe that for a minute and neither do I. Whatever she's up to, I'm betting it's dangerous. You've already been run off the road. Next time, it might be more than a warning."

After his brother had left, Laramie pulled out his phone. "Do you have plans for tonight?" Laramie asked when Sid answered. "I know it's kind of late, but the Cardwell family gets together to decorate cookies and drink hot chocolate, with marshmallows of course, and sing carols."

"Seriously? I can't even imagine such a family."

"It probably sounds awful to you, but I thought if you didn't have any plans…"

"I do have plans," Sid had said. She'd sounded surprised by the invitation. "Otherwise, I would love to."

"Really? I'm glad to hear that. Maybe next year."

"Next year?" She'd laughed. "You can plan ahead that far?"

"Can't you?"

She hadn't answered that.

"Dana also wanted me to tell you that we're having steaks."

"It sounds wonderful, but I can't," she'd said before she could weaken. "Thank you for the offer, though. Please give my regrets to Dana."

"I will. She'll be disappointed. Not as much as me, though," he'd added. "Well, enjoy your holidays if I don't see you before then. Maybe I'll see you after?"

"Maybe."

SID FELT A TIGHTENING in her throat and felt her eyes blur as she thought about his earlier call. She could envision the family in that large living room she'd only gotten a glimpse of through a window.

Steaks at Cardwell Ranch sounded wonderful. But to spend a holiday in that house with that family? There would be music and laughter. Knowing what little she did about Dana, there would be food and drinks. She could almost smell the evergreen tree, almost taste the gingerbread men fresh from the oven, almost hear the sound of Christmas carols being sung by the family.

Laughing at her foolishness, she pushed the vision

away. She'd only seen family gatherings like that in movies and television soap operas. Did they really exist?

She thought of her own childhood and the goofy little tree she and Zander had dragged in one year. They'd made ornaments for it and bought presents to put under it. They hadn't been much. Those had been the lean years before things got really bad.

Swallowing the lump that had formed, she realized she was hugging herself. What would Laramie think if he knew the truth?

She shoved that thought away. For all she knew, the invitation was just him still trying to track down his elusive cat burglar. The invitation was just to let her know he wouldn't be home tonight. The trap was set.

Sid hated being this suspicious. Especially of a man she was developing feelings for. *Did* have feelings for, in spite of the circumstances. The thought made her laugh. She really needed to finish this and move on.

As ROCK DROVE into his ranch, he was glad to see that Taylor's SUV wasn't parked out front. He wouldn't have been surprised if it had been. Taylor could be a hothead. He drove straight to the back of the studio where his car would be out of sight just in case the fool came searching for his wife. He wasn't looking forward to a face-to-face with the artist, drunk or sober. There was too much history between them, not to mention the one big secret that had them locked in a death grip for life.

At the back of his studio, he was surprised to see where someone had beaten on his padlock trying to break in. Had it been Taylor when he'd found his wife's car in the barn? Or his not-ex-enough wife, Carla? He hadn't given her a key. He wasn't stupid.

Opening the lock with his key, he was glad to see that everything was as he'd left it. But the evidence couldn't stay here, not when he planned to bring Jade home with him. He popped open the back of the SUV. He had a storage shed rented in town that no one knew about, not even Carla, since he'd put it in his other ex-wife's name. He was damned glad of it right now.

With any luck, he would never need any of this again, he thought, as he loaded everything into the back of the vehicle. If things worked out with Jade, he wouldn't need to make extra money and could get rid of all the evidence soon. He still couldn't believe his luck.

He tried to relax, to be happy. Hell, he should be celebrating right now. He had it all. Or at least he would soon. But he'd never been one to count his chickens before that last egg hatched. His life had been too tough not to know that things could turn sour at a moment's notice. Especially when dealing with a woman like Jade…

It didn't take that long to load everything and drive down to the storage shed. On the way back, feeling confident he was in the clear now, he had a feeling he'd forgotten something. He swore as he remembered what it was, then he drove back toward the ranch. Glancing at his watch, he told himself to hurry. Jade would be getting antsy. He called her and, sure enough, she was finished and waiting for him.

"Go next door to the bar. I'll be there before you know it."

LARAMIE WAS DISAPPOINTED that Sid couldn't be here with him as he entered the Cardwell Ranch main house. He wondered what her plans were as he made his way to the kitchen where Dana was at work.

"Sid's busy?" Dana asked as she slid warm cookies from a pan onto a cooling rack. "I'm sorry."

"Me, too." Would she take advantage of him being gone and take the painting tonight?

On the drive to the ranch he'd told himself he should cut this visit short after Christmas and return to the warmth of Houston—and the job he was getting paid to do. But watching over the Texas Boys Barbecue empire didn't take much watching. If he was being truthful, the company now had accountants and secretaries that did most of the work. He was more of an overseer. Maybe that was why he'd been getting a little bored with it.

Bored enough that he'd been looking forward to catching an art thief. The only thing worse would be falling for the thief.

His father, Angus, came into the kitchen and slapped Laramie on the shoulder, wishing him a merry Christmas. He hadn't seen his father yet on this trip to Montana. Dana was so excited that the whole family could be together, even Austin, who had been terrible about missing family get-togethers.

"The steaks are about ready," Angus said to Dana. "Hud wanted me to let you know." He took the huge platter Dana handed him and headed back outside.

"Everything else is ready," she called to Angus's retreating back, then turned to Laramie. "I'm sorry. But Sid probably has plans for the holidays, don't you think?"

He had no idea. In the time he'd spent with her, he had learned little about her. His gut told him, though, that she was in trouble, and that alone made him want to save her. It was a Cardwell trait that ran in his family, one he'd never felt so strongly before. Cardwell men were into helping women out of tight spots, he thought, as his brothers, father and uncle came in from the outside grill, followed by a flock of small laughing children.

Laramie had just never experienced what he was feeling for Sid. But now he understood its power. He realized he would do whatever it took to save Sid—even if it meant saving her from herself.

The smell of beef steaks filled the dining room as everyone began to take their seats, the kids all at a smaller table nearby. Laramie tried to enjoy himself, but he couldn't get his mind off Sid. What was she doing right now? He hated to think.

Earlier that day he'd found an article on a famous art forger who was so good that a lot of art experts would no longer authenticate paintings for fear of being wrong. Was there a cowboy artist that good here? Taylor had said the only person good enough was the deceased H. F. Powell.

Laramie barely heard the chatter around the table, the clink of glasses or the rattle of silverware. As the meal wound down, he looked out the window. It was already dark in the canyon even though it was still relatively early. Cardwell Ranch sat at the foot of the mountains alongside the Gallatin River. Earlier he'd driven over a wooden bridge to get here, the entire landscape shrouded in ice-cold white.

"Why do you keep looking at your watch?" Austin

demanded from next to him at the huge dinner table in cousin Dana's dining room. A burst of giggles came from the children's table. Dana got up to see what was going on.

Laramie shook his head. He just had a feeling he couldn't shake. It wouldn't be enough to catch Sid on camera. He needed to catch her red-handed. He needed to see it for himself.

"You need to let it go," Austin said as they all rose to take their dishes into the kitchen. "You need to let *her* go."

Laramie looked at his brother. "What if I can't?"

His brother groaned and shook his head. Austin actually looked sorry for him.

"Tell Dana I had to go," Laramie said, realizing he had only one choice as he handed his brother his dirty plate. "She'll understand."

WHEN HE GOT BACK to Rock Jackson's ranch, Taylor was disappointed to see that they still hadn't returned even though it was getting dark. He settled in again with a new bottle. He'd gotten a quart since he was determined to stay until Rock returned and he'd realized that could take all night.

He kept the gun handy as he parked under some pines at the edge of the property where he could see any vehicle that pulled in, but where Rock wouldn't notice him.

Too much bourbon mixed with lack of sleep and food, and he found he couldn't keep his eyes open. Laying the seat back, he decided to take a nap, telling himself he'd hear Rock when he drove in.

The dream started out nice enough. A sunny, bright

day in summer. He had been for a ride that morning after doing his chores. His father had gone to Fargo, North Dakota, to pick up a bull he'd bought. He'd wanted Taylor's older brother to go along, but Buzz didn't want to go.

"Then you're coming with me," his father had said.

Taylor couldn't think of anything worse than being trapped in a truck with the old man for two days. Not to mention, he'd been the old man's second choice. He knew his father would browbeat him the whole way. He'd always been a disappointment to his father.

On impulse, he had pretended to be sick to his stomach. His father had changed his mind about taking him and left alone. It was perfect. Buzz had some girl he planned to spend all his time with in town. Nothing could keep Taylor from doing what he loved.

He'd retrieved his paints and canvas from under the bed where he'd kept them hidden and went downstairs to the well-lit kitchen. A wave of nostalgia hit him now at the thought of the many hours he used to sit here with his mother when she was alive. She said she loved to watch him paint. She always protected him when his father caught him painting.

"You're making a sissy out of that boy," he would bellow. "I need a ranch hand, not some worthless, namby-pamby kid who likes to paint pretty pictures."

That day, with the sun coming in the kitchen window along with a warm breeze, he'd gotten lost in his art. He was so absorbed in what he was doing, he didn't hear his father return. He didn't hear his footfalls until the man was behind him and then it was too late.

All he felt was the first blow—the one that broke

his arm. He never painted after that. Not until he'd escaped the ranch and his old man.

Taylor stirred, the dream making him moan with pain in his sleep. He blinked. Had he heard a vehicle?

his store's inventory. Except for a few spare boxes, crumped the store. He lit up his flashlight and began his search. Along one aisle of stock, he quit three minutes to step on a step ladder. Had he known someone was

Chapter Fourteen

Sid had little to thank her sister Zander for, and yet tonight as she climbed on her snowmobile, pulling the ski mask down over her face, she was thankful for the part of Zander that loved breaking the rules. Her sister had acquired a talent for breaking and entering at a young age. A couple of times she'd dragged her unsuspecting little sister into her mischief. When Sid had gotten caught, she hadn't told on Zander.

Instead, Sid had used that leverage to force her sister to teach her the tricks. Since then, she'd picked up a few of her own thanks to the internet. That and making the right friends. Her childhood friend Maisie had been quick to help with Sid's plan by coming to Big Sky and getting the job at the security company.

Along with being able to shut off the power to a house for up to ten minutes, Maisie was also able to give Sid computer access to the cameras Laramie had installed. She could see him coming and going that way. Her computer beeped whenever the camera was activated.

Earlier, she'd watched on screen as Laramie came out of the house, all dressed up and carrying a bottle of wine as he got into his rental SUV and left. No doubt headed for Cardwell Ranch. She felt a pang of regret. If only she was going with him. She thought about the horseback ride and the kiss. There was something about this Texas cowboy that tugged at her heartstrings—the worst thing that could happen to her right now.

As she drove her snowmobile up the mountain, she told herself that Laramie Cardwell's only interest in her was as an art thief. If she thought it was more than that—which she wanted to be true—then she was setting herself up for a heartbreak.

Zander had called earlier asking about what kind of wine Sid preferred.

"Seriously?" Sid had said.

Zander had laughed. "So you're still a beer drinker. You're such a Montana girl. Okay. I can't wait for tomorrow night. Maybe I'll drop by a few things I've picked up later tonight. Would that be all right?"

She'd said she had to go out for a while. "But I trust you know how to let yourself in."

Her sister had chuckled. "See you later, then."

Sid hoped she had plenty of time to get this job done and return before her sister showed up. She didn't like the idea of Zander having too much time alone in her cabin.

Taking the back trails she knew so well, she put the Texas cowboy out of her mind. She was on a job. Just business—plain and simple. She would get in and out. And that would be the end of it. If Laramie suspected she was the one who'd taken the painting, well…let him prove it. Not even Laramie Cardwell could seduce the truth out of her. But she would like to see him try, she thought for only an errant moment.

If he was merely trying to catch a thief, then once

she had the painting, he would lose interest in her. It would be over. She'd have the proof she needed about his feelings for her. That thought did little to warm the cold winter night.

She stopped a short distance from the house and killed the engine. Working her way through the snow up to the side of the house, she checked her watch and waited until the outside light behind the house blinked out.

A few moments later, she was climbing up the side of the house onto the roofline. She went in the same way she had the first time—through an upstairs window. She'd disabled the lock the first time she was there and doubted Laramie had noticed. Most windows this high above the ground were never locked anyway.

Lowering herself by the rope she'd attached to the chimney, she dropped down to the window, opened it and slipped inside. As long as she moved quickly, no one would be the wiser. In and out. Five minutes tops.

As she slipped into Laramie's master bedroom, she dropped to the floor and checked her watch. She waited a moment, listening, before she turned on her penlight.

"It was good to see you, son," Laramie's father said as he left. "I hope you think about spending even more time up here now." It was what Angus always said. It was no secret that he hoped all of his sons would return to Montana.

Once outside, Laramie breathed in the cold night air and headed for his SUV. He couldn't shake the feeling that Sid would hit his house tonight. The cameras he had installed would prove it. But he knew that what he needed more than anything was to catch her in the act.

Maybe then he could get some answers out of her. And then he could corral these feelings he had for her.

But it was still early. He told himself she wouldn't attempt the theft until later—just as she had done last time. Laramie knew he was hoping he was wrong about her. Maybe she really was busy tonight—doing something other than robbing him.

It had begun to snow again as Laramie drove toward Sid's cabin. Huge lacy flakes spiraled down from the darkness in a dizzying white. He told himself he was on a fool's errand. He would find her in her cabin wrapping presents, visiting with friends over a bottle of wine, possibly even spending a quiet evening with another man.

That thought jolted him hard. He hadn't even considered that there might be a man in her life. A woman who looked like her? Of course, there would be a man.

Or not, he thought. Wouldn't a man have to know what Sid did late at night? The man would either have to be in on it or...

He found her cabin from the directions the waitress who knew her at Texas Boys Barbecue had provided.

"You can't miss it. Small cabin, stuck back in the woods. It's the last place on that road."

As the cabin appeared in his headlights, he saw that there was no light behind the windows. He slowed, aware that he would now have to turn around. What if she was home...and sitting in the dark, waiting for him to drive by to check on her? He shook off that ridiculous idea.

She wasn't home, he told himself as he turned around. Probably out on a date. Or shopping for groceries. Or out on a date. Or finishing up her Christmas shopping.

Mentally he kicked himself. What was wrong with him? He'd never acted like this with any other woman.

But when he stole a look in his rearview mirror as he pulled away, he knew that Obsidian "Sid" Forester was like no other woman he'd ever met. He also realized as the dark cabin disappeared from view, that it was probably no coincidence that she lived on such an isolated road. He couldn't see any other cabins near hers but it was dark and the pines were thick on the mountain behind her cabin. Maybe this place wasn't as isolated as he thought, but he wouldn't have bet on it.

The snow was falling harder now. It blew past horizontally on a gust of wind, shaking the SUV, shaking his thoughts. Sid wasn't out buying groceries or last-minute Christmas presents. Nor did he believe she was on a date.

No, if he was right about her, she was at his house right now stealing the painting like the thief she was.

JADE CALLED RIGHT AS Rock was pulling around the back of his studio. "I'm on my way."

"Are you trying to get me drunk?" she asked, sounding pouty. "I'm already on my third drink."

Just what he needed—her sloppy drunk before he rescued her. "I forgot to ask. How was the spa treatment?"

"Wonderful."

"Good. Sip that drink. I'll be there in ten minutes." He disconnected, pocketed his phone and got out. Even with darkness upon him, the temperature was in the forties. He loved a good holiday thaw when the snow disappeared at lower elevations and he didn't have to be bundled up as much. He was sick of winters. Maybe he and Jade should move south. They could get a place in Arizona. Jade might like that.

He unlocked the back door of the studio again and stepped in. The room smelled of chemicals and the odor hit him like a two-by-four in the face. He quickly moved to the windows and opened them even though this thaw couldn't last much longer.

Breathing a little easier, he looked around the room for what he might have forgotten. Maybe he was just being paranoid. No, he realized as he spotted it. He'd forgotten to clean up the garbage with the empty bottles of acetone and bleach, masks and gloves. He shook his head at how close he'd come to blowing it. Pulling out a garbage bag, he quickly filled it and spun around as a shadow filled the open doorway.

Alarmed, he dropped the bag. "Oh, you startled me there for a moment." He reached for the garbage bag, telling himself to play it cool. "I was just leaving, but maybe we can talk—" The rest died on his lips as he saw the gun. "Wait a minute." He held the full garbage bag in front of him as if it would stop a bullet, and he took a step back, his mind racing. "This is a mistake. You don't want to—"

The first shot caught him in the chest at heart level. He barely felt the second or third or even fourth shots as he fell to the concrete floor.

LARAMIE DROVE ONLY partway up the mountain to his house. He hadn't seen another soul on the road tonight once he'd left Meadow Village, other than the faint light of a snowmobile through the falling snow shortly after he'd turned around at Sid's cabin.

In a wide spot where the snowplow had turned around, he parked and got out. The walk up the mountain had him breathing fairly hard. Even though he was in good shape, he still wasn't used to the altitude.

As he reached the top of a rise, he slowed. Fortunately there was no moon tonight and clouds obscured even the stars. The darkness would have been complete if not for the blanket of reflective snow that covered the ground.

That gut feeling he'd had earlier at dinner had proved right, he thought as he looked toward the house. A tiny light bobbed in the master bedroom. *Sid was here.*

His heart began to pound with both excitement at finally catching her—and disappointment. He realized he'd been hoping he was wrong all this time. Or that there was a good explanation. Clearly he didn't know this woman. For that reason, he felt a sliver of concern that he might be walking into something more dangerous than he thought.

His plan on the way up the mountain had been to catch her in the act. Now that he was almost to the house, he realized she could be armed. He thought of the woman he'd kissed. She wouldn't shoot him, even if she was armed, he told himself.

You'd stake your life on a kiss? It was Austin's cynical voice in his head. He knew his brother had staked his life on even less.

Laramie reached the side door, unlocked it and stepped in. He had only a matter of seconds to disarm the silent security system. Or had she already disabled it? He couldn't take the chance that it might go off and alert her.

As quietly as possible, he stepped to it to punch in the code and saw that the system was off. He looked toward the stairs.

SID PICKED UP the painting and hesitated. Why had he left both of the paintings here together? Because he knew she would be back for one of them. She slid the light over the canvas of one and then the other until she found what she was looking for.

The difference between the two paintings was impossible for anyone else to discern. But she knew where to look. She picked up the forgery and, her penlight guiding the way, started toward the window with time to spare.

But still her footsteps faltered. Laramie would know she'd taken it. He'd been waiting for her to return. He'd had the cameras installed so he could catch her. She remembered his lips on hers, the taste and feel of him.

She shook off the memory. All the kiss had been was a ruse. Him making her doubt he was onto her. She mentally shook herself, telling herself she had known the score from the beginning. It wasn't as if she'd fallen for it. The irony didn't escape her. She was the thief, the liar, the one who wasn't being honest with *him*.

Sid wasn't sure if she heard or just sensed something.

Someone else was in the house.

She froze, listening. A faint sound two floors below. All houses had their own unique sounds, but this was human.

Her gaze shot up to the cameras. No light. They

weren't on yet. She checked her watch. Time was running out. She had to move.

Hastily, she snapped off the penlight and slipped it into her pocket. As she started to step out the window into the falling snow, Sid belatedly realized the mistake she'd made in her hurry. The penlight, not all the way into her pocket, fell out, dropped to the floor and clattered on the hardwood.

LARAMIE LOOKED UP as he heard the sound. She was here, on the top floor. He felt his heart take off at a gallop at the thought of catching her red-handed. They could quit playing this game of cat and mouse.

The thought should have brought him more satisfaction. Wasn't this what he'd wanted since that first night? No, he thought as he turned toward the stairs. At first all he had wanted was to find the woman—not fall for her. Had he found her in Obsidian "Sid" Forester? He was about to find out.

He took a step toward the first stair, telling himself it would be over soon, one way or another. Behind him, he heard a floorboard creak and frowned in momentary confusion. Until that moment, he hadn't considered that there might be more than one of them.

As he spun around, he had only a moment to take in the person before him. "Sid?" The glare of the falling snow outside the window lit her face. Too late he caught the movement of her arm—and the weapon in her hand.

Instinctively, he tried to step back, bumping into the stairs. The blow to the side of his head staggered him. He fought to keep his balance, but his eyesight was dimming to nothing more than a pinpoint.

He felt himself falling, blackness filling his vision, filling his head. The last thing he saw was her standing over him with the weapon in her hand.

Chapter Fifteen

"You hit him too hard," Sid said with a curse as she knelt down beside Laramie. She hadn't known what was going on downstairs and had been shocked to find her sister standing over him.

"I had no choice. He would have caught you."

Sid quickly felt for a pulse and then checked his pupils. "What are you doing here anyway?"

"I thought you might need my help. When I saw him come by the cabin…"

She shot her sister a look over her shoulder. The last thing she needed was help. In a few more seconds she would have been out the window and gone.

"He saw me," her sister said, raised her hands in surrender when Sid turned to glare at her in disbelief. "Don't worry, he thought I was you."

"Great. That's perfect."

"Maybe he won't remember anything," Zander offered.

Sid shook her head in exasperation as she turned back to Laramie. "Get me a cold cloth out of the kitchen."

Zander returned a few moments later. "Here." She thrust the cold wet cloth into Sid's hand. "So what are *you* doing here?" Her gaze went to the painting leaning against the wall where Sid had dropped it. "Is that one of them?" she asked in a hushed voice.

Sid didn't bother to answer as Laramie moaned, his eyelids fluttering.

"You should get out of here before he wakes up."

"We both should," Zander said, her eyes riveted to the painting. "And why all the concern over this guy? Is there more going on here than even I think?"

"Wait for me at my cabin. We can talk later." Zander still hesitated. Laramie moaned again. "Go! I don't want him catching both of us here."

Her sister finally moved, slipping out into the night. Laramie was coming to.

LARAMIE WOKE WITH a killer headache. He tried to get up from where he lay on the floor, but he settled for sitting on the lower step until his head cleared a little. He had a bump on his temple that throbbed and hurt like hell when he touched it.

At the sound of footfalls, he looked up, shocked to see he wasn't alone. "What did you hit me with?"

"I'm sorry about your headache."

"Are you?"

"How's your head?" she asked, ignoring the question.

"It hurts." He narrowed his eyes at her, trying to understand what she was still doing here. Why hadn't she just taken the painting and left? "I figured you'd be long gone."

She nodded. "So did I." She took a step toward him. "Here, I found these in your medicine cabinet. I'll get you a glass of water." She dropped two white pills into his open palm.

He stared at them.

"They're just aspirin," she said.

"Right."

"If I was going to drug you, don't you think I already would have?"

"Quite frankly, I never know what to expect with you," he said.

He took the two white pills she handed him and stared at them while she went into the kitchen. They looked like two over-the-counter pain pills.

She handed him a glass of water. He met her gaze, held it for a moment and downed the pills and the water.

"So are we going to be honest now?" he asked. When she didn't say anything, he added, "I hope you aren't going to tell me that the real cat burglar was the one who hit me."

"It's a long story."

"One I'm dying to hear."

"Maybe we'd better go into the living room where it is more comfortable, then," she said.

He got up from the step, still feeling woozy, but anxious to hear any explanation she had to give.

"I don't know where to begin," Sid said when they were seated across from each other.

"Why don't you start with why you need that painting so much," he said pointing to it where she'd left it by the stairs.

She sighed and looked away for a moment. When she looked at him again, he saw that her beautiful eyes had filled with tears. "I need it to catch the men who murdered my father."

Laramie felt a start. Her father was *murdered*? "Who was your father?"

"H. F. Powell."

LARAMIE STARED AT HER. "You're his *daughter*? So Forester is your...married name?"

She shook her head. "My parents never married. I told you it was a long story."

His head ached. He rubbed his temples, trying to make sense of this. "You said your father was murdered? I hadn't heard anything about that."

"Because his death was ruled an accident. The investigators believed my father had started the fire that destroyed his studio and everything in it—including him."

"But you think it was murder?"

"I *know* it was murder, and I've been working to prove it."

He sat up a little straighter. While his brain probably wasn't functioning as well as it could have been under the circumstances, he couldn't help suspecting he was being conned.

"Excuse my skepticism, but I don't see how stealing paintings will help you solve his...alleged murder."

"At first, I thought that the investigators were right and that my father *had* started the fire," Sid said. "Until the forgeries started showing up."

"Maybe it's my headache, but I'm having trouble—"

She sighed again and got to her feet to pace. "You have to understand. My father was an eccentric genius and because of that he made enemies." Sid waved an arm through the air as if that was putting it mildly. "Admittedly, he was often his own worst enemy. He wasn't…conventional. He hated rules. Which is probably one reason he and my mother never married. He'd married once before and the woman had left him. My father also didn't make the best husband—or father, for that matter. He would lock himself in his studio for days on end until he was too exhausted to paint."

Laramie said nothing, just letting her talk, as he tried to make sense of what she was telling him.

"When the Old West Artists Coalition was started, my father just assumed they would invite him to join." She stopped pacing to let out a laugh. "He would have turned them down flat. He *hated* organizations. But instead, they shunned him, saying that while his paintings were all right, his character was lacking."

Laramie thought he could see how that might affect a man like the one she'd described. "He was angry?"

Sid barked out another laugh. "He was *furious*. He swore he would show them that he could paint so much better than any of them that they wouldn't be able to tell his forgeries from their own work." She nodded. "He became obsessed. He quit painting his own work, determined to show them up."

"They found out and tried to stop him," he guessed.

"He must have bragged to someone about what he was doing. He planned to expose them at their annual conference."

Laramie saw where she was headed with this. "The forgeries were in the studio the night of the fire?"

She nodded. "I've always questioned why he would go to all the trouble of painting the copies only to change his mind and destroy not just them, but also himself." Sid met his gaze. "That's just it. He wouldn't have."

"So whoever took the forgeries…"

"Killed my father."

Laramie blew out a breath of air as he leaned back. "And you think you know who took them. If you're right, then you do realize how dangerous this pursuit of yours is, don't you?"

She smiled at that.

"Right," he said, feeling foolish. This was a woman who ran along rooflines in the middle of the night, broke into houses, chancing everything to get these forgeries back. This was his cat burglar.

"So have you figured out who is responsible?"

"I suspected it was one of the four founders of OWAC, but now I'm thinking all four of them were behind it. They are the ones who kept my father out of organization, the ones he despised the most. They are the ones who had the most to lose by his plan to expose them and their organization. They'd been pulling some fast ones, using the organization to raise money for charities and pocketing most of it. They had reason to fear him. By then my father was being recognized as a great artist. Once he revealed the forgeries, there would have been a lot of bad publicity that would have hurt them and shone a light on their organization. They would have been lucky if they hadn't ended up in jail."

Laramie closed his eyes for a moment, glad that the aspirin seemed to be doing the job of relieving his headache a little. "What I don't understand is why did the person who killed your father take the forgeries? Why not leave them to burn?"

"I assume the killer was worried that the fire might be put out before all the evidence burned. Maybe they planned to destroy the copies. If I'm right and all four of them were in on it, then one of them must have been responsible for getting rid of the forgeries—but didn't."

Laramie nodded. "You're sure these are forgeries that your father painted?"

"Yes."

He thought about what Taylor West had told him. There was only one artist who was so good that he could make a forgery that even the artist believed was his painting—H. F. Powell. That explained why West got so upset once he realized the significance of the painting Laramie had brought to him. It was one of the forgeries.

"Still, it makes no sense," he argued. "Why would one of them take the chance of letting these forgeries get back on the market?"

Sid shrugged. "Money, would be my guess. Also, maybe he thought enough time had passed that the duplicate paintings wouldn't come to light."

He studied her beautiful face, realizing what she'd been doing. "So you're stealing back the forgeries."

She didn't deny it.

"So you have all of them?" Laramie asked.

"With the one you have, yes."

"And with them, you'll be able to prove who killed your father?"

She looked away. "I thought I would, but it isn't going to be as easy as I'd hoped. And now I have one more forgery that has turned up that I need to get. Unfortunately, I don't have an original to trade."

"Was that him?" Zander asked as Sid came in the back door. Her sister was sprawled on the couch, a half-empty bottle of wine on the floor next to her.

She was already furious with her sister. "What?"

"The man you're falling for," Zander said, grinning as she sat up. "Don't try to deny it. I saw the way you were with him." She shook her head. "I can't see any way this is going to turn out well."

"Don't you have somewhere to be?"

"Not really. You never told me why you went there tonight."

She had no patience for this. "Guess."

"Another so-called forgery." Zander shook her head. "I was hoping you had turned into a real cat burglar. I guess it was too much to hope for. Seriously, when are you going to stop this?"

"When I'm finished with what I started. Thanks to you, I didn't get away clean tonight." She turned her back to her sister, too angry to deal with her right now. "I had to tell Laramie what I was doing."

Zander swore. "That was a mistake."

"Maybe." She trusted him, probably a mistake. But she'd had no choice, thanks to her sister.

"If you'd told me what you were doing, I could have helped you."

Sid turned. "*Helped me?* You could have helped by staying away."

"Isn't it possible that I want justice for our father, too?"

"I thought you didn't believe he was murdered?" Sid demanded. Then she saw her sister's expression. "You *do* believe it."

Zander's gaze met hers. "Does it matter? I still can't see how any of this is going to help. He's gone. Nothing you do can bring him back."

She didn't want to argue about this. It wasn't revenge.

It was simple justice. But maybe it would end just as her sister had predicted and she wouldn't be able to prove who killed him—let alone see that the men responsible got what was coming to them.

"Just let me finish what I started."

Zander got up from the couch. "Tonight aside, you're pushing your luck. I don't even want to know what you told Laramie Cardwell after I left. If any of this gets out and the killer finds out you're after him… The way I see it, you *need* my help."

Sid would love to have argued that her sister was wrong. Unfortunately, if she had any hope of pulling off the next part, she could use Zander's expertise.

Seeing her weaken, her sister smiled. "You know I'm good because I taught you everything you know."

"Not *everything*. If I thought I could trust you…"

Her sister looked excited. "Whatever it is, I'm in."

"You might not be when I tell you my plan."

LARAMIE DIDN'T KNOW what to think after Sid left. She'd trusted him with her story. He'd believed her. And while he'd done his best to talk her into going to the marshal, she'd refused, telling him that while she had all the paintings, she didn't have any proof. Yet. She made him promise he wouldn't go to the authorities, either.

"I went to the police when the first forgery turned up," she'd said. "I saw it at a gallery in Bozeman. The police didn't believe me."

"How can you be so sure it was one of your father's?" he'd asked, hating how skeptical he sounded.

She'd gone to the painting she'd left leaning against the wall by the stairs and brought it over to him. "I know this looks identical to the original, but my father had too much ego to copy it exactly. He had to leave his mark on it." She'd cocked the painting so the overhead light fell across it. "It's very small but if you look closely," she'd said pointing to a spot.

"It looks like a wolf's face."

Sid laughed. "Like I said, my father's ego made him leave a little something of himself behind. The lone wolf. But it is camouflaged and easily goes unnoticed—unless you know what to look for and where." She'd seen his still-skeptical expression and had left the painting to go upstairs to retrieve the original. "See for yourself."

He had.

Now he found himself pacing the floor as she had done. He couldn't help being worried about her. Like he'd told her, this was dangerous. It probably explained why someone had tried to run him off the road after his visit with Taylor West. He was reminded as well of Cody Kent's reaction to the painting as well as Taylor's. Had Taylor called Cody as soon as he'd left? He probably called all of the others, if Sid was right and they were responsible for H. F. Powell's death.

"They know now that the forgeries were never destroyed," Laramie had told her. "They'll be running scared and who knows how far they'll go to keep this from ever coming out. It isn't just about ruining their reputations. We're talking murder."

Sid had smiled. "If I'm right, they'll start turning on each other—if they haven't already."

"Or they'll all come after you."

"They don't even know that I am H. F. Powell's

daughter," she'd said with a shake of her head. "But I'll be careful."

He had seen that she was touched that he was worried about her. He had moved to her, cupping her cheek with his palm. "Let me help. Two of my brothers are private investigators and I—"

"No." She'd moved away before turning to look at him again. "I can't tell you how sorry I am that you are involved at all."

"Sid, can't you see that I... I care about you?"

She'd smiled and nodded. "But now I need you to trust me. Can you do that?"

He'd said he could. "But if you need me—"

Sid had stepped to him to give him a quick kiss. "I'm almost finished with this. Any interference now could destroy all the work I've done."

Against his better judgment, he'd agreed to stay out of it. What choice did he have? Go to Hud with what he knew? He couldn't do that to Sid. Nor did he know how to help her—other than letting her finish what she'd started.

Getting to his feet now, he walked into the kitchen and saw the wet cloth on the counter. Frowning, he picked it up as a flash of memory came rushing at him. Sid leaning over him, pressing the cold washcloth to his forehead.

More of the memory teased at him. Sid with something else in her hand, only...only something was wrong. He shook his head, regretting it as he felt his headache kick in again. The bottle of aspirin was also on the counter. She must have gotten it from the medicine cabinet upstairs.

A slice of memory wove its way in. He'd heard a

sound upstairs, like someone dropping something on the hardwood floor. Or was it behind him? He remembered turning. The falling snow in the doorway. He'd seen a woman's face the instant before he'd felt the blow. Sid's? No.

His pulse jumped.

It hadn't been Sid who'd hit him.

Chapter Sixteen

Laramie had believed Sid. But if there'd been someone else in his house last night, another woman who looked like Sid, then Sid had left out a key part of her story.

The problem was that this morning, in the light of day, he couldn't be sure of what he'd thought he'd seen before taking the blow. Wouldn't Sid have mentioned it if someone else had been there last night before he came to?

He'd quickly checked the security cameras he'd had installed. And hadn't been surprised to find the cameras had been turned off during the burglary. The woman knew how to cover her tracks. That should have given him some assurance that she knew what she was doing going after her father's killers.

His headache had subsided, but he still had a knot on his skull from where someone had nailed him. A mystery woman who looked enough like Sid to fool him? Or Sid herself?

He'd had trouble getting to sleep last night under the weight of what Sid had told him. He reached for his cell phone. Last night, he'd promised to stay out of it. But how could he? If he did and something happened to her—

Sid's number went straight to voice mail.

"It's just me. I was thinking about you this morning." He disconnected knowing there was no reason to ask her to call him. He doubted she would anyway. She'd been pretty clear last night.

Gingerly touching the bump on his head, he tried to remember what exactly he'd seen. He'd barely pocketed his phone when it rang again. He hoped it was Sid.

"It's Dana," his cousin said cheerfully. "I hope I'm not calling too early. I just wanted to remind you that the ball and auction is tonight." He groaned silently, having forgotten about it. "I took the liberty of having them hold three different costumes, but you need to let them know which one you want."

He swore silently. "Thank you," he said.

"I promise you will be glad you went to it," Dana said. "Everyone will be there."

Not everyone, he thought, thinking of Sid.

"I'll go and pick up my costume this morning," he told her.

"See you tonight. Let us know if you need a ride."

He had to smile as he pocketed his phone. There was no one quite like Dana. Whether or not he'd be glad he attended the ball was debatable, but he would go nonetheless because he adored her. Not because he thought for a moment he would enjoy it.

He couldn't get his mind off Sid and what she'd told him last night as he went to pick up his costume for tonight. She was so sure that the four founding members of the Old West Artists Coalition had been involved in her father's death.

They'd apparently stolen the forgeries and trusted one of them to destroy them. He hadn't. At least that was Sid's theory. Now she thought they would turn on each other. Laramie wished he believed that. They'd kept quiet about what they'd done, if Sid was right, for all these years.

It wasn't until later in the day, after running errands, that he turned on the television. He made up his mind that he couldn't sit back and do nothing. He would find out everything he could about the artists she thought were involved, he told himself, as he dressed for the ball.

That's why, when the local news came on, he couldn't have been more shocked. Maybe Sid was right after all.

ROCK JACKSON'S MURDER topped the news. Even more shocking was the arrest of Taylor West.

Laramie stood in front of the television, having a hard time believing what he was hearing. Taylor West had apparently been found passed out in his vehicle outside the Jackson residence, holding what was believed to be the murder weapon.

West had been intoxicated, resisted arrest and was now charged with multiple offenses, including homicide.

"The cowboy artist's death has now been linked to a counterfeit money operation," the broadcaster was saying. "It is uncertain if West was involved in the counterfeit operation with Jackson. But items found at the scene along with that found in a storage unit implicates artist Rock Jackson in the counterfeiting operation."

The broadcaster cut to an interview with Cody Kent and another man identified as cowboy artist Hank Ramsey. He recognized Cody and turned up the volume. Cody was saying he was shocked by the turn of events. He said he hadn't seen either man in some time.

"What a tragedy," Cody said. "Two such talented artists. They'll both be missed."

Hank Ramsey was as dark as Cody Kent was blond. Unlike Cody, he was clean-shaven with his dark hair cut short. He nervously turned the brim of his Stetson while he talked, his voice breaking at times.

"A tragedy. I only know what I heard on the news this morning. I talked to Taylor recently. I knew he was upset, but I never dreamed... Just a tragedy."

The television station cut back to the broadcaster, who moved on to other news. Laramie's phone rang.

"I assume you've seen the news," his brother Austin said.

"Do they know why Taylor West killed him?" Laramie had to ask. His head swam. Did this have something to do with the forgeries?

"I talked to Hud. Apparently Rock was having an affair with Taylor's wife. Taylor swears he didn't kill the man, but his gun appears to be the murder weapon, and he was in possession of it at the time of his arrest. Hud thinks it might also have something to do with the counterfeit money operation. Taylor swears he had nothing to do with that, either."

Laramie thought about telling his brother what had happened at his house last night. But apparently it had nothing to do with the murder or the counterfeit operation. At least he hoped to hell it didn't.

"Glad Hud caught the counterfeiter," he managed to say, wondering if anyone else was involved. And if Taylor West was telling the truth about not killing Rock, then who did?

He tried Sid's number again only to have it go straight to voice mail. He didn't leave a message. As he pocketed the phone, he feared she might be up to her neck in all this.

THE HOLIDAY BALL and Art Auction was held each year at the Big Sky Pavilion. Laramie saw the lights from miles away. Valets parked cars in one of the huge snowy lots above it. Along with arranging for a costume, Dana had made sure that Laramie had his ticket.

She had a one-in-three chance of figuring out who he was, given that she had arranged the costumes. But he wasn't sure what she and Hud would be wearing. His brothers had been equally secretive.

Waiters moved through the crowd with bubbling champagne flutes and fancy hors d'oeuvres. The lobby was a roar of voices. Beyond it, Laramie could hear music playing. He asked one of the waiters about the art that would be auctioned off tonight and was pointed to a door off the ballroom.

The three paintings were displayed under spotlights along one wall. A dozen people milled around the room. A bored-looking older man wearing a jacket that read SECURITY stood in the corner.

Laramie moved in closer to look at the three cowboy paintings. One by Taylor West, one by Rock Jackson and the last by H. F. Powell. As he caught bits of conversation, it appeared that everyone had heard the news tonight. The expectation was that both the West and Jackson paintings' bids would go quite high.

But he realized the real prize in this room was the H. F. Powell painting—if the low murmurs he'd picked up were any indication. There was talk of the painting going for more than a couple hundred thousand, but that it could go even higher because it was one of the few works of the deceased artist anyone had seen in years.

"Excuse me." Laramie addressed a woman who was studying the Powell painting. "I take it H. F. Powell paintings are rare?" he asked, remembering what Sid had told him.

The woman lifted one fine shaped brow. "He was one of the most prolific artists of his time, but he stopped painting a few years before he died." She leaned in closer. "It was rumored that he had personal problems. It was such a tragedy. He was killed in a fire at his studio. A lot of his work was lost in the fire so any painting of his is even more valuable now. This is one I've never seen before."

Interesting, Laramie thought as he studied the Powell painting. It was of a beautiful woman on a galloping horse, a rock-and-pine landscape behind her. The colors were warm as if the day had been, as well. The woman's face was filled with joy. He got the feeling she was riding toward her lover.

He studied it, surprised that not only could he feel the warmth of the day, he could almost smell the dust being kicked up by the horse's hooves. Surprising himself, he also realized he was going to have to bid on the painting. He wanted it like he had never wanted anything before because, given the resemblance, he would swear the woman on the horse was Sid's mother.

He'd never cared that much about material things. But he had to have this painting—no matter what it cost. He just hoped that wasn't what everyone else in the room was thinking, as well.

SID SPOTTED THE MAN dressed as Zorro standing in front of the H. F. Powell painting. She had cheated, waiting outside until she'd seen Laramie Cardwell's SUV pull up. She hadn't wanted to take any chances, but the truth was she would have recognized him no matter his disguise.

She'd spent her life studying forms as an artist. Laramie's form was quite fine. As she slipped through the small crowd standing around the paintings, she realized she would love to paint him. The thought surprised her, since it had been so long since she'd gotten to paint what she really loved.

Sid could see that Laramie was taken with the H. F. Powell painting. The painting was one of her father's best compositions, she thought, as she admired it under the soft lights highlighting it. Then out of the corner of her eye, she watched Laramie.

He couldn't seem to take his eyes from the painting. She guessed he had seen the resemblance between her and her mother. Around her, she heard everyone talking about the painting, all of them wondering how high the bidding would go and ultimately, who would be taking it home.

It saddened her to think that most of her father's career, this kind of art hadn't been popular. With the influx of people like the ones in this room with money and a desire to rediscover the Old Wild West, paintings like this one were now coveted. Too bad he hadn't lived long enough to see how badly people wanted an H. F. Powell painting.

But then again, her father had never painted for the money. And he certainly wouldn't have been caught dead at an affair like this. She smiled to herself, remembering that she'd told Laramie the same thing about herself. She still hoped it was true.

As Laramie moved on to Rock Jackson's painting, Sid stepped closer to the H. F. Powell painting. She stared at it with a mix of emotions. The painting caught her mother's beauty as well as her wild spirit with brushstrokes that spoke of the love the artist had felt for this woman. Her mother had been caught with that excited look in her eyes, that unmasked joy in her face... Until that moment, Sid hadn't felt the emotion captured in the painting. Her mother had been a woman in love.

"It is beautiful, isn't it?" asked a woman on the other side of her. "It moves me to tears, as well." The woman pressed a tissue into Sid's hand as she moved away. Sid hadn't realized she was smiling through her tears.

LARAMIE CAUGHT A WHIFF of perfume in a room full of warring fragrances. But he couldn't be sure that light citrusy scent was what had made him aware of a woman standing in front of the H. F. Powell painting. Maybe he'd just sensed her.

When he looked over at the masked woman, he felt a start. She was dressed in all black, from the old-fashioned hooped-skirt dress to the large floppy hat that hid her hair. She turned her head. He caught only a glimpse of cool blue eyes framed by a dark mask— just as they had been the first time he'd ever laid eyes on her.

It couldn't be Sid. She'd said she wouldn't be caught dead here. And yet this woman was the right height and the right frame from what he could see of her. Her elaborate dress hid her figure and her face was obscured by the hat and mask along with the high neck of the dress.

But it was Obsidian "Sid" Forester. He moved closer, following the faint scent of her perfume. Why had she lied about coming here? Or had her plans changed since the time he'd ask her?

He was next to her now. All his senses told him it was her. But when she raised her lashes to meet his gaze, she gave no indication that she'd ever seen him before.

In the other room, someone announced that the ball was about to begin. Music soared and the crowd began to thin. As the woman in black began to move away, he grabbed her hand. Without looking at her, he whispered, "Dance with me."

He felt her freeze. When his gaze met hers, he saw both surprise and wariness in those beautiful eyes. He tried to hide his own shocked expression. This woman wasn't Sid, not the woman he'd kissed, not the woman he'd dreamed about every night since. But he was convinced that they'd met before. Last night, when she'd put the knot on his head.

He felt her hesitate and started to let go of her hand, when she nodded slowly and did an old-fashioned curtsy. As the crowd began to move toward the ballroom, she said, "If you will excuse me for just a moment…"

Before he could protest, she disappeared into the ladies' room. He waited patiently. A few moments later, she returned. He saw the change instantly and yet he questioned if he was losing his mind as he led her out of the art room, onto the dance floor and into his arms.

Her eyes met his briefly, almost shyly, before she lowered her lashes. He felt his heart cartwheel in his chest. This wasn't the same woman he'd asked to dance.

He glanced around for another woman in black, but didn't see one. What game were they playing with him? Sid moved gracefully in his arms. His cat burglar had been light on her feet. No wonder she was such a graceful dancer. But what was she doing here? Shouldn't she be burglarizing someone else's house right now?

"Enjoying the dance?" he whispered near her ear. He felt her shiver.

"I am," she replied in a whisper that had intrigued him the first time they'd met.

He breathed in the citrus scent of her, reveling in the feel of her in his arms. How badly he wanted to kiss her again, knowing that if he did, there would be no more hiding behind the mask. He would have to demand what she was doing here because all his instincts warned him that she was up to trouble.

But as they danced, he was so happy to have her in his arms that he didn't want it to end. Unfortunately, the song did end, though, and she stepped back. He reached for her, but she slipped from his grasp.

And with a slight shake of her head, she gave him another quick curtsy and disappeared into the crowd.

He thought about going after her, cornering her, unmasking her, but good sense kept him from it. He'd promised to stay out of her business. But what was she up to? He hated to think, as he glanced toward the art room. The door was closed, the older security guard standing in front of it.

When someone touched his shoulder, Laramie jumped.

"Is anything wrong?" his cousin Dana asked him.

Laramie shook his head, but he feared a lot of things were wrong.

"You're the only cousin I haven't danced with tonight," she said.

Laramie was happy to dance with Dana. He understood how she had become the matriarch of the family even at her young age. She'd brought them all together as a family because of her loving nature. Everyone loved Dana.

"Are you having fun?" she asked as they danced.

Fun didn't really describe it, but he nodded and smiled. "I'm glad I'm here," he said truthfully, which made her smile.

"I saw you dancing with a woman dressed all in black," Dana said.

"Did you recognize her?" he asked quickly.

"No." She frowned, looking surprised. "You didn't know who she was, either?" That seemed to amuse her. "That explains why you keep looking for her."

"I'm sorry," he apologized. He hadn't even realized he'd been doing that.

Dana laughed. "I'm just glad to see you enjoying yourself."

When the dance ended, she said, "There are some people I want you to meet." She led him back to the lobby.

For the next half hour, he tried to remember the names of the ranchers, business owners and neighbors Dana introduced him to. More champagne was forced on him as he nodded and smiled and thought about the woman he'd danced with.

It wasn't until someone announced it was almost

time for the partygoers to reveal their identities that he escaped back into the ballroom. He had to find the woman.

He worked his way through the crowd, looking for her.

She'd left, he decided. And yet he'd been in the lobby. He hadn't been so distracted that he wouldn't have noticed if she'd passed him. Was there another way out of here? There would be emergency exits, but those would set off alarms.

Just when he thought he'd only imagined her—or she'd evaporated into thin air—he spotted her. She was coming out of the ladies' room. He hadn't thought that was where she might be. He hesitated, realizing also that she probably hadn't attended the ball alone.

He waited for her to make a beeline for some handsome man. The countdown began. Ten. Nine. Eight. The huge room went quiet as everyone anticipated the unmasking. Except his woman in black. Seven. Six. Five. She seemed to be making a beeline not for some handsome escort, but for the door.

Laramie stepped in front of her. Four. Three. Her gaze flew up to his. He saw the alarm as she tried to step around him. Two. One!

Masks started coming off all around the huge ballroom.

"Please," she said as she tried to get past him.

"It's time to unmask," he said and peeled off his own.

She met his eyes with a steely look. Her eyes had gone from cool blue to silver steel. With an arrogant lift of her head, she reached for her mask.

A blood-curdling scream filled the ballroom, followed by the sound of several people running. Laramie turned to see that the door to the art room was open. Even from where he was standing, he could see that the H. F. Powell painting was gone.

As he turned back, he saw that the painting wasn't the only thing missing. His woman in black was also gone.

Chapter Seventeen

Laramie saw the marshal and his brothers Austin and Hayes heading for the art room and quickly followed. Hud barked out orders to the pavilion guards to have all the doors blocked. No one was to leave. Then he motioned them and the guard in and closed the door.

"This door was locked?" Hud asked the guard the moment they were all in the room.

"I locked it myself."

"And there was no one in the room?"

"No." The guard glanced around the space. "Where would they have hidden?"

It was a good question. The room had been bare except for the paintings. Not a stick of furniture was in the room. Laramie looked toward the windows as Hud walked over to them.

"The windows don't open. Nor are there any footprints in the snow outside them," the marshal said as he turned back to the room. "No other doors in or out."

It must have dawned on them all at the same time, because they all looked up. Hud swore. A piece of the dropped ceiling had been left ajar.

"Seal the room," he said as he reached for his cell phone and barked, "Make sure no one leaves."

"Are you going to detain and question everyone outside this room?" Austin asked. They would be here all night and then some if that was the case.

Hud shook his head irritably. "But I need some men at the door to make sure no one walks out of here with that painting in case the burglar left that ceiling tile like that to misdirect us." He looked from Austin to Hayes and then Laramie. "Mind helping until I can get deputies and a crime-scene team over here?"

Laramie joined his brothers at the pavilion's main entrance. The Powell painting was large enough that it wouldn't fit under most costumes, so screening people as they left went fairly fast.

The whole time, he found himself looking for the woman in black. She didn't come through the lines. Which meant she'd left right after the missing painting was discovered? But Hud had asked that all the doors be covered. Maybe she slipped out before the guards could get to the doors. He thought of her hooped skirt and swore. The Powell painting could have fit under it.

Then he saw her. She had taken off her mask, but still wore the wide-brimmed hat that hid most of her face. Only when she glanced up did he catch the glint of her silvery-blue eyes. Eyes like a wolf, he thought.

She had started toward his line, then looked up and seen him. Hesitating, he saw her look to the other lines.

Something shone in those eyes for a moment. Defiance? Challenge? It must have been, because she stepped into his line. As he checked one after another ball goer through, she moved closer and closer.

It wouldn't be long before she was standing directly in front of him.

Laramie could hear people complaining. Some were threatening to call their lawyers.

He let two more people out and turned to find himself face-to-face with the woman of his nightly dreams and his growing obsession. Her head was down, the hat shadowing her face.

He hoped to hell she didn't think he would let her get out of here with the painting. "I'm going to have one of the women check under your hoop skirt," he said.

"That isn't necessary," she said and lifted the framework of the skirt. She wore black yoga pants beneath the skirt. No painting. When he glanced up at her, he saw the smile and the amusement in her eyes before he jerked back in surprise.

This woman looked like Obsidian "Sid" Forester. They would have been twins...

"Let's keep the lines moving," Hud ordered as the grumbling increased among the waiting guests.

"If that's all..." the woman said. She even sounded like Sid, he thought as he watched the woman who'd coldcocked him last night walk away.

TAYLOR WEST NEEDED a drink like he'd never needed one before. He'd awakened with a killer headache and the worst taste in his mouth. When he'd sat up, it took him a few moments to realize where he was. In jail. For murder.

Stumbling to his feet, he lurched toward the bars.

"Hey!" he yelled and listened for someone to come. No one did. "Hey!"

When a deputy finally did show his face, Taylor said, "I'll pay you to get me a drink."

The deputy shook his head and started to close the door.

"Wait! Do you know who I am? I'm Taylor West. I'll give you any painting you want. Just between you and me."

"You need to quiet down. Try to get some rest." He closed the door and even when Taylor yelled obscenities at his departing form, the deputy didn't return.

He banged on the bars of his cell and yelled, "I didn't murder anyone!"

"Didn't your lawyer tell you not to talk about your case?" asked a voice. Taylor couldn't see the man because they were in separate cells divided by a wall instead of bars.

"What's it to you?" he demanded.

"You should listen to your lawyer."

Taylor scoffed at that. "You know what they say about lawyers? Once you need one, you're already screwed." He wandered over to his bunk and sat down, his head in his hands. He would kill for a drink.

"Who didn't you murder?" the man asked.

"The two-bit artist Rock Jackson."

"I know who Rock is," the voice said. "Why *didn't* you kill him?"

Taylor wasn't about to get into it with a stranger. "He was running around with my wife."

"That can get a man killed, all right."

"I planned to kill him. I was waiting outside his house."

"So what happened?"

Taylor thought of the crime shows he'd seen on television. The incarcerated killer always had a big mouth and talked too much to a jailhouse snitch. "What's it to you?"

"I can't sleep, either."

"What are you in for?"

"Writing hot checks."

"*Hot* checks?"

"Checks you can't make good on because you don't have any money."

"At least I don't have that problem," Taylor said, and they both laughed. "When the cops found me I was passed out in my truck with an empty quart bourbon bottle in one hand and my gun in the other. The last thing I remember before that was closing my eyes to wait for my cheating wife and Rock to return."

"Sounds to me like you were framed."

Framed? He lay back on the bunk, staring up at the stained ceiling. "Who would want to frame me?"

"Good question," the man said. "Have you made anyone mad lately?"

"Who *haven't* I made mad?" Taylor said to himself and closed his eyes. But the list of the people who might want to frame him for murder was short and he'd confided in them about the forged painting.

SID WASN'T SURPRISED when she heard the knock at her door. She glanced at the clock. Almost two in the morning. She'd known she wouldn't be able to sleep, so she hadn't even tried. Instead, she'd been painting. It was what she did when she was upset.

"Your light was on," Laramie said by way of explanation when she opened the door. He glanced past her to the costume from the ball that had been tossed onto a chair. Sid now wore jeans and a T-shirt.

Opening the door wider, she motioned him in with a wave of her hand. After seeing him at the ball, she'd suspected it was only a matter of time before he showed up. What surprised her was that the marshal and a couple of deputies weren't with him.

"I thought you said you wouldn't be caught dead at the ball," he said as she closed the door and turned to look at him. He had stopped in the middle of her living room.

She could tell he was angry. But she suspected he was also scared. "Fortunately I wasn't."

He stepped toward her. "Where is the Powell painting?"

"You don't understand."

"Don't I?" He took another step. "You've been playing some kind of game with me since the first night we met. You're lucky I'm here instead of with the marshal."

"Why isn't the marshal here?"

Another step toward her. The room seemed to be closing in, getting smaller and smaller. She could smell the cold night air on him and remembered the way he'd pulled her close earlier when they'd danced. He was almost that close again.

"Because I wanted to give you the opportunity to level with me. For starters, I know you're in more trouble than you're telling me."

She smiled, holding her ground. "You think you know me?"

He was just inches away now. "I know how you feel in my arms. I know how you taste."

She felt something give in her chest as he reached out and cupped her cheek. She'd tried to forget how his mouth had felt and tasted on hers, how safe she'd felt in his arms, how her heart raced when he was this close.

"You weren't alone at my house last night," Laramie said, his voice little more than a whisper. He was so close she could smell his warm scent. "It was your twin."

"My twin? I don't have—"

"You don't have a sister or cousin or some relative who looks enough like you that you used her tonight to pull off the heist? You want to keep pretending you don't know what I'm talking about?"

She started to step away, needing to put space between them, afraid of what she would do if she didn't.

He grabbed her arm and pulled her into him. His voice was rough, his hands strong. "Tell me what's going on. All that stuff you told me last night? Was it just a crock of crap to keep me out of your hair tonight? Come on, Sid. You're too good at what you do," he said as his gaze swept over the painting on her easel.

She'd known he would figure it out. She'd let him get too close. Her mistake.

Laramie looked from the painting to her. His eyes widened as if the truth had just struck him. "You're not just a master thief. *You're* an art forger."

SID WRENCHED FREE of his grasp and stepped past him and, for a moment, Laramie thought she might be going for a weapon. His head still ached from last night. If he could help it, he wasn't going to let that happen again. He turned to watch her step into the kitchen and open the refrigerator.

"I'll take that as a compliment," she said as she grabbed two bottles of beer. She held one out to him. When he didn't reach for it, she said, "You came here for the truth, right? Now you're not sure you want to hear it."

"Try me. Or we can just call the marshal."

"Which makes me wonder why you haven't called him." She squinted, studying him openly. "Maybe because you have no proof. You cried wolf once, the first night we met. You don't want to do it again with the marshal. Am I right?"

She was. It didn't surprise him that she knew he'd gone to the marshal the first night when he'd caught her coming out of his future house with the painting.

The truth. That was why he'd come here tonight. At least in part. He took one of the beers that she offered. Twisting off the top with both anger and frustration, he took a drink, watching her over the bottle. "What you told me last night—"

"Was all true."

"But you didn't tell me everything."

Sid met his gaze. "I wasn't sure I could trust you."

"Trust *me*?" He laughed as he watched her twist off the bottle cap and toss it into the trash before taking a long drink.

She motioned toward a place for him to sit, but he was too restless. She was right. He wasn't sure he wanted to hear the truth. He'd fallen for this woman— a thief, an apparent forger, a cat burglar.

He stepped into her studio off the living room. The room was small with large windows. Because of the lack of wall space, paintings were stacked against the walls. "You painted all of these?" he asked turning to find her standing in the doorway, holding her beer. She nodded.

"I thought you didn't like cowboy art?"

She said nothing as she took another swig of her beer.

In one corner of the room was a stack of old logging crosscut handsaws. The rusted metal between the handles had Montana scenes painted on them. He noticed at once that they weren't half as good as the paintings. That wasn't all he noticed. Her cowboy art wasn't just good, it was masterful and yet she wasn't in the Old West Artists Coalition—just like her father. Nor had he seen her work in any of the galleries he'd visited.

He stared at one of the paintings for a long moment, something stirring inside him. He could feel her watching him. It came to him like another knock to his head.

Turning quickly, he stared at her. "Tell me I'm wrong about you."

"I wish I could."

"I don't get you."

"I think you do."

He smiled at that and shook his head. "I *want* to. You're obviously talented. *Very* talented. So I ask myself what is she doing painting old saw blades? What is it she's hiding other than her obvious talent?"

She lifted her chin. He'd seen that defiant look on her before. "Now you think you have me all figured out."

"Nope, I suspect it could take a lifetime to do that." He put down his beer and closed the distance between them in two long strides. He took her bottle from her and set it aside as he drew her to him. "The H. F. Powell painting that was stolen tonight? I wanted it more than I have wanted anything. Except," he drawled, "*you*. It was because, on some level, I knew. You painted it. But what about the auction?"

"I couldn't let it be auctioned off as one of my father's paintings. It was stolen from his art studio the night he was killed. One of the members of the OWAC donated it anonymously. The killer knows I'm coming for him. Don't worry. I'll make it right with the charity."

"If you're still alive. Sid, we have to go to the marshal."

"Are you sure we have to go right now?" She looked up at him, her blue eyes bright as diamonds, her lips parting. He dropped his mouth to hers.

Then he swung her up into his arms and carried her to the bedroom just off the studio.

SID LOOKED INTO his eyes as he gently laid her on the bed. His expression made her weak inside. His touch was so tender as he crawled onto the bed next to her and drew her close again. He dropped his mouth to hers, exploring her intimately as if there was still so much he wanted to know about her.

She felt the same way. As he drew back from the passionate kiss, he traced his thumb over her lower lip.

"I fell in love with your mouth that night," he said quietly. As he lifted his gaze, he said, "And your eyes. You have the most incredible eyes. I feel as if I can look into your soul."

Sid shivered. "Don't look too closely."

He shook his head. "You're not as bad as you want me to believe," he said just as quietly. "What do you see when you look into my eyes?"

"Kindness, compassion…" She halted seeing something that tied her tongue in a knot for a moment. "Caring."

He smiled. "Caring? Look deeper."

She let out a nervous laugh even as she was filled with pure joy. "Love?"

Laramie nodded. "I've fallen for you, Obsidian Forester. Fallen hard."

Sid couldn't speak, which was just as well because in the next moment he stole her breath away as he cupped her face in his big hands and kissed her again.

She felt wrapped in wisps of soft, warm clouds as he began to unbutton her shirt. His fingers brushed over the tops of her breasts, hardened her nipples to aching pebbles. He followed his fingers with his mouth, suckling at her until she cried out with a desire that burned to the heart of her.

With fumbling fingers, she helped him remove her own and his clothing. She sighed at the feel of his naked skin, the taut muscles of his chest and arms and stomach. Wrapping her arms around him, she pulled him to her.

When they came together it was as if they had been missing pieces of a puzzle that finally had found each other. They moved with the ancient rhythm of passion and love.

Sid arched against him, crying out when he brought her to the peak of desire, and she shuddered in his arms as she collapsed on the bed. The cool night air moved over her perspiring bare skin like a caress.

They might have stayed like that the rest of the night—if it hadn't been for the back door banging open.

Chapter Eighteen

Laramie sat up with a start, grabbing for his jeans as heavy footfalls could be heard from the other room. He glanced at Sid, her face pale and worried in the soft glow coming through the window. From her expression, she had no idea who had just broken into her cabin.

She was reaching for her robe and he'd only managed to drag on his jeans and button all but the top button when a figure filled the doorway, a second larger figure behind it.

The overhead light came on, momentarily blinding him.

"Sorry, it wasn't my idea to come barging in," a woman said. Laramie did a double take at her—and the armed masked man holding the gun to the woman's head.

"What have you done now, Zander?" Sid demanded as she pulled on her robe and tied the sash tight around her middle.

The woman who was the spitting image of Sid shrugged. "You know me, sis. Trouble just seems to find me. But this time I have a feeling this is more about you than me."

"She *is* your sister," Laramie said as he realized this

had been the woman who'd knocked him out the previous night at his house.

"*Half* sister," Zander said and smiled. "The bad half, if you ask Sid."

"Enough. Give me the paintings," the man said. "All of them, including the one you stole tonight, or I kill her."

"I don't think so," Sid said.

Laramie recognized the man's voice. Cody Kent. "You'd better listen to him, Sid. If you're right, he's already killed once. Isn't that right, Cody? You killed H. F. Powell the night you stole the paintings."

"What?" the artist was clearly taken aback. "I didn't kill Powell." He ripped off the ski mask as he shoved Zander into the room. Waving the gun, he said, "Just give me the paintings and no one gets hurt."

"Is that what you told our father?" Sid demanded.

"*Your father*?" Cody asked in confusion. "I didn't think H.F. had any family."

"He didn't have much regard for marriage," Zander said with a sigh. "But, like his daughters, he believed in justice. He planned to nail you and the others to the wall. He would have shown you all up and you knew it."

Cody waved the gun at them. "Look, we just went to his studio to talk to the crazy old coot. No one was supposed to get hurt. But H.F. was determined to ruin us all and destroy everything we'd built with the coalition. We didn't even believe he'd forged our paintings until we entered the studio and saw them."

Sid made a disparaging sound. "But once you did, you couldn't let the public see them. Were you afraid that if you just took them, he would only repaint them? He wasn't a man easily persuaded."

Cody swore. "I saw that we were getting nowhere with him, I wanted to leave. But we weren't leaving without the forgeries. H.F. put up a fight, but finally he gave in. We carried the paintings to the car."

"Including the one that was up for auction tonight," Laramie said.

"That was Rock. He had to have it. We tried to talk him out of it, but he wouldn't listen," Cody said.

"So how did you end up with all of the paintings?" Sid asked.

The artist looked surprised. "What makes you think—"

"You're the one standing here with the gun," she said.

Cody chuckled. "Rock promised to get rid of the forgeries, but I didn't trust him. I was right. I discovered where he'd hidden them. That's why he couldn't tell anyone when he discovered they were missing."

Laramie wanted to rush the man, but he couldn't take the chance that Cody wouldn't get off a shot. In the small cabin, it would be too easy to wound or kill one of them.

"Why didn't *you* destroy them?" Laramie asked.

Cody shook his head. "They were beautiful." He looked at Sid. "Your father was the most talented artist I've ever met. He was brilliant. Crazy as a loon, but a real genius. I knew I should destroy them, but I couldn't. After a few years, I sold them. They were worth a lot more by then because our careers were going better. I figured the chances were good no one would ever find out."

"It wasn't easy, but I found them," Sid said.

He didn't seem to hear her. "Once I saw the one you brought to the gallery, I pretended to be as upset as Taylor was," he said to Laramie. "We were all trying to get ahold of Rock. I knew he'd admit that they'd been stolen from him, but no one would believe him. But I had bigger problems. There was talk of a cat burglar in Big Sky. Only this cat burglar didn't take anything. I paid a couple of houses a visit and realized quickly what was going on when I saw some of the originals H.F. had used to make his forgeries."

"Is that when you panicked and anonymously donated what you thought was an H. F. Powell painting to the auction? That painting was a new one still on the easel in his studio the night he was killed."

"You have no idea how hard it was to part with it," Cody said. "That painting is worth a small fortune."

Sid shook her head. "It would be—if my father had painted it. During the last years of his life, H.F. quit painting his own art to make forgeries of all your work. To keep the creditors at bay and the three of us fed, I painted in my father's style."

"It was a *forgery*?" Cody let out a bitter curse. "You're just a family of forgers."

"Exactly," Zander said. "Our family was all smoke and mirrors."

Cody looked sick. "I knew someone was switching the real paintings and collecting the forgeries once I heard about the so-called cat burglar. I just didn't know who until tonight. I thought you would try to steal the painting. But I didn't know how you would do it. Imagine my shock when I saw you in that black dress jumping down off the roof with it. I planned to follow you, but you got away. I thought I'd blown it, then low and behold, I spotted your double and she led me right to you."

"Hank Ramsey was in on it, too, right?" Laramie asked. "Why isn't he here?"

"I stopped by his place tonight." Cody sighed. "I found him hanging from a beam in his kitchen."

"You might as well put down the gun," Laramie said. "It's all going to come out now."

Cody shook his head. He looked broken, like a man who had nothing to lose. "My art is all I have. Destroy that and I have nothing." He leveled the gun at Sid. "No matter what happens to me, those forgeries have to be destroyed." He pulled a bottle from his coat pocket. Laramie recognized it for what it was. A homemade firebomb—probably like the one he had used the night of H. F. Powell's studio fire.

SID HAD BEEN watching everything play out in front of her, feeling a little dazed. Since her father's death, she'd been grieving for all that had been lost. Once the first forgery had turned up, she'd been on a mission to catch her father's killer.

Cody Kent. She'd known it would be one of the original cowboy artists who started the coalition—or all four of them. She'd just never guessed it would be Cody who showed up at her door.

Laramie took a step toward Cody. She could tell he was trying to gauge his chances. He had to know that there was no one more dangerous than a man backed into a corner.

Sid stepped in front of Laramie. Her heart broke at the thought that she might get him killed over all this.

If only she hadn't gotten him involved. Zander, as well. She was going to get them all killed, and for what? Some artist's ego? Or the price of an artist's reputation?

"I didn't want it to be you," Sid said to Cody. "I guess we all wanted to believe it was Rock Jackson. But when I heard the news, I wondered why Rock would be making counterfeit money if he was the one who'd been selling the paintings he'd stolen from my father that night."

Cody nodded, a bitter smile coming to his lips. "I realized that something like this could happen. That some fool might take H.F.'s copy of one of the paintings to an expert. I wasn't stupid."

"So why sell them?" Laramie asked.

Cody shrugged. "In retrospect, I should have destroyed them."

Sid shook her head. "If Rock had already taken the forgeries that night...you didn't have to go back and kill my father. H.F. was old and tired. He wouldn't have redone the forgeries. But you couldn't let him show you up. It was more about your pride, your ego, than the paintings or even what the organization had been doing. By then, I'm sure your group had covered up the charity scam." She glanced at the glass jar clutched in his hand. "You went there to end it once and for all."

"I thought I could talk some sense into the old fool." Cody shook his head. "It's all water under the bridge now, though. There won't be anyone left who will be able to say differently and the forgeries will be destroyed for good."

"What about Taylor?" Laramie demanded, moving up beside Sid, determined to protect her. How she loved this gallant man. "Taylor's going to sing like a canary. He'll tell everything he knows."

"Even if anyone believed a word he said now that he's facing a murder charge, Taylor doesn't know anything," Cody said.

"That's too bad because I'm betting he didn't kill Rock," Laramie said. "Or that Hank Ramsey didn't hang himself, either."

"If you're expecting a confession..." Cody said as he took a step back.

"You toss that in here and you'll never get out in time to save yourself," Sid said seeing him look toward a candle that still burned next to the bed. "I don't think you've thought this through. Also you will destroy some of my father's paintings. Thanks to you, they're worth more now than when he was alive." He hadn't been able to destroy the forgeries. He wouldn't be able to burn her father's originals. "Not to mention..." She looked toward the bank of windows in the studio.

Cody looked angry and upset as he followed her gaze. He realized as she had that the windows were large enough that at least one of them might be able to get out before the fire killed them.

"Thank you for pointing that out," he said. At gunpoint, he forced them all into a windowless storage room at the back of the cabin where Sid kept the old saws and milk cans she'd collected for her crafts.

"I'm sorry you have to die," Cody said. "You have your father's talent. But you also don't follow the rules. You could never be a member of the Old West Artists Coalition."

Laramie balled up his fist and took a step forward, but Sid caught his arm as Cody retreated from the room, slamming the door behind him and pitching them into darkness. Sid heard him lock the door and shove what sounded like her heavy buffet in front of it.

Chapter Nineteen

Laramie snapped on the switch he'd seen by the door. The small storage room was suddenly illuminated by a dim bulb hanging from the ceiling. He turned to Sid. "Tell me there is a reason you wanted him to trap us in here."

"Other than my sister is as crazy as our father and is determined to get us all killed?" Zander asked.

Sid stepped to the door, putting her ear against it. "Just as I thought, he's looking for the forgeries and stealing some of my paintings. I'm just thankful Cody appreciates good art. Now that he knows I'm H.F.'s daughter…he probably figures they'll be worth a lot of money once I'm dead." Her lips turned up in a knowing yet bitter smile. Then she quickly turned toward the old metal milk cans stacked in a corner. "Help me move these as quietly as we can."

"See what I mean? Crazy, just like our father," Zander said. Laramie thought the last thing Sid had done was lose her mind, so he hurried to help her and saw what had been hidden under the milk cans—a hatch in the floor.

He moved quickly to lift it. A blast of freezing cold

air rose with the door. He looked down at the steps that disappeared into the darkness. "An escape tunnel?"

Zander laughed as her sister handed her a flashlight. "So this is where you hid the forgeries."

"Quickly," Laramie said as Zander snapped on the light and began to climb down. "We have to get out of here before he sets the place on fire." He looked at Sid. "If he burns the cabin, your work will go up in flames."

She smiled almost sadly and descended the stairs.

Laramie followed on her heels. They moved through a long tunnel that ended with a set of crude steps that went up.

"This is that other cabin in the woods," Zander said as they climbed up into a small laundry room lit with daylight coming through the windows.

The moment they stepped out of that room into a larger one, Laramie saw the paintings. Along with the forgeries, he saw dozens of Sid's. Still, he couldn't imagine letting Cody Kent destroy even one of her works.

"Alert the authorities," he said as he headed for the door.

"It's already been done," Sid said. "The moment the hatch was opened an alarm was set off. I have a friend who works at the security company. Wait, where are you going?"

"I can't let him destroy your paintings, let alone get away."

"They aren't worth dying over. I can paint more," she said grabbing at his sleeve. "Neither is catching Cody."

Laramie heard sirens in the distance. "Stay here with your sister." With that, he rushed out the door into the snowy morning.

Chapter Twenty

Sid quickly changed into the clothing she also kept in the second cabin. She'd tried to be prepared for anything that might happen. What she hadn't seen coming was Laramie Cardwell.

"Stay here," she said to Zander as she opened the door to follow Laramie.

"Like that is going to happen," Zander said, right behind her.

Sid couldn't see Laramie as she rushed down the steps and started through the snow-laden pines toward her cabin. One of the reasons she'd bought the property was the tunnel between the two cabins. The owner had told her the tunnel had been dug back in the fifties as a bomb shelter when nuclear war had seemed imminent. The owner had kept the tunnel maintained.

It had saved them temporarily and given her a place to stash the forgeries as well as the bulk of her paintings.

Snow began to fall. At first it was only a few flakes drifting past on the breeze. Then a flurry of them whirled around them as they hurried toward the cabin obscured by trees and snow. Sid could hear sirens coming up the mountain, but feared they would never get there in time. Laramie had the advantage, she told herself. Cody would be busy trying to make his escape. But he was greedy. He would also try to pack up as many of the paintings as he could before he realized the forgeries weren't there and burned the cabin.

The cabin was old. It would burn quickly. Had they still been locked in the storage room, she doubted any of them would have survived.

Ahead, she could see the cabin. Cody had come by snowmobile, forcing Zander along. It was still sitting out front. There was no sign of either Cody or Laramie through the pines.

"Shouldn't one of us have a plan?" Zander said behind her.

She saw that her sister had picked up a limb from the snow. It was thick enough that it could make a pretty good dent in Cody's head—if Zander got the chance to use it.

They slowed as they approached the cabin. "I have a gun just inside the back door in the wicker basket with my scarves and gloves," Sid whispered. "It's loaded. So if something happens—"

"I've got you covered, sis."

LARAMIE SPOTTED THE snowmobile sitting outside the cabin with a half dozen paintings leaning against it. Sid had been right. The bastard couldn't pass up stealing even more paintings. He treasured them more than the lives he'd planned to snuff out in the storage room.

Laramie moved cautiously along the side of the cabin. He could hear Cody inside ransacking the place, no doubt looking for the forgeries. Which meant that he'd have had to put down the firebomb he'd made.

As he neared the open doorway of the cabin, Laramie peered inside. He couldn't see Cody, but he could hear him. Stepping in, he made his way to the fireplace where the poker leaned against the stone chimney.

"What the hell?" Cody swore as he came out of Sid's studio. He held a painting in both hands. "How did you...?" The rest of his words were lost as he realized that the tables had turned. He threw the painting he'd been holding at Laramie and reached into his pocket for the gun.

From the confused look on his face, Laramie realized that Cody must have laid down the gun somewhere—just as he had the firebomb.

As Cody looked around wildly for both weapons, Laramie spotted the gun lying on the kitchen table about the same time that Cody did. Cody dived for it. Laramie charged. He caught the artist in the back with the poker. Cody let out a loud grunt and staggered, but he didn't go down. Instead, he lurched toward the gun, his fingers within inches of it when Laramie again swung the poker.

This time it caught him in the side of the head. The sound of sirens filled the air as Cody dropped to his knees. Laramie quickly stepped around him and pushed the gun out of the artist's reach.

"You don't understand. That crazy old fool was going to ruin me," Cody said.

Laramie spotted the homemade turpentine firebomb on the kitchen counter where Cody had left it as Sid and Zander rushed in, with Marshal Hud Savage and his deputies on their heels.

THE NEWS HIT the canyon as if it were Cody's firebomb. Cody Kent had been arrested. The homemade turpentine firebomb and Cody's gun had been taken as evidence. Trapped, Cody had broken down and told the authorities everything. He confessed to killing H. F. Powell after the man had tried to destroy his career. After that, he'd confessed to killing Rock and trying to frame Taylor and making Hank Ramsey's death look like a suicide.

The broadcaster was saying, "H. F. Powell's story is one of madness and genius. When he was denied membership in the organization, Old West Artists Coalition, he swore retribution, which ultimately led to his murder. And Cody Kent would have gotten away with it if not for Powell's daughter, Obsidian Forester."

Sid got up to turn off the news as, on screen, Cody was being led into the courthouse. "You don't understand," he told reporters. "All I have is my art."

"Maybe he'll teach an art class in prison," Zander said as Sid turned off the television.

"Maybe," she agreed and looked at Laramie who was frowning at the television. "Is something wrong?" she asked him.

"Just a little confused," he admitted. "If all the paintings but the ones that were stolen burned in the fire…"

"The originals my father copied from were in a safe at the house," Sid said. "He planned to expose the artists at their annual conference, which was to be held here in Big Sky a few days after his death. More than likely our father bragged to someone about what he was going to do."

"Not all of the originals were in the safe," Zander

said, shooting a look at her sister. "What Sid isn't telling you is that her sister stole several of the paintings from the safe and she had to buy them back before she could replace the forgeries." Zander smiled sheepishly at Sid. "I'm sorry I made things harder for you. Because of me, we lost the family ranch."

Sid shook her head. "Dad was so in debt by the time he died, there wouldn't have been a way to save it anyway. You were right. This…quest I've been on… I should have let it go, but I wanted justice and I hated the idea of everyone believing he was so crazy he would kill himself."

"He *was* crazy," Zander said and laughed. "We should know. We're his daughters and the apple doesn't fall far from the tree."

"Well, your father has justice now," Laramie said. "And his daughters have found their way back to each other. I'd say you accomplished more than you set out to." He rose to leave. "The invitation is still open for Christmas Eve at Cardwell Ranch. Open to both of you," he said to Zander.

"So what now?" Zander asked after Laramie left. "You don't have a murderer to catch, no houses to break into… What will my little sis do to keep herself busy?"

"Wipe that grin off your face, Z," she said playfully.

"He's in love with you, you know."

Sid said nothing. She still couldn't believe it. She loved Laramie as well, but their lives were in different states. "He's going back to Houston after the holidays."

Zander lifted a brow. "So go with him."

She shook her head. "My life is here."

"Painting cowboy art." Her sister shook her head

and laughed. "I thought Dad messed *me* up, but he really did a number on you."

"We can't spend the rest of our lives blaming H.F. for our choices," Sid said.

"Maybe you can't," Zander said with a laugh. "But I can. I'm just like him. I'll never settle down."

"Don't say never. Who knows what the future holds."

Her sister seemed to study her for a long moment. "This is the most contented I've ever seen you. Those years when you worked so hard to keep a roof over our heads when Dad had locked himself in his studio and refused to paint his own work and support us... You always did what you had to do."

Sid wished she could believe that. "I forged his work while he was forging others'. You're right. We really *are* messed up, huh?"

Zander smiled. "The ironic thing about all of it? You're a better artist than even the great H. F. Powell." She held up her hand to keep Sid from arguing the point. "It's true, sis. That painting..." She pointed to the one of Sid's mother on horseback that Cody had stolen from her father's studio. "It's a masterpiece. It would have sold for a fortune."

She heard the wistfulness as well as the larceny in her sister's voice.

"We could have both retired on that money," Zander continued. "Instead, you had to give up one of the real H. F. Powells you managed to keep me from stealing to keep us from going to prison."

Sid chuckled. "I don't want to retire. I want to paint. What about you? You have our father's gift, as well."

"Gift? More like a curse." Zander shook her head.

"No, you couldn't make me paint even at gunpoint. I've always hated it. Maybe because it takes practice and I don't care enough to hone my skills. I'll leave art to you. Anyway, look what Cody's artist talent did for him." She stood and reached for her bag. "The difference is that you have more than your art. You have a chance for real happiness with Laramie Cardwell."

"Wait a minute, where are you going? It's Christmas Eve. You said we were going to—"

"We're going to Cardwell Ranch."

"I already told Laramie that we were spending Christmas Eve here," Sid said.

"Well, there's been a change of plans. He invited us both to a real Christmas celebration," Zander said. "It sounds incredibly cheesy, but I'm not about to let you miss that. Come on."

"Are you sure, Z? Hot chocolate, tree trimming, carols around the fire?"

Zander put her arm around her sister. "I can stand it for one night. There will be presents, though, right?"

Sid shook her head at her sister. "I really am glad you came here for Christmas."

LARAMIE HADN'T REALIZED he'd been watching for her until he saw the SUV pull up out front of the ranch house.

Dana grinned at him as he headed out to the porch. It had been a crazy time after the ball, but his cousin was determined that they would have their Christmas Eve come hell or high water.

"Invite Sid and her sister," she'd insisted. "The more the merrier."

"She's having Christmas with her sister at the cabin,"

he'd told his cousin. "It's just as well. I don't see how anything can come of this. I live in Houston. Sid has her own life here."

"You can't see any way to overcome that obstacle?" Dana had asked in exasperation.

"It's more than the fact that our lives are thousands of miles apart," he'd said. "We don't really know each other."

His cousin had given him an impatient look. "You don't believe that any more than I do. And even if it is the case, surely there is some way you can rectify it. Is Houston really calling you back? Or are you just like your brothers were and afraid of giving away your heart?"

Laramie had smiled at Dana. "You just can't stand one of your cousins making a clean getaway."

She'd looked as if she might cry. "No, I can't. Nor do I want Sid to get away. Look what she did to try to bring her father's killer to justice. She risked her life and her reputation and prison."

Fortunately, once the Holiday Masquerade Ball and Auction committee members had learned how it was that the H. F. Powell painting was a forgery and Sid had offered them a real Powell to replace it, they'd dropped any legal charges. Also, Sid had promised to donate one of her paintings for the auction next year. Her paintings were now sought after as much as her father's had been.

"Hello," Laramie called from the porch as Sid and her sister climbed out of the SUV. "Glad to see you changed your mind."

"I changed it for her," Zander said.

He smiled. "That was nice of you." As the two climbed

the steps, Zander went on past, letting him pull Sid in for quick kiss. "Merry Christmas."

SID STEPPED INTO his arms as if it was the most natural thing. She parted her lips for his warm, sweet kiss and could have stayed in that very spot forever.

At the door, Zander cleared her throat and said, "The kids are watching you two."

They turned, laughing, to see all of the Cardwell brood at the window, hands cupped around their eyes, making faces and laughing.

"Must be time to go in," Sid said, straightening her coat and bracing herself to meet the rest of the family.

Later, Sid sat listening to the sound of a family at play. It was loud and unruly and wonderful.

"Are you doing all right?" Laramie whispered next to her.

She nodded and smiled. "This is normal?"

He laughed. "As normal as the Cardwells get."

"I love it." She'd met his brothers, their wives, Dana's sister and two brothers and their mates, along with Dana's father, Laramie and his brothers' father and mother and his mother's new husband and all the children. There was also Dana's best friend, Hilde, and her husband, a local deputy.

It was insane. The air was filled with noise and the smells of holiday food. There'd been eggnog and hot chocolate and gingerbread men just as she'd predicted…and homemade fudge.

When it got late, the children were put to bed. The finishing touches were put on the tree. Sid had expected a huge, beautiful pine. Instead, it was a large ungainly tree.

"Dana can't stand the idea of an ugly tree not getting to be a Christmas tree," her husband the marshal explained with a shake of his head. "We do what we can for it."

When the lights came on, the tree was transformed. As the fire crackled they gathered to sing "Silent Night." Laramie put his arm around her shoulders and pulled her close. She stared at the sparkling lights of the tree and reached for her sister's hand.

"This is the best Christmas I've ever had," she whispered when the song ended.

"It's only the first of many if I have anything to say about it," Laramie told her as he drew her into his arms. "I'm not letting you get away from me again."

From the opposite side of the room, Dana gave him a wink.

* * * * *

"Are you really here?" she asked, feeling immediately foolish.

"Feels a little unreal, doesn't it?"

She nodded. "I didn't think I'd ever see you again." He lifted her hand to his mouth, brushing his lips.

"I used to have dreams of you. That you were beside me again. . .sitting close enough that I could feel the warmth of your body by mine. Hear your breathing. And then I'd wake up and—" He let go of her hand and dropped his own hands to his knees. "Doesn't matter. Here you are. Warm and breathing."

She caught his hand, holding him in place. "Don't go."

He looked down at her hand on his. When he spoke, his voice was a low rasp. "Are you sure you want me to stay?"

She knew what he was asking.

"Know what I missed?" His voice deepened. Roughened.

Her heartbeat sped up immediately in response. When she spoke, her own voice sounded breathless. "What?"

"This." He leaned forward, closing the space between them, and touched his mouth to hers.

SMOKY MOUNTAIN SETUP

BY
PAULA GRAVES

First Published in Great Britain 2016
By Mills & Boon, an imprint of HarperCollins*Publishers*
1 London Bridge Street, London, SE1 9GF

© 2016 Paula Graves

ISBN: 978-0-263-91891-5

46-0116

Our policy is to use papers that are natural, renewable and recyclable products and made from wood grown in sustainable forests. The logging and manufacturing processes conform to the legal environmental regulations of the country of origin.

Printed and bound in Spain
by CPI, Barcelona

Paula Graves, an Alabama native, wrote her first book at the age of six. A voracious reader, Paula loves books that pair tantalizing mystery with compelling romance. When she's not reading or writing, she works as a creative director for a Birmingham advertising agency and spends time with her family and friends. Paula invites readers to visit her website, www.paulagraves.com.

For my chat pals, Kelly, Jenn and Donna.
Thanks for keeping me laughing.

Chapter One

The ligature marks on his wrists had long since healed, but the stinging phantom pain of the raw spots the shackles had chafed into his skin sometimes caught him by surprise. Odd, he thought, given the other injuries he'd sustained during his month of captivity, that those superficial wounds were the ones to continue tormenting him.

He'd had cracked ribs, for sure. A dislocated shoulder he'd been forced to reduce himself, since the rough men who'd taken him captive hadn't cared much about his comfort.

Cade Landry had escaped on the thirty-first day of his captivity, and he'd been running ever since.

Given the icy chill in the air and the heavy clouds overhead threatening snow, he should have headed south to Mexico instead of wandering around the Southern Appalachians while he tried to figure out what to do next. He could be sipping cerveza on a beach somewhere, flirting with pretty cantina waitresses and soaking up the tropical sun.

It wasn't as if he had any kind of life to get back to now.

And still, somehow, he'd never completely given up on the idea of clearing his name, though he'd spent the past several months avoiding the issue altogether.

No more. It was time to see if there was anything left of his life to reclaim.

Clouds overhead obscured the sun he'd been using as his compass, but he was pretty sure he was still headed west, which would take him out of these mountains sooner or later. Sooner if he was on the Tennessee side, later if he was in North Carolina.

Either way, he was heading for Purgatory.

Where *she* was.

You don't know if you can trust her anymore.

Maybe not, he conceded to the mean little voice in the back of his head. But she was the best shot he had.

He squinted up at the gray sky overhead, enough sunlight still filtering through the clouds to make his pupils contract. Definitely still headed west, he decided, but he hoped he'd reach civilization sooner rather than later. He had to make a stop in Barrowville first. He'd made a point to shave that morning, to clean up and look his most presentable. Maybe he'd get lucky and somebody would give him a ride into town.

The money he'd hidden away before his abduction had still been there when he'd escaped, thank God, but months of living under the radar had taken a toll on his cash reserves. He needed to see if the money they'd put away a couple of years ago was still in the bank. It was a risk, but one he had to take if he wanted to get through the long, cold winter.

Technically, the account was in *her* name, but he was on the account, as well, and as far as he knew, she'd never closed it out.

Maybe it had been as hard for her to let go as it had been for him.

Landry could tell from the color of the sky and the chill in the air that snow was coming, and he'd lived in eastern Tennessee long enough to know that snowstorms in the

Smokies could rise up fast, like a rattlesnake, and strike with power and fury.

Just like the men he'd escaped.

OLIVIA SHARP POKED at the fire behind the grate and wrapped her sweater more tightly around her shoulders. Winter in the Smoky Mountains had so far proved to be a cold, damp affair, but tonight they were supposed to get the first snow of the season for the lower elevations.

Growing up on Sand Mountain in Alabama, she'd seen snow now and then, but rarely enough to blanket everything and shut a person in for more than a day or two. But the TV weathermen out of Knoxville were calling for as much as a foot and a half in the higher elevations, and the lower elevations could expect five or six inches by morning.

She was safe and snug, tucked in with about a week's worth of background checks to read through. In a company like The Gates, which specialized in high-stakes security cases, everything lived or died on the quality of personnel who worked the cases and kept the company running at peak performance, and the CEO, Alexander Quinn, had put her in charge of profiling prospective hires.

She was lucky to still have a job at all, she knew. Her first big job at The Gates had been a spectacular failure. Tasked with finding a traitor in their midst, she'd failed to smoke him out until it was nearly too late. Quinn would have been well within his rights to terminate her employment on the spot, but he'd given her another chance.

She had no intention of screwing up again.

She had made it through three files and was starting a fourth when her cell phone rang. No information on the display, which usually meant her caller was Quinn or another agent who didn't want his identity revealed. "Sharp," she answered.

"Hey, Olivia, it's me." The distinctive mountain drawl on the other end of the line belonged to Anson Daughtry, the company's IT director and one of the people who'd saved her bacon during the investigation into the mole at The Gates, mostly by putting his own ass on the line.

Of course, he'd had a good incentive—the pretty payroll accountant he'd fallen hard for had been right in the middle of the danger.

"I thought you were on your honeymoon."

"I am." She could almost hear him grinning. "Ginny says hi."

"Hi, Ginny." She couldn't stop her own smile. She might like to play the role of a tough woman of action, but two good people crazy in love still had the capacity to make her go all squishy inside. "Seriously, Daughtry, why are you calling me on your honeymoon?"

"You remember that bank account you asked me to start monitoring for activity a few months ago?"

She sat up straighter, the muscles of her stomach tightening. "Of course."

"I got an alert in my email. Someone accessed the account a little after one. Withdrew five thousand dollars."

Olivia glanced at the clock over the mantel. About an hour ago. "Any idea what branch?"

"That's the interesting thing," Daughtry said. "It was the one in Barrowville."

"Oh." A cool tingle washed over Olivia's body, sprinkling goose bumps along her arms and legs. "Okay. Thanks for letting me know."

"Is there anything else you need me to do?"

"No," she said quickly. "I just needed the information."

She could tell from Daughtry's thick silence that he had questions about her request and what the information he'd just imparted to her meant. But she simply said, "Thanks. Go enjoy your honeymoon," and hung up the phone before he could ask anything else.

She could be in Barrowville in fifteen minutes. Ten if she drove fast, although the first flurries had already begun to fall outside her cabin window.

No. He wouldn't still be there an hour later. And the information she needed from whichever bank teller had handled the transaction, she could get over the phone.

She looked up the phone number for the bank and made the call, finally reaching the teller in question after a long wait. "How can I help you?"

"My name is Olivia Sharp. I have an account at your bank." She rattled off the account number she'd memorized ages ago. "I just received an alert that some of the money has been accessed and you were the teller who handled the transaction."

"Yes, ma'am," the teller answered. She sounded young and worried.

"He gave his name as Cade Landry?"

"Yes, ma'am. He had the right identification and he knew the account number. He's on the account."

"I'm sure you handled things by the numbers. I just need to know if you remember what he looked like."

The teller was silent for a moment, long enough for Olivia to fear the connection had been lost. But as she was opening her mouth to speak, the teller answered her question. "He was tall. Dark hair. Nice eyes. I don't remember what color, just that they were nice. Friendly, you know?"

Olivia knew about Landry's nice eyes. She knew their color, as well, a soft hue somewhere between hazel and green. "What about his build?"

"His build?"

"You know—heavy, slim—"

"Oh, right. It was…nice. You know, he looked good."
There was a nervous vibration in the teller's voice. "Built
nice."

"Athletic?"

"Yes, definitely. He looked athletic."

Olivia closed her eyes. "What about his voice? Low?
Medium? Did he have an accent?"

"It was deep, I'm pretty sure. And he didn't have an accent, exactly. I mean, he was from down here somewhere."

"Down here" meaning the South, Olivia assumed. If it
was really Cade Landry, he'd have spoken with a Georgia
drawl. "I see."

"Is there a problem? Our files show Mr. Landry is still
authorized to withdraw funds from the account." The teller
was starting to sound worried. "Should I put the bank man-
ager on the phone?"

"No," Olivia said quickly. "Mr. Landry is authorized to
withdraw funds. I just wasn't aware he was planning to.
Thank you for the information." She hung up the phone
and tugged her sweater more tightly around her, trying to
control a sudden case of the shakes.

So, someone claiming to be Cade Landry, someone who
fit his description and spoke with a Southern accent, had
withdrawn $5,000 out of a savings account she'd set up al-
most two years ago, back when the relationship between
her and her FBI partner had been going strong.

Before the disaster in Richmond.

But if it really was Landry who'd withdrawn the money
from the account, where the hell had he been for the past
year?

THE CHILL IN the air had grown bitter as the cold front rolled
in, sending the temperature plunging. Overhead, clouds
hung low and heavy, threatening snow.

The bank in Barrowville hadn't given him any trouble with the withdrawal, so clearly Olivia hadn't removed his name from the account.

Maybe that was a good sign.

He pedaled harder as the newly purchased thrift-store bike started uphill on Deception Lake Road. Getting her new address had been easy enough—he'd asked for and received the latest copy of the bank statement, which included her home address in Purgatory, Tennessee.

It had been a little too easy, really. What if he'd been an ex-boyfriend stalking her?

Isn't that sort of what you are? The mean voice in his head was back.

Fine, he thought. *I'm her ex-boyfriend. And I'm about to drop by her place unannounced. And I'm armed.*

But the last thing he'd ever do was hurt Olivia, no matter how badly she'd hurt him. He just needed to talk to her. He might not be sure he could trust her, but he knew there was nobody else he could trust.

He'd learned that painful truth the hard way.

By the time he reached the turnoff to Perdition Gap, sleet had begun to fall, making crackling noises where the icy pellets hit the fallen leaves blanketing the roadside. He picked up speed as the road dipped downhill toward the narrow gorge cut into the mountains by Ketoowee River, hurried along by the bitter westerly wind that drove sleet like needle pricks into his bare cheeks.

He'd made his choice. Set himself on a course it was too late to alter, at least for today. Snow was coming, and he had to find shelter soon.

And the cabin looming out of the curling fog ahead was his only choice, for good or for bad.

There was a car parked on the gravel driveway, the same sleek black Mazda she'd driven when they had been together. It gave him pause, the sight of something so achingly familiar in a world that had turned alien on him almost two years ago.

He dismounted the bicycle and walked it slowly up the driveway, still staring at the Mazda, noting a tiny ding in the right front panel that hadn't been there the last time he'd seen it. And there was a small parking decal on the front windshield, as well.

The sound of a door opening drew his gaze back to the house.

She stood there in the doorway, dressed in jeans and a snug blue sweater that hugged her curves like a lover. In one hand she held a Mossberg shotgun at her side. He knew from experience that she could whip that thing up and fire before he could reach for the pistol tucked in his ankle holster, so he froze in place.

He realized he could see her better than she could see him. He was bundled up against the cold and damp, a scarf wrapped around the lower part of his face and a bike helmet perched atop his head.

"Hey there, Sharp."

She stopped short.

"Sorry to drop by without calling," he added, moving slowly toward her again, pushing his bike closer to the cabin.

She took a few steps closer to the porch steps, a tall, fierce warrior of a woman blocking the entry. "So it *was* you at the bank."

He stopped at the bottom of the steps and looked up at her. God, she was beautiful, he thought, taking in the perfect cheekbones, the snapping blue eyes and the windblown blond waves framing her face. She'd cut her hair since they'd worked together. The short style suited her.

"It was," he admitted. "I was afraid you'd closed the account, but I thought I'd take a chance."

"Is that how you found me? Through the bank?"

"Your address was on the account."

"And you found a way to get the teller to show it to you." The faintest hint of a smile made the corners of her mouth twitch.

"I did."

She took a deep breath and released it. "But now you've left a paper trail. You have to know it won't take long for people to connect you to me and come looking for you."

"It was a calculated risk." He was beginning to feel a potent sense of unreality, standing here in the cold, gazing at a woman he'd once loved more than anyone or anything in his life.

Sometimes, he thought he still did.

"You should turn yourself in."

"Already tried that," he said bluntly, the heat of old anger driving away some of the cold. "Ended up chained in a backwoods cabin for a month. You'll forgive me if I'm not eager to try it again."

Her eyes narrowed. "Is that supposed to be a joke?"

"No. Believe me, there was nothing funny about it." The phantom sting in his wrists returned. He tried to ignore the sensation, hating the frisson of dread that jolted through him each time he experienced the burning pain.

"You look cold."

He couldn't stop a wry laugh, looking around him at the light snowfall. "You think?"

She made a huffing noise but stepped back, opening a path to her door. "Get inside before you freeze."

He grabbed the used duffel full of thrift-store clothes and climbed the stairs slowly, keeping an eye on her and her Mossberg. She didn't look as if she was inclined to shoot him where he stood, but a lot had changed between them since Richmond.

She entered the cabin, leaving the door open for him. A wave of delicious warmth washed over him when he entered, and he quickly closed the door to shut out the cold.

As he started to turn around, he felt cold steel against his neck.

"Put your hands on the door where I can see them." Olivia's voice was calm and cool. "And spread your legs."

"I'm armed," he warned her as he dropped the duffel bag and complied.

"I figured as much." She started to pat him down, her hands moving quickly over his arms, then slowing as she reached his waist. He couldn't quell a shiver of pure sensual awareness as she slid her hands over his hips. "You've lost weight."

"Meals have been hard to come by recently."

She discovered the pistol stashed in his ankle holster and relieved him of it. "Where have you been?"

"Here and there." He felt her retreat, cool air replacing the warmth of her body. "Can I turn around now?"

"Knock yourself out."

He turned to find her emptying the magazine of his Kel-Tec P-11 onto a rolltop desk by the wall. His duffel bag was on the floor by her feet. "Is that really necessary?" he asked with a nod toward the pile of ammunition.

"For now." She removed the round in the chamber and added it to the pile of ammo on the desk before she set the pistol down and turned her cool blue gaze on Landry. "Why did you come here?"

"Nice seeing you again, too, Sharp. It's been such a long time."

She shook her head, her eyes narrowing. "You disappeared nearly a year ago after McKenna Rigsby's undercover mission went very wrong. At least one corrupt FBI agent has gone missing, and the Bureau is scrambling like crazy to find out what other agents might be compromised. You are on the top of their list."

"I know."

"And yet, here you are. Did you think I would just turn a blind eye to the fact that you're wanted by the FBI for questioning?"

She was magnificent when she was angry. Always had been. Her blue eyes took on an amazing electric hue, and the atmosphere around her crackled with energy. He felt drawn to her, despite himself, and took a helpless step forward. "Livvie—"

"Don't." She held up her hand, a pained look replacing the fire in her eyes. "Please don't call me that."

"I know you have questions. But I've spent the last two hours riding a bicycle in the bitter cold. I'm tired. I'm freezing. I haven't eaten since yesterday. It's snowing out, and I need shelter. Food, if you can spare any. In exchange, I'll tell you everything I've been doing for the past two years, and if you still want to turn me in to the FBI after that, then fine. I'll accept that. Because I'm sick to death of running."

Her forehead creased as she considered what he'd just said. "You'll turn yourself in if I say so?"

He nodded, meaning it. He hadn't realized it until he saw her again, but he really was through running. He'd trusted the wrong person once and lost his freedom for a month— and damned near lost his life in the process.

But he had to trust someone, or what was the point of going on? He couldn't keep living under the radar forever.

And he'd already gone nearly two years without seeing Olivia Sharp. There had been a time when he couldn't have imagined such a thing, couldn't have considered even a week without her, much less a lifetime without her spreading out in front of him as far as the eye could see.

"Were you working with the Blue Ridge Infantry?" she asked, breaking the tense silence between them.

He met her gaze, took a deep breath and answered the question with the truth.

"Yes," he said.

Chapter Two

Hearing Cade Landry admit what she'd spent the past year trying not to believe shouldn't have felt like a kick in the teeth. But somehow, it did. It hit her hard enough that she took an involuntary step backward, her foot catching on the braided rug in the cabin's entry.

As she started to lose her balance, Landry lurched forward and caught her before she could fall, his arms wrapping around her waist. His hands were cold—she could feel the chill through her sweater—but his touch sent fire singing through her blood.

He'd always had that effect on her. Even when he shouldn't.

She pulled free of his grasp, steadying herself by clutching the edge of the desk. "How long?"

He stared at her, a puzzled expression on his face.

"How long did you work for the Blue Ridge Infantry?" When he didn't answer right away, she added, "Are you still working for them? Is that why you came here?"

He took a deep breath and let it out in a soft *whoosh*. "I was never working *for* them."

She shook her head, shock starting to give way to a fury that burned like acid in her gut. "Don't play semantics games with me, Landry."

His dark eyebrows arched, creasing his forehead. "Are

you going to listen to what I have to say or should we just cut to the part where you call the cops to come haul my ass out of here?"

"The latter, I think." She went for her shotgun.

He beat her there, jerking it out of her grasp. "Don't," he said sharply as she changed course, going for the P-11 she'd just emptied.

She froze in place, turning slowly to look at him. Something hot and painful throbbed just under her breastbone as she met his hard gaze. "Just get it over with."

"I'm not what you think I am," he said, lowering the Mossberg to his side. "That's what I was trying to tell you."

"You'll forgive me if I have a little trouble believing you."

His lips pressed to a thin line. "I was really hoping you, of all people, would look beyond the obvious."

She pushed down a sudden flutter of guilt. "You don't get to play the victim card. You're the one who disappeared almost a year ago without telling anyone where you were going."

"I did tell someone," he said quietly, lowering the shotgun to the floor, still within his reach. "I told my SAC at the Johnson City RA that I had information the FBI needed to know about the Blue Ridge Infantry. And the next thing I knew, I was being bludgeoned and hauled to some backwoods hellhole and beaten to within an inch of my life."

For a second she pictured what he was saying, imagined him tied up and pummeled by the vicious hillbillies who comprised the mountain militia known as the Blue Ridge Infantry, and nausea burned in her gut. She knew from her own investigations that the hard-eyed men who ran the so-called militia as a criminal organization were capable of great cruelty. If they'd ever lived by a code of honor, those days were long past.

Money and power drove them. In these hills these days, money and power too often came from drugs, guns and extortion.

"You told your SAC?" She repeated his earlier statement, trying to remember the name of the Johnson City resident agency's Special Agent in Charge. "Pete Chang, right?"

He nodded. "I didn't think he was corrupt. He's a brown-noser, yeah, so maybe he told the wrong person the wrong thing. I don't know."

"You've been a prisoner all this time?" she asked, looking him over with a critical eye. "Take off your coat."

He looked down at the heavy wool coat he was still wearing, a frown carving lines in his cheeks. "I wasn't a prisoner the whole time," he said gruffly as he unbuttoned the coat and shrugged it off. Beneath, he still wore a couple of layers of clothes—a long-sleeved shirt beneath a thick sweater—but while he looked leaner than she remembered, he definitely didn't look as if he'd been starved for nearly a year.

"Then why didn't you go to the FBI once you were free?"

"I just told you that the last time I told anyone with the FBI what I was doing, I ended up a prisoner of the Blue Ridge Infantry." He pushed the sleeves of his shirt and sweater up to his elbows, revealing what they'd hidden until now—white ligature scars around both wrists.

Olivia swallowed a gasp. It was stupid to react so sharply to the scars—in the pantheon of injuries she'd seen inflicted in this ongoing war between the Blue Ridge Infantry and the good guys, the marks on Landry's wrists barely registered.

It was what they represented—the loss of freedom, the indignity of captivity—that made her heart pound with sudden dread.

Or they could be a trick, she reminded herself sternly as she felt her resistance begin to falter. He could have inflicted the marks on himself to fool people into believing his story.

The fact remained, he'd just stood here minutes ago and admitted he'd been working with the Blue Ridge Infantry. And nobody who worked with the Blue Ridge Infantry was ever up to any good.

"What are you thinking?" Landry spoke in a low, silky voice so familiar it seemed to burrow into her head and take up residence, like a traveler finally reaching home after a long absence.

She fought against that sensation and gripped the edge of the desk more tightly. "That's really none of your business."

"You're not curious?" he asked, his eyes narrowing as he took a step closer to her. "You don't want to hear all the details?"

She held his gaze but didn't speak.

"Or maybe you really don't give a damn anymore." He spoke the words casually, but she'd known him long enough to recognize the thread of hurt that underlay his comment.

"You're the one who left," she said.

"Are you sure I was the one?" He took another step toward her, and she tried to back away. But the wall stopped her.

"You packed your things and left."

"You'd already left. Maybe not your body, but the rest of you—the part of you that really mattered—" He stopped his forward advancement, looking down at the rough planks of the cabin floor beneath his damp boots. "Doesn't change the outcome, does it? We both walked away and didn't look back, right?"

"Why did you come here?" she asked again, not because she believed he'd answer her any more truthfully than before, but because it was better than thinking about just how many times over the past two years, with how much regret, she'd looked back on the life she and Landry had once shared.

"Because I thought—" He looked up at her, pinning her to the wall with the intensity of his green-eyed gaze. "It doesn't matter what I thought, does it? You've made up your mind about me. I get it." He turned away, heading for the door.

She hurried forward and picked up the shotgun. "I didn't say you could leave."

He turned to look at her. "You're going to shoot me to stop me?"

"If I have to." She sounded sincere enough, even to her own skeptical ears. But her heart wasn't nearly as sure.

She'd loved him once, as much as she'd ever loved anyone in her whole life. Hell, maybe she still did.

If he tried to leave, would she really pull the trigger to stop him from fleeing?

"You won't shoot me," he said softly. "At least, that's what I want to keep believing. So I won't put you in that position."

"You'll turn yourself in?"

He frowned. "I'd rather not. At least, not yet. There's a lot I still need to tell you before you'll understand exactly what we're up against and why."

"What *we're* up against?"

He nodded. "I have to assume someone at that bank in Barrowville will remember the name Cade Landry. And why it's so memorable. They'll call the authorities to report my visit to the bank. And like you said, it won't take long for them to connect us. We were partners, Olivia." He moved toward her, walking with slow, sure deliberation. "Lovers."

His voice lowered to a sensual rumble, bringing back a

flood of memories she'd spent two years trying to excise from her brain. "Don't."

"It's too late to undo it, Livvie. I took a risk coming here, and maybe I shouldn't have." He came to a stop just a few inches from where she stood, and she made herself remain in place, though the pounding pulse in her ears seemed to plead for her to run as far and as fast as she could.

Losing him once had nearly unraveled her. If she let him back into her heart—into her bed—again...

"I said I was working with the Blue Ridge Infantry, and that's the truth. But it's only part of it." His hand came up slowly until his fingertips brushed her jawline, sending a shiver of sexual awareness jolting through her. "Did you know they were targeting The Gates?"

She swallowed with difficulty. "Of course. We've been trying to bring them down since Quinn first opened the doors of The Gates."

"I'm not on their side, Olivia. That's not what I meant by working with them—" He stopped midsentence, his head coming up suddenly. It took a moment for Olivia to hear what he'd obviously heard—a car engine moving up the road toward her cabin.

Landry moved away from her and crossed to her front window, sliding the curtains open an inch.

"Could be a neighbor," she said quietly, suddenly afraid he was going to bolt, even though a few minutes earlier, she'd been hoping he'd leave and not look back.

It was just curiosity, she told herself, the need to know what he'd been starting to tell her about his connection to the BRI. It certainly had nothing to do with the way her jaw still tingled where he'd touched her or the quickened pace of her heart whenever she looked his way.

"They're stopping here," he said bluntly, turning back to look at her. She saw fear in his eyes, raw and wild, and realized she had only a few seconds to keep him from doing something reckless.

She pushed past him and looked through the curtains. The truck that had stopped outside her house was a familiar but, under the circumstances, not exactly welcome sight. "It's Alexander Quinn."

Landry groaned. "Your boss."

She looked at him, wondering how much he knew about Quinn. "You said you're not on the BRI's side. Neither is Quinn. If you know anything about The Gates, you have to know that."

"That doesn't mean he's going to turn a blind eye to the warrants out for my arrest."

"You might be surprised."

He shook his head and picked up his duffel bag. "I'm going out the back. Just give me a head start."

She caught his arm as he started past her, not letting go even when he tried to tug free of her grasp. "Don't run. Not yet. My bedroom is through that doorway. First room on the right. Let me find out what Quinn wants."

Landry stared at her as if he were trying to read all the way through to her soul. Finally, the sound of footsteps on the front porch spurred him into action. He went through the doorway and veered right into her bedroom, closing the door behind him with a soft click.

Olivia took a deep breath just as Quinn knocked.

Showtime.

HER ROOM SMELLED like Olivia, that half-sweet, half-tart scent he'd never been able to identify as anything other than her own unique essence. For a few seconds all he could do was breathe, fill his lungs with that scent, store it away for another drought like the two years they'd been apart since he'd left Richmond—and Olivia—behind.

The bedroom was small and sparsely furnished—a bed, a chest of drawers and a small trunk at the foot of the bed. The bedding was simple and neat—two pillows in pale blue cotton cases, sheets that matched and a thick quilt that looked handmade.

Despite the tension running through him like currents of electricity, despite the muted sound of the door knock just a room away, Landry couldn't stop himself from smiling. It faded quickly, but the flicker of sentiment remained— she hadn't really changed in the past two years if she was still decorating with handmade quilts.

She made the quilts herself, a secret she'd kept from her fellow FBI agents with the ferocity of a mother bear guarding her den. "If you ever tell anyone about this," she'd sworn when she'd finally let him in on her secret, "I will hunt you down and kill you."

The sound of voices drifted down the hallway. The rumble of a male voice, barely discernible, followed by Olivia's alto drawl.

"New bike?" the male voice asked.

"Picked it up at a yard sale," Olivia answered.

Landry pressed his ear to the door, trying to hear the conversation more clearly.

"It's a man's bike," Quinn said in a tone that was deliberately nonchalant.

"I bought it from a man," she answered, a shrug in her voice. "Women's bikes are usually too small for a woman my height."

Good save, Landry thought.

"I got a call from Daughtry," Quinn said, still sounding like someone making small talk. "He said you got a hit on some bank account you'd asked him to monitor."

"That man doesn't know the meaning of *honeymoon*,

does he?" Olivia laughed softly, but Landry heard the faint strain of tension behind her words.

Did Quinn hear it, too?

"One of the reasons I hired him," Quinn answered. "But that doesn't answer my question."

"You didn't ask a question."

Still as smart-mouthed as ever, Landry thought.

"Whose account did you ask him to monitor?"

"Mine," she replied. "I've been noticing some discrepancies in my bank statement, so I thought maybe someone had hacked my password for that account. It's not a lot of money, but still."

"So there's someone tapping into your account? Why didn't you just change the password?"

"That would only stop them from accessing the account. I wanted to catch someone in the act."

"Did you?"

"Maybe. I have some feelers out."

Landry didn't hear anything else for several long seconds, not even an unintelligible murmur that would suggest they'd merely lowered their voices. The silence was unnerving. If he couldn't hear them, he had no way of knowing where they were.

Or how close they were getting to his hiding place.

Come on, he thought. *Start talking again.*

"As much as I relish the screwball comedy potential of being snowed in with you, Quinn, you're not going to be able to get that truck back down the mountain if you don't make tracks in the next few minutes."

"Now you're just tempting me, Olivia." There was a warmth to Quinn's voice that made Landry's gut tighten.

What the hell?

"Funny," Olivia said, but there was no censure in her

voice, only a soft amusement that made Landry want to kick down the door.

"Are you sure you're going to be okay here alone? A few of the agents are bunking down at the office for the duration. It's a little college dorm for my tastes, but I think you can handle the frat-boy atmosphere if you'd rather tough it out in a crowd."

"No, thanks," she said with a laugh that was too friendly for Landry's peace of mind. "I'll be fine here. I have a load of résumés to go through and some housework I've put off for the past couple of months. But thanks for the concern."

"Are you sure everything's okay?" Quinn asked in a tone so quiet and intimate Landry had to strain to make out the words.

"Everything's fine."

"Olivia, I know you're blaming yourself for how close Daughtry and Ginny came to losing their lives, but you're not infallible. Nobody in this business is. We all make mistakes."

Olivia's response was spoken too quietly for Landry to hear. But Quinn's next words gave him a pretty good idea what she'd said.

"There are a lot of ways to pay for mistakes. Sometimes your own conscience is the harshest judge of all. I think you've already given yourself more penance than I'd have ever suggested. That's why I let you come up with your own punishment."

"I would have fired me."

"That's why you're not the boss."

There was another long silence. Landry clenched his fists to keep from reaching for the door handle.

"Call if you need anything. I might know how to get my hands on a snowmobile." Quinn's voice, tinged with amusement, broke the silence, and Landry started breathing again.

He heard the door close and waited until he heard Olivia's footsteps outside the door.

"Still in there?" she asked quietly.

He opened the door to face her. "I was contemplating escape."

"He's gone."

"I heard."

One sandy eyebrow arched over a sky blue eye. "You were eavesdropping?"

"Was there something you didn't want me to hear?"

The other eyebrow joined the first, creasing her forehead. "What's that supposed to mean?"

He meant to change the subject, talk about what a bad idea it was for him to stick around the cabin with her in case her boss decided to come back to check on her in that snowmobile he'd mentioned. But those weren't the words that came out of his mouth.

Instead, to his dismay, he asked, "What the hell is going on between you and your boss?"

Chapter Three

"You were right," Quinn said. "He's there."

Anson Daughtry's voice over the phone picked up a little static as Quinn eased his Ford F-150 pickup around a mountain curve. "What are you going to do about it?"

"Right now? Nothing. She's going to be snowed in with him for a couple of days, and maybe she'll get some information out of him."

"Did you bug the place?" Daughtry's question was delivered bone dry, but Quinn knew his IT director's unfavorable opinion about eavesdropping, especially on employees at The Gates.

"If I did, I wouldn't tell you," Quinn answered just as drily.

"So, you're just leaving her alone with him, without any way of knowing whether or not she might be in trouble?"

"She knows how to call for help if she needs it."

Daughtry made a sound of pure frustration. "Don't you think he's dangerous?"

"I'm *sure* he's dangerous. To someone. The question is, to whom?"

"So you're just letting Sharp find out for you? In a snowbound cabin?"

"If I can't trust my agents to handle themselves in dangerous situations with dangerous people, what the hell am

I doing running a security firm?" Quinn had hired Olivia Sharp because everything he'd ever heard about her told him she was perfectly capable of holding her own in a high-risk situation. She'd been a member of an elite FBI SWAT team for six years, and in every dangerous situation he'd put her in since hiring her, she'd proved her mettle. "Sharp is every bit as dangerous as Cade Landry ever thought of being, and she doesn't have any illusions where he's concerned."

"She was involved with him before."

"What makes you think that?" Quinn asked carefully.

"I hear things."

"Then maybe you heard that they're no longer together. And that it ended badly. Which means she's not going to assume his motives for showing up at her cabin in the middle of a snowstorm are entirely pure."

"Love's not that straightforward," Daughtry said bluntly, in the tone of a man on his honeymoon.

"Let me worry about my agents, Daughtry. You worry about your wife. I'm sure she's shooting you glaring looks by now, considering how long we've been on this call." He pressed the end-call button on his phone and stifled a smile. One of his still-single agents had recently groused that the marriage bug was spreading like a contagion at the office, and Quinn couldn't really deny it.

Take a pair of single, physically fit, energetic and bright people, toss them in the middle of a high-risk, high-stakes situation and step back, because sparks were going to fly. A lot of the time, those sparks fizzled out to nothing once the danger was over, but in some cases, his agents had made real connections with each other, the kind that had a chance to last a lifetime.

Quinn was about as far as a man got from being a romantic, but he'd learned a long time ago not to interfere when a man and a woman wanted to be together.

Very bad things could happen.

OLIVIA STARED AT Cade Landry, certain she'd misunderstood his question. Because there was no way in the world he'd just stood there and asked her what was going on between her and Alexander Quinn, as if it was any business of his. He wasn't a fool or an idiot, and only one of those would stand here in her bedroom doorway, two years after walking out of her life without even a goodbye, and question anything at all about her personal life. Especially in that particular tone of outrage.

But here he was, gazing at her with green eyes blazing with fury, his jaw muscles tight and his nostrils flaring.

"We're going to pretend you didn't just ask me that question," she said in a deceptively soft voice. But she could tell from the troubled look in Landry's eyes that he heard the undertones of danger.

"I'm sorry. You're right. I'm in no position to question anything about your life." He looked down and started to move around her, heading toward the front room.

"Where are you going?" She caught up with him as he was reaching for the unloaded pistol still lying on her rolltop desk.

"I shouldn't have come here."

She caught his hand, stopping him as he started to pick up the pistol. "Why *did* you come here? Why now?"

He looked down at her hand covering his, and she felt the muscles in his wrist twitch as he slowly turned to look at her. "Because I don't know what to do next. And you were always my go-to."

Her heart squeezed into a painful knot. "Even now?"

"Maybe especially now." He eased his hand from her

grasp. She made herself let go as he took a step past her, back toward the center of the room. "Maybe it's better we're more like strangers to each other these days. You can be objective about what I should do next."

She couldn't be objective about him, but she didn't bother saying so. She needed to hear where he'd been and what he'd been doing for the past seven months.

"Look, why don't you sit down in front of the fire? You still look cold." She picked up the knit throw blanket draped over the back of the sofa and handed it to him. "Get warm. I'm going to heat you up a bowl of soup. You want a sandwich, too?"

He took the blanket but shook his head. "I didn't come here for you to take care of me." A look of frustration creased his face.

"Then why did you come here?" she asked softly when he didn't continue.

"I needed to see you." The words seemed to escape his mouth against his will. The look of consternation in his green eyes might have been comical under other circumstances.

But Olivia couldn't laugh. She knew exactly what that raw ache of need felt like. She knew what it was like to wake in the middle of the night and feel compelled to reach out for someone who was no longer there beside her. For almost two years, she and Landry had been a unit. Inseparable.

She should have known it would never last. Forever was the exception in most relationships, not the rule. And with her family history, she should never have allowed herself to think she might be able to beat the odds.

"I wish you'd wanted to see me two years ago when I tried to reach you."

Landry looked down, one hand circling his other wrist

as if to soothe the scars that formed a circle there. "I should have listened to you when you tried to explain."

"You were too angry."

"I felt betrayed."

Her heart ached at the pain in his voice, but she didn't let herself fall into that morass again. She'd spent too much time blaming herself for Landry's anger when there had been nothing else she could do but exactly what she'd done. "I'm sorry you felt betrayed. But short of lying about what I remembered, I couldn't help you."

His gaze snapped up. "I know. I expected too much."

"You expected me to lie?"

He shook his head. "I expected you to believe me, without question. I thought you would know I was telling the truth, even if you didn't remember."

She stared back at him, guilt niggling at the back of her mind. "I do believe that you remember hearing an order to go into the warehouse instead of holding our position. But that's not what you were asking me to say."

He let out a gusty sigh. "I don't know that I was really asking anything of you except your trust and belief in me. But you never could really give me that, could you? Not wholeheartedly."

Guilt throbbed even harder, settling in the center of her chest. "You know blind trust is a problem for me. You knew that going in." She looked up at him. "I warned you, Landry. And you said you could deal with it."

"Because I thought *you* could." He looked away from her, his gaze angling toward the window beside the fireplace. After a second she followed his gaze and saw that the snowfall was starting to reach blizzard proportion, whiting out everything around the cabin.

"The power probably won't hold out much longer," she warned him, moving toward the hall. "If you want something hot for dinner, we should heat it up while we still have electricity."

He followed her down the short hallway to the kitchen at the back of the cabin. "I don't want to put you out."

"It's soup from a can. I'll heat it in the microwave. You're not putting me out." She pulled a large can of beef stew from the pantry and showed it to him. "How's this?"

"It's fine. Thank you. Can I help with anything?"

"Again, soup from a can, heated in the microwave." She shot him a look of amusement. "Sit down, Landry. You look as if you rode a bicycle here all the way from Bitterwood."

"Barrowville," he corrected her with a wry grimace. "Which was a breeze compared to hoofing it here on foot from North Carolina."

Olivia set the can on the counter and turned to look at him. "North Carolina?"

"I don't want to talk about it right now, okay?" As he met her gaze, waning daylight cast his face in light and shadows, emphasizing how much older he looked now than the last time she'd seen him. The past two years had been hard on him. Aged him, left fine lines around his eyes and mouth.

"Okay," she said quietly and returned to the task of preparing soup for their dinner.

He ate as if he hadn't eaten in days, though, as she'd noticed before, he didn't appear thin enough to have skipped too many meals over the months he'd been missing. Without being asked, she opened another can of soup and heated it up for him.

"Thank you," he told her after he'd finished the second can of soup. "I haven't had anything but protein bars and water for the past two days."

She wanted to ask him what had happened to him, but

there was a warning light in his eyes when she leaned toward him, as if he'd read her mind.

She sat back and finished her own soup slowly as he took his bowl and spoon to the sink and washed them. When he was done, he walked past the table and went to stand by the kitchen window to watch it snow.

"How long is the snow supposed to last?" he asked.

"It should snow all night. We should get about six or seven inches, and the temperature isn't going to get above freezing for a couple of days after that. There's a slight chance for more snow day after tomorrow, but the weather guys aren't as sure about that." So he hadn't been near a television or radio in the past few days, either, she noted silently.

Just where the hell had he been all this time?

OLIVIA'S CABIN WAS large and tastefully rustic, but Landry had a feeling the place had come fully furnished. Outside of her bedroom, there was little in the cabin that reminded him of her apartment back in Richmond, a small loft apartment that she'd decorated in cool colors and clean lines. Even her beloved quilts had been stitched together in straight patterns, using fabrics in blues, greens and whites. Uncluttered and organized—that had been the Olivia Sharp he'd known and loved.

But he could tell she'd changed, just as he had. She'd left the FBI first, left him and his anger behind. He'd been both furious and hurt at first, but after what he'd gone through over the past few months, hanging on to resentment seemed pointless.

"I don't have a spare bed."

He looked up to find her standing in the living room doorway, holding another thick quilt like the one he'd seen on her bed. "You have a sofa. That'll do."

She handed him the quilt. It was another of her creations; he could tell by the geometric precision of the pattern.

"Still quilting?" he asked as she started to leave the room.

She stopped and turned to face him. "When I have time. Which isn't often these days."

He set the quilt on the sofa next to him and waved toward one of the armchairs across from where he sat. "You like working at The Gates?"

She sat and folded her hands in her lap. "I do."

"Your boss seems very interested in your welfare."

The look she sent slicing his way was sharp enough to cut.

"Sorry. Too soon?"

"Quinn takes an interest in all of his employees," she said flatly.

"He's trying to take down the Blue Ridge Infantry."

She didn't answer, her eyes narrowing.

"I'm not a traitor, Olivia."

"You never told me how you got mixed up with the BRI." She crossed her long legs and sat back, pinning him with a challenging stare. "I know you tried to help McKenna Rigsby when she was targeted by the Blue Ridge Infantry. You talked to one of our agents, tried to warn him about Darryl Boyle's involvement with the BRI. But one question never really got answered, once you disappeared—"

"How did I know about Boyle?"

"Exactly."

He tried to relax, as well, even though he suspected that some of Olivia's placid composure was an act. He knew his unexpected arrival on her doorstep that afternoon had been a shock to her system, but as usual, she was trying not to let it show.

"I suspected, when Rigsby supposedly went rogue, that

something very bad had driven her there. She struck me as a good agent. She sure as hell hadn't joined the Blue Ridge Infantry—she hated them with a passion, hated everything they were doing and how they were twisting things like honor and patriotism for their own purposes." He couldn't hold back a smile remembering Rigsby's tirades. "She vented to me. A lot. She was undercover, trying to get close to some of the female militia groupies, so she had to pretend she thought they hung the moon when she was with them."

Olivia's lips curved with amusement. "She's so not groupie material."

"So you know her."

"I do." She didn't elaborate.

"Is she okay?"

Her smile faded. "She's fine."

"I didn't get to find out what happened to her after she was taken."

"Because you were grabbed by the BRI guys."

God, he hated the skepticism in her voice, the hint of disbelief, as if he'd have disappeared for a year just for the hell of it. "You don't believe me."

"I never said that."

He pushed to his feet. "You didn't have to."

She stood, as well, and caught his arm. "Don't do this. I'm trying to understand what's happened to you."

"You're looking at me as if I'm crazy. Is that what you think?"

"Of course not." Her grip softened, her fingers sliding slowly down his arm to his wrist, where they settled against his scars. "I just need to know why you stayed away so long. Where have you been?"

"After I got away from the guys who took me, I headed

east into North Carolina." He gave a little tug of his arm and she let go of his wrist.

"Why east?" she asked.

"Because when I got out of that hovel where they were keeping me, that's the way I was facing. So I ran and didn't look back." He looked down at his scarred wrists.

"Until now. Why did you come back now?"

He looked at her, saw the curiosity in those summer-sky eyes and blurted the truth. "Because you're a target. And you needed to know."

Chapter Four

"That's why you're here? You thought we didn't know we were on the BRI's hit list?" Olivia shook her head, not buying it. "I told you already. We know—"

"I don't mean The Gates is the target," Landry said in a quiet tone that made her chest ache. "I mean *you*, Olivia. The BRI is trying to get their hands on *you*."

She stared at him, trying to read past the mirrorlike calm of his green eyes. "How would you know this? You said you hadn't had anything to do with the BRI since your escape."

"I didn't say that."

She thought for a moment and realized he hadn't. She'd assumed it, given that the BRI had taken him hostage and, according to what he had told her, beaten him terribly to get information out of him.

"Maybe you should sit down and tell me what you know." She waved at the sofa and sat facing him on the coffee table, crossing her long legs under her. "How do you know I've been targeted?"

He leaned forward, resting his elbows on his knees. The action brought him close to her, close enough to touch. All she'd have to do is reach her hand toward him and—

"I got away from the BRI. But I still know some people who lurk around the edges of that group. People who aren't on the inside but are close to men who are."

A cold tingle rippled through her. "Women, you mean. The groupies."

"A couple. Also a few guys who sympathize with the stated goals of the group but don't like their methods or trust that they're what they say they are. There are a lot of people in these parts who've seen the mess government interference has made among their kinfolk and neighbors. You have multiple generations who've known nothing but life on welfare."

"The draw," Olivia murmured. At his quizzical look, she added, "That's what people here call it. 'The draw.'"

"They can't live without it, but some of them hate what it's turned them into, too." He stood up and paced toward the fireplace, leaning toward the heat as if he'd felt a chill. "It makes it very tempting to hook up with people like the BRI."

"I know." She'd grown up poor herself. Had struggled to escape the cycle of poverty and bad choices that had haunted her family for a couple of generations. "People don't want to feel victimized. Being part of the BRI gives them a sense of power."

"There's a young man I got to know over the past couple of months. Little more than a kid, really. We worked a few day labor jobs together over near Cherokee. His uncle is part of the Blue Ridge Infantry, but this kid is smarter than that. They keep trying to recruit him, but he resists. He's saving up all his money, planning to go to a technical college over in Asheville."

"He's the one who told you the BRI is targeting me?"

"Not exactly." Landry crossed to the coffee table and sat on the edge, facing her. He leaned closer, his gaze intense.

Once again, the desire to reach across the narrow space between them hit her like a physical ache. She curled her hands into fists and kept them in her lap. "Then what, exactly?"

"He got me into a meeting where they were planning their next move in the war against The Gates."

She stared at him. "You were in a meeting with the BRI and they didn't shoot you on sight?"

"Well, they didn't know I was there," he said with a grin that carved dimples in both cheeks, sending her heart into a flip. "The meeting was at his uncle's place, and there's a big vent in the den where they met. My friend lived with his uncle's family for a while when his mama was in rehab a few years ago, and he found out that if you listen through the vent in his old bedroom, you can hear what they're saying in that den clear as day."

"He let you listen in? Does he know who you are?"

Landry shook his head. "I told him I was thinking of joining the BRI because I was tired of how the federal government was taking over every aspect of our lives. He sympathized, but he told me the BRI wasn't the way to go. They were nothing but trouble and he could prove it."

"By letting you listen in on a meeting."

"Yes."

"And you overheard them making a threat against me?"

"Not by name."

"Then how do you know?"

"They called you Bombshell Barbie."

She arched an eyebrow at him. "And that told you it was me?"

"No. What told me it was you was that one of them said you were dangerous as hell and wouldn't go down without a fight. The combination of the two—the nickname and the statement about your fighting spirit—that's what told me it was you."

She stifled a smile, not sure she should feel quite as complimented as she did. "Bombshell Barbie, huh?"

He held up his hands. "I didn't come up with it."

"I know. I'm pretty sure a guy named Marty Tucker did. He was up to his nasty eyeballs in the BRI until he shot himself trying to escape a colony of bats."

"Bats?"

"Long story. He lived. Now he's in state prison, serving time for kidnapping and other assorted crimes. Sadly, he's chosen to keep all his secrets about the BRI to himself, so we're not any closer to bringing them down than we were before." She frowned. "Matter of fact, they've been really quiet recently. No chatter coming out of there at all that we've heard."

"Until now."

"Until now." She cocked her head. "How long have you known about this target on my back?"

"Two days."

"And you didn't think to call and warn me?"

He slanted a look at her. "You'd have believed it was me on the other line?"

"Probably not," she admitted.

"I knew you'd need proof."

"What kind of proof?"

"An audio recording of the BRI's plans."

An electric pulse of excitement zinged through her. "You have that?"

He shook his head. "Not on me. I didn't want to risk getting caught with it. I put it in a safe place."

"Where?"

"I can't tell you that. Not yet."

Her spine stiffened, and angry heat warmed her face. "You can't tell me? I'm the one in danger and you can't tell me?"

His gaze flicked around the cozy room. "How do you know this place isn't wired for sound?"

"I check it periodically for bugs," she said flatly, trying to control her frustration.

"Using what equipment? Something you got from work?"

"Yes." She met his questioning look without flinching, even though she knew where he was going with the question. "And yes, I realize Quinn probably has a way to get around a bug detector he himself supplied. But I trust him with my life."

Landry's eyes narrowed and he pulled back. "Really? Well, I don't."

She bit back a protest and counted to ten. Landry had no reason to trust Quinn, after all. Or anyone else, she supposed, considering what he claimed he'd been through over the past few months. "Fair enough."

"It's safe for now."

"But the BRI is still after me?"

He nodded, easing forward again. "I don't know the timing of what they have in the works. I know only what they're planning to do. What you need to look for."

Another chill washed through her, raising goose bumps on her arms and legs. "Do you mean to keep that a secret, too?"

A small flicker in the corner of his eye was his only reaction to her blunt question. "No, of course not."

"So what do I look for?"

"First, it's not going to be your standard hit. No sniper shot, nothing like that."

She had an unsettling sense of unreality, listening to Landry speak of her impending death as if it was just another case to be investigated. "Is that good news or bad news?"

His gaze snapped up to meet hers. "None of this is good news."

"Right."

He suddenly reached across the space between them, closing his hand over hers. As if he'd read her earlier thoughts, in an urgent tone he added, "This is not just another case for me, Livvie. No matter what happened between us two years ago, you will never, ever be just another case for me."

As she stared at him, heat spreading through her from the point where his fingers had closed around hers, he let go and sat back, clearly struggling to regain his cool composure.

"I'm sorry," she murmured. "Go on."

"They're going to take you when you're alone. So you need to make sure you're never alone."

"That's impossible."

"Look, I know your boss offered you the chance to stay at the office with some of the other agents. Maybe you should do that."

She looked at the whiteout conditions outside the cabin window. "Too late for that."

He followed her gaze. "I'm sure your boss could come up with some way to get you out of here."

She shook her head quickly. "Landry, I'm safe enough here. For now, anyway. I'm armed and it's not easy to get here in the snow. And you're here, right?"

He nodded toward the rolltop desk. "But I'm unarmed."

She met his warm gaze, trying to be objective, to put everything from their past, good or bad, out of her mind and just assess the situation as an agent.

He'd shown up unannounced, after having disappeared for nearly a year, and told her that he'd been working with the same dangerous militia group he now said had made her a target for assassination. But he'd come alone and warned her of the danger against her. He'd had the opportunity to hurt her earlier, when he'd got the drop on her with her Mossberg shotgun, but he'd done nothing to hurt her.

Was he trying to pull some sort of scam? Was this story about hillbilly assassins part of some bigger plan the BRI had hatched?

Or was he telling her the truth?

"Why?" she asked finally.

His eyebrows twitched upward. "Why did I come? I told you—"

She shook her head. "No—why has BRI targeted me specifically? Do you know?"

"They didn't say. At least, not the part of their discussion I was able to overhear."

"What about your friend? The kid whose uncle is a BRI member. Would he be able to find out why they've targeted me?"

"If I could get in touch with him, yes. But that's very dangerous. Even more so for him than for me. He took a big chance letting me sneak in to eavesdrop on the meeting. If either of us had been caught…"

She quelled a shudder as her mind finished the sentence for him, in vivid, brutal images. She'd seen the lengths to which the BRI would go to carry out a plan. "I get it."

"After the snow thaws, I'll see if I can reach him. But I'll have to be very careful."

She pushed to her feet, nervous energy getting the better of her. "There has to be something I can do while we're waiting. Research or something—"

He stood and crossed to her, closing his hands around her arms and pulling her to face him. His expression was fierce at first, but it softened when she met his gaze.

"I'll tell you everything I can remember from what I overheard," he said in a tone so earnest, so familiar, it made her heart ache. "This all has to be confusing and disturbing—"

"Don't do that," she murmured. "Don't handle me."

Slowly, he dropped his hands away from her arms, but the sensation of his touch lingered, making her feel jittery and unsettled. "Let's sit down, okay? Take a second and breathe."

He was still handling her, but at least he wasn't touching her. She returned to the armchair, and he sat on the coffee table in front of her.

So close. So palpable a temptation.

"They managed to get someone inside The Gates—Marty Tucker, I presume—but he was inside before you got there. They don't assume their limited success with Tucker can be repeated, especially since you're still there, sniffing out any possible traitors in your midst."

"How do they know that?"

"They said Quinn's not trying to hide that information. In fact, he made sure it got out through some of the information channels the BRI already knows are compromised."

Olivia straightened, alarmed. "Quinn put information about me and my role at The Gates out there for the BRI to hear? Deliberately?"

"You didn't know?"

She shook her head.

"See why I'm not sure we can trust your boss?" he asked softly.

She pressed her lips to a thin line, not ready to speak ill of Quinn to anyone, especially Cade Landry. But Quinn should have warned her, damn it! He'd deliberately made her a target by putting the information out there about her role at The Gates.

Was her life a bargaining chip in his plan to take down the BRI?

"He set you up as bait." Landry's voice was a soft growl. "*If* you're telling me the truth."

"I am."

She wished she could say she didn't believe him. But the truth was, setting her up as bait without warning her was exactly the kind of thing Alexander Quinn would do. He was always, *always* about the bottom line. Get the job done whatever it took.

Even if what it took was putting one of his employees in the line of fire to set a trap.

"So they're targeting me? Do they think he won't find someone else to do what I'm doing?"

"They're not going to kill you."

"But you said I was a target."

"You are. But remember when I said they were going to take you? I really meant take you. They're looking to take you captive."

"Why?"

"They seem to think they can use you to break someone."

She frowned. "Someone? Who?"

Landry dropped his gaze, his expression enigmatic as he silently studied his hands for a long moment. When he finally looked up again, an unspoken question darkened his green eyes. "After listening in to Quinn's conversation with you this afternoon, I think they're planning to use you to get to him."

"Why? Why do they think that would get them anything?"

He held her gaze, the questions in his eyes multiplying. "You tell me. I asked you this before, but you didn't really answer. Is something going on between you and Quinn? Are you lovers?"

"No," she answered bluntly. "I mean—"

His eyebrows quirked. "You mean?"

"We're not lovers. But there have been times—" She

swallowed with difficulty, suddenly overcome by the acute awareness that Alexander Quinn might have her cabin wired for sound. She took a bracing breath and continued. "There have been times I thought he wanted to be."

"He's in love with you?"

"I don't think Quinn has ever loved anyone that way," she said with a soft laugh. "But he's a man."

"And you're a beautiful woman. Who seems very alone."

She looked up at him. "I choose to be alone."

"Why?" He shook his head. "You're not a loner, Livvie. You enjoy being around other people. You like companionship."

"That was two years ago. My life is very different now. For one thing, I'm too busy for relationships. My job is dangerous and thankless, and I don't want to inflict that kind of stress on someone else."

"Even one of your fellow agents at The Gates? They're working the same stressful job. They understand the long hours, being on call—"

"Why are you pressing this issue? Do you want me to tell you I've moved on from you? I have. It was two years ago." Her voice rose with emotion. "When I left the FBI, I didn't look back. Are you happy?"

"No." He stared back at her, his nostrils flaring. "No, I'm not happy."

She snapped her mouth shut and looked away.

"I know I drove you away. To this day, I don't know how to trust you again, but I have missed you every single moment. The smell of you haunts my dreams. I can close my eyes and conjure up a vivid memory of the sun glinting off your hair that long weekend we spent on Assateague Island. I can feel the thunder of horse hooves beneath my feet when that wild herd ran past us on the beach. I can remember the way your laugh rang in my ears like music."

He hadn't moved an inch closer, hadn't reached out across the distance between them, but his voice caressed her, seduced her, until she felt a throb of desire pulsing low in her belly.

"I didn't come here to get you back. Or ask for another chance," he said in a deep growl that made her think of long, hot summer nights naked in his arms. "But I don't know if I could keep on living if you weren't."

He moved then, rising to his feet and pacing across the room to the window. Outside, the snowfall continued, barely visible in the deepening dusk. Soon night would fall, silent and deep in the snowbound woods.

And she would be alone with the only man she'd ever let herself love.

She couldn't stop herself from rising to join him at the window. He turned slowly to face her, his face half in shadow.

"They're wrong," she said. "The BRI, I mean."

"About what?"

"Alexander Quinn might very well want to sleep with me. He might even feel some level of affection for me. But he wouldn't hesitate to sacrifice my life if he believed it would serve justice in some way. That's the sort of man he is. So if your friends in the Blue Ridge Infantry believe they can use me to control him in any way, they are sadly mistaken."

"That won't stop them from trying."

She lifted her chin. "Let them try."

His eyes narrowed as he held her gaze, studying her as if he'd never seen her before. "You're different," he murmured finally, reaching up to brush a piece of hair away from her cheek. His fingers lingered a moment, and she felt how work-roughened they'd become since the last time he'd touched her that way.

He dropped his hand to his side. "Do you trust me enough to give me back my weapon?"

Trust might not be the right word, she thought, but she was willing to take the risk. "Yes."

He moved away from her to the rolltop desk and retrieved his pistol, reloading it with both speed and skill. "Any chance you have more 9 mm ammo around?"

"Of course."

His gaze lifted to meet hers, a slow smile spreading over his face, carving dimples into his cheeks and taking a decade off his appearance. "Should've known."

As she started toward the hall closet where she kept her extra weapons and ammunition, the lights went off, plunging the cabin into gloom relieved only by the dying fireplace embers.

"There goes the power," she said with a sigh, detouring toward the hearth to coax the fire back to life.

"Wait," he murmured as she reached for the poker. He was much closer than she'd expected; she hadn't heard his approach.

"What?" she asked, her voice dropping to a near whisper.

"How sure are you that the snow caused the power to go out?"

"It's not unusual during a snowstorm—"

He tugged her away from the window. "Or during a siege."

Chapter Five

Only the soft crackle of the smoldering fire and the quiet hiss of their respirations relieved the sudden blanket of silence that fell over the cabin. Outside, snow continued to fall quietly as Landry listened for any out-of-place noises.

Olivia moved away from the fireplace and picked up the Mossberg shotgun leaning against the wall by the desk. She slanted a quick look at Landry before she started toward the front door and grabbed the thick leather jacket that hung on a hook by the entry.

He caught up with her, closing his hand around her wrist. "What the hell do you think you're doing?"

She shook off his grasp and turned to look at him, her blue eyes glimmering in the low light. "I'm going outside to see if I can tell what knocked the power out."

"Didn't you hear a single word I said about a siege?"

"If there are people out there who want to take me captive, I'd rather get the fight over now than hide like a coward in the cabin."

"Well, you're not going out there alone." He chambered a round in the P-11. "I'll go first."

"Why? Because you're the guy?"

He angled a quick look at her. "Because you're the target, and the target should never be the first person out the door."

She frowned but stepped back. "You need a jacket."

He backtracked and shrugged on the thick fleece coat he'd picked up earlier that day at the thrift store in Barrowville, hurrying in case she changed her mind about allowing him to join her.

But she waited for him at the door, her gaze drawing him all the way in as he closed the distance between them. She was a tall woman, nearly as tall as he was, and if anything, she looked even stronger and fitter than she'd been when they'd worked together in the FBI.

They'd always been a good team, right until the case that had broken them. He hoped the old instincts would kick back in for them now, despite all that had passed between them, because if there really were people out there lying in wait for Olivia, it would take all their skills and a whole lot of luck to make it out of the situation unscathed.

An icy blast of air greeted them as they stepped out onto the cabin porch. Wind had swirled snow beneath the porch roof, depositing about two inches halfway onto the porch's weathered wooden floor.

Landry paused at the top of the porch steps and surveyed the cold white expanse in front of him. If there had been anyone moving around out here in the past little while, they hadn't come close to the porch. The snowfield was pristine and undisturbed.

"The snow probably knocked a branch on a wire somewhere between here and the nearest transformer." Olivia's low voice, only inches from his ear, sent a ripple of pure sexual awareness darting down his spine.

He turned to look at her. "We should check all the way around the house before we let down our guard."

Her eyes narrowed, but she didn't protest as he led her down the steps into the thickening snow. Almost five inches covered the ground, even more gathering at the edges of the porch where the wind had blown the snow into rising drifts.

It was a soft, wet snow, flattening under his boots as they slowly circled the cabin, looking for any signs of intruders.

But nothing had disturbed the snow around the cabin, save for a small set of tracks belonging to what he guessed was probably a foraging raccoon, looking for a meal.

"It was just the snow," Olivia murmured, giving him a nudge toward the front of the cabin.

He trudged back through the tracks they'd left in the snow and nodded for her to precede him up the porch steps. She climbed the steps with a soft sigh he recognized as a sign of impatience and turned to face him when he joined her in front of the door.

"Fine," he said. "It was just the snow. This time."

Olivia shook the slush from her boots and opened the cabin door to head inside. He knocked the snow from his own boots before he followed her in.

She closed and locked the door behind him, shrugging out of her damp coat. "Are we going to do this every time you hear a noise you can't identify?"

He tamped down a flood of annoyance. "If I think it's necessary."

She released another sigh as she hung the coat back on its hook. "Okay, fair enough. Let's get the fire cranked up. I'm freezing."

He took off his coat and hung it on the hook beside hers. "How can I help? Need more wood?"

"It's in a bin by the back door. Straight down the hall."

He found the wood bin and grabbed a couple of pieces for the fire then returned to the front room. He found Olivia kneeling in front of the hearth, adding newspaper as kindling to the charred logs still glowing faintly red. He added the wood to the fire and looked around for matches.

Olivia reached into a small steel canister on the mantel and withdrew a narrow fireplace lighter. "Here."

He touched the butane flame to the kindling. It ignited with a soft *whoosh*, and the logs soon caught fire, emitting a delicious wave of heat into the room.

"Nice," Olivia murmured, extending her hands toward the flames.

He pulled the room's two armchairs close to the fire. "Sit."

She did as he said, leaning toward the warmth. "Thanks."

He sat in the chair next to her, holding his icy fingers toward the fire until some of the numbness subsided. "No, thank *you*."

"For what?"

"For extending a little Southern hospitality to a poor, weary traveler?" he suggested with a smile.

Her lips curved in response. "You didn't give me a lot of choice."

"Maybe not. But I am grateful to be here in front of this fire instead of out there in all that cold white stuff."

Olivia fell silent, her gaze directed at the flickering fire. Settling back in the chair, Landry allowed himself to study her profile, take in the lean lines of her body only partially hidden by her sweater and jeans. His earlier observation was correct; she was in excellent shape. She'd always been a curvy woman, and that hadn't changed, but the curves were matched with toned muscles and an overall look of vibrant health.

Leaving the FBI and going to work for The Gates seemed to have been good for her, at least physically.

But what about her spirit? The Olivia Sharp he'd known and loved had been a firecracker, full of explosive energy and a fierce inquisitiveness that had taken her very far very fast in the FBI.

But not this woman in front of him. She was quiet, contemplative and remarkably still.

She stirred as he watched her, turning her gaze to him. "I could heat up some milk over the fire for hot chocolate. Or even water for coffee, if you'd prefer that—"

"You've changed." He hadn't meant to blurt the words aloud, but he couldn't take them back.

Her eyelids flickered and she looked away. "So have you."

Now that he'd started down this conversational path, he decided, he might as well go all in. "Are you happy?"

"I'm...content."

He felt an ache settle in his chest at the hint of melancholy in her tone. "Is contentment enough?"

"For now."

"Do you anticipate finding more than contentment at some point in the future?"

She slanted a look his way. "Why don't you just come out and ask whatever it is you want to know?"

"Do you miss me?" He clamped his mouth shut as soon as the words escaped his lips. He hadn't intended to ask such a blunt, self-serving question.

"Yes." Her answer, equally blunt, caught him by surprise.

They fell quiet, letting the crackle of the fire fill the lingering silence. Landry wasn't sure how much time had passed before she spoke again, but the flames in the hearth had already begun to die down.

"I loved you. Like I'd never loved anyone in my life." Her gaze remained directed forward, toward the fireplace, the flickering light from the flames bathing her face in a warm glow. "When things fell apart, I had to keep going. Keep working the job, not let the loss derail me. But I just couldn't keep going, day in and day out, working alone when I'd gotten so used to you being there."

The ache in his chest intensified. "I'm sorry."

"You'd been transferred by then. It's not like we'd have been working together anyway."

"I was a mess," he admitted. "It was hard to care about anything for a long time. I worked the job, but it just didn't mean anything to me anymore."

"I heard you'd started going through the motions."

Guilt flooded him, hot and sour. "I did. Much to my shame. I don't really have an excuse. I just knew I wasn't ever going to get any further up the ladder than I already was, and any screwup would probably be the end of the line for me."

"Easier to keep your nose clean if you're not rocking the boat."

"Yeah. I guess. I'm not sure I gave it that much thought. It's just—nothing meant anything. Every time I cleared a case, three more would pop up to take their place. Bureaucratic crap kept creeping further and further down the line into the field offices. We were dealing with federal-level politics in the Johnson City RA, for Pete's sake."

"Why didn't you just leave the FBI, then?"

"And do what? I spent over a decade solving crimes and protecting lives. It's all I really know how to do at this point."

"You could have come to work for Quinn at The Gates, for one thing." She picked up the fire poker and gave the logs a nudge.

"I wasn't ready." He stopped short as she snapped her gaze up to meet his.

"You weren't ready to work with me again."

"That's not it, exactly."

She turned back to the fire. "Then what is it?"

"I know Ava Trent probably didn't have anything good to say about me. Or McKenna Rigsby, either. But my job was to watch their backs, and I didn't want to leave them in the lurch."

"So you stayed for your partners?" She arched an eyebrow but still didn't look at him.

"I wanted my job to mean something again. I thought if I stuck around, if I did what it took to get through the day, I'd feel that fire again." He shook his head. "As if that fire came from outside of me."

She remained silent for a long time, her singular focus on the flickering fire beginning to make him squirm inside. The Olivia Sharp who'd been his partner, in his work life and his personal life, had been a vibrant force of nature. Quiet contemplation had never been her style.

Maybe that woman really was gone. Maybe he'd lost her in the aftermath of the Richmond debacle just as surely as he'd lost himself.

"I never understood why you couldn't forgive me for not remembering what happened." Her low murmur seemed loud in the snowbound hush of the cabin, yet he was certain he'd misunderstood her.

"What?"

She slowly turned her gaze to meet his, her blue eyes blazing with a mixture of anger and pain. "I had a head injury. I couldn't remember anything that happened right before or right after the explosion. But you seemed to think I should be able to pull those memories out of nothing to prove you weren't lying. That wasn't fair."

"It wasn't what you couldn't remember that was the problem. It's what you told the investigators."

Her brow furrowed. "I didn't tell them anything. I couldn't. I didn't remember anything."

"Yet you somehow managed to remember me pushing you and the other team members to disobey the hold order." His voice sharpened.

"I did no such thing."

He shook his head. Why was she denying it? Did she think he hadn't learned what she'd said in her official statement?

The agents who'd interrogated him had shown him a transcript of her testimony, signed off by Olivia, that had laid the whole mess on his shoulders.

Surely she remembered what she'd told the investigators. The words were certainly burned in *his* mind— "Agent Landry believed that waiting would allow the hostage-takers to escape, so he decided to countermand the official orders and go into the building."

Her eyes narrowed. "What aren't you telling me?"

"Nothing." He was starting to feel sick, his dinner roiling in queasy waves in his gut. "It doesn't matter."

Her lips flattened with anger. "You're right—it doesn't. The real problem is that you never trusted me. Not really."

How could he argue with her? His lack of faith—in anyone and anything—had long preceded Olivia's presence in his life.

He closed his eyes. "You, of all people, know why I didn't trust anyone easily."

Her fingers closed around his jaw, tugging his face around, forcing him to open his eyes and look into her pain-filled gaze. "I am not her. I never was. I never will be."

He didn't know what to say in response. She was right. Of course she was right. And yet...

She dropped her hand away from his face and turned back to the fire. "We were doomed from the start."

We were, he thought bleakly.

So why hadn't he done the wise thing and walked away before it blew up in their faces?

THE SNOW STOPPED around midnight, but the electricity didn't return. The cabin had been built to keep out the cold mountain winds, but with only the fire in the hearth to keep the place warm, it hadn't taken long for the temperature inside the cabin to drop precipitously.

"This is the last of the quilts," Olivia told Landry as he sat in silent misery by the fire. Without talking about it, they'd both settled on the thick rug in front of the hearth, huddled together for warmth.

What they hadn't done was speak any more about the past, about the mistakes they'd both made that had led them from the closest of companions to the awkward strangers now sitting side by side under a mountain of handmade quilts.

She'd made it seem that the end of their relationship was entirely his fault, but that wasn't fair, was it? She had her own demons, had made her own mistakes.

"I should have confronted you when you just left without a word."

He made a low, growling sound deep in his throat. "It doesn't matter, does it?"

"I guess not."

He sighed. "I was always a mess. I never should have inflicted myself on you in the first place."

"It never felt like an affliction."

He slanted a skeptical look at her, making her smile self-consciously.

His own lips curved in response. "You can say it. I may be a mess, but I can be honest about my shortcomings."

"I had my own shortcomings. I never felt good enough for you."

He uttered a profane denial.

"No, it's true," she said. "You came from a rich family, and I was from Hick City, Alabama—"

"My rich family left me so screwed up, I walked away from you."

"And my poor family left me so screwed up, I let you go without a fight. Because I'd always figured you'd go, sooner or later." She looked down at her hands, at the short nails she used to wear long and well manicured, and realized so much of the life she'd once lived had been a disguise, a facade she'd invented to make herself feel good enough for the rest of the world. "Little Sand Mountain rednecks like Olivia Sharp don't get to be with rich Savannah boys like Cade Landry. Not for long."

She felt the anger rising off him, as tangible as the waves of heat flowing from the hearth. "You were always the better person, Olivia. You have to know that. You were smarter, stronger, wiser—"

"I never felt that way. And the first time things between us went sideways—"

"I proved you right by walking away," he finished for her.

A soft buzzing sensation from her hip pocket startled her. She'd figured the power outage would have created cell-phone coverage issues, as well, but when she checked the phone display, the signal was strong. "It's Quinn," she said with a glance at Landry.

He nodded at the phone. "Take it."

She answered. "Sharp."

"Quinn," he responded as bluntly. "Is the new bike still parked outside your cabin?"

He knew. She hadn't really doubted he would. "Actually, it's back in the mudroom by the kitchen. Didn't want the snow to rust it."

Quinn sighed. "Damn."

"What do you have against my new bike?"

"Someone's looking for it. Someone with a wallet full of credentials and the full force of the United States government behind him."

Damn it. "You're not suggesting I put the bike back out in the snow to fend for itself?"

Quinn dropped the games. "Landry's a wanted man. If the FBI tracks him to your place—and given his little trip to the bank in Barrowville, it's really only a matter of time before they do—things could get very uncomfortable for you both."

She looked at Landry, who was watching her with troubled eyes. "Any suggestions?"

"I realize travel at the moment is hardly optimal, and you should have at least another couple of days, because the FBI isn't likely to try to make it up the mountain before the snow thaws. But if I were in your place, I would be planning not to be there by the time the roads are passable again."

"Understood."

Quinn hung up without saying goodbye. She closed her own phone and shoved it back in the pocket of her jeans.

"Something's happened," Landry said.

"The FBI is looking for you here in Tennessee. Quinn doesn't think they've tracked you to the bank in Barrowville yet, but it's only a matter of time."

Landry pushed to his feet. "I'll get out of here."

She scrambled up, catching his arm as he reached for his boots. "They won't come tonight. Or tomorrow, most likely."

"That'll give me time to get far away from here."

"Don't," she said, her heart suddenly pounding wildly.

He looked down at her fingers closed around his forearm. "Don't what?"

She swallowed hard, forcing the words from her tight throat. "Don't leave me behind again."

Chapter Six

"Forget I said that." Olivia took a step back and let go of his forearm, turning away.

Landry didn't let her retreat. Not this time. He closed the distance she'd opened up, until the heat of the fireplace filled what little space remained between them. Its glow bathed her face with gold and added sparkling glints to her blond hair. Desire snaked through him, but he ignored its sibilant seduction. Wanting her wasn't enough. It had never been enough.

Maybe that had been the problem. Wanting was easy. Visceral.

Trusting—that was the hard part.

"I can't forget you said that." He laid his hand on her shoulder, keeping the touch light and undemanding. But her gaze snapped up to meet his, her blue eyes darkening with arousal as if he'd caressed her.

He still had that effect on her, just as the mere sight of her made him long for her touch.

"This is a mess of my own making. You're not part of this. I can go, and you can pretend I never darkened your door."

"I can't pretend that." She looked away quickly, as if she could hide the desperation her eyes had just revealed. But it was too late. He'd seen the fear. It echoed the same desperate emotion burning in the center of his chest.

Need. Pure, unadulterated need.

He needed her. His partner. Set aside everything else—the desire, the complicated history, the perceived betrayals and the two-year separation—and the partnership remained, a connection between them that time and distance hadn't been able to sever after all.

"You were a good agent," he said. "A damn good one, actually. And I need my partner one more time, okay? I won't deny it. But it's still your choice. I'm not a good bet here. I'm in a mess and I can't even offer you ironclad proof that I'm telling you the truth."

She turned slowly to face him. "I believe you."

Her simple declaration jolted through him like an electric shock. "Livvie—"

She held up her hand. "I believe you came here to protect me. That's what I believe. But I'm going into this with my eyes open. And the second you keep secrets from me and tell me a lie, that's it. I'll know it. And you'll be out there on a shaky limb all by yourself, because I'll be going to the FBI and telling them everything I know. Including your last whereabouts."

He couldn't hold back a smile of relief. That was the Olivia Sharp he'd known and loved, the tough-minded, no-nonsense agent who'd watched his back and saved his ass more times than he could count.

"Fair enough," he said, holding his hand out to her.

She looked at his outstretched fingers for a tense moment then clasped his hand in hers and gave it a firm shake. "I think we're safe here until morning. So let's pack up the supplies we're going to need to hike up the mountain in half a foot of snow and then get some sleep so we can head out before daylight."

He should have known she'd have a cabin full of survival gear and supplies. Olivia Sharp had set the standard for preparedness during her years in the FBI field office in Richmond. She already had a prepared "bug out" kit, as she called it, containing camping supplies, tools and a 72-hour supply of Meals Ready to Eat as well as changes of clothing.

She had a second backpack stored in the hall closet. Within a half hour, she'd added another three-day stock of supplies and food to that backpack, as well, filling in the blanks with clothes from his duffel bag.

"The cold will be a pain, but these hills are full of places to find shelter," she said in a tone that was all business. He mimicked her brisk attitude as he carried the two backpacks to the front room and set them near the fire while she retrieved extra weapons for them, adding a compact Glock 19 to her Mossberg and handing over a spare pistol.

He looked at the Kimber Stainless II pistol in his palm and smiled. "You remembered."

"It was two years ago, not two decades," she said in a flat tone. "It's loaded, and I put extra ammo in your kit. Now let's try to get some sleep before morning, okay?"

She settled down on a bed of quilts and pillows that had been warming by the fire while they'd gathered supplies, her back to Landry.

He tucked the Kimber in the borrowed backpack and sat down beside her on the makeshift bed. "We should sleep back to back," he said, glancing at her quilt-covered form.

"Knock yourself out," she murmured.

He stretched out beside her and covered himself with a quilt, as well, easing back until his body collided with hers. "Sorry."

"Shut up and go to sleep, Landry."

Stifling a smile, he tucked the quilt tightly around him and closed his eyes. There were only a few scant hours before morning, and they both needed as much sleep as they could muster.

But he had a feeling, no matter how few hours remained between him and dawn, this was going to be one of the longest nights of his life.

DAYLIGHT WAS STILL an hour or two away, nothing more than a faint gray glimmer in the eastern sky, when Olivia woke. The fire had died down to warm embers, allowing a bone-aching chill to settle over the cabin's front room. Only the solid wall of heat pressed against her back kept her from shivering and burying herself more deeply beneath the two quilts covering her from chin to toe.

The hot body behind hers shifted and uttered a familiar groaning sound that made her breath catch in her throat.

Landry.

"You awake?" His voice was like rumbling thunder, muffled by the quilts.

"I am."

He shifted, turning over until he was practically spooning her. "I think my fingers fell off during the night. Can't feel them."

She rolled over to face him. His green eyes met hers with sleepy humor, and she felt something hot and tight release inside her, allowing her to breathe deeply again. "You'd better find them," she said with the hint of a smile. "You're going to need them."

He brought his hands out from beneath the quilt and touched her neck. His fingers were like ice.

She batted them away, laughing despite herself. "Stop!"

"Cold hands, warm heart."

Her smile faded. "We need to hit the road soon."

He sighed. "If we can find the road."

They ate a breakfast of protein bars and left the cabin

while it was still mostly dark out. As Olivia had hoped, once they got past the clearing around her cabin and into the woods, the snow was thinner on the ground, thanks to the shelter of the trees overhead.

"Keep an eye on the trees," she warned as Landry fell into step behind her. "Limbs can snap without a lot of warning."

"Duly noted."

She'd tasked him with hauling the crude travois she'd fashioned from a rake handle, a hoe handle and a canvas tarpaulin, which she'd loaded with the supplies she'd packed into a waterproof duffel in case they had to find shelter before they reached their destination.

"What is our destination, exactly?" Landry asked as they headed deeper into the woods.

"Well, for tonight, I want us to reach a place called Parson's Chair." When he didn't say anything else, she turned to look at him. "No comment?"

His green eyes narrowed as he met her gaze. "I come from Georgia. I have no standing to make fun of strange place names."

She smiled. "It's a tall outcropping that kind of looks like a tall, straight-backed chair, hence the name. But beneath the chair is a large cave that will give us shelter if we can reach it by nightfall."

"And if we can't?"

She turned and started walking faster, tugging her jacket more tightly around her. "Let's just make sure we do."

PARSON'S CHAIR WAS near the top of Fowler Ridge, the southernmost peak of the two mountains that flanked Perdition Gap. On a warmer day, with good weather, Olivia could reach the outcropping within a three-hour hike. She and a couple of the female agents at The Gates had made the hike several times over the summer.

But climbing the winding natural trail in subfreezing temperatures, with a slick carpet of snow underfoot, was turning out to be a grueling test of endurance. She had nearly fallen once already, and as she neared the halfway point of their hike, she heard the sound of a hard thud and a guttural curse behind her, turning in time to see Landry slide almost ten feet back down the mountain on his side, the travois he was pulling tumbling with him.

She reached for the end of the contraption, where she'd strapped the poles together, and caught it before it went over the side of the trail, keeping a sharp eye on Landry as he struggled out from beneath the travois and regained his footing. As he crawled back up the mountain, she held out her gloved hand to him, and he grasped it with a grim smile of gratitude.

"Clearly, I don't have any pack-mule DNA in my ancestry," he muttered as he joined her near a clump of boulders.

She shrugged her backpack off her shoulders and settled on one of the smoother rocks. "Let's rest a minute. Rehydrate and warm up." She pulled out a thermos of warm broth she'd stowed in the backpack before they'd left the cabin that morning.

Landry settled on the boulder beside her, retrieving his own flask. They drank in silence for a few moments before he closed the flask and put it back in his pack. "How much farther?"

She looked at him and saw with alarm that he was wiping blood from the side of his face with the sleeve of his jacket. Rising quickly, she eased his hands away to get a better look at the injury. It was a nasty scrape that started in the middle of his cheek and went into his hairline, disappearing under his black ski cap.

"It's just a scratch," he protested.

"It's bleeding like crazy," she growled, grabbing her backpack to find the compact first-aid kit she'd put inside.

"Seriously, it's a scratch. My head's not even hurting." He winced when she pressed an antiseptic pad against the scrape.

"The travois is obliterating our tracks, for the most part, but if you're leaving a blood trail, I'm not sure the snow we're supposed to get tonight is going to be enough to hide it."

He closed his eyes. "And we're about to spend the night in a cave."

"We're not unprepared."

He opened his eyes, giving her a curious look. "When did you learn all this doomsday prep stuff, anyway?"

"I was born with survival skills," she murmured, mopping up the blood from his face. The scrape continued oozing, but it wasn't as bad as the bleeding had made it look. She tucked the used wipe into a disposal bag and shoved it back in the pack, then made quick work of applying adhesive bandages along the length of the scrape. "All better."

He caught her hand as she was about to let it drop away from his face, pressing her palm against the day's growth of beard scruff on his jaw. Dimples flirted with his cheeks. "But do I still have my boyish good looks?"

He was flirting with her, the beast. And worse, she was falling for it, hard. Damn his charming hide.

She tugged her hand free of his grasp and picked up the first-aid kit. "You're assuming you ever had boyish good looks."

He put his hand over his heart, feigning injury.

She put the first-aid kit in the backpack and swung it up on her shoulders. "We should get moving again if we want to reach Parson's Chair before nightfall."

She didn't wait for him to gather his things before she started hiking up the trail again. Behind her, she heard the sounds of his scrambling to catch up, and she took a little pity on him, slowing her pace until he had.

"You've developed a cold side." His voice drifted to her on the icy wind.

"I've always had a cold side."

As the trail widened, he moved up until he was walking side by side with her. "Not like this. Is it because of me? Because I'm not worth it."

She slanted a look at him and saw he was serious. "Trust me when I say you are only a single line on a lifelong list of reasons not to let myself be vulnerable to other people."

"You never talked much about your past."

"It wasn't important."

"It should have been." He caught her wrist as she continued forward, forcing her to turn and face him. "I should have asked."

"It doesn't matter," she said, tugging free of his grasp once more and continuing up the mountain. What was done was done, and there wasn't a thing either of them could do to change it.

SNOW STARTED FALLING again late in the afternoon, a blizzard of tiny flakes at first, creating a fine mist that looked like the tendrils of mist that gave the Smoky Mountains their name. But within an hour, the flakes grew larger and the snowfall thicker, reducing visibility to almost nothing.

Landry had no idea how they'd be able to find Parson's Chair when they couldn't see ten feet in front of them.

"Stay close," Olivia called, her voice almost whipped away by the wind.

"Wouldn't dream of letting you out of my sight," he muttered.

After what felt like another hour of hiking, though a glance at his watch told him only fifteen minutes had passed, Olivia slowed to a halt. "There it is," she said.

He followed her gaze and saw the faint outline of a rocky outcropping visible through the wall of falling snow. "Parson's Chair?"

"Let's go," she said, hiking forward at a reinvigorated pace.

Tightening his grip on the travois, he followed, ignoring the ache in his calves and thighs. When they finally reached the mouth of the cave beneath Parson's Chair, he eased the front of the travois to the ground and stretched his sore limbs. "Remind me to hit the gym more often when I get back to civilization."

She shrugged off her backpack and shot him a look of amusement. "And here I was thinking you were looking lean and ripped."

"That's from walking everywhere I went, hauling around a backpack and eating only a couple of meals a day." He eyed the dark opening of the cave. "Any chance there's a bear inside?"

"They'd be hibernating at this time of year anyway."

"I heard black bears don't hibernate."

"Why don't you take this, go in there and find out?" She handed him a flashlight from her backpack and waved her hand toward the cave entrance.

"Gee, thanks." He took the flashlight and took a step inside, swinging the light in a slow arc to get his bearings.

The cave was larger than he'd expected, a cavern about twenty feet wide with a high ceiling. The back of the cave disappeared into darkness, suggesting there might be a tunnel that went even farther into the mountainside.

"Any bears?" Olivia's voice was right in his ear, giving him a start. He hadn't even heard her approach.

"If there are, they're hiding." He shone the flashlight in her face, making her squint.

"Give me that." She took the flashlight and headed back outside to grab her gear. He joined her, unloading the travois and helping her take their supplies deeper into the cave.

He had to give her credit; she'd prepared well for a night in a cave. The well-packed duffel he'd been dragging behind him on the travois contained a portable propane heater, two fleece-lined sleeping bags and extra bottled water. "You forgot the portable toilet." He slanted a sly look her way.

She waved her hand toward the cave entrance. "The toilet came with the accommodations."

"Yeah, I've used it before." He folded one of the sleeping bags into a square and sat cross-legged in front of the duffel bag, looking through the rest of the supplies. "No wonder that bloody thing weighed so much. You packed half your cabin."

She followed his example and folded her own sleeping bag into a makeshift seat cushion. "I wasn't sure how long we'd have to be out in the elements." She opened a bottle of water and took a drink.

He grabbed his own bottle of water. It was icy cold, which might have been good about six months ago when he was living through the hot North Carolina summer, but now served to add chills on top of his existing shivers. "How long does that heater last?"

"Six to twelve hours, depending on the heat level. I figured we'd start as low as we can so we can make it last longer. These sleeping bags will help. And we should probably change into dry clothes now, too."

"You want me to wait outside?"

She met his questioning look with one arched eyebrow. "I don't think either of us grew anything new since the last time we saw each other naked. I know I haven't."

He smiled at that as he stood up. "I'll turn my back anyway."

"Chicken," she murmured.

His grin faded as he heard the zip of her jeans and struggled to keep a memory of her sleek curves and warm golden skin from taking over his brain. After shucking off his own wet clothes, he pulled on the jeans and sweater he'd stashed in his backpack. The dry clothes warmed him immediately.

"All done," Olivia said.

Turning, he shook the melted snow out of his hair and used his discarded sweater to soak up some of the remaining moisture. "You became quite the Girl Scout while we were apart. I used to beg you to go camping, with very little luck, and here you are earning your merit badge in disaster prep."

"There's a difference between knowing how to survive in the wilderness and actually wanting to do it for recreation." She settled on her sleeping bag again and took off her boots and damp socks. Her toenails, he noted, were neatly pedicured and polished a bright sky blue that seemed to reflect the azure tint of her eyes. "Hopefully, we won't be up here more than one night."

He sat next to her on his own sleeping bag and followed her example by taking off his snow-stained boots. His socks were still mostly dry, so he didn't take them off. While she donned dry socks and another pair of boots, he asked, "Why *did* we come up here, anyway?"

"Because it's halfway to where I want to go. And I knew we could find shelter here for the night."

"And where is it you want to go?"

She stopped in the middle of tying her boot and looked up at him, her expression hard to read. "We're heading for The Gates."

Chapter Seven

"I thought you didn't trust Quinn."

The words, spoken quietly but urgently, were the first words Landry had uttered since she'd told him of her intentions to hike to The Gates for refuge. She had expected resistance, and when he'd merely turned away from her and started sorting through the rest of the supplies to see what food was available for supper, she hadn't known what to think.

The Cade Landry she'd spent almost two years of her life loving had been quick-tempered and just as quick to get over it. But she wasn't sure this slow-simmering version was an improvement.

"I don't trust him to put my safety above whatever mission he's running at any given time," she admitted, taking the MRE he was holding out to her and reading the packet label. "Spaghetti. Discriminating choice."

He managed a smile, though she could tell he was still disturbed by the thought of putting his own safety—and freedom—in the hands of Quinn and the agents of The Gates. "Eat up. It's going to be another long hike into Purgatory tomorrow, right?"

She sighed. "I know you're not happy about going to The Gates, so you can stop pretending that everything's fine."

"What's the point? You're going to go whether I do or

not. And since it's your life in danger, I can't exactly let you head off there alone, can I?"

"Why not?" She dropped the MRE on the cave floor in front of her and angled her chin toward him, her own anger rising in a rush. "You had no trouble leaving me behind two years ago, did you?"

"Maybe we should talk about who left whom."

"Maybe we should."

For a moment tension crackled between them like a live wire. Olivia's chest started to ache from the hurt and anger she'd kept pent up for too long. But was a cave in the middle of a snowstorm really the place to have this argument?

"I'm sorry," she said, picking up the MRE she'd thrown down. "This isn't the time or place—"

"You'll tell me when you find that time and place, right?" he asked in that quiet tone she was beginning to recognize as his slow boil.

"Do you really want to hash this out here and now?"

"No," he admitted. "Not here or now."

"Let's just get some food and some sleep, in that order." She opened the MRE and pulled out the packets inside. The entrée was the first place to start, she decided. The most calories, and she could eat it hot. She could save the items that didn't require heating for breakfast. "You know how to use one of these things, right?"

"Yeah." He picked up the flameless ration heater. "Been a while, though."

"These come with saltwater packets to activate the heater." She poured the water into the heater, activating the chemicals that produced heat. The packet warmed quickly, and she held it as long as she dared, until the heat began to sting her fingers. She shoved the entrée into the heater packet and set it aside. "What sides came in your packet?"

He went through the small packets that had come in his

meal. "Cheese and crackers, fig bar, shortbread cookies, raisins—"

"Trade you my peanut butter for the cheese spread, and this yummy oatmeal cookie for the shortbread." She waggled the packets at him.

"Deal on the cheese spread, but I don't know. These shortbread cookies sound pretty appetizing." He held out the packet toward her, pinning her with his gaze. "But I might be convinced to trade it for something else."

Despite the icy chill of the cave, the air between them heated instantly. The familiar fire in his gaze was pure temptation, and damned if she didn't want to tumble in headfirst.

She looked away. "If you want the shortbread cookies, keep them."

He let out a little huff of air. "Here. You can have them. I'll take the oatmeal cookie." He laid the packet of shortbread cookies on the cave floor in front of her.

She looked up and saw something in his expression she hadn't expected.

Sadness.

"Landry—" She stopped. Started again. "Cade."

His eyes snapped up at her use of his first name. "You never called me Cade when we were together. No need to start now."

"Maybe that was a mistake. I mean, you called me Olivia. Why did I have to put that distance between us?"

"That wasn't what put distance between us." He looked down at the shortbread cookies she hadn't yet picked up. "And it wasn't just you. I need you to know that I know that I was a big part of the problem."

"Maybe we were just too damaged for anything between us to have a chance to work." To her dismay, she felt hot tears stinging her eyes, threatening to fall. She blinked hard, keeping them at bay.

"I wish I wasn't in this situation." He growled the words, his voice deep with frustration. "I wish I'd just come to you before, when there weren't people hunting for us both. I wish I'd told you that I loved you and we could figure out a way to make it work."

"I could have tracked you down and said the same thing." She made herself look at him, to face the choices she'd made. "I wasn't ready to make that move, and I wouldn't have been ready to give you a second chance if you'd shown up at my door, either."

"Then why don't I feel like it's really over?" The words seemed to tumble from his lips, fast and desperate, as if something inside him was determined to get the question out before his better judgment found a way to shut him up.

"I don't know," she answered as truthfully as she could.

"You don't feel that way, do you?"

She could lie, she supposed. Tell him what he clearly believed to be the truth. But she'd never been able to lie to him with any effectiveness.

"I do," she admitted, forcing herself to say it. Get it over with. "I do feel that way. I never felt as if we got any closure, the way it ended. You know?"

He nodded. "I know."

"I need you to know. I really loved you. Like I've never loved anybody in my whole life. And when things fell apart, I felt ripped in two." She couldn't stop the tears, as much as she wanted to. She pushed them away with her fingertips, shooting him a watery smile. "Sorry. I know you hate it when I cry."

He reached across the space between them, the pad of his thumb brushing a tear from her cheek. "I know you loved me." He dropped his hand away. "You just couldn't believe in me."

"You said that before. When you first showed up at my cabin yesterday. You said I just couldn't believe in you enough. But I don't know why you think that. Is it just because I didn't tell the panel that I remembered getting an order?"

"No, of course not." He looked puzzled by the question. "I knew you had a head injury, so I get that you might not have remembered the order."

"Then what did I do that was so unforgivable?"

"It's what you told the panel about my obsession with the BRI."

Now she was the one who was confused. "What?"

"Olivia, it's okay. Maybe you were right. Maybe I was getting a little too focused on bringing them down. I mean, look at the mess that obsession has gotten me into now."

"But I didn't say—"

"Peterson sneaked me a copy of the transcript of your debriefing. I read your statement."

She shook her head. "There's got to be some mistake. I mean, yeah, I was still suffering from the concussion, but I remember really clearly what I told the investigation team, and I didn't say anything like that about you."

"But your statement—"

"Either you misread it, or you didn't see the real transcript," she said firmly, anger rushing heat into her cheeks. "Because I never said anything like that to the debriefing team. Concussion or no concussion."

"How can you be sure? If you had a head injury, maybe you said things you were thinking that you wouldn't have said aloud if you weren't suffering a concussion—"

"I know I didn't say it, because I never thought it. I never thought you were obsessed with the BRI. You were passionate about bringing them to justice, yes. But so was I. We both wanted that group of terrorists stopped."

A look of dismay crossed his face. "Then if you didn't say it—"

A chill washed over her that had nothing to do with the snowy weather outside the cave. "Someone falsified my deposition."

"But who?"

"Peterson's the one who gave you the sneak peek. Could he have changed it?"

"I guess he could have, but why would he? He'd gain nothing from it. He wasn't on the SWAT team that day." Landry rubbed his chin, his palm making a soft swishing sound against his beard stubble. "Who was in the debriefing with you?"

She frowned, trying to remember. "Definitely the squad leader, O'Bannon. Agents Thompson and Lopez of Internal Affairs."

"What about Darryl Boyle? Was he there?"

She met his urgent gaze. "Yes. He'd been the unit leader that day."

"I've been thinking a lot about that day in Richmond. I've gone over it and over it in my head, replaying every second."

"I wish I could remember."

"No. You don't. I never thought I'd say this, but I'm glad you don't remember." He looked queasy. "You don't remember two of our friends—our brothers—blown up in front of us."

She reached across the space between them, touching his hand. His gaze snapped up to hers, but instead of pulling away, he covered her hand with his own.

"I'm sorry. I'm sorry I wasn't well enough to attend the

funerals for Davis and Darnell. I should have been there with you."

"I missed you," he admitted, giving her hand a light squeeze before he pulled away and rose to his feet. There was a faint glow of lingering daylight coming from the mouth of the cave; he walked toward it slowly until he stood in the opening.

She tugged her jacket more tightly around her and followed, stopping next to him in the cave opening. "Snow's starting to slow down."

He glanced at her. "How much more do you think fell?"

She gazed into the gloom, making out only faint impressions of their trek to the cave in the snow. "At least three or four more inches. Looks like maybe nine inches altogether."

With a little shiver, he turned and walked deeper into the cave. "How long before we can turn on the heater?"

"I'd like to wait until we bunk down. Let's eat. The food should be heated by now, and that should warm us up for a bit."

He lowered himself onto the folded sleeping bag and reached for the box holding his MRE.

"Use your—"

He growled an oath and dropped the now-open box on the cave floor.

"Glove," she finished.

"Thanks for the warning." He slipped on his glove and fished the hot entrée out of the box while she did the same. Steam rose from the packets, filling the air around them with the smell of food.

They ate in silence from the entrée packets and drank a whole bottle of water each before stowing away the trash for disposal when they reached town the next day. Outside, night had descended, snuffing out almost all the light from the world beyond the cave.

"I want to get a predawn start tomorrow," she warned as she handed him the flashlight. "Here, hold this where I can see what I'm doing with this heater."

He pointed the flashlight beam toward the small propane heater. "Is it dangerous to run that thing in an enclosed space like this?"

"It shuts off automatically if the oxygen level gets too low." She made sure the fuel tank was safely seated in place. She turned on the power, and heat rose from the vents. "Plus, this cave has an opening deeper inside. If you wet your finger and hold it up, you'll feel the breeze."

His lips curved and his dimples made a quick appearance. "I'll take your word for that."

"We should probably try to sleep with our backs to the heater," she suggested as she unfolded her sleeping bag and laid it out by the unit.

He followed her lead, setting up his bag on the other side of the heater. "How much more battery time does that flashlight have?"

"Should be plenty for the trip. But let's not waste it." She switched it off, plunging the cave into inky darkness.

For a few minutes, the sounds of movement, hers and his, filled the silence as they unzipped their sleeping bags and slid inside, then zipped themselves up within the fleece-lined cocoons.

Silence reigned again for a long while, broken only by the soft whisper of their breathing and the hiss of the propane heater warming the air between them.

"I'm sorry." His voice rumbled in the darkness a long time later, just as she was starting to relax.

"For what?" she asked, resisting the temptation to turn over to face him.

"For being reckless. Getting that money out of our joint bank account yesterday, even though I knew it was possible—probable—that the account would have been flagged."

"So why did you?"

"I guess I was just tired of being out there alone," he said after a long pause. "I missed having someone who gave a damn about my life, and since you were the last person who really did—"

"I'm not sorry," she said quietly.

When he didn't respond, she wondered if he'd heard her.

"I'm not sorry," she said more loudly, turning her head to make sure he could hear her. "I've been so worried about you, for a lot longer than just the time you've been missing. I'm glad you came to my cabin. I'm glad I know you're okay."

"For now."

She sighed, turning her back to him again, suddenly overwhelmed by a heavy sense of danger creeping closer.

"For now," she conceded and closed her eyes, giving in to the bone-aching weariness from a day's hike up the mountain.

She didn't think she'd fall asleep easily, despite her fatigue, but the comforting flow of warmth from the propane heater and the soft, steady cadence of Landry's breathing soothed her into deep, dreamless slumber.

LANDRY OPENED HIS eyes and stared into the black void of the cave, listening to Olivia's slow, steady breathing. It felt a little ridiculous, really, to be forcing himself to stay awake just so he could listen to her sleep nearby.

That was how much he'd missed her. Enough that something as simple as hearing her move oxygen in and out of her lungs was the most comforting sound he'd heard in two long years.

Why had he let her go? His reasons had seemed so right,

so overpowering, in the heat of his anger and the burning humiliation of what he'd perceived as betrayal. But he believed her now when she said she'd told only the truth.

He should have believed it all along. He should have told her what he'd read and heard her side of the story. She'd have told him the truth, that she hadn't painted him as an unstable obsessive, and then maybe—

Maybe what? Maybe they'd still be together?

He'd have found a way to screw it up. He'd never had a relationship last longer than a few months before Olivia. Looking back, he wasn't sure how she'd put up with him as long as she had.

Maybe her own emotional baggage had made her more patient than she might have been. She'd come from poverty, from an unstable home with a young and irresponsible mother. Her father had been little more than a stranger, and while she'd sworn nothing terrible had happened to her during her childhood, he'd begun to suspect her father's behavior with her when she reached her teens had made her uncomfortable.

"I was lucky," she'd said firmly the one time he'd brought the subject up. "My mom might have been a major mess as a parent, but she never let anyone hurt me that way. Besides, after I hit my teens, we moved away from Sand Mountain, and I never saw him again."

He hadn't said what he'd been thinking, that maybe her mother had chosen to leave their hometown behind to get her away from her father and his discomfiting behavior.

Whatever the reason, he was glad she'd got out of that situation mostly unscathed.

But she hadn't got away without emotional baggage, any more than he'd escaped his own troubled youth without deep and lingering trust issues.

An unfamiliar sound drifted toward him through the

inky darkness, dragging his mind out of the past and back into the cold, uncertain present.

Not unfamiliar, he realized as the noise came inexorably closer.

Just unexpected.

Footsteps approached the cave at a slow, steady pace, crunching the crusty snow underfoot.

They had a visitor.

Chapter Eight

Consciousness returned to Olivia in a nerve-rattling rush, leaving her disoriented. Something had awakened her. But what?

"Don't make a sound." She recognized Cade Landry's voice, quiet but urgent. "Someone is moving around outside the cave." His voice was little more than a whisper of breath against her cheek that time.

She tried to sit up and realized she was cocooned in her sleeping bag.

She heard the faint sound of a zipper, and cold air flooded over her, scattering goose bumps across her skin. Wriggling free, she rose to her feet.

Cold steel pressed against her fingers. Her Glock 19. She didn't bother to check the magazine—she'd loaded it before they left the cabin.

"How do you know someone's out there?"

As if in answer, she heard the crunch of boots in the snow outside. She went very still and silent, her nerves instantly on high alert.

Landry touched her arm briefly then moved toward the mouth of the cave, staying out of the semicircle of faint illumination that lightened the cave floor just in front of the entrance.

She joined him there, just a few feet from the world outside, peering through the darkness for any sign of movement.

"Do you see anyone?" She felt his question more than she heard it, a huff of warm breath tickling her ear.

"No."

Suddenly, shockingly close by, a male voice uttered a low oath.

Next to her, Landry's body reacted with a slight jerk. She put her hand on his arm, recognizing the voice. "It's okay. I know who it is."

"Sharp, if you're in there, I think I just broke my damn ankle." The male voice outside spoke in a whisper.

With a sigh, she started toward the cave door.

Landry caught her arm, jerking her back against the hard heat of his body. "Are you crazy?"

"I told you—I know who it is."

"It could be a trap."

"It's not a trap," came the voice from outside, sounding both pained and annoyed.

She pulled free of Landry's grasp and went outside. Sitting on a low boulder nearby was a lean man with spiky brown hair and a pained look twisting his feral features. He had one leg crossed over the other, massaging his ankle through the hiking boot.

"Hammond, what the hell do you think you're doing up here in a snowstorm?"

Seth Hammond made a face. "I could ask you the same thing."

She shot him a pointed look and he shrugged.

"Rachel and I bought a place just up the gap from where you live. I took the baby out to see her first snow and I spotted two idiots climbing up the mountain in a bloody blizzard. One of 'em was dragging something behind him like a pack mule. So I went and got my binoculars. You can imagine my surprise when I saw one of those idiots was you."

"Funny."

"Anyway, I thought I should see what you were up to. And who was with you."

She sighed, looking at her colleague from The Gates. "What if I didn't want you to know what I was up to and who I was with?"

He eased his foot to the ground. "Well, the good news is, I don't think I can hike down the mountain to tell anybody what I saw. I'll probably just sit here and freeze to death, and nobody will ever find out what you're up to."

"Do you really think it's broken?"

"It's not broken." Landry stepped out of the cave, taking up a protective stance close to her. "You would have screamed when you put your foot down on the ground that way if it was broken."

Seth peered up at Landry through narrowed eyes. "You a doctor?"

"No. I'm a guy who's had a broken ankle."

Seth pushed to his feet, testing the injured limb. He seemed to be holding his weight easily enough. "What do you know? It's not broken."

"Told you it was a trap," Landry muttered to Olivia.

"It wasn't a trap." Olivia looked pointedly at Seth. "Did Quinn send you?"

"No. I told you—I saw you from my house."

"You're not seriously trying to sell me that story."

The look on Seth Hammond's face was pure innocence. "Would I lie?"

She rolled her eyes. "Uh, yeah, you'd lie. You were a con artist for years. It's kind of what you do."

"Con artist?" Landry asked.

"Reformed," Seth said with a feral grin.

"Or so he says." Olivia glanced at Landry. "Think we should just leave him out here? Since he's not crippled or anything?"

"Oh, come on, Sharp. It's damn cold out here, and I think I hear the sound of a heater running in that cave."

"Should have packed your own," Landry said.

Seth gave him a considering look. "Don't believe I got your name."

"Don't believe you did," Landry agreed.

"Might as well let him get warm or he'll sit out here whining all night and keep us awake." Olivia nodded for Seth to enter the cave ahead of her.

Landry caught her arm as she started into the cave after Seth. He kept his voice low. "I don't like this."

"He's a colleague at The Gates."

"I don't care. I don't trust anyone at The Gates except you."

"But I do. And we're going to need help if everything you've told me is the truth."

"Of course it's the truth."

"Then we don't need to try to go up against a whole army of well-armed, morally bankrupt rednecks by ourselves."

Seth's voice wafted out of the cave. "Got any extra MREs in here?"

"No," Olivia and Landry called in unison. She looked up at him, struggling against a smile.

He didn't fight it, grinning down at her, his dimples making an appearance that even the dark night couldn't quite hide. "I don't know, Sharp. You and I always made a pretty good team. Just the two of us."

She took a step back from him, alarmed by the sharp tug of longing that gripped her by the heart. "There hasn't been just the two of us in a long time."

His grin faded. "You trust your buddies at The Gates, but you don't trust me."

"*You* don't trust *me*," she countered, lowering her voice further. "That was always our problem."

"I guess it was," he conceded. "And it went both ways."

She couldn't argue. "But maybe it's not too late to learn to have a little trust in each other." She glanced toward the cave. "I'm telling you, Seth Hammond is a lot of things, but he's not a traitor. He takes his work at The Gates very seriously, and part of his work is watching the backs of other agents. Including me."

"So you're asking me to trust your judgment about a man who claims he hiked who knows how many hours up this mountain just to see what you were doing?"

She couldn't stop a soft huff of laughter at his dry tone. "Yeah. I guess that's exactly what I'm asking."

He looked toward the cave entrance then back at her. "That's a hell of a lot to ask, Sharp."

"I know."

He sighed. "Okay. Fine. We'll let the huckster join our slumber party."

"Reformed huckster." Seth's voice drifted out from the cave.

"Ears like a bat," Landry murmured. "Kinda looks like one, too."

"I heard that."

"Shut up and grab yourself one of those protein bars," Olivia called to Seth. "But keep your mitts off my MREs."

Landry nodded for her to come with him, a little farther from the cave. She followed, trying to hide her growing amusement at his irritation. When they reached the edge of the rock formation that formed Parson's Chair, he stopped and turned to look at her.

"You don't think he really just spotted us hiking up the

mountain and took it upon himself to follow us all the way up here on a whim, do you?"

"I'm not an idiot."

"So what do you think? Quinn had him staked out to watch your place?"

"Maybe. Or more likely, he's tracking us electronically in some way."

"You mean GPS?"

She glanced back toward the cave. "Some of the equipment I brought with us came from The Gates. I guess there could be trackers inside some of them."

"Quinn tracks his agents? He doesn't trust you?"

"We had a problem with leaks. We had a mole in the agency, and Quinn's very touchy about it. So for a while, he was tracking all the agents to see where they went. I guess it's hard for him to let go of his CIA instincts."

"So the hillbilly con man in there might be removing all the trackers while we're out here chatting?"

She shook her head. "No. Quinn doesn't care if I find out about the trackers. He's making a point to me with them anyway."

"And that point would be?"

"I might be one of his agents. I might even be one of the ones he's most likely to confide in. But he's never going to fully trust me. Or anyone else."

"Sounds like a couple of people I know."

She made herself meet his gaze. Now that her eyes had adjusted to the dark, she could make out the details of his familiar face, the lean planes of his cheeks and the curve of his full bottom lip, a hint of softness in his otherwise chiseled features. She couldn't make out colors, but she knew from experience that his green eyes held a touch of hazel, shifting hues with his emotions. Right now, she knew, his eyes would be a deep, smoky green, like a forest pool reflecting the earthy colors around it. A hue of green she'd learned long ago meant he was troubled and tense.

"It's freezing out here. Why don't we go back into the cave?" She lowered her voice to an intimate murmur.

He slanted a look at her. "Right now, hearing you talk to me in that tone, I'm really wishing your good buddy the con man wasn't waiting for us in that cave."

She felt a jolt of pure sexual thrill whip through her body like electricity. She'd forgotten how easily he'd been able to seduce her out of a bad mood or a fit of anger. One soft, oblique hint of desire in that sexy growl of a voice, and she was on fire from the inside out.

"Landry—"

He smiled, sighed and gestured toward the cave. When he spoke, his voice was soft with understanding. "Come on. Let's get inside before he eats all our food."

LANDRY HADN'T EXPECTED to get much sleep with a stranger sharing the cave with him and Olivia, but her sense of ease must have been contagious, for he was asleep nearly as quickly as she was and woke to morning light seeping into the cave and the sound of a whispered conversation taking place close by.

"Of course he sent me." That was Seth Hammond's quiet drawl.

"He doesn't trust me?"

"He doesn't trust sleeping beauty over there."

"Landry's not a danger to me."

"Are you sure about that?"

There was a brief pause before her answer, long enough for Landry's stomach to tighten.

"Positive," she answered, and even in a whisper, conviction rang in her words. "He needs my help. I didn't know how to give it to him before, but I'm not going to stop this time until we figure it out."

Deciding to stop his eavesdropping while he was ahead, Landry rolled over and made a low, sleepy groaning sound as he stretched.

"Good morning," Olivia said.

He turned to look at her and his breath caught. Her face was free of makeup, her hair was a tousled mess, but she was still the most beautiful thing he'd seen in ages, and even the presence of Seth Hammond didn't keep him from wanting to cross to her and take her to bed right there on the icy cave floor.

He managed to control the urge and pushed up to a sitting position. "No more unwanted visitors while I was asleep?"

"No, just me," Seth said with an unperturbed grin. "Let's just get this out in the open, okay? I know who you are. I know the FBI is looking for you. And I know Olivia here doesn't think you're one of the bad guys. And since my track record with the authorities isn't exactly clean, I'm in no position to judge your decision to run instead of turn yourself in."

"How did a guy like you ever get a job with The Gates in the first place?" Landry grabbed his jacket as an icy draft raced through the cave, making him shiver. Olivia had already turned off the heater, and most of the residual heat had dissipated.

Olivia tossed Landry his half of the leftovers from their meal the night before. "Eat some breakfast. We can talk about Quinn's hiring practices later. We need to get on the trail again."

"At least it's downhill from here," Seth said in a cheerful drawl that made Landry want to throw his breakfast at the man.

Instead, he examined the packets Olivia had tossed to him. Peanut butter and crackers, a toaster pastry, raisins and an oatmeal cookie.

"Yum," he muttered.

"Food is fuel," Olivia said briskly as she started rolling up her sleeping bag. "Eat up. Daylight's burning."

HIKING DOWNHILL IN the snow wasn't a lot better than hiking uphill, Landry decided a couple of hours later as he hit a slick patch and landed hard on his tailbone. The impact knocked the wind out of him for a moment, and the poles lashed together at the pointed end of the travois cracked hard against his chin.

Olivia and Seth both stopped to help him back up. "You want me to pull the mule cart for a while?" Seth asked, nodding at the travois with a friendly grin.

"Let him do it," Olivia told Landry in a dry tone, already heading back onto the trail. "Serves him right for letting Quinn turn him into his personal bloodhound."

Landry handed over the travois poles and caught up with Olivia on the trail. "Are you sure heading into town is the best idea? Quinn clearly doesn't trust me or he wouldn't have sent your huckster buddy back there to make sure you were okay in my company."

Hammond's voice piped up behind them. "Reformed—"

"Shut up!" Landry and Olivia snapped in unison.

Olivia slanted a quick look at Landry, her lips curving in a half smile. "I don't know if it's the best idea," she admitted, her smile starting to fade. "But it's the best one I have. You have any better ideas?"

"No," he had to admit.

"At the rate we're going, we should hit town in about two hours. Then the pace should pick up because the streets are relatively flat, and you won't be tripping over hidden stones every few yards."

"What's between here and town?"

"Enemy territory," Hammond said, his voice closer. He'd caught up with them despite his heavier load.

"There's a small enclave of people who claim allegiance to the BRI," Olivia explained. "Their cabins are a little ways off the trail, so if we're lucky, we shouldn't have any trouble with them."

Landry caught her arm and stopped her in her tracks. "If we're lucky?"

"It snowed nearly a foot up here in the mountains. Power up this way is spotty on a good week, so they're probably hunkered down, trying to stay warm. It'll be all right."

"You hope."

"I expect," she said firmly. But he saw her grip her Mossberg shotgun more tightly as she started hiking forward again.

They walked awhile in silence before Olivia broke it with a soft question. "Where is your evidence?"

So much had happened between the time he'd shown up at her cabin and this laborious hike down the mountain, it took Landry a moment to understand what she was asking.

"Evidence?" Hammond prodded when Landry didn't answer immediately. "Evidence of what?"

"Of the BRI putting a hit out on me," Olivia answered in a flat tone that belied the feral alertness behind her blue eyes.

"It's not a hit exactly," Landry corrected her.

"So they interrogate me roughly for a few days before they put me out of my misery. Close enough to a hit for me," she said.

"Wait—what?" Hammond wriggled out from under the travois and trudged forward to join them. "Someone's trying to take you prisoner, and you're out here hiking into town by yourself?"

"She's not by herself," Landry protested.

Hammond shot him a hard look. "Close enough. Why didn't you tell Quinn? He could have put a half dozen agents on your place to stand guard."

"So then I'm Quinn's prisoner instead."

"At least Quinn's not looking to put a bullet in your brain," Hammond snapped, all of the folksy humor gone from his demeanor. "Damn it, Sharp, why do you always play it this way? Why don't you let anybody help you?"

Landry looked from Hammond to Olivia, taking in the bristle of anger in her expression and the frustration in Hammond's voice. Apparently, this wasn't the first time Olivia had clashed with her fellow agents at The Gates about her lone-wolf attitude.

He guessed a few things about Olivia hadn't changed in the past few years after all.

"Let's just get to your office and get warm." Landry nodded at the travois Hammond had dropped. "You can call Quinn and tattle on her when we get there."

The sharp-eyed look Hammond threw Landry's way would have intimidated a different man. But after all that Landry had gone through over the past few months, it would take a hell of a lot scarier man than Hammond to make him flinch.

Hammond released a harsh breath and stalked back to the travois.

"You want me to spell you for a bit?" Landry asked as the other man jerked the lashed poles over his shoulders.

"I'm good," Hammond growled.

"You have such a way with people," Landry murmured to Olivia as he caught up with her.

"I don't want people at the agency thinking I need to be wrapped in cotton and put away somewhere safe."

"Do they do that as a rule?"

She cut her eyes at him. "I haven't tested the theory yet."

"If you're so worried that's what's going to happen, why are we going to The Gates in the first place?"

Her voice rose. "Because I have nowhere else safe to go, okay?"

They walked on in silence for another half hour, battling a rising wind that whipped up the mountain, blowing snow around them and limiting visibility to a few dozen yards. The watery sunlight that had offered a brief reprieve against the icy chill had faded behind a sheet of low-lying clouds that threatened more snow.

"What was the forecast the last time you checked?" Landry asked. He'd lost his cell phone months ago and had never bothered to replace it. Whom did he have to call? But he'd seen Olivia checking her phone that morning before they hit the trail.

"It might snow a little more," she answered. "They weren't sure."

"How much more?"

Coming to a sudden stop, she didn't answer. Landry followed her gaze into the blowing snow and saw what she'd seen. Movement, straight ahead.

There was someone out there in the woods ahead.

"How close are we to the BRI enclave?" Landry asked softly.

"Too close," she answered.

Behind them, Seth Hammond uttered a soft expletive.

"Well, now," came a low drawl, "look who just wandered into our territory, boys."

Landry froze, a flash of images flooding his memory so hard and fast he felt as if he'd been gut-punched.

He knew that voice. He'd heard that voice every day for a month, the deceptively gentle tones that had been a sound track for the brutality of his henchmen.

He'd never seen the face—they'd made sure of it. But he'd know that voice anywhere, even in his nightmares.

Landry turned slowly, bracing himself for his first look at the monster who haunted his dreams.

But before he could move, a crack of rifle fire split the icy air, and he threw himself at Olivia, shoving her to the ground beneath him.

Chapter Nine

The idiot was trying to protect her!

But in the process, he'd damn near knocked the Mossberg out of her hand. She shoved him off her and rolled onto her stomach, leveling the barrel toward the last place she'd seen their gun-toting intruders.

But they were gone, running through the snowy woods like wraiths, fading into the whitewashed scenery.

As Olivia turned her head to check the rear, Landry pushed her down again, his weapon hand whipping toward a spot behind her. "Don't move."

"Landry—" Hammond began.

"Shut it," Landry barked. "Put the guns down."

"You're outnumbered." The familiar voice sent a shudder of relief ratcheting through her body. She shoved Landry off again, ignoring his growling order to be still, and looked up to confirm what she'd heard.

Six men in arctic camouflage stood in a semicircle around them, eyes alert and rifles raised. One man was clearly in charge, a dark-haired man with dark hazel eyes and lean, chiseled features. He wore the camo like a second skin, which made sense, she supposed, given his decade in the US Army.

"They're friendlies," she said sharply to Landry, putting her hand over the hand that held his gun.

"Says who?" he growled, shoving her hand away.

"I say," she said firmly, circling to stand between his pistol and her colleagues. The second she got a look at his wild-eyed expression, a quiver of pure terror ripped through her gut. In that moment, she realized, he could just as easily shoot her as not.

Then his gaze focused on her. His expression softened a notch, and he slowly lowered the Kimber to his side.

"Friendly to whom?" he asked, his voice raspy and unsteady.

"To me. And you." She held out her hand to him.

For a moment he looked at her as if she'd lost her mind. But she didn't budge.

After a long, breathless moment, he turned the Kimber grip toward her and handed it over.

She slid the Kimber into the waistband of her jeans and turned to face the men from The Gates. "You should have brought Ava," she said to the leader. "He knows her."

"Yeah, well, she and Solano are down in Alabama. Solano's sister had her baby a week early." Sutton Calhoun shrugged and nodded toward the men flanking him. "Somebody go help Seth out. He's too damn scrawny to be a pack mule."

Hammond made a rude gesture at Calhoun, earning a laugh from Calhoun and the other guys on the squad. But he stepped forward and gave Sutton a downright brotherly hug. "How'd you know to come to our rescue?"

"We didn't. We just knew from your last text that y'all were heading down the mountain in the morning, so we figured you might run into trouble here in the redneck red zone. Quinn asked for volunteers, but when nobody spoke up, he made us draw straws." Calhoun grinned. "We got the short ones."

"Funny."

"This him?" Calhoun nodded toward Landry but looked at Olivia for a response.

"What, you don't have my mug shot hanging on the office wall?" Landry's sarcastic tone almost hid his underlying tension.

Almost.

"I'm Sutton Calhoun." Calhoun extended his hand.

Landry ignored it.

"Manners," Olivia murmured.

He looked at her as if she'd lost her mind. When he answered, his coastal Georgia drawl kicked in. "This ain't a cocktail party, darlin'."

Calhoun shrugged and finished the introductions. "This is Fitzpatrick to my right. That's Dennison on the left. Cooper's the big guy. Jackson's the guy on the end."

"And I believe we've spoken before." Nick Darcy stepped forward.

"You answered the pay phone at the Econo-Tel," Landry said, showing the first hint of relaxing. "The guy with the British accent. You were protecting Rigsby."

Darcy nodded. "You probably saved her life with that call. If we'd been even a few steps behind Darryl Boyle—"

"Olivia says Rigsby's okay."

"She's splendid," Darcy answered in a tone so besotted, Olivia couldn't quell a smile.

"I see," Landry murmured, glancing at Olivia.

"We probably shouldn't stick around here much longer," Calhoun warned. "Those fellows might have gone for reinforcements."

"Don't suppose you brought any skis with you?" Hammond muttered.

"You can't ski worth a lick anyway," Calhoun said, clapping his friend on the back before barking an order in the sharp tone he must have learned during his days in the Army. "Move out."

THE LITTLE TOWN of Purgatory looked like a Christmas card, covered with snow and sparkling with lights in the deepening twilight. The temptation to stop his weary trudge forward and just enjoy the sight was more than Landry could resist.

He'd been in and out of civilization over the past months, slipping into bigger towns when he needed supplies or information, but most of his time had been spent in the hills, bunking down wherever he could find a kind soul who would take pity on his homeless state and give him a hot meal and a place to stay for the night.

He hadn't stayed overnight in a town since he'd got away from the BRI, and he'd begun to wonder if he ever would again.

"Can't linger." That was Sutton Calhoun's voice, gentle but firm in his ear as he nudged Landry forward. "We're almost home."

"Home," it turned out, was a deceptively shabby-looking mansion on a large, tree-shaded corner lot near the center of town. An engraved plaque near the large iron gates read "Buckley Mansion, est. 1895." A smaller, less ostentatious sign on the gates themselves, however, proclaimed that they'd arrived at The Gates.

"Why The Gates?" Landry asked Olivia as they entered through the iron portal and started up the snowy walk.

"I'm not sure," Olivia admitted.

"The gate of purgatory," Dennison offered as he passed them on the way to the front porch. "Though some of us think it's the gates of hell instead. Occasionally."

It looked like heaven to Landry, welcoming lights glowing warm in the windows, though when they walked inside, the front lobby was empty. But there was light and blessed heat, and an instant sense of safety, however transitory it might prove to be. The temptation to relax his guard was almost more than Landry could resist.

"Who else is here?" Olivia asked.

"Rigsby's here," Dennison drawled. "You know Darcy— never leaves home without her. Brand is up with Quinn at his office."

"Delilah's working the storm shift?" Olivia asked.

"Along with Sara and Ivy."

"Sara's Dennison's wife—Ridge County sheriff's deputy," Olivia told Landry. "Delilah and Ivy are married to Brand and Calhoun, respectively."

"They're both local cops over in Bitterwood."

"Y'all have some sort of law-enforcement dating service going on the side?" Landry asked softly as Olivia led him to the winding stairway leading to the second floor while the other men headed out of sight, shedding their outerwear as they went.

She smiled. "Easier to date someone who gets your crazy hours. You should know that better than anyone."

He did. Of course, he and Olivia had shared most of those crazy work hours, which could have been a problem, he supposed. But somehow it never had been. Work was one part of their shared lives that had never been an issue.

Until Richmond.

He put the dark memories out of his head and followed Olivia down a dimly lit hallway to a room at the eastern corner of the house. She gave a soft knock but didn't wait for a reply before she entered.

A sandy-haired man in his forties sat behind a large oak desk, leaning back in his chair with his hands steepled over his chest. He looked up, unsurprised. "You're an hour later than I expected."

Olivia sighed. "We ran into a couple of BRI boys. Slowed us down."

"Everybody unscathed?"

"I'm sure Sutton or someone on the team has already texted you the details," she drawled, nodding at the other man in the room, a tall, dark-haired man with blue eyes who had turned at the opening of the door. "Brand."

Landry froze. "You're Adam Brand."

Brand's dark eyebrows lifted. "And you're Cade Landry."

"You were on the FBI's naughty list, too."

"I was," Brand said with a nod and a faint whisper of a smile. "Unfairly in my case. What about yours?"

The smile hadn't disappeared, but the room felt instantly colder and less hospitable.

"Definitely unfair in my case," he said firmly. "All the way around, as a matter of fact."

"So we've concluded," Quinn said mildly, waving at the empty chair beside Olivia. "Sit. You must be exhausted."

Landry wished he could make a stand, but his aching legs told him to stop being a stubborn fool. He sank gratefully into the armchair, turning so he could keep both Quinn and Brand in sight.

"We know Darryl Boyle was working with the BRI. We have no reason to think you were, despite your unexplained disappearance. Would you like to explain it?"

Landry glanced at Olivia. "Not at this time."

"Understandable. There's hot food in the kitchen downstairs, and you'd probably like to take advantage of indoor plumbing about now. Sharp can show you where everything is."

"That's it?" Landry asked.

Quinn's sandy eyebrows lifted a notch. "Did you expect something else?"

"You're an ex-spook. I guess I anticipated some sort of enhanced interrogation techniques."

"You've already been through enough of those. Haven't you?" The gentleness of Quinn's tone caught Landry off guard. Apparently, it came as a surprise to Olivia, as well; she stared at her boss with a look of confusion.

"Go get settled. Get warm. Eat some food, drink some water and then get some sleep. We'll all still be here in the morning. Maybe you'll feel more like talking then."

Olivia rose first, heading for the door in stony silence. Landry followed her out, catching up with her halfway to the stairs.

She turned to look at him, her eyes snapping with anger. "That bastard's trying to play you."

Landry nodded. "Yeah, I know. We used to interrogate suspects, too, remember?"

She let out a long, slow breath, visibly trying to relax. "I know. And I know he needs the information. Hell, I still don't know everything that happened to you, either. And I'd like to."

He shook his head. "No, you wouldn't."

She put her hand on his arm, her fingers still icy from the hike in the snow. "I need to know. So when you're ready—"

He covered her hand with his for a moment then gently pulled her hand away, taking a step back from her. "I'm not sure I'll ever be ready, Olivia. Can you deal with that?"

She gazed up at him, her blue eyes troubled. "Can you?"

He nodded toward the stairs. "Quinn said something about food and water?"

She pressed her lips to a thin line. "Yeah. Follow me."

She headed down the hallway toward the staircase, her spine rigid with annoyance. He couldn't hold back a smile at the sight of a pissed-off Olivia Sharp stalking ahead of him like a lioness on the hunt.

He'd missed the hell out of this woman.

OLIVIA WAS FINALLY, blessedly warm. A hot meal, a long, steamy shower and the marvel of central heating had managed to drive away the last of her chills and leave her feeling toasty and half-asleep.

In fact, she must have dozed off for a few moments, for when the soft knock at her dormitory door jarred her awake, the shock left her nerves jangling and her head buzzing.

"Olivia?" Landry spoke quietly from the other side of the door.

She pushed herself to a sitting position on the bed. "Come in."

He slipped inside, stopping just inside the room. "I'm sorry. Did I wake you?"

She resisted the urge to rub her gritty eyes. "No. I'm up. For now."

He walked a few steps closer, flashing a lopsided smile. "Same here. I just wanted to check on you. It was a long hike."

"I'm fine." She patted the edge of the bed. "Sit."

He sat, turning to face her. "I know I gave you a hard time, but thank you for making me come down here. I guess over the past year, I forgot I don't always have to be an army of one."

She'd had to learn the same lesson, she realized. Especially since she'd come to The Gates specifically to investigate a few of her fellow agents suspected of being the source of the devastating information leaks that had put people's lives at risk.

"The people who work here are rough around the edges, but they're good agents. And we really do have each other's back. Quinn wouldn't have it any other way."

"I'm still not sure I like him. I know I don't trust him."

She couldn't blame him for that. "I don't trust him to pick me over the mission. But I trust his passion for protecting this country and its people."

"But you're a security and investigations company. Not a branch of the military."

"And yet, we stand in the breach. There are a lot of people in these hills who just want to live a decent life without fear. And there are a lot of people in these same hills who prey on those good people because they can. Because they're ruthless and better armed."

He flashed her a bemused smile, triggering the dimples that knocked a decade off his age and made her insides twist with desire. "Still protecting and serving, huh? Without all the bureaucratic crap that used to make you nuts."

"It's not all small-scale like trying to take down the BRI. We have some big clients who pay a lot for our training and expertise. It's just—taking down the BRI is Quinn's passion right now."

"Why's that?"

She shrugged, realizing she'd never bothered to ask the question of her wily boss. "I guess maybe it has something to do with his having grown up in these hills. I don't know. Maybe he knows what it's like to be a victim of the predators."

"Or he was a predator himself," Landry murmured. "And maybe he wants to make up for it."

Olivia looked at her former partner through narrowed eyes. She hadn't ever considered the possibility that Quinn had once been one of the human vipers who stalked the Appalachian Mountains. "I don't know. Maybe you're right."

Landry reached across the narrow space between them, taking her hand. "It doesn't matter what inspired him, I guess. We all have mistakes in our pasts we can't correct. At least he's trying to make things better around here instead of worse."

The feel of his rough palm against hers felt right, she realized, dropping her gaze to their joined hands. She'd missed him so intensely over the past two years that having him here, touching him and hearing him speak in that deep Georgia drawl she'd always loved, seemed like a dream she'd wake from any moment.

"Are you really here?" she asked, feeling immediately foolish.

He smiled at her again, making her heart skip a beat. "Feels a little unreal, doesn't it?"

She nodded. "I didn't think I'd ever see you again."

He lifted her hand to his mouth, brushing her knuckles with his lips. "I used to have dreams of you. That you were beside me again. Nothing big. Just beside me, sitting close enough that I could feel the warmth of your body by mine. Hear your breathing. And then I'd wake up." He let go of her hand and dropped his own hands to his knees. "Doesn't matter. Here you are. Warm and breathing."

"Are you never going to tell me what happened to you when you were taken captive?"

"It's not important."

"I can tell it's still important to *you*."

"I'm okay." He flashed another smile, but even the distracting dimples couldn't make it look anything but forced.

But she didn't want to push him. If he needed to talk about what he'd gone through, he'd do it in his own time.

She hoped.

"I don't want to keep you up if you're tired." He started to get up.

She caught his hand, holding him in place. "Don't go."

He looked down at her hand on his. When he spoke, his voice was a low rasp. "Are you sure you want me to stay?"

She knew what he was asking.

"Yes."

He sat in front of her again, closer this time. He turned his hand until it was palm to palm with hers, their fingers twining. "I like your hair short."

She laughed at the non sequitur. "I like yours longer."

He grinned again, the expression deliciously sincere. "Couldn't find many barbershops out in the wilderness."

"That's where you've been all this time?"

"Most of it." He took her other hand, twined his fingers with hers.

"Where did you stay?"

"Camped out a lot. Stayed at cheap roadside motels now and then, when I could spare a little cash."

"How'd you get any cash?" She leaned closer, letting the warmth of his nearness envelop her. "Did you steal?"

"Define *steal*." He grinned at her frown. "I might have eaten a crab apple off someone's tree now and then. But mostly I used money I'd stashed away in case of emergency."

She rubbed the back of his hand with her thumb. "You were expecting an emergency?"

"*Expecting* might be too strong a word. I just anticipated the possibility. And tried to prepare for the worst-case scenario."

"And was what happened the worst case?" She looked up at him.

"Not the worst."

"But bad enough."

He gave her hands a squeeze. "Let it go for now, Livvie. Okay?"

She would have liked to argue, but she didn't want to risk making him get up and leave. "Okay."

"Thank you."

"For now," she added.

He smiled again. "Yeah, I know you don't give up. You're like a bulldog with a chew toy."

"Flattering."

"A beautiful bulldog. A svelte bulldog."

"I think that's an oxymoron."

"Who're you calling an oxymoron?"

She laughed. "I missed this."

"Talking nonsense?"

She stroked his hand again. "Talking nonsense with you."

"Know what I missed?" His voice deepened. Roughened.

Her heartbeat sped up immediately in response. When she spoke, her own voice sounded breathless. "What?"

"This." He leaned forward, closing the space between them, and touched his mouth to hers.

Chapter Ten

When they'd been lovers, there had been passion. Tenderness. Laughter. Even sometimes anger. But never, ever this tentative, questing sensation, like two strangers coming together for a stolen kiss.

Landry drew back and studied her face, trying to read the nuances of each expression flitting across her features as her gaze met his with the same quizzical alertness.

"You're different, aren't you?"

He nodded. "So are you."

"But I still want you." Her raw admission sent a blazing arrow of desire shooting straight to his core. "I just don't know—"

He curled his hand around the back of her neck and gently pulled her into an undemanding embrace, struggling to dial back his body's physical response to her touch. He wanted to reconnect to her, as the friends they'd always been, even if they couldn't be lovers again. Rushing into something they'd regret was a bad idea.

"That feels good," she said as he stroked his hand lightly up and down her spine.

"I don't want to lose you again." He brushed his cheek against her temple, starting to enjoy the exquisite tension of holding her close without any intention of taking things any further. "We were friends first, and I'd like to be friends again."

She lifted her hands, cradling his face between her palms. "I'd like that, too, but—" Her words cut off with a little huff, and she bent toward him, covering his mouth with hers.

There was no hesitation in her kiss. No tentativeness. Just a slow, thorough taking that made his head spin and his heartbeat crank up to hyperspeed. Any thought of differences, of unfamiliarity, were swallowed up by the rising heat between them.

This. He wanted this.

He wanted *her*. Right now, just as she was.

She tugged him down to the bed, parting her thighs to let him settle on top of her. One long leg wrapped around his legs, pinning him to her.

"Don't think," she breathed against his lips.

Threading his fingers through her hair, he deepened the kiss, tasting the minty hint of toothpaste on her tongue. She curled her fingers in his T-shirt and tugged the fabric upward, grumbling when he pulled away from the kiss long enough to whip the shirt over his head.

As he bent to kiss her again, she splayed her fingers against his chest, running them through the coarse hair. She hadn't forgotten how much he liked her hands on him, tracing, teasing, arousing—

A hard rap on the door sent a ripple of raw shock through his nervous system. Olivia growled a soft profanity against his throat and dropped her head back to the pillows.

"What?" she barked toward the closed door.

"Quinn wants to see Landry." Seth's quiet drawl held a touch of amusement, as if he knew exactly what he was interrupting.

"Tell him I'm not his employee, and I'll talk to him in

the morning." Landry glanced at Olivia, who was watching him through slightly narrowed eyes. "What?" he added more quietly.

"It's possible he has information you might need," she said in an equally hushed tone.

"It's possible I need a cold shower before I can appear anywhere outside this room," he growled, rolling up to a sitting position and leaning forward in an attempt to get his body back under control.

"I'll go stall Hammond, see if I can find out more about what Quinn wants." She stood and unhurriedly straightened her clothes. Landry watched her smooth the fabric he'd held bunched in his hands mere moments earlier, his heart still pounding a steady cadence of lust.

"Maybe if we hurry——"

Smiling, she bent and kissed him, a slow, wet, deep kiss that made his blood ignite. "Stay put. I'll be back."

As he retrieved his discarded T-shirt, he tried to make out the muted conversation Olivia was having with Seth Hammond outside, but they'd apparently moved too far away from the door. He gave himself a quick once-over and realized she'd managed to unbutton his jeans and get the zipper halfway down without his realizing it. Talented girl!

He zipped up and finger-combed his hair, wishing the dorm rooms in the basement of The Gates had come equipped with a mirror. He didn't need to show up at his command performance with Alexander Quinn looking as if a tall, blonde bombshell had just tried to have her way with him.

Even if she had.

The door opened suddenly and Olivia slipped inside, her expression serious.

"What is it?" he asked.

"An agent has gone missing. Grant Carver. Quinn thinks the BRI have taken him hostage."

A chill washed over Landry, despite the cozy warmth of the room. "When?"

"Sometime this afternoon. His wife called Quinn when he didn't come back from a quick run."

"Couldn't he have just gotten stranded somewhere?"

"That was the assumption. Until she followed his tracks and came upon a patch of snow that looked as if there'd been a struggle. Carver's hat was in the snow. So was an alarming amount of blood. She called the local cops. One of the cops who took the call was Dennison's wife, Sara. She called Dennison to let him know."

Landry sank to the end of the bed, feeling sick. "Any reason why the BRI would go after this guy Carver? Has he had run-ins with any of them?"

Olivia sat next to him, close enough to touch. But he kept his hands on his knees, too wound up to trust himself to touch her. There was a lot about his time in BRI captivity he hadn't told her. Things that he didn't like to think about, things that showed up in his nightmares all too often recently.

"Quinn asked Carver's wife that question. She said no. Some of her distant relatives are involved with the local BRI cell, and she thought that was probably why they could live where they do without too many troubles with the militia members."

"Live where they do?"

She turned to look at him. "They live on the bottom slope of Fowler Ridge. Near that BRI enclave we hiked through today."

"You said it happened this afternoon?" Landry's tone was neutral, but his expressive eyes gave away the emotions roiling behind his mask of calm—anger, worry and guilt Olivia had expected, given the possibility that the mountain rescue The Gates agents had pulled off earlier that day might well have led to the BRI's retaliatory attack on one of the company's agents.

But the fear that roiled behind his green-eyed gaze caught her by surprise.

Landry was afraid. And in all the time she'd known him, she'd rarely seen him afraid of anything.

"If you're wondering if it's connected to you, we don't know." Quinn spoke in a calm tone that didn't manage to hide the fact that he believed Landry's presence in their midst might have precipitated Carver's abduction.

"You know," Landry growled, "I should get out of here. All I'm doing is making things that much harder for you."

Quinn shook his head. "We don't negotiate with terrorists. We certainly don't hand over innocent people to them to get our agents back. Carver knew what he signed on for."

"Carver has a wife. A family." Landry glanced at Olivia.

She'd told him about Carver's pregnant wife and two kids because he'd asked, and she wasn't going to lie to him, even to protect his feelings.

"Nobody has come to us with any demands," Adam Brand said from his seat next to Quinn at the conference table. Besides Landry and herself, there were nine agents seated at the long oak table—Adam Brand and Sutton Calhoun at the head with Quinn, Mark Fitzpatrick, Cain Dennison, Kyle Jackson, Nick Darcy, McKenna Rigsby and Caleb Cooper. All good men in a nasty fight—Brand and Rigsby were former FBI agents, while Calhoun, Dennison, Jackson and Fitzpatrick had all been in the military. Darcy had been with the Diplomatic Security Service for several years, Caleb Cooper had been a narcotics cop in Birmingham, Alabama, and Quinn had been in more dangerous hot spots around the globe than any of them, and he'd lived to tell.

Landry could do a lot worse for backup. But Olivia had

a feeling it wasn't the quality of people willing to watch his back that was fueling his fear.

She'd seen the same look in his eyes up on the mountain just before the guys from The Gates had shown up to run off their assailants. It had started when that man from the BRI had spoken.

Had Landry recognized the voice?

"Let's just sit tight for now. The local law is out looking for Carver. Let's let them do their jobs," Quinn suggested.

"Do you have any idea what kind of things they might do to him?" Landry's voice came out in a strangled growl. Olivia put her hand on his arm but he shrugged away her touch.

Quinn nodded. "We have some idea, yes."

"If he's not leverage—"

"There's a limited amount of information Carver could share with the BRI," Quinn said calmly. "Because of his familial connection to the group, we've kept him away from cases involving the militia group. I'm sure they know that."

"So he *is* leverage."

"Possibly. But there's nothing we can do about it at the moment, so I'd concentrate on something else." Quinn's gaze settled on Landry. "Calhoun says you reacted strongly this afternoon on the mountain, when one of the men who challenged you spoke. You had your back to him, so you must have recognized the voice?"

Landry looked reluctant to speak, but after a moment he nodded. "I think I did."

"Do you know who he was?" Quinn asked.

Olivia could tell from Quinn's tone that he already knew exactly who had accosted them on the mountain earlier that day. He just wanted to establish whether Landry knew.

"I don't know the man's name," Landry answered, looking down at his hands twisting together in his lap. He pulled them apart and gripped the arms of his chair. "I couldn't tell you what he looked like, either. But I'd know that voice in a noisy crowd."

"He was one of your captors?" Olivia asked quietly.

His gaze snapped up to meet hers, full of anger and no small measure of humiliation. "One of them. The worst of them."

"I realize you probably would prefer not to remember what happened during your time in captivity—" Quinn began.

Landry cut him off. "If you're thinking of hooking me up with a shrink or hypnotist or whatever you spook types like to use to poke around in a person's brain, forget it. I don't remember anything that could help you find your missing man. When I got away, I just ran as far and as fast as I could. I'm sure they've already moved operations somewhere else. They moved me around a lot before I got away, so I don't think they have a permanent base for their snatch-and-grab operations."

"Fair enough. Meeting adjourned." Quinn stood, the look he gave the other men sitting around the table serving as a silent warning—Cade Landry was off-limits, for the time being, anyway.

Olivia could tell most of the other agents weren't happy about their boss playing softball with Landry, but they knew better than to voice their dissent at the conference table. They could take it up with him privately later—and from the displeasure in their expressions, Olivia was pretty sure that at least two or three of them would.

But for now, she and Landry were free to go.

"I need to get out of here," Landry murmured as he caught up with her down the hall. "I should never have tried to play this straight. Those bastards don't know the meaning of playing it straight."

She caught his arm as he started toward the stairs. "You're not leaving."

"I'm not staying."

"You know what the conditions out there are like. It's only going to get colder now that the sun has set."

"How cold do you think Grant Carver is right now?" His voice lowered to a deep growl. "Do you have a clue what they might be doing to him?"

"Yes," she answered tightly. "I do have an idea. Maybe you should go compare notes with one of our agents, Hunter Bragg. The BRI took him hostage last year. He has the scars to prove it."

Landry looked away from her, his expression queasy. "They're relentless. They're not really any good at interrogations. They don't know how to play the game, how to get any real information. They just do it because they're sadistic bastards who get off on the feeling of power it gives them to make a grown man scream." He tugged his arm away from her grasp and started down the stairs.

She ran down the steps after him, tripping in her hurry to keep up. He caught her before she tumbled, pulling her tightly against him. A jolt of pure animal awareness bolted through her from the point where her hips met his, and she dug her fingers into the muscles of his upper arms.

"Don't go," she whispered.

"I can't stay."

"You can. At least tonight. Stay tonight."

He looked away from her, his gaze scanning the room before it returned to lock with hers. "You know we can't pick up where we left off."

"You mean you don't want to."

For a second his expression softened, and he looked like the man she used to know, the man who had loved her and made her as happy as she could ever remember being.

"You know I do."

"Then stay. We don't have to pick up where we left off, but please, don't go away again. Not yet, not while you're in trouble. Let me help you."

He brushed her hair back from her cheek, his touch so impossibly tender it made tears sting her eyes. She blinked them back, not willing to let them fall. "I don't know if you can. I don't know if it's fixable."

"Then you can just get some rest. Most of the guys will be up all night trying to piece together what happened to Carver and how we proceed at daylight. We should get some sleep so we can spell them in the morning."

"We?" He tugged lightly at her hair.

"You used to be a damn good FBI agent. I don't think you've forgotten everything you learned at the academy, have you?"

"Trying to bend me to your will by dangling a mystery in front of me?"

"Is it working?"

"Maybe." He bent toward her until his forehead touched hers. "You win. I'll stay. For now."

She gave his arms a squeeze. "Come on. Let's get some sleep. Tomorrow's going to be a long day."

He didn't resist as she led him back down to the basement dormitory rooms, stopping outside the door of her room. "As tempting as it is to go back in there with you…"

She smiled. "The goal is sleep?"

He nodded toward the room across from hers, where he'd stashed his own things. "I'll be there in the morning. I promise."

She pressed her hand to the front of his shirt, feeling the reassuring thud of his heartbeat against her palm. "If you aren't, I'm hunting you down."

He sneaked a quick look around, as if reassuring himself they were alone, then bent and gave her a quick kiss. "Get some sleep."

She waited in her doorway until he entered his own room and closed the door behind him, then turned and entered her own dorm room, flicking on the light.

The bed was the way she'd left it, slightly rumpled and full of recent memories of Landry—the way he smelled, the sensation of his hands on her bare skin, the electric thrill of their bodies pressed close and straining for more. She closed her eyes and sank on the edge of the bed, swamped by memories. Of their first meeting, the literal electric shock that passed between them as they shook hands, making them laugh and snatch their hands away.

The more visceral shock of desire the first time they'd taken a step past the slow burn of attraction and kissed at the end of a long day at work.

She lay back on the bed, opening her eyes to stare at the ceiling. They hadn't planned to start a relationship. For weeks, even months, they pretended what was happening between them was just chemical. Two people enjoying each other, no strings attached.

But there had been strings. Probably from the beginning. Despite her tumultuous childhood with a promiscuous and reckless mother, despite his parents' distant, businesslike marriage, somehow, they'd been foolish enough to believe in the possibility of forever.

And then the bombing at the warehouse in Richmond had blown everything apart.

The tears she'd been fighting earlier leaked from her eyes and slid down her cheeks. She brushed them away, angry at the sign of weakness and glad that Landry wasn't here to see it.

She couldn't start thinking about forever again. She just had to focus on getting through one day at a time. She had to figure out a way to get Landry out of the mess he was in. Give him back the life that the BRI had stolen from him when he'd ended up their captive.

Then maybe she'd figure out how to say a proper goodbye this time.

HE'D ARRIVED AT his apartment after midnight, the metallic taste of fear in his mouth and his mind reeling with questions he didn't know how to answer. He'd tried to help Agent Rigsby, hadn't he? It had been a risk to try to call her and warn her that someone else from the FBI was coming after her.

But before he'd hung up the phone with Darryl Boyle, supervisory special agent with the FBI's Knoxville field office, he'd known McKenna Rigsby was in big trouble.

Boyle was railroading her. The man had said nothing incriminating, but Landry had heard the flicker of eagerness in his voice when he told Landry Rigsby had called him, as well.

He was going after her. And he had no intention of bringing her back alive.

Landry had tried to help her, but he couldn't reach her before Boyle did. He wasn't even sure where she'd be—she'd set a trap, hoping to ensnare the person who had tried to kill her before, and she might not have been in either of the two locations where she'd told him and Boyle she'd be.

He'd just hoped she'd got away. He'd done all he dared. He had his own trouble with the FBI, with a career that was already on life support. He couldn't risk sticking his neck out, in case he was wrong about Boyle.

What a coward he'd been.

When the four men materialized out of the shadows of his living room, he'd been unprepared for a fight. They took him down with ease, binding him with duct tape and hustling him out to a van he hadn't noticed parked outside his unit.

That had been the beginning of his trip to hell.

Chapter Eleven

Olivia woke to darkness and a gnawing sense of unease she couldn't place. She knew she was in one of the dorm rooms in the basement of the old Buckley Mansion that Alexander Quinn had transformed into The Gates. She hadn't been awakened by a sudden noise or an unexpected touch in the night. She'd just gone from sleep to animal awareness in one fluid motion, without any idea why all of her senses were suddenly tingling.

She listened to the darkness, waiting for some noise, some sensation to remind her what had summoned her from sleep, but there was nothing but the languid silence of a mostly unoccupied space. Down here, in the rooms built out of the mansion's stone foundation, even the creaks and groans of the old house settling rarely penetrated this quiet sanctuary.

Maybe one of the other agents had come down to catch some sleep before morning, she thought, pushing off the covers and swinging her feet down to the cold floor. Shivering, she felt around for the slip-on shoes she'd retrieved from her desk in the agents' bull pen and slid them on her feet.

She padded to the door, stopping to listen before she opened it and stepped outside into the dimly lit main room. The basement dormitory consisted of one long, wide corridor with six small bedrooms branching off on either side, three to the right and three to the left. There was a large bathroom at the end of the hall. That door was open, as were four of the other doors in the dorm.

Only Landry's door remained closed. Apparently, all of the other agents remaining on the premises were still upstairs with Quinn.

She crossed the hallway and pressed her ear to the closed door, wondering if she'd heard noises coming from the room across the hall. But she could hear nothing from inside, except a faint creaking noise that might have been the bedsprings shifting under Landry's weight.

Or was she simply imagining that she could hear sounds of occupation, because the alternative—the possibility that what had jarred her awake had been Landry sneaking out of the dorm—was something she didn't want to believe?

Just open the door, her anxiety whispered in her ear. *Open it and you'll know if he bugged out on you.*

She turned the door handle, half expecting it to be locked. But it moved easily in her grasp, the door swinging quietly inward.

Landry was there, still in the bed. The creaking noise she'd heard repeated twice, louder now.

He was moving in his sleep, jerky twitches rather than thrashing that might hint at a violent nightmare. But the light angling through the open doorway fell on his face, revealing an expression that was nothing short of terror.

Landry jerked up to a sitting position so suddenly, she couldn't hold back a gasp of surprise. Her hand flexed, rattling the doorknob, and his gaze whipped up to meet hers.

"I'm sorry," she breathed. "I didn't mean—"

He pulled his knees up under the twisted sheets and rested his elbows on them, pressing his face into his hands for a long moment. The muscles in his back flexed, revealing pale streaks she hadn't seen before.

She reached for the switch on the wall and flooded the room with light.

Landry squinted up at her. "What the hell?"

"What are those?" she asked, crossing to the bed to get a better look at the pale scars marring his back. "Oh, my God. What happened to you?"

He looked away from her. "The Blue Ridge Infantry happened."

She touched one of the pale scars. He flinched and she pulled her hand back quickly. "They beat you."

"You didn't think it was a trip to the beach, did you?"

"What did they hit you with?" She tried to school her expression, to approach the question without emotion. She'd seen terrible things as an FBI agent and also working at The Gates. She'd seen some of the worst things people could do to their fellow human beings, and she'd always thought herself to be stoic and controlled.

But the thought of someone wielding a whip or a stick or whatever had made these scars—

"They're healed. They don't matter." He reached over and picked up his discarded T-shirt, pulling it over his head. "You should be trying to get some sleep."

"I was. Something woke me."

He frowned. "You think you heard something?"

"I'm not sure." She sank onto the side of his bed. "I guess maybe I'm still on edge."

"I can't imagine why," he murmured in a dry tone.

She managed a smile. "Are you sure you're okay? You were tossing and turning when I came in."

"Unfamiliar bed."

"Yeah." She plucked at the bedsheets. "You haven't really

had a chance to talk to anybody about what the BRI put you through, have you?"

"Couldn't exactly go into therapy while I was running for my life."

"You know it's not healthy to try to bury a traumatic experience."

He laughed softly. "I seem to remember a beautiful, hard-headed FBI agent who chafed at the idea of post-operation counseling."

"And that same agent didn't cope very well after Richmond, remember? I lost so much after what happened at the warehouse. I lost myself." She blinked back the rush of hot tears burning her eyes. "I lost you."

He looked up at her, his green eyes glistening with pain. "You really think post-trauma counseling would have saved us?"

"I don't know." She shook her head, feeling suddenly helpless. "I just wish we'd fought harder. I wish we'd valued our relationship more."

"You think I threw it away, don't you?" His lips thinned to a hard line. "You think I pushed you away."

"I used to." She rubbed away a tear that trickled from the corner of her eye. "But I pushed you away, too. I knew you were angry with me. I should have worked harder to be certain I understood why. Maybe if I'd tried, you'd have confronted me after what the debriefing team told you about my statement, and I could have assured you they were lying."

"I'm not sure I'd have believed you," he admitted, looking away.

"I'd have made you believe me."

"You shouldn't have had to make me believe you. I should have believed you because of who you were. What you were to me."

His use of the past tense made her stomach ache. "You never could. Could you?"

The sadness in his eyes hurt her heart. "I wanted to." He shook his head. "I guess I was so used to lies spoken as casually as small talk. There were so many things I wanted desperately as a kid to believe. Promises my parents made that they never kept." He laughed bleakly. "You'd think all those years later, I could have just let it go. They never really wanted kids, and when they had one by accident, they figured out a way to go on with their lives as if I had never happened. It had nothing to do with me. Not really. I didn't matter enough for it to be about me."

Growing up poor with a flighty, promiscuous mother, Olivia had pictured the lives of wealthy people as a utopian promised land, where every child had two parents, all they wanted to eat, all the clothes they wanted to wear and every luxury she could imagine.

She'd never realized there were privations that money couldn't alleviate, until she'd met Cade Landry.

"I guess you haven't spoken with your parents since you went missing?" she asked.

"I don't imagine they care."

She shook her head. His parents had done one hell of a number on him with their casual, thoughtless neglect. "What about Mary? Does she know you're still alive?"

He shook his head. "Mary's safer thinking I'm dead."

"You don't think the BRI's reach goes all the way to Savannah, do you?"

"No point in risking it." He shrugged. "Mary's got a new batch of kids to raise. Did you know that? Last time I talked to her, she was working for a lawyer and his wife. Seem like nice people, from what she said. And the kids are stinking cute. She emailed me photos from Christmas a year ago."

His nanny, Mary Allen, had been the closest thing he'd had to a parent growing up. She'd been only twenty years old when his parents had hired her, shortly after Landry's birth, and she'd given him the attention his parents had withheld.

But even she had kept a certain distance, emotionally. Or tried to, Olivia supposed, thinking of a few things Landry had let slip about his relationship with his nanny. Mary had seemed determined to give Landry's parents every chance to be what he needed them to be. She hadn't wanted him to replace his parents with her.

Olivia had met Mary once, on a weekend trip to Savannah early in her relationship with Landry. She'd been a trim, pretty woman with curly brown hair liberally streaked with gray and kind blue eyes that had made Olivia instantly wish she'd had a Mary Allen in her own life growing up.

"I've had a lot of time to think. To navel-gaze, I think was how you used to put it." Landry slanted a lopsided smile at her. "I do wish you'd come to me and told me the truth. I don't know if I'd have believed you right away, but in time, I think I would have."

An ache of regret throbbed in her chest. "You think so, do you?"

"You probably wouldn't have forgiven me for doubting you, so I'm not sure it would have solved anything," he admitted. "But it would have been comforting anyway. Knowing you didn't think I was lying about the order to go into the warehouse."

She turned to face him, catching his hands in hers. "I never once believed you were lying about that. Not once. No matter what other trust issues I had, I never doubted you were a good FBI agent. You didn't ignore orders on a whim, and you didn't put people's lives in danger for selfish reasons. I know you wanted to stop those guys. I did, too. But I wouldn't have defied orders and blundered into that warehouse just because I was eager to make an arrest. And neither would you."

His eyes narrowed briefly. "You mean that, don't you?"

"I do."

He blinked rapidly, and she didn't miss the hint of moisture in his eyes as he looked down at their clasped hands. "Thank you."

"I know a lot has happened since Richmond. I know we can't go back to what we had then. I don't really want to."

He let go of her hands. "Yeah, a whole lot of water under that bridge."

She took his hands again, giving them a sharp tug to make him look at her. "It wasn't enough then. Not for either one of us. It's not something we should aspire to now."

His eyes narrowed. "Aspire to?"

"I don't want to live this way anymore. I want more than half a relationship. I want to be able to trust someone else. I want someone else to be able to trust me, too."

He nodded. "I get that."

"Maybe that person will never be you. That's something you're going to have to figure out. I just know that as much as I loved you then, it wasn't enough. It would never have been enough, not the way it was. Not with everything we held back."

He released a huff of air. "Yeah. You're right. It wouldn't have been."

She let his hands go and stood up. "I'm going back to my room now. You try to get some sleep. And if you need me, you know where to find me."

It took strength to walk out of his room and not look back, but she made herself do it. Made herself walk across the wide corridor, enter her dorm room and close the door behind her.

And if she cried herself to sleep, it was nobody's business but her own.

"We STOCKED UP for the snowstorm," Mark Fitzpatrick told Landry as he passed him a plate of eggs, bacon and toast, steaming hot from the stove.

"Did you buy up all the milk and bread?" Landry asked with a smile, knowing that a fellow Southerner would get the joke.

"What was left." Fitz grinned. "Don't you wonder why people don't make a run on charcoal and grills instead when snow is forecast? Seems those things would be more useful."

Landry joined the other agents who'd gathered at the conference table for breakfast. Their numbers had expanded, he noted. There was a small, dark-haired woman sitting next to Sutton Calhoun, and across from her, a taller brunette had joined Adam Brand and Alexander Quinn, her head close to theirs in conversation.

"Ivy Calhoun and Delilah Brand," Olivia told him as he settled beside her at the table. "They're both cops in Bitterwood. They worked the overnight shift as part of the department's snow contingency plan or something."

"And there's another guy's wife who's a cop, too, right? You said she was called out on Grant Carver's disappearance?"

"Right. Sara Dennison. Dennison headed out last night to meet up with her and see if she could tell us any more about the investigation. I guess they haven't made it back here yet."

Two more people came into the conference room, still dressed in heavy clothing and red-cheeked from the cold outside. One was a tall, rawboned man in his midthirties with wavy brown hair and dark eyes, while the woman beside him was petite, blonde and sweet-faced. They both gave Landry a curious glance.

Then the man did a double take. "Cade Landry."

Landry sighed. He'd spent the past few months trying to look as different from his FBI photo as he could, but apparently there were some things a man couldn't change about himself.

"Landry, this is Anson Daughtry, our IT director, and his wife, Ginny, one of our accountants." Olivia gave Anson and Ginny a pointed look. "Who're both supposed to be somewhere sunny on their honeymoon."

"And miss the fun? Who do you think we are?" Daughtry set down their plates of food and pulled out a chair for his wife before settling across from Landry and Olivia. "We just walked in—anything new on Carver?"

"Not that we've heard," Olivia answered.

Daughtry gave Landry a curious look. "I heard you'd shown up, but I thought you two were stuck in your cabin."

"You knew I was at her cabin?"

"He was the one I had monitoring that bank account in Barrowville," Olivia murmured.

"I see." He arched an eyebrow at Daughtry. "And from that, you figured out who I was and where I was?"

"Well, we knew you had once had a relationship with Bombshell Barb—" Daughtry's mouth snapped shut, and Landry saw Ginny dig an elbow into her husband's ribs. "We knew you were once involved with Agent Sharp, so when the bank activity showed up—"

Landry lowered his voice. "Your boss likes to stay on top of what's going on in all his agents' lives, doesn't he?"

Daughtry rolled his eyes. "You have no idea, man."

At the head of the table, Quinn's cell phone trilled. He answered it with a brief "Hello" and just listened for a moment. "Okay, thanks."

The room had grown quiet, all eyes turned to their boss.

"That was Dennison. A call came in to Sara's radio while they were checking in on his grandmother. Patrol officers just got a call about a body found in the snow about a mile south of Fowler Ridge."

Brand was the first to ask the obvious question. "Carver?"

"We're not sure. Dennison's heading over there with Sara to take a look." Quinn's gaze landed on Mark Fitzpatrick. "You know Carver's wife pretty well, don't you?"

Fitz nodded. "Lexie and I went to high school with her. You want me to go wait with her in case we get bad news?"

Pressure built inside Landry's chest and swelled upward, making his head pound. He had to get out of this room, out of this building.

He had to get as far away from these people as he could, before anyone else got hurt.

He was on his feet and halfway out the door before anyone else reacted. He heard Quinn call his name, heard the scrape of chair legs on the floor as he swept through the door and down the hall.

Footsteps padded after him, hurrying to catch up as he reached the stairs. Olivia's voice rang out behind him. "This is not your fault."

He turned swiftly to look at her. "You're trying to tell me you honestly think the BRI would have taken your colleague if I hadn't shown up at your cabin two days ago like a stupid fool?" He felt sick, the half a plate of bacon and eggs he'd eaten heavy in his gut. "I knew there was a risk. I knew it. I just thought I would be the only one who would suffer if it all went wrong. I should have known better."

"You don't know this had anything to do with you."

"Of course I do. That man on the mountain—he knew exactly who I was! I could tell from the tone of his voice."

"Just because you recognized his voice doesn't mean he recognized you."

"Then why, after all this time of your friend Carver living safely on that mountain, did he get grabbed the very same day that bastard ran into us on the mountain? Can you answer me that?" Agitation rose like bile in his throat, spurring him into motion again. He started down the stairs at a reckless pace, two steps at a time, and bolted toward the front door.

Olivia raced down after him, grabbing him as he reached for the handle. "Damn it, no! Don't you dare walk out on me again! Not like this."

"It could have been you, Livvie." He turned to look at her, his heart contracting at the concern that darkened her blue eyes. "You could be that body they found in the snow. I never should have come here. I never should have brought this nightmare to your doorstep."

"It's not Carver." Alexander Quinn's voice rang in the foyer, making them both turn to look at him. He walked unhurriedly down the stairs toward them, coming to a stop a few feet away.

"Dennison called back?" Olivia asked, sounding relieved.

"Yes. Halfway to the site, they got a call from the patrolman on the scene. The body had ID on it. Driver's license. Some professional credentials."

Beside Landry, Olivia frowned. "Professional credentials?"

Quinn walked closer, his gaze sliding from Olivia's face to Landry's. "To be specific, FBI credentials. Someone you both know, actually."

Olivia exchanged a glance with Landry before she looked at her boss again. "Are you telling us—"

"After all this time, Darryl Boyle finally turned up," Quinn said.

Paula Graves

"...no emotion and skill. It's about the man behind the
trouble. I feel like it is more so presenting to..."
Olivia all the emotion that Boyle finally hit which
humanity.

Chapter Twelve

"I thought we'd never find Boyle's body. I figured he was
somewhere down a hole in the mountains where nobody
but the bears would find him." McKenna Rigsby looked
up at Nick Darcy, carrying out a whole silent conversation
in that one glance.

Olivia had been tangentially involved in the ruse Rigsby
and Darcy had set up to trap Darryl Boyle, an FBI agent
who'd stupidly tried to co-opt the Blue Ridge Infantry to
create a domestic terror act devastating enough to make the
government finally start rooting out radicals from within
the US borders. But Boyle had turned the tables on Rigsby,
and if she and Darcy hadn't been able to convince the head
of the Blue Ridge Infantry that Boyle wasn't the ally he
made himself out to be, it might have been Rigsby lying
dead in the snow rather than Boyle.

"I wonder how long he's been out there," Darcy murmured, looking troubled. Olivia knew he had never fully
made peace with trading Boyle's life for Rigsby's, no matter
how much he loved her. Like the rest of The Gates agents,
he didn't like leaving anyone behind, even someone who'd
gone into league with the bad guys.

"Not long." Quinn walked into the conference room,
sliding his phone back into his pocket. "Sara said the body
was pretty fresh."

"He disappeared months ago," Landry said.

"I know." Quinn glanced at Landry. "There were signs that Boyle had taken more than one beating during the time he's been missing."

Landry's face went pale, and he looked down at his hands clasped tightly together on the table.

Olivia quelled the urge to touch him, knowing he'd just shrug her hand away. But she needed to get him somewhere alone, soon, and see if she could get him to talk about what he'd been through. Whatever the BRI had done to him—and she couldn't imagine they'd been kind in any way—he was still suffering the emotional aftermath.

Repressing that trauma wasn't going to make it go away. And anything he could remember about his time in captivity with the BRI might be important in their quest to take down the vicious militia group.

Quinn crossed until he was standing close to Landry. He waited for Landry to look up before speaking again. "You realize the discovery of Boyle's body after all this time is only going to reenergize the FBI's investigation into what happened last spring."

Landry gave a solemn nod. "I know. I should get out of here before the FBI comes knocking on your front door."

"I didn't say that." Quinn bent and planted his palms on the table. "But we need to consider what to do with you while the FBI is sniffing around."

"Maybe it's time to turn myself in."

"No." Olivia closed her fingers over his arm. "The last time you tried turning yourself in, the BRI took you captive."

"But I was alone then." He squeezed her hand. "Now I'm not."

Warmth flooded her. "No, you're not."

"I don't think we've reached that point yet," Quinn said.

"We're pretty sure there are still people left in the FBI who are sympathetic to the Blue Ridge Infantry."

"Darryl Boyle made that pretty clear. We just don't know who or how many." McKenna Rigsby looked across the table at Landry. "I'm sorry, Landry. I feel as if I'm the reason you went through what you did, because you were trying to help me."

He shook his head quickly. "Don't. You were a target, too. You had every right to try to figure out who in the FBI was trying to kill you. I'm sorry I didn't work all that out before things went so wrong. I should have been paying better attention." His gaze dropped and he tugged his arm away from Olivia's grip. "I should have been a better agent."

"You can flog yourself later," Quinn said in a dust-dry tone. "Right now I need you to concentrate on what you might know about the people who took Carver captive. I don't want to lose an agent. We've been damned lucky so far, and I'd like the record to hold."

Landry nodded but didn't say anything more.

"I think we're safe from the FBI until the roads clear, but once they do, we're going to be racing the clock." Quinn looked at the agents surrounding him. "I'd like to stash Landry somewhere the FBI wouldn't think to look for him, but I'm not sure at this point that our established safe houses are a good option. They're too easy to connect to The Gates. Any other suggestions?"

"Rachel's uncle and aunt live over in Bryson City," Seth Hammond suggested. "They've got a guesthouse out back of their place. Rachel and I have stayed there a few times. Nobody'd think to look for Landry there."

"Rachel's his wife," Olivia murmured to Landry.

"A decent option. Any other suggestions?"

"I have family in Alabama who are damned good in a fight," Caleb Cooper said.

"I've considered that option, but I don't want Landry that many hours away."

"What difference does that make?" Olivia asked, not liking the dark gleam she saw in Quinn's eyes.

Her boss glanced at her briefly before turning his pointed gaze to Landry. "Because sooner or later, I believe Mr. Landry will understand the vital need for him to tell us everything he remembers about his time in BRI captivity. And when he does, I don't want to have to drive six hours to hear him out."

Next to Olivia, Landry looked down at the table, his jaw tight with anger. She put her hand on his leg under the table and felt his muscles twitch. "Why don't we start with Bryson City?" she suggested. "As soon as the roads are cleared for travel, I'll drive him there. We'll play tourists for a few days until the FBI gets tired of sniffing around here."

Quinn's gaze remained on Landry's lowered head. "Very well. The temperature is supposed to rise above freezing this afternoon, with enough sunshine to give us a decent melt-off. The roads could be clear enough to drive by morning."

Olivia squeezed Landry's leg. "Then we'll head out first thing in the morning."

"THE HUNTERS ARE nice people." Olivia had spent most of the past hour folding the clothes for their trip to Bryson City. She kept a couple of changes of clothing at the office for emergency situations, she'd explained to Landry when she'd pulled the small overnight bag out of her locker in the agents' bull pen. Added to the clothes they'd brought with them on the hike over the mountain, she had enough to wear for four days. If they could find a laundry in Bryson City, they could stay longer if necessary.

But Landry knew it wouldn't be necessary.

He'd put off facing everything that had happened to him in BRI captivity for long enough.

He caught Olivia's wrist as she placed a pair of socks in one of the suitcases Quinn had provided. "We don't have to go to Bryson City."

She frowned. "You want to go somewhere else?"

"I can tell Quinn everything he needs to know tonight. Get it over with and get out of here so you and everybody else can get on with your lives."

The look on her face nearly unraveled his resolve. "You want to leave? Now? After—" Her lips snapped to a thin line and she turned away.

"It would be better for you, Livvie. Surely you can see that. Even if we can somehow prove I'm not a traitor, there's no way the FBI lets me come back. I'm done there. And I'm not sure what other sort of job I can get that's going to be worth anything. I don't know how to be anything else."

"Quinn would hire you."

"No, he wouldn't. I'm too big a risk. He knows that. So do you."

"Because you worked with the Blue Ridge Infantry? Obviously, you were trying to bring them down." Her brow furrowed. "Right?"

She was trying so hard not to have doubts, but she couldn't quite pull it off. He couldn't really blame her. He hadn't exactly given her a reason to believe in him anymore.

"I was. But I wasn't doing it for the FBI or any other organization that could back me up. I have only my word that I was on the side of the angels, and Quinn can't trust my word." He touched her face, letting his fingers slide lightly over the perfect curve of her cheek. "You can't, either, can you?"

Her jaw tightened, her chin lifting. "I believe you."

"Without any proof?"

Her gaze leveled with his, her eyes a cool, crystalline blue that should have chilled him but warmed him to his core instead. "Your word is the proof. I believe you."

She almost convinced him she did.

She released a soft sigh, as if she could read his own doubts. "Let's just go through with the plan, okay? We'll go to Bryson City to stay for a few days. Once we're there, if you want to tell me everything you can remember about your time in captivity, great. If you feel you need to wait a little longer, that's fine, too. I know you'll do the right thing for Grant Carver."

Landry couldn't stop a soft laugh. "Oh, Livvie. Still twisting the knife with a smile, aren't you?"

She arched an eyebrow at him. "Me?"

"I will do everything I can to help find Carver." God knew, the guilt was starting to eat him up.

"I know you will."

Alexander Quinn stopped by the dorm room a few minutes later. "The roads into North Carolina have been deemed passable by the Tennessee and North Carolina Highway Patrols." He handed over a key to Olivia. "There's a Chevy Tahoe parked out back, gassed up and ready to go. It should be able to handle any icy patches left on the road."

Olivia glanced at Landry. "Is Rachel's uncle expecting us?"

"Yes. He's setting up the guesthouse for you. If anyone asks, you're distant relatives from Georgia, up here to enjoy the winter season in the Smokies."

"I don't want to put anyone else in danger," Landry said. The closer he got to leaving The Gates, the more he feared he was making a mistake. "Maybe I should just wait here for the FBI to show up and take me into custody. I can call a lawyer I know in Richmond, make sure he makes noise with the Richmond field office so they'll know someone's watching."

"Why didn't you do that when you got away from the BRI?" Quinn asked.

He wasn't sure he had a good answer. At the time he got away from his captors, his only thought was to get clear of their reach and find a place to hunker down until he could figure out what to do next.

The problem was, he never really figured out what to do next.

"Go to Bryson City. Do some thinking without the pressure of the FBI breathing down your neck," Quinn suggested. "Maybe you'll figure out how you want to handle things with the FBI from a place of clarity."

Clarity, Landry thought. He wasn't sure he knew what the word meant anymore.

THE DRIVE TO Bryson City took two hours on slick roads through the Smoky Mountains, but the Chevy handled the conditions as well as Olivia could have hoped, and the scenery was so breathtaking she had to struggle to keep her eyes on the road instead of the snowy landscape.

"I wish this was a pleasure trip," Landry murmured as they rounded a curve and came upon another breathtaking mountain vista.

"So do I."

"Do you know anything about this place where we'll be staying?"

"It's actually an extension of a restaurant and music venue, Song Valley Music Hall."

"A music hall?"

She glanced at him, taking in his confusion. "It belongs to Rafe Hunter, Rachel Hammond's uncle."

"Wife of the con man."

"Former con man."

"Whatever."

"Her aunt and uncle have run this place for years. They're actually quite well-known for what they do. Apparently, Rafe Hunter is known in music circles as a brilliant judge of talent. Seth says playing at the Song Valley Music Hall is a badge of honor for a new artist."

Landry was silent for a moment while Olivia eased the Tahoe into a slushy curve. Once they'd reached the straight-away, he added, "Does this Rafe Hunter know who we are and why we're there?"

"He knows I work with Seth. He thinks you're my boy-friend and this is a winter getaway for us." She glanced at Landry and saw him frowning. "Is that a problem? It seemed like the easiest cover story."

"No, it's fine."

"We aren't going to see much of Mr. Hunter, so you don't have to pretend anything."

"That's not the problem, believe me."

"Then what?"

"Are we going to share a room?"

She slanted another look at him and found his intense green gaze on her. Heat flitted up her neck and into her cheeks, and she forced her gaze back to the winding road. "It's a guesthouse. There are two bedrooms."

His voice dropped to a soft growl. "That didn't entirely answer my question."

Her breath caught. "I don't know," she admitted.

"Then maybe that's the answer." He leaned back against his seat. "I think we should both be really sure about any-thing that happens between us this time. We both ignored a lot of doubts the last time and jumped into things reck-lessly."

"That's how you remember our relationship?" She tried

to quell the sense of hurt that rose in her chest, but she didn't have much luck. "As a reckless mistake?"

"I didn't say that."

"I think you did."

He fell silent for the rest of the drive, tension stretching between them until Olivia felt that she'd snap in two. The sight of the Song Valley Music Hall through the front windshield of the Tahoe was a palpable relief.

The place was packed, parking hard to come by, but Olivia found a slot for the Tahoe near the far end of the parking lot and cut the engine. "You stay here. I'll go find Rafe and tell him we're here."

"Where's the guesthouse?" he asked, giving the low-slung saloon-style facade of the music hall a skeptical look.

"I'm not sure," she admitted. She'd assumed there would be some sort of residential structure attached to the building, but there was nothing like that in sight as she crossed the gravel parking lot and entered the music hall.

An early dinner crowd filled the place with talk and laughter that rang in her ears after the long, mostly silent drive through the mountains. The smiling man at the bar at the back answered her query by pointing to a short, jovial man talking to customers at a nearby table.

Olivia waited for him to finish the conversation, stepping into his path as he turned toward the next table. "Mr. Hunter?"

He had to look up to meet her gaze. His smile widened. "Lord, you must be Olivia. Seth described you over the phone." The twinkle in Rafe Hunter's eye made her wonder if the nickname "Bombshell Barbie" had come up. She tried not to take it as anything but a compliment, but she tired of everyone focusing on the fact that she was tall, blonde and on the curvy side. She was also smart, resourceful and dangerous.

Then again, being underestimated could often work in her favor.

"How far is the guesthouse from here?" she asked as she followed him to a back room in the music hall. The cramped little space was clearly his office; he dug through the lap drawer of the desk and retrieved a key.

"Not far," he said with a smile, nodding for her to follow him back to the main hall, where a four-piece bluegrass band was warming up for their first set. Rafe motioned for her to wait a moment while he crossed to speak with the mandolin player. They exchanged a few words and laughter before Rafe returned to Olivia. "Sorry about that—new act, and there's a record-label scout in the audience tonight. They're as nervous as pigs at a barbecue joint." Rafe laughed at his own joke. "I like to put 'em at ease. They play better if they're laughing."

They stepped out into the chilly twilight air. Overhead, stars and a waxing moon glowed through wisps of clouds visible above the trees. "Y'all get a lot of snow over there in Tennessee?" he asked conversationally as they walked toward the side of the music hall, not far from where she'd parked the Tahoe.

"Enough," she answered, his friendly mountain twang coaxing her own Sand Mountain drawl out to play.

He led her around the building and waved his hand at what the music hall's bright facade had hidden. About twenty yards behind the music hall stood a lovely two-story wood cabin, glowing with warm light from within. "That's where my wife, Janeane, and I live. And right behind that house is the guesthouse. We built it for Janeane's mama, thinking she'd come live with us after Janeane's daddy died. But Donna fell in love with the funeral director and eloped about four weeks later." Rafe laughed, apparently finding the story hilarious.

"That was fast," Olivia commented.

"Well, that's Donna. Fast and brash. It's a big part of her charm." Rafe stopped walking and turned to her, handing her the key he'd brought with them. "Just head on down the flagstone walk past the house and you'll see the place. Janeane knows you're arriving, but be sure to pop your head in the back door and let her know you're here so she won't go for her shotgun." He walked back toward the music hall, laughing.

Olivia started for the Tahoe, but Landry met her halfway, carrying their suitcases in both hands, the shoulder strap of the duffel bag full of their supplies draped across his body.

She relieved him of one of the suitcases. "That was Rafe Hunter."

"I figured." He looked past her at the wood cabin. "Is that it?"

"No, that's Mr. Hunter's place. He said the guesthouse is behind their house, down this flagstone path." Nodding for him to follow, she walked down the dark path, animal awareness prickling the hairs at the back of her neck. How much of her unease could be attributed to the danger lurking around them and how much to the prospect of several days alone with Cade Landry in a scenic mountain cabin, she couldn't say.

The guesthouse came into view as they passed the back corner of the Hunters' cabin, a small, pretty one-story cabin decorated with the slow-melting remains of the earlier snowstorm. Boxwood shrubs flanked the steps up to the porch, giving the log cabin the appearance of a quaint country cottage.

"Cute," Landry commented.

Olivia slanted a look at him.

He met her gaze, smiling. But his smile faded in an instant, and his eyes widened as he looked at something behind her.

She heard the unmistakable clatter of the fore-end of a pump-action shotgun sliding back, ready to fire.

"State your business." The voice behind them was female, mountain-accented and deadly.

Dropping the suitcase to the ground beside her, Olivia lifted her hands and slowly turned to face the small, silver-haired woman pointing a shotgun at her chest.

Swallowing the instant flood of terror that came with facing a shotgun barrel, Olivia forced her voice through her tightened throat. "Janeane Hunter, I presume?"

Chapter Thirteen

"I told her to poke her head in the back door and tell you she'd arrived." What Landry assumed was Rafe Hunter's plaintive voice was audible over the phone Janeane Hunter held to one ear. The shotgun remained in her other hand, though she'd dropped the barrel until it pointed toward their legs instead of their midsections. Landry wondered if they could make a run for it before Janeane Hunter could whip the barrel up and give the fore-end a pump. After another look at her sharp-eyed gaze, he decided it would be folly to try.

Janeane made a face at the phone. "That might've got her shot for sure, you old fool."

"I would have knocked," Olivia offered helpfully.

Janeane flashed her a pointed look, and Olivia pressed her mouth to a thin line. Landry quelled the urge to laugh, despite the jittery adrenaline flooding his system.

"Did she show you any ID?" Janeane asked.

"No, but hell, she looked like what Seth described, and there can't be too many that do," Rafe said. Landry couldn't argue with his logic. Rafe was right. There weren't many women in the Smokies, or anywhere else, like Olivia Sharp.

"Well," Janeane said doubtfully, "if you're sure."

"Let the kids go, hon. I've got to run. A new set is starting."

Janeane hung up the phone and engaged the safety on the shotgun before she set it down in the corner by the fridge. "Sorry about that. Been having some home invasions in these parts recently. Damn meth heads." She extended her hand. "Janeane Hunter."

"Olivia." Olivia shook the woman's hand. "This is my friend Jack." Jackson was Landry's middle name, and Quinn had suggested using that name instead of Cade, since it was a little less uncommon.

"You work with Seth?"

Landry could tell from the woman's smile that she liked her niece's husband. He was a little surprised, given the man's rather colorful history.

"I do," Olivia said with a smile.

"He's an interesting character," Janeane said drily. "But good people, deep down. Loves our Rachel, and he's real good to her. Have you seen pictures of the new baby?"

"Yes, ma'am," Olivia said with a laugh. "Beautiful like her mama."

Janeane beamed. "I think so, too." She caught herself up, her smile turning a little sheepish. "Here I've held you at gunpoint and now I'm talking your ear off about my little grandniece. You folks must be tired. You hungry? I could have Rafe send something from the music-hall kitchen down to the cabin."

"Actually," Olivia said, "I think we're going to head back to the music hall after we unpack. I've heard good things about the food and the entertainment."

"Well, you know I agree," Janeane said with a bright smile as she walked them to the door. "I've got to get this month's books done tonight or I'd join you." She remained on the back porch, watching while they walked to the guest cabin a few yards away.

Inside, the small cabin was clean and casually furnished

with a cozy leather sofa and a pair of matching armchairs filling the front room. They explored the rest of the cabin, finding a small but complete kitchen in the back and two bedrooms, each with its own full bath, on either side of a narrow central hallway.

Unlike Olivia's cabin, which had been originally built as a tourist rental cabin and was outfitted with the sort of luxuries vacationers preferred, the Hunters' guest cabin was simpler, designed for everyday living. The bedrooms were reasonably large, but there was no hot tub on a back porch or roomy claw-foot tub in the bathrooms, just a simple toilet, tub and sink. Landry washed up, unpacked his bags and met Olivia in the front room a half hour later.

"Were you serious about going to the music hall?" he asked, noticing she'd changed out of her travel clothes into a pair of tweed trousers and a slim-fitting sweater the color of the Gulf of Mexico in the summer, a brilliant blue green reflected in her bright eyes.

"I thought it might be nice to get out and eat something besides a protein bar or a can of soup. Seth says the music's really good if you like bluegrass, and I know you do—"

"What if someone spots us?"

"You can wear that farm-supply cap I packed for you. You haven't shaved in a couple of days, and a beard always makes you look a little different. And here." She reached down and picked up a tweed newsboy cap and a pair of steel-rim glasses he hadn't noticed sitting on the coffee table nearby. She set the cap on her head, covering most of her short blond hair, and donned the glasses. "I'll wear these instead of contacts. My own mother wouldn't recognize me."

"If you don't want to be noticed, you probably shouldn't wear that sweater," he said with a wave of his hand.

She grinned so brightly at him as she took a step closer, he felt certain his heart skipped a couple of beats. "You like?"

"I love. But you'll turn every head in the place if you wear that."

She sighed. "I can keep my jacket over it. I don't want to change because it's cashmere and it's so soft."

He reached out and touched her shoulder, letting his fingers trail down her arm. She was right. The cashmere was as soft as a kitten's fur and warm from her body heat. The urge to let his fingers continue exploring the warm, soft curves of her cashmere-clad body was nearly impossible to resist.

He shoved his hands in the pockets of his jeans. "Yeah."

Those azure eyes locked with his for a long, electric moment before she looked away. "I know it's a little bit of a risk, but I'm getting cabin fever already and we just got here." Her lips curved up in the corners. "And I bet it's been a long time since you just went out and had some fun, isn't it?"

"You have no idea."

Her smile faded. "I guess I don't. I'm sorry. I didn't even think—"

He caught her cheeks between his palms, making her look at him. "It's okay. I'm glad you don't dwell on it. It helps me feel more normal, and it's been a really long time since I've felt that way."

"I know what you mean." She covered his hands with hers, holding them in place against her cheeks. "Let's just do this. Let's go, eat some good food, listen to some good music and pretend like we're both normal for a little while. What do you say?"

Impulsively, he gave her a quick, fierce hug and let her go. "Just point me to that cap and we'll get out of here."

SETH HAD TOLD Olivia the truth. The food at the Song Valley Music Hall wasn't fancy or complex, but it was delicious, fresh and prepared with care by someone who clearly knew his way around a country kitchen. The music didn't disappoint, either; the band Rafe Hunter had booked for the evening was young but wildly talented, doling out an inventive blend of bluegrass, country, rockabilly and blues that kept the patrons clapping.

After a trip to the bathroom a little after nine, Olivia returned to find the waitstaff clearing out a space in the center of the restaurant. Circling around the buzz of activity, she found Landry at their table, chatting with Rafe. Both men stood at her approach, the courtly gesture making her smile.

"What's going on?" she asked, nodding at the hustling waiters hauling tables away from the center of the room.

"Dancing, darlin'," Rafe drawled, winking at Landry as he wandered away to talk to a couple of patrons nearby.

"Dancing, darlin'," Landry repeated, holding out his hand. "Shall we?"

She let him draw her onto the dance floor as the band fired up a brisk two-step.

"If I'd known about this place when we were both in Richmond, I would have suggested a weekend trip to check it out," he murmured in her ear a few minutes later as they swayed to a bluesy arrangement of "The Tennessee Waltz."

"Do you ever wish—" She stopped herself.

"Do I ever wish what?" he prodded when she didn't continue.

"It's stupid. Never mind."

He leaned back to look at her, his green eyes warm and soft in the mellow light of the dance hall. "No, tell me."

She took a deep breath. "Do you ever wish you could go back to the day of the warehouse explosion and do things differently?"

"Of course. All the time."

"What would you have done differently?"

"I would have questioned the order to go in, for one thing. I should have questioned it then, but I thought maybe someone had seen something inside the warehouse, some move by the bombers to take out hostages—"

"I know. I mean, I don't know what that moment was like, because I can't remember it. But I can imagine it. I think my reaction would have been the same as yours. Maybe it was. I wish I remembered."

"I'm glad you don't." His plaintive murmur made her heart hurt. "I'm glad you don't remember any of that moment. I wish I didn't."

"It wasn't your fault." She touched his cheek, enjoying the sensual scrape of his beard stubble against her palm. "You did what you were told."

"How many people's lives have been ended at the hands of someone who was just doing what he was told?" His eyes darkened to a murky forest green, his expression etched with regret. "I should've made a better choice without being told."

She dropped her hands to his shoulders and squeezed, trying to contain a sudden rush of anger for the hell he'd clearly gone through since that horrible day in Richmond. The lives lost, the careers damaged, the nightmares, the second-guessing and the ravening sense of guilt—none of it ever should have happened.

But it had. Neither of them could change a damn thing about that fact.

She kept her voice low, well aware of the crowd around them, but what she was going to say needed to be said. For her sake as well as Landry's. "Look, I know what it's like to have regrets. I get trying to figure out what you could have done differently—God knows I've pored through the notes on that case for two years now, trying to figure out what could have been done to stop any of it from happening.

That's natural. But *you* didn't strap a bomb to your body and take innocent people hostage. *I* didn't hit the detonator in a room full of civilians and FBI agents. That's on those BRI bastards, not us."

"Can we get out of here?" he asked, his gaze sliding away from her face to take in the crowded music hall.

"Of course."

They called for the check, paid and tipped the server and headed out into the cold night after saying a quick good-night to Rafe on their way out.

After the doors of the music hall closed on the noise behind them, only the hiss of their frosty breaths in the night air and the thump of their shoes on the flagstones broke the frigid silence until they reached the guest cabin. Olivia unlocked the door, let them in and locked up behind them.

"Thanks," Landry said as he shrugged off his coat.

"I'm sorry. I shouldn't have pushed you to go out."

He turned quickly toward her. "No. I enjoyed it. I did. It's been a long time since I've been able to sit in a crowded restaurant with a beautiful woman, eating good food and listening to good music."

"I shouldn't have brought up Richmond."

He touched her cheek, his fingers cold against her skin. "It won't go away if we don't talk about it. It might be worse if we don't."

Taking his hand, she led him over to the sofa. She pulled him down beside her, turning to face him. "You want to talk about Richmond?"

"No. But I think I need to."

IT HAD BEEN a pretty day, he remembered. Bright blue sky and mild temperatures as fall edged toward winter. The scene was so clear in his head—the sprawling warehouse south of Richmond, gleaming a creamy bone white in the midday sun, the black-clad SWAT team surrounding all the exits while the negotiation team held a tense standoff with the bombers.

"I go over and over that day in my mind. We'd been there less than two hours." He met Olivia's gentle, direct gaze. "That's nowhere near the longest we've waited for a hostage negotiation to produce results. I don't remember being tired or impatient. I just remember worrying that nothing we were doing that day was going to stop someone from dying."

Her expression was so serious, so intense, her brow furrowed as if she was trying to wring a memory from somewhere deep inside her forgetful brain. "Was there any indication that the bombers were about to make a move? I've read the incident-report files, but maybe you've remembered something since then you didn't remember at the time?"

"There was nothing. It was quiet. Eerily so. When we first got there, I could hear hostages talking and crying. But after a while, even that stopped. It was like they were resting. Holding their breaths for something to happen." He managed a faint smile. "You know that feeling."

She nodded. "The incident report said we got the order to move by radio, but the other teams said they heard no such order."

"I know. I'm not sure how it happened. Believe me, I've relived those moments a thousand times, trying to figure out how it could have happened."

"Do you remember changing the frequency at any point?"

He shook his head. "Definitely not."

"Were you in possession of your radio the whole time?"

Frowning, he replayed the moments before the radio order. He and Olivia had been on the east side of the warehouse, along with the other two agents on their team, Len Davis and Kevin Darnell. Both Davis and Darnell had died in the bomb blast. Olivia had suffered a concussion when debris had knocked her backward into a wall.

Landry's injuries had been minor scratches from shrapnel. Even though he'd been in the lead, by some fluke of fortune, he and Olivia had just moved behind a large air-conditioning unit, which took the brunt of the blast, sparing them more serious injury.

Davis and Darnell, who'd gone in the opposite direction as they started to spread out, had been hit with a blast of metal shrapnel that had killed them instantly.

Landry would never be free of those images, watching the split-second, senseless deaths of two good men. But he was damn glad Olivia had been spared that particular memory.

"Any chance someone else could have changed the radio frequency?" Olivia prodded.

He dragged his mind back to the present, meeting her curious gaze. "Yes. There was. I don't know why I didn't consider that possibility."

She licked her lips. "When?"

"Just about fifteen minutes before all hell broke loose, Agent Boyle came by with water. Remember?" He kicked himself when she ruefully shook her head. "I'm sorry. Of course you don't. It was the first time we'd seen him all morning. I guess I must have assumed he was back at the staging area, conferring with the negotiators. He gave us each pep talks."

She frowned. "Boyle gave us pep talks?"

"I know that wasn't his way, but we both know the way he felt about domestic terrorists. He was rabid, and that's kind of what the pep talks were about. He told me, and I guess he told the rest of you, too, that whatever happened, we were patriots for trying to stop the bombers."

She shook her head. "Patriots. Interesting choice of words, now that we know he was working with the BRI to stage a big incident."

"In retrospect, I have to wonder if he didn't stage the incident in Richmond."

"Or maybe it was just a target of opportunity. Maybe he let his zealotry get the better of him and took advantage of the situation to create an incident."

"We weren't supposed to live, were we?"

She met his gaze solemnly. "I don't think we were. When we did, and you told the debriefers about the radio call, it sounded like a lie."

"A bad agent covering his ass." Landry shook his head. "And suddenly the story became about FBI malpractice instead of a domestic terror attack. No wonder Boyle sabotaged me. He must have been so furious."

"You said it was the main negotiator, Williams, you heard on the radio. Are you sure it wasn't Boyle?"

"As sure as you can be about a voice over a radio. I didn't know Williams that well, but he has that distinctive Brooklyn accent. Definitely not a Baltimore accent like Boyle had."

"Their voices are around the same depth, though," Olivia murmured. "A Brooklyn accent is so distinctive, it's easy to mimic, especially over a radio. And none of us on the team were from Brooklyn, so it's not like we'd have been able to distinguish a real accent from a fake one."

He followed her unspoken logic. "Fifteen minutes before the radio call, Boyle came by and took us one by one to talk to us. I remember he put his hands on my shoulders because at one point, he made my shoulder radio squawk with static, and I nearly jumped out of my skin."

"He was changing the radio frequency." Olivia let out

a soft curse. "The bastard set us all up to be killed for his obsession."

A shivery sense of relief washed over Landry, spreading goose bumps along his arms and legs. In the rush of excitement, he reached up and cradled Olivia's face between his palms. "That's it. Oh, baby, that's exactly how it happened. You have no idea how much that question has haunted me. How did I not see it before?"

She closed her hands over his. "You just needed your partner to help you talk it out."

Emotion swelled in his chest, choking him. A flurry of thoughts, of images and pent-up feelings, swirled through his brain, but the lump in his throat wouldn't let them come out in words.

But he could see those unspoken thoughts shining in Olivia's eyes.

Two words finally escaped his tight throat. "I forgot."

Her lips trembled in a whisper of a smile. "Forgot what?"

"Us. I forgot us." Swept up in an irresistible whirlwind of emotion, he curled his hand around the back of her neck and pulled her closer, fitting his mouth to hers.

The first time he'd kissed her after so long apart, it had seemed like kissing a beautiful stranger. The desire had been there, but not the familiarity. Not the sense of knowing.

The second kiss, initiated by Olivia, had been an explosion of fiery desire, almost faceless and nameless in its intensity. Two mouths, two bodies, looking for pleasure and completion.

But this kiss, this melding of lips and tangling of tongues, this symphony of touches and breaths and long, deep sighs—

This kiss felt like home.

Chapter Fourteen

Us, she thought. *This is us.*

Landry's hands moved in a slow, sweet exploration of her face before sliding down to her shoulders and sweeping lightly down her arms. His fingers clasped hers. Entwined with them. And it felt so familiar, so perfect, that she wondered how they ever could have let go of this sense of completeness.

She let go of his hands and lifted her fingers to his face, tracing the little nicks and contours she'd once known as intimately as she knew her own face. That scar on his chin was a high school baseball injury, when he'd taken a cleat to the face diving to tag out a runner stealing base. The dimples that creased his cheeks when he laughed had come from his grandfather on his mother's side, he'd once told her, though his mother didn't have dimples.

"At least, I don't think she did," he'd said when she'd asked about the dimples that still had the power to make her heart skip a beat. "I never saw that much of her, and when I did, she wasn't smiling."

The image of his distant, unsmiling mother made her heart break a little each time she thought of it.

She drew back from the kiss, opening her eyes. Landry stared back at her, his gaze soft but intense. Slowly, he smiled, triggering the dimples, and she couldn't stop a soft laugh.

"What?" he asked.

"Those dimples."

His smile widened, the dimples deepening. "Missed 'em, did you?"

"I did."

"I missed *you*. Every single inch of you."

"All seventy of them?"

He laughed. "Yeah. And even more when you're wearing heels."

She pressed her forehead against his. "How did we let it fall apart? One day we were fine, and the next—"

"I don't think we were fine." He leaned back, putting a little distance between them. Cool air seeped in between them, giving her a chill.

She rubbed her arms. "You're right. We weren't."

"This is such a bad time to be considering this." He rubbed his jaw, his palm rasping against his beard stubble. "I have no idea what's going to happen next. I'm wanted by the FBI, and you've been targeted by the BRI, and in case it's not clear, those bastards aren't going to just let me go unscathed if I run into one of them in the woods one day and they figure out who I am."

"All the more reason we should stick together." She lifted her chin and pinned him with her more determined gaze. "Maybe it'll all go wrong again. Hell, maybe it's inevitable. But right now we need each other, as partners if nothing else. We just work better together than apart, and you know it. Tell me I'm wrong."

"You're not wrong." He bent toward her and pressed his lips against her forehead. She snuggled closer and he wrapped his arms around her, holding her close. "I just don't think we need to get ourselves all tangled up in plans and promises when we're not sure what tomorrow's going to hold."

She sighed, wishing she could argue with his logic. But he was right. Rushing into things never worked out well, in her experience. "Okay. We'll slow it down and just concentrate on the work for now. Agents Landry and Sharp, back on the job."

"That sounds good." He gave her a quick kiss on the temple then let her go. "In the morning, that is. It's late and we've had a few long, stressful days. Let's get some sleep and we'll get started first thing in the morning. Deal?"

"Deal." She extended her hand toward him.

He shook her hand, his grip lasting a little longer than necessary. In his green eyes she saw a sweet, intense longing that echoed in her own chest. Finally, he let go and smiled. "I really did miss the hell out of you."

"Back at ya." She made herself turn around and head for the bedroom she'd staked out earlier in the evening, closing the door behind her. By the time she'd snuggled under the warm blankets, she heard Landry's footsteps enter the hall outside her room.

His footsteps faltered as he neared her door. Olivia waited, breathless, for him to make another move.

When his footsteps moved on, and the door to his bedroom opened and closed, she let out a pent-up breath, well aware he'd made the smart decision.

But she didn't have to like it.

Her cell phone hummed on the bedside table where she'd left it. It wasn't her normal phone; she'd left that back at The Gates locked in her desk. Instead, Quinn had provided both her and Landry with untraceable burner phones for their trip to Bryson City. Her late-night caller could be only one person.

"It's nearly midnight, Quinn," she said into the phone.

"You didn't check in when you arrived."

He was right. She hadn't. "Sorry."

"Everything okay?"

"Everything's fine," she assured him, tucking her knees up to her chest. "No problems on the road, got here in time to have some good food and listen to some good music and now we're safely tucked in our beds for the night."

Quinn was silent for a long moment.

"Is something wrong?" she asked when he didn't speak.

"Are you alone in that bed?"

Her spine straightened. "Is that any business of yours?"

"No. Not the way you mean."

"Then in what way *is* it your business?"

"I remember the Olivia Sharp who walked into my office looking for a job. She was— I'm not sure I even know the right word for it. Broken, I guess. Not in a way that was obvious. But there were pieces missing, and I could see it."

"Thank you for the analysis, Dr. Phil."

"I'm not trying to psychoanalyze you, Olivia. I'm not sticking my nose where it doesn't belong. If you're going to continue to be a vital member of my team, you have to be smart and focused and emotionally centered."

"I am all of those things."

"Good. Keep it that way." Quinn's voice lowered. "I take it from your answers that you really are alone in your room?"

"Quinn—"

He laughed softly. "That time, I was sticking my nose where it doesn't belong."

"I'm fine," she said, realizing he'd thrown in the last question just to break the tension. "And I know what I'm doing. I promise."

"I hope whatever happens with Landry is a good thing

for you. I really do. But I need you to put your own safety first. Carver's missing, and for all we know, he's already dead. I don't want to have to call up your mother and tell her that you're gone, too."

She tamped down a flush of guilt. She hadn't talked to her mother in over a week, she realized. Carla Sharp hadn't exactly been a great role model, but Olivia had never once doubted her mother loved her. And she loved her mother, too, even when Carla exasperated her beyond words. Maybe especially then.

"I don't want you to have to do that, either," she said. "I'll be careful."

"You do that," Quinn said. "Call if you need anything."

"Will do." She hung up, set the phone on the bedside table and stared up at the darkened ceiling, wondering if she was going to be able to keep her word. Carver was missing; she and Landry were both hunted. She'd chosen the work she did willingly, knowing the dangers, but she was nearly thirty-five now. Her window of opportunity for having a child of her own was closing quickly, if having a child was even what she wanted.

Was it? She and Landry had been partners and lovers, but one thing they'd never seriously talked about was getting married and starting a family. In fact, in retrospect, she could see that they'd gone out of their way to avoid talking about marriage and kids.

Why? What had they been afraid of? That they wanted different things out of life? In some ways, she knew Landry as well as she knew anyone in the world, but in others, she didn't think she knew him at all.

Because he'd wanted it that way? Because she had?

Maybe they were crazy to think they could make their relationship work this time.

Maybe they were crazy to try.

Olivia was already up the next morning, scrambling eggs, when he wandered into the kitchen. She turned around to flash him a quick smile. "Good morning."

Her face was freshly scrubbed and free of makeup, and her hair was damp and tousled from the shower, but she was still the most beautiful thing he'd ever seen, especially in that Alabama T-shirt and houndstooth-patterned running shorts, her long, tanned legs stretching for miles beneath the hem.

"Good morning," he replied, looking over her shoulder. "Need any help?"

"The toaster is over there on the counter. There's bread in the pantry—the Hunters stocked the place with some essentials for us, it seems. Janeane left a note so we'd know everything's fresh."

The kind gesture touched him more than it probably should have. "That was nice of her."

Olivia must have heard something odd in his tone, for she turned away from the stove to look at him. "It was."

He smiled. "I guess it's been a while since I've experienced much human kindness."

Olivia reached out and touched his arm briefly. "Give yourself a little time to get used to it again." She turned back to the eggs.

He hoped he'd have reason to get used to it. The thought of returning to a life of running and hiding was deeply disheartening. He'd grown accustomed to living a mostly solitary life, his only relationships shallow and transient.

But he'd never grown to like it.

The toaster took four slices at once. He put bread in the slots and pushed down the lever. "If we can't figure out a way to prove someone in the FBI set me up, I'll have to go back under the radar."

"We'll figure it out," she said, her voice firm.

"You can't know that."

She moved the skillet from the stove eye and turned to look at him. "I will not rest until we figure it out."

God, he loved her when she stuck out her chin and made declarations of intent. She was fierce and formidable and as sexy as hell.

He lifted his own chin in response. "Then neither will I."

She flashed him a big, toothy grin. "There's the Cade Landry I remember."

He hoped she was right. He hoped he was the man he used to be, because the man he'd become didn't seem to be a damned bit of good to anyone.

As they were cleaning up after breakfast, Olivia outlined her plan for the morning. "I brought files with me that I want you to go through. They're dossiers we've gathered on the bigger players in the Blue Ridge Infantry, and I was hoping maybe you could tell us if any of them were involved in your abduction."

"I didn't see faces. They wore masks."

"Maybe there will be something else that you'll be able to identify about them. Or maybe something in their files will spark a memory." She put the last cup in the dishwasher and straightened. "I set up everything for us in the front room."

He followed her into the living area and saw that she'd stacked fifteen manila folders in a neat line on the long coffee table in front of the sofa. "How long have you been awake?"

"A couple of hours." She slanted a sheepish smile at him as she took a seat on one end of the sofa. "Early riser, remember?"

"I remember." He sat beside her and picked up the first dossier. "Calvin Hopkins."

"Head of the Tennessee branch of the Blue Ridge Infantry.

Anything familiar about him?" Olivia asked as he flipped open the folder.

The photos in the dossier appeared to be candid shots taken with a telephoto lens. "Who took these shots?"

"Grant Carver, among others," she answered soberly. "One of the benefits of his living near the Fowler Ridge enclave."

"If you know where they're living, why hasn't someone gone in and staged a raid?"

"Because they learned a little something from the meth cookers with whom they've aligned themselves. They don't bring their drug business home. We think they've set up meth labs in other places in the hills. Abandoned cabins up high in the hills, maybe. Or even some of the old, abandoned marble quarries north of here. A few of those places are still private property, with absentee owners. All kinds of activity could be going on there without anybody but a few locals knowing it."

Landry rubbed his jaw, realizing he was already falling back into the habit of not shaving. Reentering civilization after nearly a year of living on the fringes was proving to be more difficult than he'd expected.

"Take a close look at some of the people with Hopkins," Olivia suggested as he flipped to a photo of Hopkins talking to a clean-shaven man wearing khakis and a light blue golf shirt. "That guy isn't in the BRI, we're pretty sure."

"Maybe he's just some tourist asking for directions."

"Maybe. Or maybe he's one of those other FBI agents Darryl Boyle spoke about before he disappeared."

He looked up at her, frowning. "What other FBI agents?"

"You said you thought there was someone in the FBI who had contacted the BRI when you tried to report Boyle's treachery to your superiors. I just figured you knew that Boyle wasn't the only one."

"I did but I didn't realize Boyle had actually admitted

it." Landry looked at the photo of the man in the khakis. "I don't recognize him. Do you?"

She shook her head. "But I left the FBI before you did. I was hoping maybe he was someone in one of the local field offices. Probably not an agent, but maybe one of the support staff?"

"He might be with the Knoxville office, I guess," Landry said doubtfully. "Though you'd think Rigsby would have recognized him."

"She didn't."

"If he was with the Johnson City RA, he was either there before I came aboard or after I left."

Olivia sighed. "I guess it was too much to hope for."

"Sorry."

She shook her head. "Don't be. We have a lot more files to go."

They continued working their way through the files, concentrating on photographs first. Then when none of those pictures triggered any memories, they started to go through the written reports The Gates had gathered from their agents as well as civilians who lived or worked in areas influenced by the Blue Ridge Infantry.

"Your files are amazingly thorough," Landry commented a couple of hours later when they stopped for a break. She had coaxed him into his jacket and boots for a walk in the woods behind the guesthouse, where the evergreens had sheltered much of the remaining snow from the melting rays of the sun.

"Unfortunately, we've had a lot of run-ins with members of the Blue Ridge Infantry. And a few of their drug-dealer and anarchist buddies."

"I'm not sure the FBI's files on these groups are as detailed."

"The BRI has become really savvy about covering their

tracks. We can outline how we think they're committing crimes, but producing evidence of their involvement is another thing altogether."

"I know. I was part of a task force trying to round some of them up, remember?"

"Right." She gave him a sidelong look. "You never told me how you were working with the BRI. I know you weren't sanctioned to get involved with the BRI undercover while you were on that task force. When Quinn got us involved in trying to keep McKenna Rigsby safe, we did a lot of digging with our FBI sources and we found out that much. But you ended up working with them anyway. How did it happen?"

"The contact fell into my lap. A guy who lived in the apartment next door was doing some jobs for them. Transporting contraband, that kind of thing. They made a mistake with him—he wasn't a meth head, but he was a drinker, and when he got drunk, he liked to talk. I figured out that I could pick his brains easily enough if I made sure to be his designated driver. So I ended up spending my nights at his favorite bars, looking for a chance to scrape him up off his bar stool and take him home."

"What kind of information did he give you?"

"Upcoming runs for the BRI. When they'd be moving drugs from one place to another. I went to Chang and told him what was up. I figured we could interdict the next run, if that's the way they wanted to go, but they didn't think there was sufficient evidence to warrant a raid." He frowned at the memory.

"That's ridiculous," she said, sounding confused. "What was their reasoning?"

"They didn't say. And I wasn't in any position to push them on it, given my shaky status with the Bureau." He shook his head, angry with himself. "I should have pushed anyway. I knew there was something hinky going on. But I just—I just didn't much care at the time."

"You must have started caring at some point, if you ended up working with the BRI anyway."

He nodded. "I did."

"What happened?"

"Rigsby disappeared."

The curious look she sent his way was tinged with suspicion. "I knew you were part of the team running her undercover op, but I wasn't aware you'd become close."

He almost laughed at the thought. "We weren't close. But I knew she was a good agent. She certainly didn't go rogue for the hell of it, so I knew something had gone really wrong. And I might not have been running on all cylinders as an agent, but my gut told me that whatever had gone wrong had gone wrong on the FBI end of the operation."

"What did you do?"

"I tried to get Chang to let me go undercover and see what had gone wrong. I had a ready way in, through my neighbor, and I was still pretty new to Tennessee, so it wasn't like anyone in the BRI would know my face. At least, that's what I figured. I didn't know about Boyle at that time."

"Chang said no?"

"He ran it up the Bureau chain of command and came back with a no," Landry corrected her. "I think he might have contacted the Knoxville field office and got the no-go from Boyle. He was the Knoxville liaison person."

"So he would have known you were trying to go undercover. He must have tipped off the BRI."

"That's the thing. I don't think he told them anything. At least, not at first." Snow crunched beneath their boots as they hiked through the woods, stretching their limbs. Landry's legs were still a little sore from their long hike over the mountain, but the exercise helped loosen the aching muscles and tendons.

"It must have suited his purposes for you to go undercover," Olivia mused. "Do you know why?"

Landry shook his head. "When Rigsby called me to meet her at the Econo-Tel, I had a gut feeling I shouldn't follow protocol. But I just didn't trust my instincts. Instead, I went through proper FBI channels. I called our task-force liaison to report the contact."

"Darryl Boyle."

"I knew when he told me not to contact anyone else, something was wrong. I even tried reaching Chang, but I never got through."

"So you called the number Rigsby had used to contact you, trying to warn her about Boyle."

He nodded. "I got Nick Darcy instead. By then, Boyle was already on his way to the other meet site Rigsby set up, along with some of his BRI buddies."

"So you knew then that whatever contacts you'd made in the BRI were compromised."

"I knew I couldn't trust Boyle. So I went home to pack some things. I knew I couldn't stay there anymore. I went to the bank and got a few thousand dollars out. Stashed it somewhere safe where I could access it if I needed to. I contacted my landlord and broke my lease. Told him to keep the deposit for his trouble."

"That made you look like you were on the run."

"I was." He looked at her. "I had no idea who to trust. Or if there was anybody left at all who could help me."

"You could have contacted *me*." The look she gave him was half fury, half dismay, as if she wasn't sure whether she wanted to give him a whack upside the head or burst into tears.

"I wanted to. I knew you were working for The Gates, so I knew where to find you. But I made a mistake."

"What mistake?"

"I gave the FBI another chance."

"I would rather know that you were working on the case without them knowing you are, because maybe ..."

"I understand."

"I appreciate your caution."

Chapter Fifteen

"Who did you contact?" Olivia asked, dread settling in the pit of her belly. Since leaving the FBI, she'd taken her share of emotional blows where the people she'd worked with were concerned. First Boyle. Then for a while, she'd come to fear that Landry was a traitor, too.

"I went over Chang's head," Landry answered. "Called someone at FBI headquarters instead. Dallas Cole."

Her eyebrows lifted a notch at the name. Dallas Cole? "The visual-information specialist at headquarters?"

Landry smiled at her surprise. "Yeah. Exactly. I figured, who would bother to corrupt a guy who designs brochures?"

She tried to picture upright Dallas Cole taking a bribe. "You're not telling me someone did."

"Honestly, I don't know. I haven't tried to contact him again to see what happened, for obvious reasons. He was always a pretty straight arrow—maybe he didn't listen when I told him to skip the chain of command and go straight to Assistant Director Crandall to tell him where to contact me."

"Actually, the Dallas Cole I remember wouldn't break chain-of-command protocol for anyone," Olivia said. "And if Boyle had thought ahead and made a few calls…"

Landry sighed. "Cole would have reported my contact

and they'd know where to find me. Which must be exactly what he did. Because it wasn't twenty minutes later, while I was waiting for a call back from Crandall, that a bunch of big, bearded guys ambushed me and hauled me off for interrogation."

Olivia touched his arm, horrified by the pictures his words painted in her mind. "No wonder you didn't think there was anyone in the FBI you could trust."

"Now you know why I didn't turn myself in to the authorities when I got away from my captors."

"I'm sorry. I'm so sorry you felt so alone. That you didn't feel there was anyone you could trust."

He touched her hand then gently removed it from his arm and took a few steps away. "We should probably get back."

"Wait." She tugged him around to face her, not ready to let him leave. Not before she told him what she'd spent most of the night before thinking about. "You know what we said last night, about the wisdom of trying to recapture what we had together?"

He met her gaze with wary eyes. "Yeah?"

She took a deep breath. "I don't think we should try."

His eyes flickered, as if she'd caught him flat-footed. "Oh."

She realized he didn't get what she was saying. "I'm sorry. I didn't say that well. What I mean is, we aren't the same people. I know I'm not, and I think you'd agree that you're not, either. Right?"

His expression shuttered. "Right."

He started to turn away from her, but she was still holding his hand.

"So let's not try to recapture our relationship." She caught his other hand in hers and stepped closer until her heat enveloped him. "Let's make something new."

She let go of his hands and rose to kiss him, her arms

wrapping around his shoulders to pull him closer. As Landry tightened his arms around her waist and pulled her flush to his body, the cold dissipated. The rustle of wind in the trees disappeared, swallowed by the thunderous pounding of Olivia's pulse in her ears.

It was so easy to let herself be swept up in the memories of their time together, the whirlwind of crazy hours, high-octane SWAT missions and stolen moments of pleasure in a world sometimes gone insane. They'd lived on passion and adrenaline, glossing over the missing pieces of their relationship as if they didn't matter. Things like trust and commitment, the building blocks of a relationship that had lasting power.

No wonder it had all fallen apart.

As if he sensed her sudden doubts, Landry's grip on her loosened, and he drew back to meet her gaze, his green eyes troubled. "What's wrong?"

"We made so many mistakes before."

His lips pressed flat as he nodded. "I know."

"I don't want to make those mistakes again."

He let her go, turning so that his profile was to her. "Okay. I get that. We should probably go back to the cabin and get back to work anyway."

"That's not what I mean." She moved closer to him, missing the heat of his body. "I want it to work this time. Don't you?"

He turned slowly to look at her. "Of course."

"We never thought past the next day." She shook her head. "Hell, most of the time we never thought past the next hour. We lived in the here and now, and we thought it was enough. But it wasn't. Was it?"

"No." He shook his head. "It wasn't nearly enough."

"If we do this, I don't want to settle for less than everything."

"You mean marriage and kids and mortgages?" His

expression shuttered, and she felt the first hard flush of dismay.

But before she could answer him, she felt a quiet buzz against her hip. "Damn it." She pulled her vibrating phone from her pocket. It was Alexander Quinn, of course.

"What, does he have you wired for sound?" Landry muttered as she pushed the answer button.

"Hello?"

"Carver showed up at home, a little scuffed but okay."

Relief swamped her. "That's amazing news! Did he escape?"

"Carver?" Landry asked softly. She nodded.

"Yes, but I'm not a hundred percent sure they didn't let him go."

"Why do you say that?"

"Because he came back with a message. And I think maybe it was one they wanted him to deliver."

"What kind of message?"

Quinn's voice lowered. "You're not on speaker, are you?"

Olivia glanced at Landry. "No."

"Carver said the men who took him told him there's a reason Cade Landry came out of hiding and sought you out. That the story he told you about being a target is true. But it's not the Blue Ridge Infantry who's after you."

"Then who?"

"It's Landry."

SOMETHING WAS WRONG. Very, very wrong. From the sudden shift in Olivia's posture to the blank expression on her face, Landry knew that whatever Quinn was telling her had hit her like a brick bat.

Was it something about Carver? Had something bad happened back in Purgatory?

"That's not possible." She spoke in a careful tone, still

looking at Landry even as her expression remained frozen in neutral.

Whatever Quinn said to her didn't do anything to improve her demeanor. She finally looked away, her gaze going south toward the guest cabin barely visible through the trees.

"I understand. You don't have to worry." She hung up the phone and took a deep breath before she slowly turned to look at him.

"Carver's okay?"

"He escaped. He was a little beat up, but Quinn says he's going to be fine." Something in her voice suggested she wasn't telling him the whole story, but she turned and started walking toward the cabin before he could ask anything else.

He hurried to catch up. "Wait a minute—what else was Quinn telling you? What's he worried about?"

"I'll tell you when we get to the cabin," she answered, picking up her pace until they were almost jogging through the trees.

The hair on the back of his neck rose as she beat him inside and disappeared almost immediately into her bedroom and closed the door. Adrenaline pumped into his system, feeding his rising alarm.

Get the Kimber, his instincts screamed. *Get it now.*

He pushed down the rising fear, held it in check. This was Olivia. Whatever had gone down between them, she wouldn't hurt him. Not without reason. He had to believe that, or he had nothing at all to believe in anymore.

Remaining where he stood in the middle of the front room of the guest cabin, he waited, his ragged breathing slowly subsiding and his pounding heart easing to a slow, steady beat.

When the door of her bedroom opened, the click of the

latch sent a little jolt through his nervous system, but he fought against the fight-or-flight instinct and made himself remain still while she slowly emerged from the hallway and walked back into the front room.

She was holding her Glock in her right hand, the barrel facing the floor. Moisture glistened in her eyes but she wasn't crying. He could see the effort it was taking not to let the tears fall.

She didn't look at him as she spoke. "Quinn thinks the BRI let Carver escape on purpose. He said that Carver overheard something his captors said, and Quinn thinks they planned it that way. They wanted to give us a message without delivering it directly."

Landry swallowed with difficulty. "What message?" he asked, though he had a sick feeling he already knew.

"He heard them say they're not the ones who are after me."

The cold certainty deepened, rippled like an icy breeze down his limbs, scattering goose bumps. "Then who is?"

Olivia's gaze lifted and locked with his. "You. They said it's you."

He saw pain in her eyes, and his heart contracted. Did she believe Quinn? Was that why she was carrying the Glock?

For her protection against him?

She lifted the Glock and he braced for whatever came next, knowing he couldn't do anything that might hurt her, no matter what she did next. When she set the Glock on the top of the glass-front cabinet that stood against the wall and dropped her empty hands to her sides, he released his pent-up breath.

"Landry, the one thing I know, the one thing I believe with absolute certainty, is that you didn't come in from the cold in order to hurt me."

Relief rolled through him, threatening to make his knees buckle.

She took a step closer, her gaze holding steady with his. "I'm not sure what the BRI is up to by sending a message through Carver the way they did. Maybe it's an attempt to turn us all against each other. Or maybe whatever operation you overheard them planning that day through the bedroom vent wasn't a sanctioned BRI operation, and this is their way of letting us know. I honestly don't know. But I know you. No matter what went wrong, no matter how many problems we overlooked instead of fixed, no matter how much time we've spent apart, I know you. You won't hurt me, because it would kill you. Just like I won't hurt you."

He glanced at the Glock she'd laid on the cabinet and forced a smile. "I have to admit, I wasn't so sure you weren't going to hurt me the other day when you pulled your shotgun on me."

She smiled back, the tears welling in her eyes trickling down her cheeks. "I had the safety on. You didn't notice?"

"I couldn't see past the barrel stuck in my face." He took another deep breath and let it out. "So the BRI is spreading the word that I'm the big bad, huh? I guess Quinn was pretty quick to buy into it?"

"Quinn's not exactly the trusting sort."

"You don't say." He walked back to the front door of the cabin and looked outside, scanning the yard. The sun was already high in the sky, hot enough despite the chilly temperatures to melt away half the snow that had been in the yard that morning when he woke. "Does the BRI have any idea where we are?"

"I don't know. Sometimes I think they have every inch of the Appalachians under surveillance."

"How much do you trust Quinn?"

"Enough," she said after a moment's thought. "You

asked if he believes this story about you. I think by calling me, he gave us the answer."

"He believes it."

"Actually, no. I don't think he does. He gave me the choice of what to do by calling me. If he truly believed you were the bad guy in this scenario, he and a dozen other agents from The Gates would have shown up without warning and gotten me out of here before calling the FBI to come get you."

"So that call was about giving you the facts at hand and trusting you to make the right decision?"

"That's how Quinn works. He says he has to be able to trust his agents to make the right decision in the field."

"So what's your decision in the field?"

"I think we're about as safe here, for the moment, as we'd be anywhere." She looked around the cabin, her eyes narrowed as if she were assessing the cabin's utility as a fortress. "I wouldn't mind shoring up our defenses a bit, though."

"What do you have in mind?"

"Short of building a moat?" She flashed him a grin that made his heart flip-flop, and for a second, he felt as if he'd been transported to three years earlier, when they had still been together, still partners. Still lovers.

He forced himself back to the present. She had been right earlier, when she'd said it was folly to try to recapture the past. The past, for all its delights, had also been riddled with mistakes and lost opportunities.

They had a chance to start fresh. And that was what he planned to do.

"How much do you think we can trust Rafe and Janeane?" he asked.

"Seth Hammond trusts them. And he's a pretty good

judge of character. He made his living off being able to read people, you know."

"Interesting choice of hires for The Gates," he murmured.

"Quinn's a pretty good judge of character, too." She crossed to him and took his hand. "We're going to figure all of this out. You're not going to spend the rest of your life running. Do you hear me?"

When she said it, he could almost believe it. "I hear you."

"We've just got to figure out a plan. Something more proactive than hunkering down and hoping nobody finds us. Making this place or any other place a fortress is the same as making it a prison. I have no desire to live the rest of my life in a prison."

She never had been the wait-and-see type, he thought. It didn't seem that the time they'd spent apart had quelled her propensity to take action.

Waiting had never been one of his strong suits, either. Which was why he'd spent the previous night working out potential plans of action in his head when sleep proved elusive.

Putting his life in the hands of the FBI wasn't something he was willing to try again, even if it was unfair to the thousands of honest, trustworthy agents and staffers in the Bureau's employ. He didn't know who could be trusted, so he had to work on the premise that he could trust none of them.

But Olivia was right. He may have escaped BRI captivity months ago, but that didn't mean he wasn't still trapped behind the invisible bars of life on the run.

It was time to come out of hiding.

"You have something in mind, don't you?" Her eyes narrowed a twitch, a faint smile playing with her lips. "Come on, Landry. Spill."

"I do have something in mind," he admitted as he crossed to the fireplace and added logs and kindling to the cold hearth. Despite the rising temperatures that continued to melt the blanket of snow outside, the cabin was chilly, sending shivers down his spine.

Or maybe it was the plan he'd been formulating that was giving him the shakes. Because he'd figured out last night, lying in a strange bed in the dark, listening to the moans of the wind in the eaves and the thud of his own pulse in his ears, that there would be no easy solution to his problem.

He was a wanted man, and he had no proof of his contentions about what had happened almost a year ago when he'd tried to do the right thing and had ended up bound and beaten for his efforts.

The only way out was to get the proof.

And the only way to get proof was to bait a trap.

"Are you going to tell me or not?" Olivia's voice was close behind him, her breath warm against his neck.

"I can't prove I'm not a traitor. Because I can't prove I was set up. Especially not while I'm hunkered down and hiding."

Suddenly, she was standing in front of him, her eyes wide and scared. "What exactly are you suggesting?"

He took her hands in his. "It was my fault that McKenna Rigsby's plan to trap Darryl Boyle went sideways."

"Because you followed protocol and contacted Boyle in his capacity as the task-force liaison?" Olivia's grip on his hands tightened. "How were you supposed to know he was one of the bad guys?"

"I think I did know, deep down," he said bleakly. "But that's not what I'm trying to get at." He tugged her hands up, pressing her knuckles against his chest. "I'm saying that if I hadn't screwed up and called Boyle, her plan might have worked. Boyle wouldn't have been forewarned, and he might have walked right into Rigsby's trap. It was a good plan. It just might be a great plan."

"You want to set a trap."

"Yes."

Her voice rasped. "With you as bait."

Chapter Sixteen

"This is a crazy idea."

Stopping in the middle of making notes on the files he was studying, Landry slanted a look Olivia's way. "Just an hour ago, you agreed it would work."

She put her hands over his, tugging the pen from his fingers. "I said it *could* work. Could is not would."

He closed his eyes. "Livvie."

"Don't Livvie me, Cade Landry. You're already working out the logistics of a plan when we haven't even considered other options."

"What other options?" He pushed aside the notepad and turned to face her, his expression tight with exasperation. "There are no other options. I've known since I got away that one day, sooner or later, I was going to have to put myself out there as a lure to get the BRI and their friends in the FBI to show their hands. It's time to stop avoiding the inevitable."

"I think you're being reckless."

"And I think you don't want to face the fact that there's no safe way out of this mess. Not for me, anyway." He took the pen from her grip. "I still think it might be a good idea for you to call Quinn to come get you. Take you back to The Gates until whatever happens to me happens."

Anger burned lava-hot in the center of her chest. "Who

do you think I am? Do I look like the kind of person who would hide behind the walls of The Gates to save myself while you're out there with your neck on the line? Do you think I could do that to the man I—" She bit off the word, not quite ready to say it aloud, even though the emotion swelled in her chest, threatening to burst forth no matter how hard she tried to keep it bottled up.

He cradled her cheeks between his palms, gentle understanding in his gaze. "No. I know you couldn't. But I'm not the man who could let you risk your life without trying to talk you out of it."

She pressed her forehead to his. "We should call Quinn, at least. Get some backup for this operation."

"Livvie, you've told me yourself that you've had leaks at the agency."

"But we stopped the leaker."

"You stopped *a* leaker. Are you sure there aren't other traitors in your midst?"

As much as she wished she could say she was sure, she wasn't. Not really. There hadn't been any sign of information leaks since the police had taken Marty Tucker into custody after he'd tried to kill Anson and Ginny Daughtry when they'd figured out his secret. But that didn't mean there wasn't another mole in the agency biding his time before he could make a move.

"No," she admitted. "I don't think there is. I really don't. But I can't be a hundred percent sure."

"Then we do it my way."

"How exactly are we going to document what happens when the bad guys spring the trap? We're not exactly rolling in cash or audiovisual equipment." She gave him a pointed look.

"There's a music hall not a hundred yards from here that has its own recording equipment."

Her brow furrowed with suspicion. "And you know this how?"

"When you went to the ladies' room last night, I chatted a bit with Rafe. You remember that balcony that goes around the whole music hall, kind of like those old-timey Western saloons?"

"Yeah?"

"I noticed there was a guy up there recording the music sets. I was curious, so I asked Rafe about it. He said he invested in some audio and video equipment a couple of years ago when he started working with talent agents to get their clients' work in front of prospective record labels. They pay him to record the sets live, and those sets go on public video-sharing sites. They can only upload the ones where the artists still retain the rights to the music, but Rafe said it's gotten several of the bands who debut here a closer look from the record labels looking for fresh talent."

"And you think Rafe will just hand over his expensive equipment to you for your sting?"

"I hope so."

"And if he doesn't?"

"I still have some money left over from the funds I took out of our joint bank account the other day. I'd just rather not tap into it if I don't have to." He flashed a smile. "Might need it for bail money."

"If this plan doesn't work," she muttered, "you're not likely to be granted bail."

He put down the pen, pushed his notes away and pulled her into his lap. She snuggled closer as he wrapped his arms around her waist and buried his face in her neck. "We have to try something, Livvie. This waiting for something to happen is going to kill me."

She kissed the top of his head, wishing she could argue. But he was right. He'd already spent nearly a year in hiding, and the longer it went on, the more dangerous it would become. He needed his life back.

She needed *him* back.

"I think you may be right about backup, though." He leaned his head back to look at her. "We have no idea how many people might be involved in the FBI branch of the Blue Ridge Infantry. If it's more than two, we'll be outnumbered."

"I don't want to be outnumbered. We don't have to be."

"I know you trust the people you work with."

"I want to trust the people I work with," she corrected him bleakly. "But after this past year and the leaks—"

"You said you thought you'd caught the only leaker."

"And you asked me if I was sure, and I said no."

"I've been thinking about that, too." He rubbed his chin against her collarbone, his beard prickling her skin, sending lovely little shivers of sexual awareness skittering down her spine. "Everybody who was in that conference room yesterday knows where we are. You trusted them enough not to change our plans."

She thought about the men and women who'd helped them figure out the logistics of their trip to Bryson City. She would trust her life to any of them. Perhaps more to the point, she'd trust Landry's life to any of them. "I did. I do."

"So they're the ones we contact. But I don't want to go through the phone system at The Gates or their cell phones. If there is a leaker at your agency, they might have access to anything that could be connected directly to the company. Do you have other ways to contact them?"

She had home phone numbers for most of them in the address-book app in her phone, coded in case someone ever managed to sneak a peek at the saved information. "I do."

"Good. We can call them when we get our plans finalized. Tell them how they can help." He gave her hip a little slap. "As tempting as it is to cuddle here with you on the sofa, we have to work out a lot of logistics."

She sighed and slid out of his grasp, settling on the sofa next to him. "Starting with figuring out if Dallas Cole is still with the FBI."

ICE CRUSTED ON the banks of the Potomac, an incongruous contrast with the cloud-streaked brilliance of the January sunset, reflected in all its fiery glory in the glassy surface of the river. The Jefferson Memorial was little more than a murky silhouette in the distance, a reminder that for all the beauty of its natural surroundings, Washington, DC, was a city built on power. Powerful men, powerful institutions, powerful ambition and powerful greed.

He had seen it all during his time in the capital. Idealism had died a million deaths on the altar of compromise. Good intentions soon became swallowed by desperation to score an elusive win at any cost.

Governing a free country could be a very nasty business, indeed.

He sighed and spoke into the phone. "When did you get the call?"

"Ten minutes ago." The voice on the other line was deep and well modulated, though even if he hadn't known the speaker already, he'd have been able to detect the hint of eastern Kentucky in the man's inflections.

Dallas Cole had tried to leave coal country behind him, but there were things a man couldn't escape no matter how hard he tried.

"Why you?"

"He said he was giving me a second chance to get it right." Cole's voice betrayed a touch of guilt, a hint of uncertainty.

"Get it right?"

"He said the last time he called, he had trusted me to do as he asked, and I failed."

"And what did he ask?"

"For me to take the message directly to you instead of going through channels."

Assistant Director Philip Crandall didn't speak right away as he watched an egret rise from the water and take flight, its wings flapping slowly as it glided across the flaming sky.

"Did I do the wrong thing?" Cole asked as the silence extended.

"Of course not," Crandall said. "You made the right call, Mr. Cole. I'll take care of it. Please don't discuss this call with anyone else."

He hung up the phone and took a couple of deep breaths. In and out, cleansing the tension from his neck and shoulders.

Finally. *Finally.*

He'd begun to think he'd never find a way to end the nightmare.

SON OF A BITCH.

Son of a *bitch*!

"What have I done?" Dallas Cole met his own gaze in the reflective glass of his office window. His office in the J. Edgar Hoover Building was little more than a closet with a single window he thanked his stars for every day, considering he'd started out in an even smaller closet without a window in sight. Support staff might be a vital cog in the FBI machine, but cogs didn't get corner offices and great views of— Well, okay, not many people at that ugly behemoth of a building had great views, period, despite FBI headquarters taking up prime property a hop, skip and a jump from the White House and other DC landmarks.

"Did you say something, Cole?"

The lilting female voice drew his mind out of self-imposed chaos and his gaze to the door. Michelle Matsumara, his supervisor, stood in the open doorway, neat and pretty in her trim blue suit.

"Talking to myself again, boss." He flashed a sheepish smile, feeling sick. Matsumara just gave a delicate shrug and continued down the hall.

He pressed his face into his hands. To say he'd been shocked by the phone call from a man claiming to be Cade Landry was an understatement of epic proportions. He'd spent the past year utterly certain Landry was dead and buried in some deep, dark hollow in the southern Appalachians.

Cole was from Harlan County, Kentucky. He knew all about deep, dark hollows.

Landry hadn't answered any of his questions, just told him to get it right this time. "Tell AD Crandall where he can meet me. And tell him I want him to come alone."

This time Cole had done as Landry asked. Bypassed Matsumara and her superior, Kilpatrick, and gone directly to Crandall, even though he knew, gut-deep, that both Matsumara and Kilpatrick were honest, trustworthy public servants—as good as they came, especially in a place like the capital.

After his phone call with the assistant director, Cole didn't think he could say the same of Crandall.

It hadn't been anything Crandall had said. His response had been everything anyone could have expected—an expression of concern about the contact from Cade Landry, reassurance that he'd done the right thing by calling him directly and, of course, an admonition to keep the call to himself.

But there'd been something else in Crandall's voice.

Something as deep and dark as any hollows a man could find in the hills of Kentucky.

Cole looked at his office phone, his mind reeling. The phone Landry had used to make the call had apparently been equipped with number blocking, for the phone display had been blank. It wasn't likely redial would work, he thought, but he picked up the phone and tried it anyway.

Nothing happened.

Damn it, Landry. How could he warn the man about Crandall?

Would Landry even believe him? Nothing Crandall had said would strike anyone as suspicious. Hell, if Cole hadn't heard the man himself, he wouldn't have given a second thought to Crandall's responses.

Never ignore your instincts, boy. His grandmother's voice rang in his mind. Leona Halloran was a big believer in hunches and listening to the still, small voice in a person's head. "It's the warnin' voice of angels, Dallas. They're tellin' you, watch out! There's trouble ahead."

He pulled out his cell phone and stared at the screen, thinking about his options. Who might know how to reach Landry after all this time?

The answer hit him like a gut punch. *Of course.*

He pulled up a search application on his phone and found the number he was looking for. As he started to dial it, the hair on the back of his neck rose, prickling the skin as if a cool finger had traced a path across the flesh.

Warning voices of angels, he thought, and shoved the phone back in his pocket. It was almost six o'clock on a Friday. Like most of the employees who worked in the J. Edgar Hoover Building, he didn't exactly watch the clock. But he'd worry about trying to impress management another day. He had a phone call to make.

And not from a phone that could be connected to him.

"Do you think he went straight to Crandall this time?"

Landry looked up at the sound of Olivia's voice. She stood in the open doorway of his bedroom, dressed for bed in a sleeveless T-shirt—the Atlanta Braves this time instead of Alabama. Her shorts might have hit midthigh on a shorter woman, but Olivia was a statuesque Amazon goddess, and there was enough skin visible to inspire some of his favorite fantasies.

"I have no idea," he admitted, dragging his mind back to business. "I guess we'll find out tomorrow. Are Quinn and the others set for tomorrow?"

She nodded. "All set."

He patted the edge of the bed, well aware that he was wearing nothing beneath the sheet covering his lower half. He could tell by the flicker of awareness in her blue eyes that she was aware, as well.

But she crossed slowly to the bed and sat down beside him, facing him. Slowly, she reached out and pressed her palm against the center of his bare chest. "I guess this could be it. Freedom or—" Her throat bobbed as she swallowed the rest of the thought.

"I have to believe it's going to be a win. I think we've both earned one, don't you?"

Her fingers brushed over his chest muscles, lightly tracing the contours and sending delicious shudders down his spine. "I'm not sure wins can be earned. Not in a world this ruthless."

He curved his palm around her hip and saw, with visceral pleasure, the way her eyelids flickered at his touch. He could still affect her. Still elicit a physical response, deliver on the unspoken promise of pleasure.

"So it's all luck?" he asked in a growl, pressing his thumb against a point just below her hip bone that he knew could make her squirm.

Her soft gasp sent a jolt of raw desire racing straight to his core.

"Landry—" Her response ended on a soft groan as he flicked his thumb across the sensitive point again.

When he reached for her, she came willingly, her long limbs tangling with his. Her hips settled flush with his, and he was the one who groaned as his arousal amplified a thousandfold.

"I want you," he whispered against her throat.

She arched her neck as he flicked his tongue against the tendon just below her jaw. "You don't say."

Cupping her bottom, he positioned her more snugly over his sex. "Need proof?"

Her laugh was like cello music, deep and fluid. She stretched out, her body sleek against his, and he felt his heart begin to pound. "I was willing to take it on faith," she said, "but if you insist."

Suddenly, her hips began to vibrate against his, sending shock waves through his whole nervous system. In the middle of lowering her mouth to his, Olivia stopped short and growled an impressively profane word.

Pulling back until she straddled his thighs, she pulled her cell phone from the pocket of her shorts and glared at the display.

"Really, Quinn?" she snarled at the offending device.

"His sense of timing is really something to behold," Landry murmured, trying to get his breathing back under control.

She answered the phone in a low, hostile voice. "What?"

Landry watched her expression shift from frustration to puzzlement. "Really. He called the agency?"

"What is it?" Landry asked.

"Hold on. I'm putting this on speaker so Landry can

hear." She pulled the phone away from her ear and tapped the screen.

A moment later Quinn's voice came over the phone. "Cole called around six thirty, asking for you. We told him you were gone for the day and he flat out asked if you were with Landry."

Olivia arched her eyebrows at Landry. "And you responded how?"

"We told him we'd make sure you got his message."

"And did he leave one?"

"No. But we were able to get a trace on the number he was calling from. It's a gym not far from the National Mall. We haven't dug any deeper, but we'd probably find out that Cole is a member there."

"No, you wouldn't," Landry disagreed. "If he bothered to use a phone that doesn't belong to him, he'd use a number that isn't easily traced back to him. What we need to do is call him back on his cell phone."

"You think he'd answer?" Quinn asked.

"I think he'd have to chance it," Olivia said. "He called me for a reason. I don't think it's to catch up on my life these days."

"He thinks you know how to reach me," Landry said.

"He called for a reason. We need to find out what it is." She shifted until she was sitting on the bed instead of his thighs. Missing her warmth immediately, he stifled a sigh.

"Well, give it a try and call me back." Quinn hung up the phone.

Olivia edged closer to him on the bed until her hip was warm against his, as if she needed to be close to him as much as he needed to be close to her. "You have his number handy?"

Landry had it memorized. It had been the last phone number he'd dialed before the BRI had ambushed him, and he'd spent a good bit of his captivity repeating the number to himself to keep from thinking about his predicament.

He rattled it off to Olivia, who arched her eyebrows at his quick reply. But she didn't say anything as she dialed the number and put the phone on speaker so he could hear the call.

The phone rang four times before Dallas Cole's voice answered with a cautious "Hello?"

"You called," Olivia said bluntly.

"Right. I can't believe you actually called me back."

"Why did you call?" she asked, not bothering to hide her impatience. Olivia could be a sweet, considerate woman, but there were times when she could intimidate a bull moose. This was one of those times.

"Cade Landry called me."

"I know."

"He's with you, isn't he? I knew he would be."

"Why did you call back?"

"I did what he asked this time. I bypassed Matsumara and Kilpatrick and went straight to AD Crandall."

Olivia darted a look at Landry, clearly surprised. "What did he say?"

"He thanked me for telling him and said he'd handle everything as you asked."

"Well, that's good, then." Olivia frowned at Landry, clearly disappointed that Cole hadn't reacted as they'd thought he would. He wasn't happy himself. Now they'd have to figure out another plan—

"No, it's not." Cole's blunt tone interrupted Landry's thoughts. His accent, which usually was carefully neutral, held a strong hint of the Appalachian backwoods. "You and Landry thought I'd go through channels again, didn't you? That's why he called me again, even though the last time he came to me for help, he ended up in a hell of a tangle."

"Yes," Landry said.

"I'm sorry about that, man. You told me what to do, but I did it my way and you ended up paying for it. So this time, I did it your way. But Crandall's not what you think. He's not what I thought, either."

"But you said he agreed to handle it."

"He did. But I don't think he's going to—" Cole's words cut off on a soft expletive.

"What?" Olivia prodded.

"I've picked up a tail. At least I hope it's just a tail." His voice rose a notch, tight with tension. "Two sets of head-lights, coming up fast."

"Where are you?"

"Driving south on 231, north of Ruckersville. Thought I should get out of town for the weekend— Son of a bitch!" His words were almost drowned out by the squeal of tires audible over the phone line.

Then the call cut off.

Olivia stared at Landry. "What just happened?"

Feeling sick, he reached for his phone. "I think Cole just got run off the road."

Chapter Seventeen

Mulberry Creek Diner wasn't nearly as picturesque as its name, but it offered Alexander Quinn the three things he was looking for in a staging point—lots of strong, hot coffee, free Wi-Fi and a large private room where eight men and four women could meet in relative privacy to discuss their plans to set a trap for a traitor.

"Still nothing from the Virginia State Police," Sutton Calhoun informed them after getting off the phone with his wife. "Ivy has a friend there who's promised to keep her informed if they get any accident reports from the Ruckersville area, but nobody's reported anything so far."

Almost twenty-four hours had passed since Dallas Cole's phone call had come to an abrupt end, and still no word about his whereabouts. Quinn didn't have a good feeling about Cole's chances for survival, but he was the FBI's problem. Quinn had his own agents to worry about.

"Maybe they weren't intending to kill him," Landry muttered. He was sitting near the end of the table, his chair pulled close to Olivia's, as if he didn't want to get too far away from her.

"Landry thinks someone might have taken him captive to question him," Olivia explained.

"Because that's what happened to you?" Nick Darcy

asked. He sat to Quinn's left, McKenna Rigsby on his other side.

"Cole told me he didn't trust Crandall. He said something about their conversation made him feel really uneasy." Landry turned his coffee cup in circles in front of him. "I figure if a graphic designer's warning bells were going off during that conversation, an assistant director of the FBI might have had some suspicions, too."

"I wish there was a way to track Crandall. See if he's really on his way or if this is another wild-goose chase," Rigsby said.

"I'm working on that," Quinn said vaguely. Nobody asked him to elaborate. He wouldn't have done so if they had. He might not be in the spy business anymore, but he still knew what "need to know" meant. "I'm not sure it matters right now if Crandall shows up himself. To be honest, it's not that likely. You don't get to be an assistant director of the FBI if you do your own dirty work."

"Then what are we doing here?" Darcy asked, his dark eyes snapping up to meet Quinn's. "What do we think is going to happen?"

"We're setting a trap," Rigsby said.

"A trap Crandall's probably already seen through if he's sent people after Dallas Cole," Olivia muttered.

Adam Brand took a sip of coffee and grimaced. "We still run with our plan, in case that's where Crandall wants to make his stand."

"He won't," Olivia insisted.

Quinn didn't think he would, either. "He's put Dallas Cole on ice for a reason. What reason?"

"Setting up a new scapegoat?" That suggestion came from Seth Hammond, who sat across the table from Quinn. Covert Ops weren't his area of expertise, but he'd been in on this case from almost the beginning, tracking Landry and Olivia up the mountain and keeping an eye on them for Quinn. He'd wanted in on the finale, so Quinn had added him to the team.

"You mean, he wants to pin everything on Dallas Cole?" Rigsby asked. "But what about Landry? I thought he was already the designated patsy."

"Thanks, Rigsby." Landry made a face at her.

"You know what I mean. Crandall must know you suspect him by now. Or does he think you still believe he's one of the good guys?"

"I don't know. Maybe he sent people to grab Cole in order to keep him from communicating anything more to Olivia or me." Landry looked at Quinn. "Cole went to the trouble of not using a phone that could be connected to him. So Crandall may not know he's been in touch with us already."

"Wonder if Cole had reason to think he was under surveillance?" Hammond suggested.

"I think most people in the government assume their communications can be accessed easily. Especially someone in the FBI," Olivia said.

"And Crandall knows that." Quinn pushed away the half-drunk cup of coffee in front of him. "I think Olivia's right. Phil Crandall won't show his face here. That's not how this game is played."

"It's not a game," Landry muttered.

Quinn sighed. "You're right. Bad choice of words."

"You think nobody will show up at all?" Olivia asked.

"I didn't say that. Landry's a wild card, and if I were Crandall, I'd take one more shot at eliminating him. I'd be thinking, maybe Landry can't connect me to any of this mess, but what if he can? And I hate to say it, Olivia, but Landry is probably right about your being a target. Crandall must know by now that Landry's made contact with you."

"But if they know we're setting up a trap, why would anybody show up at all?" Hammond looked confused.

"They're not going to show up at the meeting point," Brand agreed. "We know that much already."

"But they'll do their own surveillance and go after Olivia and Landry once we close down the operation," Quinn explained. "This is a trap on top of a trap on top of a trap."

"Like running a long con," Hammond murmured.

"Sort of."

"I don't think we'll be able to prove Crandall was behind any of this just because someone tries to take out Landry and Sharp," Brand warned.

"No, but we may be able to finally bring some provable charges against some members of the Blue Ridge Infantry. Then the police can get search warrants, warrants to pull phone records, and maybe that will lead to even more warrants and searches—"

"*If* we can pull this off," Landry finished. "It's a big if."

"That could very well depend on the two of you," Quinn warned him. "We're going to have to fall back and leave you two exposed for a little while. I'm not going to lie and tell you it won't be dangerous. It will."

Landry's gaze shifted toward Olivia. "I don't think Olivia has to be part of the bait this time. She can fall back with you, and I can go it alone."

"No." Olivia shook her head. "Not happening."

"She's right." Quinn didn't like the idea of Olivia in the crosshairs, either. She was a good agent, a very good asset to his company, and he'd come to like and trust her during her time as one of his agents, as much as he ever allowed himself to trust anyone. "They almost certainly know you're together. They'll be very suspicious if you part company now."

"It's a chance I'm willing to take."

"I'm not," Olivia said. "This could be your best chance to clear your name and get your life back."

"If you're talking about the FBI, there's no way they'll take me back, even if I get out of this without criminal charges."

"There's more to life than working for the FBI." Olivia put her hand over Landry's, just a brief, firm touch, but in the gesture Quinn saw all he needed to know about where Olivia's loyalties ultimately lay.

Good thing they were chronically understaffed at The Gates these days. If everything worked out this afternoon, it looked as if he'd be adding a new investigator.

"We don't have time to fight this out," he warned. "We're an hour from meeting time, and the roads are still messy. We need to get rolling."

"I'm not leaving you, Landry. So deal with it." Olivia's low, fervent tone left no room for argument. Landry met her gaze and sighed.

"Okay. Fine." He looked at the rest of the men and women at the table. "Let's get this party started."

Quinn pulled Olivia aside as they lined up to pay their dinner checks. "I meant what I said—our best chance to make this plan work is if you stick with Landry. But it's your choice. If you have any doubts..."

"I don't." Her chin lifted and her gaze met his without wavering.

"Good luck." He touched her arm and walked past her to the checkout counter, hoping this was one of those rare operations that went off without a hitch.

OLIVIA SUPPOSED THAT sometime in history, somewhere in the world, an operation had gone exactly as planned.

She'd just never been part of such a thing herself.

The meeting time had come and gone about an hour ago,

and as they'd expected, Crandall had been a no-show. So had Dallas Cole or anyone from the Blue Ridge Infantry. But Seth Hammond had sent her a text message a few minutes ago to inform them the covert backup team had spotted about a half dozen men observing the meeting place from a distance.

Quinn and half the crew from The Gates were now headed back to the agency, while Landry and Olivia were on the road to Bryson City. The trip would take them through any number of potential ambush points, with only their stealthy backup team to help them out until more reinforcements could arrive.

By midnight, they'd passed almost all the potential ambush points the operation team had mapped out for them. They were five minutes from the Song Valley Music Hall and the Hunters' guest cabin.

"Do you think they figured out our plan?" Olivia asked as she forced herself to stay relaxed and focused.

"Check with the backup team."

Before she typed a letter, a text from Seth Hammond came in. "The men they've been following have just peeled off and seem to be heading back to Tennessee."

"I don't like this," Landry muttered.

Olivia didn't, either.

The Song Valley Music Hall was dark when they pulled into the driveway that wound past the restaurant toward the houses behind it. A couple of lights were still shining in upstairs rooms of the main house, but the guest cabin was dark and quiet.

Prickles of unease crept down Olivia's spine. "Do you think the Hunters are still awake? There are lights on."

"What are you thinking?"

"I don't know," she admitted. "My danger radar is still

going off like crazy, but I don't know if it's because I'm still on high alert from playing out this plan."

"I can't shake the feeling that it's not over," Landry admitted. "I don't trust that they've backed off tonight. Patience isn't something I've ever associated with the Blue Ridge Infantry."

Olivia felt sick. "And we've just put the Hunters in danger."

Without warning, Landry pulled the Tahoe to a stop in front of the Hunters' cabin and cut the engine. "We'd better tell them what's going on."

The sense of unease strengthened exponentially once they left the relative safety of the Tahoe and headed up the flagstone walk to the Hunters' cabin. The weight of the Glock tucked in the holster under her jacket was a partial comfort, but every instinct Olivia had was screaming warnings to stay on guard.

"Wait," she said as Landry started to reach for the screen door.

He glanced at her. "What?"

She reached in her pocket and pulled out the flashlight she'd carried with her on the operation. She flicked on the light and ran the narrow beam up and down the front of the screen door. She was about to shut off the light when something glinted in the beam, catching her attention.

"Do not move," she said with quiet urgency.

Landry went still. "What did you see?"

"There's a wire sticking out between the door frame and the screen door. It might be a loose wire from the screen, but—"

"But it might be a trip wire."

"Right." She took a step backward. The floorboard beneath her boot gave a loud creak, and her heart skipped a beat.

A moment later she heard a muffled shout coming from inside. "Get away! The house is rigged!"

"That was Rafe," Landry growled, stopping his retreat. Olivia saw him eyeing the windows, looking for another mode of entry, but she had a feeling the windows might be rigged with explosives, as well.

She put her hand on his arm and pulled out her phone, punching in a message to Hammond. "We're not bomb-disposal experts. We can't get them out of there by ourselves."

"This is all my fault."

"No, it's not." Her phone vibrated and she checked the screen. Hammond's text in reply was blunt and profane. "He's informing Quinn. Quinn has contacts in the local law-enforcement agencies. He'll make sure the best bomb squad available shows up to take care of this situation. But we have to get away from this house." She turned toward the door and shouted, "Rafe! We're getting help. Hang in there!"

"The guest cabin's probably rigged, as well, in case we went there first," Landry growled.

"The music hall may be, too. We need to get the experts here before we make things worse."

Cade resisted for a moment when she gave his arm a sharp tug, but finally he turned and hurried her down the steps and back to the Tahoe.

As she reached for the door handle, something thudded hard against the front panel of the SUV just as she heard the crack of rifle fire echoing through the trees nearby.

"Get in the car!" Landry shouted, already opening the driver's door.

Olivia heard the click of the passenger door unlocking and jerked it open as another bullet shattered the side mirror in an explosion of flying glass. One small shard nicked her cheek with a sharp sting.

"Go, go, go!" She flung herself onto the passenger seat and jerked the door shut behind her.

Landry jerked the Tahoe in Reverse and whipped it around in a semicircle until they were facing the road.

Where three dusty pickup trucks blocked the driveway, each one manned guerrilla-style by men in camouflage standing in the truck beds, rifles aimed directly at them.

Chapter Eighteen

"Get down, get down!" Landry jerked the Tahoe in Reverse and swung into a sharp J-turn even as rifle fire split the night air. He heard more than saw Olivia hit the floorboard, putting three rows of seats between her and the shooters. She started speaking and he realized she'd called 911.

"We're taking rifle fire and we're hemmed in. I'm not sure there's any way to evade them." Olivia's voice was breathless and pitched a little higher than usual, but there was no sign of rising panic, no hint of fear taking over.

He wished he could say the same for himself. The mere thought of bringing in the authorities had his heart pounding and his mind reeling. He'd been stuck in fight or flight so long, the idea of turning over his fate to the authorities was almost more than he could fathom.

But they were out of options. Even as he swung the truck across the uneven yard behind the music hall, twisting the steering wheel back and forth to avoid the obstacle course between him and the other end of the music hall, he knew there was little chance of mistake. In the cracked glass of the rear window, he saw that only two of the trucks had taken up the pursuit, which meant the third vehicle was probably circling around to cut them off.

There was a small gap between the two trucks behind him, but if he timed it right—

He jammed on the brakes and the Tahoe's wheels slid on the lingering patches of melting snow as he jerked the wheel around to reverse course again and aimed for the narrowing gap between the two pickup trucks now barreling across the slippery ground straight at him in a terrifying game of chicken. Finally, as the grille of the Tahoe came a few short feet from the front of the trucks, the drivers swerved out to avoid a head-on collision.

The men in the truck beds were too busy clinging to the truck to get off any shots, and with a scrape of metal on metal as the SUV slid against the side of one of the trucks, the Tahoe shot the gap and raced up the driveway toward the road.

The trucks behind him had to avoid each other, slowing down their attempts to reverse course, and the third truck that had gone around the music hall to cut them off had no idea what had happened.

His heart pounding, Landry gunned the Tahoe down the driveway, increasing his lead as he swung onto the road in front of the music hall and tore away from the pursuit.

Olivia had pulled herself up into the seat and was giving the 911 operator a play-by-play of what had just happened, peering through the gloom ahead to make out the sign on the next crossroad they passed. "We're still heading north on Valley Road, just past Soldier Junction." She listened a moment, turning around to look out the back. "They're still behind us but falling back. No, we didn't get any license numbers."

Suddenly, headlights came on, bright and blinding, from two vehicles parked on either side of the highway. Landry's heart jumped into his throat. "Son of a—"

Olivia's hand closed over his arm, and he darted a quick look at her.

"The Gates," she said, and he realized what she was telling him.

He drove past the two trucks parked on the shoulder and kept going. With a glance in his rearview mirror, he saw that the parked vehicles had pulled out behind him, blocking both lanes of Valley Road.

"They'll have vehicles trailing the trucks," Olivia said softly, the phone pressed against her chest. "They're going to hem them in."

"There'll be a firefight."

"Maybe. But those vehicles have bullet-resistant windows and armor. Just like this one."

Landry looked at the bullet holes in the rear window and realized they hadn't penetrated the glass. He released a harsh breath. "You could have told me."

"When?" She put the phone to her ear and told the 911 operator they'd evaded their pursuers and arranged for a meeting point with the sheriff's-department deputies responding to the call.

Landry eased the Tahoe to the shoulder where she indicated they should stop and put it in Park, though instinct told him not to cut the engine. Those jerks in the trucks weren't the only dangerous people in these hills.

"Are you okay?" He turned to look at Olivia, taking in her disheveled appearance and searching for any signs of injury. He saw a dark rivulet of blood running down the right side of her face. "You're bleeding!"

She reached up and touched her cheek, looking at the blood that came away on her fingers. "I got nicked by flying glass from the side mirror. Barely even stings. I'm fine. How about you?"

If he'd been injured, he couldn't feel it. He reached for her, tangling his fingers in the hair at the back of her neck, and pulled her across the gear console and into his embrace.

Electricity seemed to flow through his veins like blood, sparking everywhere it traveled, until his whole body felt like a live wire, utterly on edge.

But slowly, as she lifted her hands to draw soothing circles across his back, the frantic energy ebbed, until he finally felt his pulse return to some semblance of normal.

Even the wail of sirens in the distance, moving inexorably closer, wasn't enough to jar his nervous system into another flight of panic. One way or another, his ordeal was over. The authorities would believe him or they wouldn't. But there would be no more running.

He might well be doomed to spend the next few years of his life behind bars, but he thought he could handle it now.

Now that Olivia was on his side.

"How much longer are they going to interrogate him?" Olivia couldn't stop her restless pacing beside Alexander Quinn. He sat with annoying calm in one of the two chairs that faced the empty desk of Ridge County Sheriff Max Clanton, who had insisted on observing the interview.

"You know the FBI. They like to swagger around and play the big dogs." The look Quinn shot her way was full of amusement, making her want to kick him in the shin with her hiking boots.

Instead, she stopped pacing, slumping in the chair next to him and stretching out her long legs, which had begun to ache. Dropping her chin to her chest, she glared at the empty desk chair and tried not to think about what Landry was going through in the interview room down the hall.

The Bryson City Police had picked up the men who'd been chasing Olivia and Landry, but so far, they hadn't been able to get much out of them. Quinn had told her it was possible they wouldn't be able to connect them to the Blue Ridge Infantry at all.

At least the Hunters had been safely rescued from their booby-trapped house. The bombs had been small pipe bombs, two hidden in the decorative urns on either side of the porch set to blow if anyone had opened a door or a window on the first floor. Fortunately, one of the officers on the Bryson City force had been an explosive-ordnance expert in the Marine Corps and had managed to disarm the simple explosives without incident.

But they still hadn't figured out how the men who'd accosted them had known to look for them in Bryson City at the Hunters' place.

"I get the feeling something's up with this interrogation," Quinn said a few minutes later, breaking the tense silence and drawing her thoughts back to the present.

"Good or bad?" She wasn't sure she wanted to hear the answer, but she couldn't go through life avoiding things that frightened her.

"I don't know. I just can't shake the sense something's changed."

She looked at him, trying to read his expression. A fool's game—Quinn never gave anything away he didn't want to. And sometimes when he wanted to, what he gave away was a lie he wanted you to believe.

Before she could ask another pointless question, the door to the office opened and Max Clanton entered, his sandy eyebrows lifting in surprise as he spotted them waiting in front of his desk. "Y'all know it's nearly five a.m., right? Figured you'd have moseyed on home for the night."

Olivia rose to face him. Max Clanton was a tall man, fit and trim, looking young for a man in his midforties, and from the handful of things she'd heard about his time on the Knoxville Police Force before he ran for Ridge County Sheriff, he was tough as a bull. But he must have seen something fierce in her expression when she turned to look at him, because his forward progress faltered and his expression shifted from affability to wariness.

"Where is Cade Landry?"

"I'm not sure." Avoiding her gaze, Clanton continued to his desk and sat in his chair, making a show of straightening the files on the corner of his desk.

"You're not sure?" she pressed, starting to grow alarmed. "An hour ago he was in your interview room down the hall, talking to the FBI. I thought that's where you were, too."

"I was called away on a different case," Clanton said apologetically. "When I checked in again, the interview room was empty."

"Empty?" Olivia took a step toward the sheriff's desk.

Quinn rose and put his hand on her elbow, holding her in place. "Thank you for allowing us to wait in your office. If you have any further questions for Ms. Sharp or any of my employees, we'll be happy to oblige." He guided Olivia out the door and into the narrow corridor outside, shutting the door behind them.

"Where the hell is Landry?" she asked, keeping her voice down.

"My guess is, he's been taken into custody by the FBI, at least temporarily."

"And the Ridge County Sheriff's Department just let them take him?"

"Technically, he's committed no crimes in Ridge County that would give the sheriff primary jurisdiction." Quinn nudged her down the hall and out into the main foyer. "I'll make some calls, see if I can track down where he's been taken."

"That won't be necessary." A tall, dark-haired man with clear blue eyes and a Southern drawl stepped in front of them as they started toward the door. He handed Olivia a card.

It read "Will Cooper. Federal Bureau of Investigation." She looked up at him, her eyes narrowing.

"Where's Landry?"

"My guess is, he's currently on the way to The Gates. The FBI has released him under his own recognizance while the details of his situation continue to be sorted out." Cooper nodded at Quinn. "Nice to finally meet you, Mr. Quinn. I've heard a lot about you. I'm Will Cooper."

"One of the Alabama Coopers, I assume?"

Will smiled. "My brother Caleb gave me a call because I'm on a multistate task force investigating and interdicting domestic terror incidents. I've just been assigned temporary duty in the Knoxville field office to review some recent undercover operations run out of that office as well as the Johnson City resident agency."

"You got Landry released."

"He's got some details to work out, but unless different evidence arises, there aren't likely to be any charges pending against him." Will nodded toward the door. "I'd like to talk to you, Mr. Quinn, about your investigation into the Blue Ridge Infantry, if you'd be willing to discuss it with me."

Quinn looked at Olivia. She nodded. "Go ahead. I'll meet you there." She peeled off toward her car in the visitor's parking lot and pulled out her phone as she settled behind the steering wheel.

It was a long shot to think Landry would still have possession of the burner phone Quinn had given him. The cops had probably confiscated it as evidence. She'd just have to hope he was waiting for her.

When she arrived at The Gates, the agents' bull pen was buzzing with activity, agents making up for lost time after the snow days. Olivia caught Ava Solano's arm as the other woman edged past her in the doorway. Ava had worked with

Landry briefly when they'd both been in the FBI's Johnson City RA. "Ava, have you seen Cade Landry?"

Ava's dark eyebrows lifted. "I thought he was at the sheriff's office, being questioned still. Did they let him go?"

"Seems to be the case, at least for now. Have you been here for the past hour or so?"

Ava nodded. "I have tons of paperwork I'm catching up on. If I see him, I'll tell him you're looking for him."

Olivia made herself slow down as she left the bull pen and headed for Quinn's office to see if he and Will Cooper had arrived. Maybe Cooper had misunderstood and the FBI agents who'd come from Knoxville to interrogate Landry had simply taken him to Knoxville for more questioning.

As disheartening an idea as it was to think he was still in deep trouble with the Bureau, it was a better option than the panicky fear starting to take up room in the back of her mind.

Face it, Olivia. There's always the chance he's run again.

But how would he run? He no longer had the Tahoe to drive. When he'd shown up in her front yard a few days ago, his only means of transportation was a thrift-store bicycle.

Which brought up another question. If he'd left the sheriff's department the way Will Cooper said, how had he managed it? On foot? Called a cab? Hopped on a bus?

She settled down in the chair in front of Quinn's desk and tried to think. Could he have caught a ride with another agent from The Gates? As far as she knew, she and Quinn had been the only ones there at the sheriff's office this afternoon, but Dennison's wife worked there as a deputy. She supposed Landry could have run into Dennison at the station and asked for a lift.

As she was dialing Dennison's number, Quinn and Will

Cooper entered the office, their pace faltering a little when she stood and took a step toward them.

"Cooper, you said Landry had left and you thought he was headed here, but he's not here. Can you tell me how he left the sheriff's department?"

Cooper looked momentarily nonplussed by the question, then apparently caught on to what she was asking. "One of the deputies going off duty offered him a ride."

"Male? Female?"

"Female. Dark hair, dark eyes, midthirties—"

That could fit Sara Dennison. "Thanks." She headed past them into the corridor and pulled out her phone. Sara's number was saved somewhere in her call list, wasn't it?

She found it as she was heading down the winding staircase to the first floor and made the call.

Sara answered on the second ring. "Dennison."

"Sara, it's Olivia. Did you give Cade Landry a ride this afternoon?"

"I did—he said he needed a lift to your place because he'd left a lot of his stuff there when y'all had to bug out. Frankly, he could do with a shower after sweating out an FBI interrogation, so I dropped him off at your cabin. I hope that was okay. I talked to Cain and he said you and Landry were friends."

"It's fine," Olivia assured her, already out the back door to the employee parking lot.

THE BICYCLE WAS still where Olivia had put it, in the small storage shed behind her cabin. The metal was icy cold but dry, protected from the snow by the sturdy shed's tin roof.

Landry ran his hand over the cold steel handlebars and remembered the ride up the mountain to this place, the snowfall increasing with every mile. He'd been terrified he was making the worst decision of his life.

He should have known better. Being with Olivia was always the right choice. How could he have ever thought anything different?

For a moment the sound of a car engine approaching up the mountain road sent a little ripple of alarm darting through him. But he made himself remain calm, though he didn't entirely relax his guard. He might not be stuck in fight-or-flight mode anymore, but there were still dangerous people out there who might be willing to take another shot at bringing him down.

The FBI hadn't given him back the Kimber or the Kel-Tec P-11 he'd had on him when they'd taken him in. He supposed they wanted to hold them as evidence until they fully settled his case.

That was fine. He had nothing to hide now.

Fortunately, he'd stashed his extra weapon in the locked cabinet in the shed, along with some ammo. He located the key in the hidden spot Olivia had shown him and unlocked the cabinet to retrieve the compact Ruger and its holster. He clipped the holster to his belt and loaded the magazine into the grip as the approaching vehicle came to a stop nearby. The engine cut, and he heard a door open, then close with a slam.

Olivia's voice rang out in the cold afternoon air. "Landry!"

He shoved the Ruger into the holster and edged through the shed door.

"Landry, are you here? Please say you're here!" The anxiety in Olivia's voice caught him by surprise, making him hurry as he rounded the side of the house toward her voice.

She was halfway up the porch steps when he reached the front yard.

"I'm here," he said.

She whirled around to look at him, her blue eyes wide. "Landry."

As he started to cross the yard, she came back down the porch steps and met him at the bottom. "Livvie."

She reached out and touched the front of his jacket, her gaze settling somewhere around the middle of his throat. "I thought you'd gone."

He put his hand over hers. Her fingers were cold and trembled a little beneath his touch. "You think I'd go without saying goodbye?"

She tugged her hand away and stepped back, her expression shuttering. "Is that why you're here? To say goodbye?"

"Let's go inside. Get a fire started and get warm." He put his hand under her elbow and nudged her toward the steps. She seemed to resist for a second, then gave in and went upstairs and unlocked her front door.

She went straight to the wood bin by the fireplace and went about the job of building a fire in the hearth, her movements quick and efficient, like everything she did.

She was radically competent, brilliantly resourceful and marvelously self-sufficient. She was, in short, a magnificent woman, and he could spend the rest of his life trying to be worthy of her without getting anywhere near his goal.

But he had to try. Because the alternative was walking away from her again. And he knew now, with utter certainty, that he didn't have it in him to do that again.

"I'm not sure my trouble with the FBI is over," he said, breaking the tense silence that had risen between them.

She gave the fire one last poke and turned around to look at him. "I really didn't expect them to let you go on your own recognizance, given that you've been a fugitive for so many months."

"I've offered to testify in front of a Senate subcommittee on domestic terrorism, which seemed to mollify my interrogators a bit." He moved closer, holding out his hands to warm them in front of the fire. "There was a new guy, Cooper—seemed to think I won't be charged with anything given the circumstances of my disappearance."

"That's good."

She still hadn't looked at him since they'd entered the cabin. Her shoulders were tense, her chin set and a little on the belligerent side.

"Livvie, I'm not leaving."

Slowly, she looked up at him. "You say that now..."

"I will never leave you again. Not if I have a choice. As long as you want me to hang around, I'm in. No doubts."

She raised one of her eyebrows a notch. "You? With no doubts?"

He caught her hands, tugged her around to look at him. In the firelight, she was a golden goddess, as beautiful and luminous a creature as he'd ever seen. His heart seemed to swell near bursting, so full of gratitude and love that he didn't know what to do with all the emotion.

"I lost you because I was a stupid idiot. But somehow, when everything seemed hopeless, I closed my eyes and looked for an answer, and there you were. Like a light in my darkness. So I found you. Because you were my hope. You're my home."

Her eyes glowed like jewels as she met and held his gaze. "Landry."

"I love you. I have loved you since almost the first day we met. There was never a point in time after that when I didn't love you, and there never will be." He touched her face, his thumb brushing against a sparkling tear that slid from one of her eyes. "So you tell me what you want."

"You." She slid her hand around his neck and pulled him to her. "I want you."

He kissed her then, a long, slow, intimate exploration that left them both breathless. Olivia finally broke away just enough to whisper against his mouth, "Say it again."

He didn't have to ask what she meant. "I love you."

Her answering smile was bright enough to light up the Eastern Seaboard. "Do you realize in all the time we were together, we never said those words to each other?"

He brushed her hair away from her cheek. "Technically, one of us still hasn't said them."

"I love you, idiot. If I didn't love you, I'd have probably shot you that first day you showed up in my front yard with that stupid bike."

"So let's do it, then."

She shot him a wicked look. "Do it? Here? Now?"

He laughed. "Well, yes, but I was actually thinking about getting hitched."

She took a step back, looking surprised. "Hitched?"

"Yeah. You know, married. Blissfully wed. Fitted with the old ball and chain."

"You were doing so well there for a minute."

He laughed again. "Marry me, Livvie." His smile faded as he realized she might not have experienced the same epiphany he had about trust and devotion. "Unless you're still not sure you can trust me."

"No, that's not it." She brushed her thumb against his lip. "I just never thought I'd marry. I thought I'd be like my mom, always looking but never finding."

"Is that what you still think?"

She looked up at him, her gaze frank and open. "No, it's not. I know what I've found. I know it's worth keeping."

"So is that a yes?"

Her slow, sexy smile warmed him to his core. "Yes," she said and kissed him again.

Epilogue

The thin gold band on her left ring finger felt right, she decided after sneaking a peek for the sixth time in the past hour. It fit perfectly, neither loose nor constricting, as if it had been forged specifically for her alone.

"It's just a wedding ring," Landry murmured from his desk across from hers in the agents' bull pen on the second floor of The Gates. "It's not going to come alive and bite you."

She looked up at him, flashing him a quick, sheepish smile. "I like the way it looks. And the way it fits."

"I like the way it looks on you." The grin he shot back at her came with a full display of dimples and a softness in his green eyes that was endearingly shy.

She looked pointedly at the thicker band on his own ring finger. "Right back at ya."

"Oh, my God. Why didn't y'all just go on a real honeymoon instead of inflicting all this newlywed bliss on the rest of us?" Seth Hammond perched on the edge of Olivia's desk, shaking his head. "Have a little mercy on us, will ya?"

Sutton Calhoun thumped Hammond on the back of his head and dropped a file folder on Olivia's desk blotter. "I seem to remember a couple of months of you on the phone babbling disgusting endearments to your own bride, Hammond. Leave the newlyweds alone."

Calhoun waited for Hammond to wander back to his desk before he motioned Landry over. "Here's everything we could find on Dallas Cole. Any chance he's not a victim? Darryl Boyle hinted to Rigsby that he wasn't the only one in the FBI who was a true believer, and so far, we're just not finding any dirt on Philip Crandall."

"We just don't know," Landry admitted. "Given my own recent history, I'm in no position to assume a man's disappearance is evidence of his complicity in a crime. But Dallas Cole could have been trying to set us up so we wouldn't go to Crandall for help. It might have been a ploy to slow us down until the BRI could get their assets in place."

"Well, it's a place to look," Olivia pointed out. "If he *is* one of the bad guys, we need to find him."

Calhoun's slate blue eyes darkened. "And if he's not one of the bad guys?"

"Then he's in trouble and could use our help," Landry answered. "If he'll take it."

Olivia reached out, putting her hand over her husband's, her wedding band clinking quietly against his. His gaze flicked up to meet hers, and his dimples made a quick appearance.

A hint of amusement tinted Calhoun's voice. "Either way, Quinn wants us to find Cole and bring him in before the BRI gets their hands on him. He wants you two in charge of the investigation, since you know the most about him."

"We don't really know that much," Landry warned. "We could pick him out of a lineup, maybe, but—"

"We're investigators," Olivia reminded him. "It's our job to find out all we can about him now."

She picked up the folder Calhoun had placed on her desk blotter and opened it to the first page, a grainy photo of a dark-haired man with brown eyes and a guarded expression on his lean face. He was thirty-four, according to the notes clipped to the photos. Six foot one, approximately one hundred and eighty pounds, no distinguishing features.

"How does a graphic designer get mixed up with a backwoods terror group?" she asked in a murmur.

"That's what we have to find out," Landry answered.

Olivia looked at the photo again, trying to see beyond the flat, expressionless surface of the image.

Who was Dallas Cole?

And which side was he really on?

* * * * *

MILLS & BOON®

**If you enjoyed this story,
you'll love the the full *Revenge Collection*!**

**Enjoy the misdemeanours and the sinful world
of revenge with this six-book collection.
Indulge in these riveting 3-in-1 romances
from top Modern Romance authors.**

Order your complete collection today at
www.millsandboon.co.uk/revengecollection

'The perfect Christmas read!' - *Julia Williams*

Jewellery designer Skylar loves living London, but when a surprise proposal goes wrong, she finds herself fleeing home to remote Puffin Island.

Burned by a terrible divorce, TV historian Alec is dazzled by Sky's beauty and so cynical that he assumes that's a bad thing! Luckily she's on the verge of getting engaged to someone else, so she won't be a constant source of temptation... but this Christmas, can Alec and Sky realise that they are what each other was looking for all along?

Order yours today at
www.millsandboon.co.uk

MILLS & BOON®

Man of the Year

Our winning cover star will be revealed next month!

**Don't miss out on your copy
– order from millsandboon.co.uk**

Read more about Man of the Year 2016 at

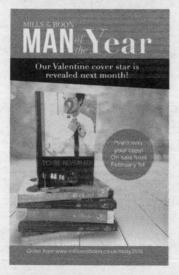

www.millsandboon.co.uk/moty2016

**Have you been following our
Man of the Year 2016 campaign?**
🐦 **#MOTY2016**